PR[A]
SEBASTIAN S[T]

WHAT D[...]

"Excellent. . . . The con[...]
cate plotting, surprising [...]
tions of the lives of the underprivileged makes this one of the
best entries in Harris's superior historical series."

—*Publishers Weekly* (Starred Review)

"A lively foray into early-nineteenth-century politics, treach-
eries, and moral indiscretions." —*Kirkus Reviews*

WHEN MAIDENS MOURN

"Regency England comes alive in Harris's seventh Sebastian
St. Cyr novel." —*Library Journal*

"Intriguing." —*Publishers Weekly*

"An absorbing mystery." —*Booklist*

"This elegant Regency mystery series continues with a seventh wonderful book. The soldier-turned–sleuth and lord is a
fascinating character who sweeps the reader into the story. The
English countryside descriptions, witty charm of the hero, and
emotional connection between Sebastian and his new wife—a
strong, independent woman—are all superb."

—*Romantic Times* (4½ Stars, Top Pick)

WHERE SHADOWS DANCE

"Page-turning adventure, international intrigue, and unlikely
romance. . . . I like the way Harris is moving through the series, especially with the multifaceted Hero."

—*The New Orleans Times-Picayune*

"I love this series. It has it all: romance, political intrigue, dark
humor, and memorable characters."

—*The Historical Novels Review*

continued . . .

WHAT REMAINS OF HEAVEN

"Harris is a master of the genre."
—*The Historical Novels Review*

"Harris combines all of the qualities of a solid Regency in the tradition of Georgette Heyer by pairing two strong characters trying to ignore their mutual attraction while solving a crime together. Anyone who likes Amanda Quick and/or is reading the reissued Heyer novels will love this series."
—*Library Journal* (Starred Review)

"[The] seductive antihero [is] at his swashbuckling best."
—*Publishers Weekly*

WHERE SERPENTS SLEEP

"C. S. Harris's attention to historical detail and sense of adventure combine to make a ripping read . . . captivated me to the final page."
—Will Thomas, author of the Barker & Llewelyn novels

"An intriguing mix of bloody murder, incest, and brutality. The author, who has done her historical homework, makes a fascinating focus of her book in Hero Jarvis, a young woman whose uncompromising independence puts her far ahead of her time."
—*The Washington Times*

"Harris does an excellent job of interweaving the mystery in this book with the larger story arc of the series . . . solidly written."
—*St. Petersburg Times*

"Outstanding. . . . Harris does a nice job of weaving the many plot strands together while exploring the complex character of her protagonist."
—*Publishers Weekly* (Starred Review)

WHY MERMAIDS SING

"A serial-killer thriller set two hundred years ago? . . . It works, thanks to Harris's pacing and fine eye for detail. A real plus: The murk and stench of the age only heighten the suspense."
—*Entertainment Weekly*

"Thoroughly enjoyable . . . moody and atmospheric, exposing the dark underside of Regency London . . . deliciously ghoulish . . . kept me enthralled."
—Deanna Raybourn, author of *The Dark Enquiry*

WHEN GODS DIE

"Like Georgette Heyer, Harris delves deep into the mores of Regency England, but hers is a darker, more dangerous place."
—*Kirkus Reviews* (Starred Review)

"Deftly combines political intrigue, cleverly concealed clues, and vivid characters . . . a fast-moving story that will have readers eagerly anticipating future volumes in the series."
—*Publishers Weekly* (Starred Review)

"Harris knows her English history and has a firm grasp of how a mystery novel is supposed to play out. . . . Fans of historicals, especially those set in Regency-era England, will snap up this triumph."
—*Library Journal* (Starred Review)

WHAT ANGELS FEAR

"Perfect reading. . . . Harris crafts her story with the threat of danger, hints of humor, vivid sex scenes, and a conclusion that will make your pulse race. Impressive."
—*The New Orleans Times-Picayune*

"C.S. Harris artfully re-creates the contradictory world of Regency England as her marvelous characters move between the glittering ballrooms and the treacherous back alleys of London. . . . Start this one early in the day—you won't be able to put it down!"
—Victoria Thompson, author of the Gaslight Mystery series

"Appealing characters, authentic historical details, and sound plotting make this an amazing debut historical."
—*Library Journal* (Starred Review)

"An absorbing and accomplished debut that displays a mastery of the Regency period in all its elegance and barbarity."
—Stephanie Barron, author of the Jane Austen Mystery series

"The combined elements of historical fiction, romance, and mystery in this fog-enshrouded London puzzler will appeal to fans of Anne Perry."
—*Booklist*

"A masterful blend of history and suspense, character and plot, imagination and classic mystery. A thoroughly intriguing, enjoyable read."
—Laura Joh Rowland, author of the Sano Ichirō Mystery series

WHAT ANGELS FEAR

A Sebastian St. Cyr Mystery

C. S. HARRIS

BERKLEY PRIME CRIME
New York

BERKLEY PRIME CRIME
Published by Berkley
An imprint of Penguin Random House LLC
375 Hudson Street, New York, New York 10014

Copyright © 2005 by The Two Talers, LLC
Excerpt from *Why Kings Confess* by C. S. Harris © 2014 by The Two Talers, LLC
Penguin Random House supports copyright. Copyright fuels creativity, encourages
diverse voices, promotes free speech, and creates a vibrant culture. Thank you for buying
an authorized edition of this book and for complying with copyright laws by not
reproducing, scanning, or distributing any part of it in any form without permission.
You are supporting writers and allowing Penguin Random House to continue to
publish books for every reader.

BERKLEY is a registered trademark and BERKLEY PRIME CRIME and the B colophon
are trademarks of Penguin Random House LLC.

ISBN: 9780451219718

New American Library hardcover / November 2005
Signet mass-market / January 2006
Obsidian mass-market / February 2014
Berkley Prime Crime mass-market / June 2017

Printed in the United States of America
10 12 14 16 18 19 17 15 13 11

For my husband,
Steven Ray Harris,
for more reasons than I could name

No place so sacred from such fops is barred,
Nor is Paul's Church more safe than Paul's Churchyard;
Nay fly to altars; there they'll talk you dead,
For fools rush in where angels fear to tread.

—Alexander Pope,
An Essay on Criticism

Prologue

Tuesday, 29 January 1811

She blamed the fog. She wasn't normally this nervous. This afraid.

It was such a foul, creeping thing, the yellow fog of London. Even without the fog it would have been dark at this hour. Dark, and January-cold. But the murky vapor made it worse, wrapping around her lantern in wraithlike drifts that had Rachel stumbling as she cut across the churchyard.

A loose stone rolled beneath the delicate sole of one kid half-boot, the clatter sounding unnaturally loud in the stillness of the night. Pausing, Rachel threw a quick glance over her shoulder, her gaze raking the faint, mist-shrouded outlines of the graveyard's scattered monuments and tombstones. From the distance came a clacking rattle and the fog-muffled voice of the charley, calling out the time. Rachel drew in a deep breath of frosty air tinged with the scent of wet earth and leaves and a stale, musty hint of old death, and hurried on.

The heavy stone bulk of St. Matthew of the Fields loomed before her. Rachel clutched the satin-lined velvet folds of her evening cloak more closely about her. She should have told him to meet her at half past eight, she decided. Nine at the latest. It was the usual time, half past eight.

Only, this wasn't a usual transaction.

She hadn't expected to be so edgy. It was a sensation she didn't like. Being nervous made her feel like a victim, and Rachel York refused to play the role of victim. Never again. It was a promise she'd made to herself at the age of fifteen, and in the three years that had passed since that fateful night when she'd seized control of her own life, it was a promise she'd never broken. She wasn't about to break it now.

At the steps leading up to the north transept door, she paused again. Beneath the deep round arch of the side portal, the darkness was nearly complete. Lifting the lantern high, she let the narrowed beam of light play over the door's weathered old oak. Through the thin kid of her gloves the iron key felt cold and heavy in her hand. To her annoyance, her fingers shook when she thrust the toothed end into the lock.

With one twist, the mechanism clicked smoothly and the door swung silently inward before her on oiled hinges. The Reverend McDermott was careful about such things. But then, he needed to be.

Rachel pushed the door open wider, one artfully curled lock of golden hair fluttering against her cheek in the sudden outward gush of air. Familiar church smells engulfed her, the scent of beeswax and damp stone and ancient wood. She whisked herself inside, carefully closing the door behind her. She did not lock it.

She dropped the key into her reticule, felt its weight heavy and solid against her thigh as she crossed the transept. The cold silence of the church closed around her, the light from her lantern wavering over candle-blackened stone walls and the scattered, recumbent figures of entombed ladies and long-dead knights lying still and cold in the empty hush.

They said it was close on to eight hundred years old,

St. Matthew of the Fields, with molded sandstone arches that sprang from thick, cylindrical piers, and small high windows that now showed only blackness beyond. Rachel's father had been interested in such things. Once, he had taken her to see the cathedral in Worchester and talked to her for hours about arcades and triforiums and rood screens. But her father was long dead; Rachel shut her mind against the memory, unsure what had brought such a thought to her now.

The Lady Chapel lay at the far end of the apse, a tiny fourteenth-century jewel of white marble and slender columns and delicately carved screenwork. Rachel set her lantern on the steps before the altar. She was early; he would not be here for another twenty minutes or more. The emptiness of the ancient church seemed to press in upon her, cold and dark. She found her gaze returning, again and again, to the blessed candles clustered together on the snowy linen of the altar cloth. For a moment longer, she hesitated. Then, kindling a taper, she began to light the candles, one after the other, their golden flames leaping up warm and bright until they seemed to merge into one comforting glow.

Rachel gazed up at the massive canvas that hung above the altar, a darkly swirled depiction of the Virgin Mother ascending gloriously into the heavens against a background of triumphant angels. Once, Rachel might have murmured a soft prayer.

Not now.

She didn't hear the transept door open and close, only the faint echo of stealthy footsteps along the choir. He was early. She hadn't expected it of him.

Turning, she shoved back the hood of her cloak and forced her lips into a practiced smile, ready to play her role.

She could see him now, a faint shadow, the outline of

his greatcoat and top hat just visible through the Lady
Chapel's intricately carved stone screen.

Then he moved into the candlelight.

She took a quick step back. "*You*," she whispered,
and knew she'd made a terrible mistake.

Chapter 1

Sebastian could hear the tolling of the city's church bells, counting out the hour; dull echoes of sound muffled by distance and the acrid fog that, even here, hugged the open ground and shrouded the bare, reaching branches of the stand of elms that grew at the edge of the field. Dawn had come, but it brought little warmth or light. Sebastian Alistair St. Cyr, Viscount Devlin, only surviving son and heir to the Earl of Hendon, propped his shoulders against the high side of his curricle, crossed his arms at his chest, and thought about his bed.

It had been a long night, a night of brandy fumes and cigar smoke, of faro and vingt-et-un and a promise made to a sad-eyed woman—a promise that he would not kill, however much the man he had come here to meet might deserve killing. Sebastian tipped back his head and closed his eyes. He could hear the sweet call of a lark at the far end of the field and, nearer, the steady swish, swish of wet grass as his second, Sir Christopher Farrell, paced back and forth in the roadside's verge. Suddenly, the footsteps stopped.

"Maybe he won't show," said Sir Christopher.

Sebastian kept his eyes closed. "He'll show."

The pacing resumed. Back and forth, boot heels squelching in the damp earth.

"If you're not careful," said Sebastian, "you're going to get mud on your boots."

"To hell with my boots. Are you certain Talbot is bringing a doctor? How good of a doctor? Maybe we should have brought our own doctor."

Sebastian lowered his head and opened his eyes. "I don't intend to get shot."

Sir Christopher swung about, his fair hair curling wildly in the damp mist, his normally soft gray eyes dilated. "Right. Well, that's reassuring. Doubtless Lord Firth had every intention of not getting shot when he stood up against Maynard last month. Pity, of course, that the bullet went through his neck."

Sebastian smiled.

"I'm delighted to see I'm amusing you. This is another of those advantages of having gone to war, is it? Staring with calm disdain into the face of death? Ranks right up there with being rendered irresistibly fascinating to members of the fair sex."

Sebastian laughed out loud.

Christopher smiled himself, then resumed his silent pacing, a slim, flawlessly tailored figure in buckskins and high-gloss top boots and well-laundered linen. After another moment, he said, "I still don't understand why you didn't choose swords. Less chance of someone accidentally getting killed with swords." Lifting his left arm in a fencer's pose, he pantomimed a quick thrust against the cold, misty air. "A neat little pink through the shoulder, a bloody scratch on the arm, and honor is satisfied."

"Talbot intends to kill me."

Christopher let his arms fall to his sides. "So you're just going to stand there and let him take a shot at you?"

"Talbot couldn't hit a ship of the line at twenty-five paces." Sebastian yawned. "I'm surprised he chose it." It was the Code Duello: as the challenged party, Sebastian selected the weapons. But the choice of distance then fell to the challenger.

Christopher scrubbed an open hand across his face. "I've heard rumors—"

"Here he comes," said Sebastian. Straightening, he swung off his driving coat and slung it over the high seat of the curricle.

Christopher turned to stare into the opaque distance. "Bloody hell. Even you can't see in this fog."

"No. But I have ears."

"So do I. And I don't hear a thing. I swear, Sebastian, you must be part bat. It's unnatural."

A minute or two later, a carriage appeared out of the gloom, a pair of showy blacks pulling a high-perch phaeton containing two men and followed at a discreet distance by a simple gig. The doctor.

A tall, lanky man with straight, thinning brown hair and an aquiline nose jumped down from the phaeton's high seat. Across the mist-blown field, Captain John Talbot's gaze met and held Sebastian's for one long moment. Then he turned away to strip off his coat and gloves.

"Right then," called the captain's second, a mustachioed military man who clapped his hands together in a false show of heartiness. "Let's get to it, shall we?"

"Those rumors I mentioned?" Christopher said in an undertone as he and Sebastian moved forward. "They say the last time Talbot fought a duel, he chose twenty-five paces, then turned and fired after twelve. Killed the man. Of course, Talbot and his second swore the distance had been settled at twelve paces all along."

"And his rival's second?"

"Shut up about it when Talbot threatened to call *him* out—for naming Talbot a liar."

Sebastian gave his friend a slow smile. "Then if Talbot should have occasion to call you out for a similar reason, I suggest you choose swords."

"You've the pistols?" said Talbot's second, as Sir Christopher walked up to him.

A brace of pistols in a blue velvet-lined walnut box was produced, inspected, and loaded by the seconds. Talbot made his choice. Sebastian took the other pistol in his hand, felt the cool, familiar weight against his palm, the deadly hardness of steel against his curled finger.

"Ready, gentlemen?"

Back-to-back they stood, then began to walk, each step measured to the steady drone of the counted paces.

"One, two . . ."

The doctor ostentatiously turned his back, but Christopher stood his ground, his eyes narrowed and watchful, his face pale, anxious. Sebastian knew his friend wasn't only worried about Talbot's intentions, that Christopher had other misgivings. Christopher didn't understand that there was a fine line between seeking death and being indifferent to its occurrence. A line Sebastian had yet to cross.

". . . three, four . . ."

He had an unexpected memory, of a misty summer morning long ago, on a grassy slope near the Hall, when his two older brothers had still been alive, and his mother. The air had smelled of the fresh scones they'd brought for tea, and ferns, and the restless sea beating against the rocks in the cove far below. They'd played Drakes-and-Dragons that morning, the four of them, counting out the movements ". . . five, six . . ." as they wove in and out, even his mother, her head thrown back, laughing, the strengthening sun bright on her golden hair. Only his sister, Amanda, had sat aloof, as she always did. Aloof and disapproving and angry for reasons Sebastian never quite understood.

". . . eight, nine . . ."

The metal of the pistol's trigger felt cold and solid against Sebastian's finger, the wind-swirled mist damp against his cheeks. He forced himself to focus on this moment, this place. The lark called again, from nearer the base of the hill. He could hear the gurgle of a distant stream, the clip-clop of a horse, ridden at a slow trot up the road.

". . . ten, eleven . . ."

It was the hesitation in the other man's stride between the tenth and eleventh count that warned him. That, and the whisper of cloth rubbing against cloth as Talbot turned.

". . . twelve—"

Sebastian spun about and dropped into a crouch at the precise moment that John Talbot fired, so that the bullet intended for Sebastian's heart grazed his forehead instead. Then, gun empty and dangling slack in his hand, Talbot had no choice but to stand, body turned sideways, jaw clenched tight, nostrils flaring with each indrawn breath as he waited for Sebastian's shot.

Calmly, purposefully, Sebastian raised his pistol, took aim, and fired. Captain Talbot let out a sharp cry and pitched forward.

The doctor scrambled out of the gig and ran toward him.

"Bloody hell, Sebastian," said Christopher. "You've killed him."

"Hardly." Sebastian let the pistol fall to his side. "But I imagine he'll find it damned uncomfortable to sit down for a while."

"I say, I say, I say," blustered Talbot's second, his mustache working back and forth. "Most ungentlemanly conduct, this. Englishmen stand and fire weapons *from their feet*. Someone ought to fetch the constables. There'll be murder charges brought for this, mark my words."

"Be quiet, man," said the doctor, snapping open his case. "No one I've treated yet has died from being clipped across the arse."

Sir Christopher began to laugh, while Sebastian stretched to his feet and walked across the field to collect the other pistol. He'd promised Melanie he wouldn't kill her husband.

But she hadn't said anything about not making the bastard suffer.

Chapter 2

*I*t was in the retrochoir that Jem first noticed the blood.

He'd known something was wrong before that, of course—known it as soon as he opened the north transept door. For thirty years now Jem Cummings had been sexton here at St. Matthew of the Fields. It was part of his job to see that the church was locked up tight every night and unlocked again the next morning.

So Jem knew.

They had a young rector what'd taken over the living three years ago—the Reverend McDermott, he was. McDermott hadn't liked the idea of keeping the church locked at night. But then Jem had told him about that time back in '92, when them bloodthirsty heathen Frogs had been rampaging across the Channel and the old reverend had come in one morning to find the high altar smashed and pigs' blood splattered across the choir walls. When he heard about that, Reverend McDermott dropped his talk about leaving the church open real quick.

It was the pigs' blood that Jem was remembering now as he staggered toward the nave, his bum leg hurting bad in the damp cold, his eyes straining as he peered into the early morning gloom. Yet the peace of the church seemed undisturbed, the high altar pristine and untouched, the sacristy door protecting the church's precious, consecrated vessels solid and locked. The pounding of Jem's heart began to ease.

Then he saw the blood.

He didn't know what it was at first. Only dark smudges, faint but growing more distinct, more discernibly in the shape of men's shoe prints as he traced the trail across the worn paving slabs toward the Lady Chapel. The cold of the ancient stone walls seemed to seep into his very bones, his breath coming ragged in his tight chest as he crept forward, his body shaking so badly he had to clench his teeth to keep them from rattling.

She lay on her back, sprawled in an obscene posture against the polished marble steps that led up to the chapel's altar. He saw bare thighs, spread wide and gleaming white in the lamplight. A froth of lace edged what had once been a fine satin flounce, torn now, and stained with the same darkness that smeared her thighs. Eyes wide and glassy stared at him from beneath a head of golden curls tipped back at an unnatural angle. At first he thought the front of her gown was black, but as he inched closer, he saw the gaping gashes across her throat and he understood. He understood, too, where all the blood had come from. It was everywhere, the blood, worse even than that long-ago day when the Jacobin fanatic had thrown buckets of the stuff around the choir. Only, this wasn't pigs' blood. It was her blood.

Jem stumbled backward, his elbow knocking painfully against the edge of the Lady Chapel's intricately carved stone screen as he squeezed his eyes shut, blocking out that horrific vision.

But nothing would ever blot out that smell, the cloying, sickening mingling of blood and candle wax and raw, sexual fulfillment.

Chapter 3

*I*t was almost noon by now, but the light filtering down through the stained-glass windows in the apse of St. Matthew of the Fields was still feeble, diffuse.

Sir Henry Lovejoy, chief magistrate for Westminster at Queen Square, let his gaze travel over the blood-splattered chapel walls, the thick pools of congealing gore standing out dark and cruel against the white marble of the altar steps. He had a theory, that the incidence of crimes of violence and passion was higher on those days when the yellow fog held London in its choking, deadly grip.

But it had been a long time since London had seen a crime like this one.

To one side of the Lady Chapel, a small, ominously still form lay hidden beneath a cloth stained dark and stiff with so much blood that Lovejoy had to force himself to walk over to it. Bending, he flipped back the edge of the fabric, and sighed.

She'd been pretty, once, this woman. And young. Any untimely death was tragic, of course. But no man who'd ever loved a woman, or watched with pride and fear the tentative first steps of a child, could look upon that youthful loveliness and not experience an added weight of sorrow, an extra edge to his sense of outrage.

His knees creaking in complaint, Lovejoy lowered himself into a squat, his gaze still fixed on that pale, blood-streaked face. "Know who she is?"

The question was addressed to the only other person in the chapel, a tall, well-built man in his mid-thirties, with fair, fashionably disheveled hair and an intricately tied cravat. As Queen Square's senior constable, Edward Maitland had been the first authority of any consequence called to the scene and had been the one handling the investigation to this point. "An actress," he said now, standing with his hands clasped behind his back, his weight rocking back and forth on the balls of his feet as if to contain his impatience with Sir Henry's slow, methodical ways. "A Miss Rachel York."

"Ah. I thought she looked familiar." Swallowing hard, Lovejoy eased the cloth from the rest of the girl's body, and forced himself to look.

Her throat had been repeatedly, viciously slashed in long, savage gashes. Which explained the sprays of blood on the walls, he supposed. So much blood, everywhere. Yet Rachel York's death had not been quick, or easy. Her fists were clenched as if in endurance, and bruises showed dark and ugly against the pale, bare flesh of her wrists and forearms. The skin high on her left cheek had been split by a harsh blow. The torn, disarrayed emerald satin gown and ripped velvet pelisse told their own story.

"He had his way with her, I take it?" said Lovejoy.

Maitland shifted his weight back onto the heels of his expensive boots and balanced there, his gaze not on the girl but on the high, blue and red stained glass of the eastern window. "Yes, sir. No doubt about that."

No doubt indeed, thought Lovejoy. The inescapable tang of semen still hung in the air, mingling with the heavy metallic odor of blood and the pious sweetness of incense and beeswax. He let his gaze travel over the girl's carefully composed limbs, and frowned. "She was lying like this, when you found her?"

"No, sir. She was there, before the altar. Weren't proper to leave her that way. This being a church and all."

Lovejoy straightened, his gaze drifting back to those blood-smeared marble steps. Every candle on the altar had guttered down and gone out. She must have lit them all, he thought, before she died. Why? In piety? Or because she was afraid of the dark?

Aloud, he said, "What was she doing here, do you suppose?"

Maitland's brows twitched together in a swift, betraying movement instantly stilled. It was obviously a question that hadn't occurred to him. "That I can't say, sir. The sexton found her when he came to open the church this morning." He pulled a notebook from the pocket of his greatcoat and flipped it open with the ostentatious display of attention to detail that sometimes grated on Lovejoy's nerves. "A Mr. Jem Cummings. Neither he nor the Reverend"—there was a brief ruffling of pages—"Reverend James McDermott say they've ever seen her before."

"They lock the church every night, do they?"

"Yes, sir." Again Maitland consulted his notebook. "At eight sharp."

Reaching down, Lovejoy carefully replaced the cloth over what was left of Rachel York, only pausing at the last moment to study, once again, that pale, beautiful face. She had a French look about her, with the fair curls and widely spaced brown eyes and short upper lip often found in Normandy. He'd seen her just last week, with Kat Boleyn in the Covent Garden Theater's production of *As You Like it*. Seen her and admired her, not simply for her beauty but for her talent. He had a clear image of her upon the stage, her hands held high in the clasp of her fellow cast members as they took their final bow, her eyes bright and shining, her smile wide and triumphantly joyous.

He jerked the cloth back over those still, bloodstained features and turned away, his gaze narrowing as he took in the layout of the old church, the aisled nave and wide transepts, the choir and broad apse. "This Mr. Cummings . . . does he say he came back here, to the Lady Chapel, before locking up last night?"

Maitland shook his head. "The sexton says he glanced back here from the retrochoir and gave a loud halloo, warning that he was about to lock up. But he didn't actually venture into the chapel itself, sir. And he wouldn't have seen her from the retrochoir. I checked myself."

Lovejoy nodded. In the damp coolness of the church, some of the pools of blood had yet to dry. Glossy and thick, they shimmered darkly in the lamplight, and he took care to avoid stepping in them as he walked slowly about the chapel. There'd been so many big, careless feet tramping in and out of the chapel in the past six hours that it would be impossible to accurately reconstruct what the floor had looked like before the sexton's arrival. But it seemed somehow disrespectful, a violation of that poor girl lying there against the wall, to be tromping heedlessly through what had once been her life's blood. So Lovejoy tried to avoid it.

He stopped in front of the small altar's white marble steps. The blood was thickest here, where she'd been found. A lantern lay on its side, its glass shattered. He twisted around to glance back at his constable. "Any idea who was the last person to use the Lady Chapel?"

Once again, Maitland thumbed through his notebook. It was all for effect, Lovejoy knew. Edward Maitland could recite the entire contents of his notebook from memory. But he thought it gave weight to his pronouncements, to be seen looking up each fact or figure. "We're still checking," he said with a slowness that was again for effect, "but it was probably a Mrs. William Nackery. She's a haberdasher's widow. Comes to the Lady Chapel here every evening at about half past four and prays for some twenty to thirty minutes. She says the church was empty when she left, just afore five."

Lovejoy lifted his gaze to the blood-spattered walls, his lips tightening into a smile that had nothing to do with humor. "It appears to be a fairly safe assumption to say she was killed here."

Warily, Maitland cleared his throat. He always grew uncomfortable when Lovejoy began stating the obvious. "I should think so, sir."

"Which seems to place our murder between the hours of five and eight last night."

"That's the way we figured it, sir." The constable cleared his throat again. "We found her reticule some two or three feet from the body. It was open, so most of the contents had spilled out. But her pocketbook was still there, undisturbed. And that's a fine gold necklace and earrings she's wearing."

"In other words, no robbery."

"No, sir."

"But you say the reticule was open? I wonder if it simply fell open when she dropped it, or if our killer was searching for something?" Lovejoy glanced again around the cold chapel, felt the damp chill of the stones seeping up through the soles of his boots. He shoved his gloved hands deep into the pockets of his greatcoat, and wished he hadn't forgotten his scarf. "I'm waiting, Constable."

The planes of Edward Maitland's broad, handsome face pinched with puzzlement. "Sir?"

"For you to tell me why you felt it necessary that I come here myself."

The frown eased into a self-satisfied smile. "Because we've figured out who did it, sir."

"Really?"

"It was this what told us where to look." Maitland took a small flintlock pistol from his pocket and held it out. "There's no doubt it was dropped by our murderer. One of the lads found it mixed up in the folds of her cloak."

Lovejoy took the weapon and balanced it thoughtfully in his hand. It was an exquisite piece, of high-grade steel, with a polished mahogany grip and a brass trigger guard intricately worked with the design of a serpent wrapped around a sword. Forty-four caliber, he decided, from the looks of it, with a rifled bore and a plate that read W. REDDELL, LONDON. There was still enough blood on the barrel to leave a dark smudge across the palm of his kid glove.

"You'll notice the trigger guard, sir. The serpent and the sword?"

Lovejoy ran the thumb of his left hand across the stain. "Yes, I did notice it, Constable."

"It's the device of Viscount Devlin, sir."

Lovejoy's grip tightened on the pistol in an involuntary, convulsive movement. There were few in London who hadn't heard of Sebastian, Viscount Devlin. Or of his father Lord Hendon, chancellor of the exchequer and trusted confidant of the poor old mad King's Tory prime minister, Spencer Perceval.

Lovejoy flipped the pistol around to hold it out, butt first, to his constable. "Careful, Constable. We're treading on dangerous ground here. It won't do to go leaping to any hasty conclusions."

Maitland met his gaze steadily. He made no move to take the pistol from Lovejoy's grasp. "There's more, sir."

Lovejoy dropped the pistol into his own greatcoat pocket. "Let me hear it."

"We've spoken to Rachel York's maid, a woman by the name of Mary Grant." This time Maitland made no pretense of needing to consult his notes. "According to Mary, her mistress went out late yesterday to meet St. Cyr. She told the maid, and I quote, 'His lordship'll pay handsomely, never you fear.' " The constable paused as if to allow sufficient time for the effect of his words to penetrate, then added, "It was the last anyone saw of her."

Lovejoy held his constable's light blue eyes in a steady stare. "What are you suggesting? That she was blackmailing the Viscount?"

"Or threatening him in some way. Yes, sir."

"I take it you've checked into Viscount Devlin's whereabouts last night?"

"Yes, sir. His servants say he left the house at about five. Claimed he was on his way to his club. But according to his friends, Devlin didn't arrive at Watier's until just after nine."

"And where does the Viscount say he was?"

"We haven't been able to locate the Viscount himself, sir. His bed was never slept in last night. Word about town is that he was set to fight a duel this morning."

Lovejoy brought one cupped hand to his mouth and blew thoughtfully against his palm and fingers before letting the hand fall again. "Whoever did this must have been drenched in blood. If Devlin is our man, he would have needed to return home for a change of clothes and a wash before going on to his club."

"It had occurred to me, sir."

"So? What do Devlin's servants have to say about that?"

"Unfortunately, before he went out, Devlin gave his entire staff the night off. His lordship seems to be a most generous employer." There was something about the way it was said—a clipping of the vowels, a tightening of the lips—that betrayed a hint of an emotion Maitland generally kept discreetly hidden. He was no radical, Maitland. He believed in the social order, in the Great Chain of Being and the hierarchy of man. But that didn't stop him from craving wealth and position, and envying those, such as Devlin, who'd been born to what Maitland himself couldn't even aspire.

Lovejoy turned away to wander about the small Lady Chapel. "His valet would know if a set of evening clothes had disappeared from his lordship's wardrobe."

"His lordship's man claims to have found nothing missing. But you know what these manservants can be like. Loyal to a fault."

Lovejoy nodded absently, his attention caught by an enormous painting of the Virgin ascending into heaven that hung high above the altar. He himself had evangelical, Reformist tendencies—a dangerous inclination he was careful to keep private, of course. He didn't hold with stained glass and incense and smoke-darkened Renaissance canvases in heavy gilded frames; considered them sinful popish remnants that had nothing to do with the austere God Lovejoy worshiped. But he noticed that blood from Rachel York's repeatedly slashed throat had sprayed across the painted Virgin's bare foot in such a way that it echoed, hauntingly, other images he had seen, of Christ on His cross, blood trickling from the wounds in His impaled insteps. And he wondered again, what the woman had been doing here, in this half-forgotten, inconsequential old church. It seemed a strange site for a beautiful young actress to select for an assignation. Or for blackmail.

Maitland cleared his throat. "I'm to tell you that Lord Jarvis is wishful of seeing you, sir. At Carlton House. As soon as you've finished here."

The phrasing was deliberately delicate and Lovejoy knew it, for this was a summons no magistrate could refuse. All the Public Offices, whether at Bow Street or Queen Square, Lambeth Street or Hatten Garden, had standing orders to report to Lord Jarvis immediately if it appeared a crime might involve some sensitive person, such as the mistress of a royal duke or the brother of a peer of the realm. Or the only son and heir of a powerful cabinet minister.

Lovejoy sighed. He had never exactly understood the precise nature of Lord Jarvis's influence. In addition to a mammoth townhouse on Berkeley Square, the man kept offices in both St. James's Palace and Carlton House, although he held no government portfolio. And while it was true that he was tied by blood to the royal family, the relationship was that of cousin only. It had often seemed to Lovejoy that Jarvis's position could best be described by that vague, medieval phrase, *the power behind the throne*, although how Jarvis had acquired that power and how he had maintained it through the course of King George's long descent into madness, Lovejoy could never understand. He only knew that the Prince of Wales now depended on the man as much as the King ever had. And that when Jarvis summoned a magistrate, the magistrate went.

Lovejoy swung back to his constable. "You've already sent him word of this?"

"I thought he'd want to know right away. Devlin's father being so close to the Prime Minister and all."

Lovejoy blew out a long, tense breath that turned into a frosty mist in the cold air. "You do realize the delicacy of the situation?"

"Yes, sir."

Lovejoy's gaze narrowed as he studied the constable's impassive face. Odd that it had never occurred to Lovejoy to wonder until now about Edward Maitland's politics. But then it had never really mattered, until now. Lovejoy tried to tell himself it still didn't matter, that their job began and ended with the need to investigate and solve this murder, and punish the malefactor. And yet . . .

And yet the Earl of Hendon, like Spencer Perceval and the other ministers in the King's cabinet, was a Tory, whereas the Prince of Wales and the men with whom he surrounded himself were Whigs. At any time, for the son and heir of a prominent Tory to be accused of such a crime would have been explosive. For the accusation to come now, when the old King was about to be declared mad and the Prince made Regent, could have profoundly far-reaching implications. Not just for the composition of the government, but for the nature of the monarchy itself.

Chapter 4

$\mathcal{T}$he privileged inhabitants of fashionable London were just leaving their beds when Sebastian climbed the short flight of steps to his Brook Street home. Only the distant, fog-muffled rumble of traffic from New Bond Street and the squeals of children playing chasey in the charge of nursemaids in nearby Hanover Square disturbed the noonday silence.

There was a kind of sweet oblivion in exhaustion, a blessed numbness, and Sebastian felt it now. Morey, his majordomo, met him in the hall, an unusually anxious look drawing the man's features together into a frown. "My lord—" he began.

Sebastian's gaze fell on a familiar cane and top hat resting on the hall table. He was suddenly, intensely aware of his crumpled cravat and the blood-encrusted graze across the side of his forehead and the inevitable toll taken by all the brandy-tinged hours that had passed since last he'd slept. "I take it my father's here?"

"Yes, my lord. The Earl awaits you in the library. But I believe it imperative that you first be made aware of an incident which occurred this morn—"

"Later," said Sebastian, and crossed the hall to open the library door.

Alistair St. Cyr, the Fifth Earl of Hendon, sat in a

leather armchair near the fire, a glass of Sebastian's brandy cradled in the hand that rested on one knee. At his son's entrance the Earl looked up, his jaw working back and forth as it had a tendency to do when his emotions were aroused. At sixty-five, he was still a powerful man, with a barrel chest and a thick shock of white hair above a heavily featured face. He had the most startling, deep blue eyes Sebastian had ever seen. For as long as he could remember, Sebastian had watched those brilliant eyes flare with an emotion he could never quite identify each time Hendon's gaze came to rest upon his only surviving son. And for the past fifteen years or more, Sebastian had watched that blaze of emotion quickly disappear beneath a tide of pain and disappointment that was all too easy to read.

"So?" said the Earl now. "Did you kill him?"

"Talbot?" Sebastian swung off his caped driving coat and tossed it over one of the cane chairs by the bowed front window. His hat and gloves followed. "Unfortunately, no."

"You're damned cool about it."

Sebastian walked to the side table and poured himself a glass of brandy. "You would wish me otherwise?"

The Earl's jaw worked furiously back and forth. "What I wish is that you curb this propensity to try to put a period to the existence of your fellow men. This makes three meetings in the six months you've been back in England."

"Actually, it's been some ten months since I sold out."

"*Damn* your impertinence." Hendon surged to his feet. "The last one—what was his name?"

"Danford."

"That's right. Danford I could understand. There are some insults a gentleman can't be expected to allow to pass unchallenged. But Talbot? My God. You were

screwing the man's *wife*. There'd have been hell to pay
if you'd killed him, I can tell you that."

Sebastian drained his brandy in one long pull and
tried to swallow twenty-eight years' worth of raw, con-
flicting emotions with it. He hadn't, in point of fact, been
screwing Melanie Talbot. But even if Sebastian had
been inclined to explain himself, there would have been
no point: the idea of simple friendship between a man
and a woman was something Hendon could neither believe nor understand. Any more than he'd understand
why Sebastian would care if a man such as Captain John
Talbot should choose to beat his gentle young wife.

"The man wants killing," Sebastian said simply.

"Why? So you can have his wife?"

Turning away, Sebastian went to splash himself another drink. "That was never my intention."

"What you need is a wife of your own."

Sebastian froze, then carefully lowered the brandy
carafe. "So we're back to that, are we?"

"If you're going to insist upon continuing this dissolute lifestyle of yours, the least you can do is have the
courtesy to ensure the succession before you drink
yourself into a decline. Or go out some morning and get
yourself shot."

"You underestimate me."

He turned to find his father studying the gash across
Sebastian's forehead through narrowed, troubled eyes.
"This one was close."

"I told you, the man wants killing."

The Earl's jaw hardened. "You're eight-and-twenty.
It's past time you settled down."

"To do what? Take over management of the estates?" Sebastian laughed at the spasm of alarm that
crossed his father's features, lifted the brandy in a mock
toast, and murmured, "Touché."

"The seat for Upper Walford is empty."

Sebastian choked on his drink. "You can't be serious." His father continued to stare at him. Sebastian lowered his glass. "Good God. You are serious."

"Why not? It would give you something to do besides drinking and gaming and sleeping with other men's wives. And we could use a man of your abilities in the Commons."

Sebastian subjected his father to a long study. "Afraid Prinny means to bring in the Whigs if he's made Regent, are you?"

"Oh, the Prince of Wales will be made Regent, make no mistake about that. It's only a question now of form, and timing. But he'll find he runs up against stiff opposition if he attempts to circumvent the Tories and resurrect the Ministry of All Talents. Or something worse."

"Not so stiff as you might wish, obviously, if you're trying to recruit me as a candidate."

The Earl lowered his gaze to his own glass, turning it slowly in his palm so that the cut facets reflected the light from the lamps that burned even now, at midday, against the foggy gloom. "One might consider it a duty, in such perilous times as these, to join right-thinking men in defense of national interest, property, and privilege."

"I don't suppose it's ever occurred to you that if I were in Parliament, I might actually choose to challenge the sacred traditions of property and privilege, and champion instead the heresies of Jacobinism, atheism, and democracy?"

Lord Hendon swallowed the remainder of his brandy in one long gulp and set the glass aside. "Even you wouldn't be such a fool." Without bothering to ring for the footman, he strode to the door, only pausing with his hand on the knob to glance back and say, "Think about it."

Sebastian stood at the window, one hand holding aside the heavy green velvet as he watched his father's powerful, familiar figure disappear into the swirling fog. Perhaps it was a trick of the light, or an effect of the mists, but his father suddenly looked older and more tired than Sebastian remembered him being. And he knew a twist of regret, an urge to reach out and stop his father, to somehow make things right between them. Except that things could never really be right between them because Sebastian could never be what his father wanted him to be, and they both knew it.

He was reminded again of that long-ago, laughter-filled morning on the slopes above the cove. Alistair St. Cyr hadn't been there that summer. Even in those days, the Earl had spent most of his time in London. But he'd come home the next day, his face tight with grief, to hold the pale, lifeless body of his eldest son and heir clutched in his arms.

With Richard dead, the title of Viscount Devlin, like the position of heir apparent, had passed to the second son, Cecil. Only Cecil had died, too, just four years later. Then all of Alistair St. Cyr's hopes, all his ambitions and dreams had fallen on the boy who'd never been meant to be the heir, the youngest and least like his father of them all.

With a shrug, Sebastian let the curtain drop and turned toward the stairs.

He'd made it almost to his bedroom when his major-domo came hurrying down the hall. "My lord, I must speak with you. We've had the constables here this morn—"

"Not now, Morey."

"But my lord—"

"Later," said Sebastian, and firmly shut the door.

Chapter 5

*H*is hat clutched in his cold hands, Sir Henry Lovejoy followed a liveried and powdered footman through the echoing, labyrinth-like corridors of Carlton House. A few months ago, Lord Jarvis would have held such an audience at St. James's Palace, where the poor mad old King George III kept his offices. That Jarvis had now shifted his base here, to the palace of the Prince of Wales, struck Lovejoy as the clearest sign imaginable that a Regency was indeed imminent.

The great man was at his desk, writing, when Lovejoy was ushered into his presence. He acknowledged Lovejoy's existence with a curt motion of one plump, ringed hand, but he did not glance up or even invite Henry to sit. Henry hesitated just inside the threshold, then went to stand before the hearth. The fire was a small one, the room cavernously large and frigid. Henry held his numb hands out to the flames. From somewhere in the distance came the rhythmic rat-a-tat of a hammer and the clanging of what might be scaffolding. The Prince of Wales was always renovating, whether here at Carlton House or at his Pavilion in Brighton.

"Well?" said Jarvis at last, laying aside his pen and shifting in his chair so that he might regard his visitor. "What have you to report about this sorry business?"

Retracting his cold hands and turning, Lovejoy executed a neat bow, then launched into a precise description of the crime scene, the victim, and the evidence they'd collected so far.

"Yes, yes," said Jarvis, thrusting up from his chair with an impatient gesture that cut Henry short. "I've heard all this from your constable. It's obvious Lord Devlin must be arrested immediately. Indeed, I can't conceive why a warrant hasn't been issued already."

Lovejoy watched his lordship fumble in his pocket for a delicate ivory snuffbox. He was an unusually large man, standing well over six feet in height and weighing some twenty to twenty-five stone. In his youth, he had been handsome. Beneath the ravages of indulgence and dissipation and the passing of the years, traces of those good looks could still be seen, in the fiercely intelligent gray eyes, the strong, aquiline thrust of the nose, the sensual curve of the mouth.

Lovejoy cleared his throat. "Unfortunately, my lord, I am not convinced the evidence is sufficient to justify such an action at this time."

Jarvis's head came up, his eyes narrowing, his fleshy face deepening in hue as he fixed Lovejoy with a hard stare. "*Not sufficient*? Good God, man. What do you want? An eyewitness?"

Lovejoy drew a steadying breath. "I admit the evidence implicating the Viscount appears on the surface quite damning, my lord. But we really know very little as yet about this woman. We don't even have a clear idea as to what the killer's motive might have been."

Deftly flicking open his snuffbox with one fat finger, Lord Jarvis lifted a pinch to his nostrils, and sniffed. "She was raped, was she not?"

"Yes, my lord."

"So there's your motive."

"Perhaps, my lord. Although the violence of the attack suggests a level of anger, of instability even, which goes beyond simple sexual hunger."

Jarvis closed the box with a snap and sighed. "Unfortunately, such outbursts of violence are not unknown amongst young gentlemen who have served king and country in war. As I understand it, Devlin has killed on at least two other occasions since his return from the Continent."

"Affairs of honor, my lord. And his opponents were wounded. Not killed."

"Nevertheless, the tendency is obviously there."

His lordship walked away to stand for a moment at a window overlooking the terrace below, his hands clasped behind his back, his profile carefully composed, as if in deep thought. It was a moment before he spoke. "You're a sophisticated man, Sir Henry. Surely I've no need to explain to you what it means, to have the son of a prominent peer—a member of the government, for God's sake—implicated in such a crime. If we are seen to hesitate"—he swept one well-tailored arm in an expansive gesture toward the streets—"if the crowds out there believe that being born to a position of privilege is enough to allow an Englishman to get away with rape and murder, with sacrilege—" Jarvis broke off, his arm falling back to his side, his voice dropping to a deep, solemn hush. "I was in Paris, you know, in 1789. I'll never forget it. The sight of blood running in the gutters. Of men's severed heads, stuck on pikes. Of gentlewomen snatched from their carriages and torn limb from limb by the howling mobs." He paused, his gaze sharpening suddenly on Lovejoy's face. "Is that what you want to see here, in London?"

"No. Of course not, my lord," Lovejoy said hastily. He knew he was being manipulated, knew there were undercurrents to all this that he, a simple magistrate, could never hope to understand. He knew it, yet that didn't stop the chill that touched his soul, the sick dread that clutched at his vitals. It was every Englishman's worst fear, that the endless, rampant, mindless carnage of the French Revolution might someday spread across the Channel and destroy everything he held most dear.

"If Lord Devlin is indeed innocent of this terrible crime," Jarvis was saying, "he will in due course be exonerated and freed. The important thing is to be seen acting now. These are perilous times in which we live, sir. The news from the war is not good. The masses are discontented and sullen, and easily stirred up by radicals. With His Majesty's health unlikely to improve and a Regency bill even now before Parliament, the very stability of the realm could be at stake. This is no time to be seen to hesitate, to dither and delay. The Prince of Wales wants Devlin arrested, and he wants it done before nightfall." Jarvis paused. "I trust I can rely upon you to handle the situation with the tact and discretion required."

It was never easy, bringing a member of the aristocracy to justice. Yet it did happen. It wasn't so many years since the fourth Earl Ferrers had been arrested for the murder of his steward, tried before the House of Lords, and hanged. As heir to the Earl of Hendon, Sebastian St. Cyr carried the title of Viscount Devlin as a courtesy title only. "Lord" he might be called, but otherwise the title conveyed upon him none of the legal rights of an actual peerage. Until the day he became Earl of Hendon in his father's stead, Devlin would not, technically, be a peer. And so he would be tried before the King's Bench, like any other common criminal, rather than in the House of Lords.

If it came to that, of course.

Lovejoy bowed sharply. "Yes, my lord. I'll see to it personally."

An unexpectedly winning, almost gentle smile spread across Lord Jarvis's face. "Good man. I knew I could count on you."

His hat gripped tightly before him, Lovejoy bowed himself out of the great man's presence. But as he turned to walk down that long, ornate corridor, his footsteps echoing hollowly, his heart feeling strangely heavy in his chest, Sir Henry Lovejoy became aware of a growing conviction that he was being used.

Chapter 6

Sometimes, dreams of the war still came to him. Dreams haunted by dying children, dark eyes filled with pain and fear and bewilderment, and golden-skinned women, swollen pregnant bellies ripped open by soldiers' bayonets. Once it had mattered to him *which* soldiers' bayonets, French or English? It had mattered desperately. That had been before he'd understood it was irrelevant, that it was only a factor of time and geography, that soldiers of all nations did these things. Once, he'd thought England a nation anointed by God, a favored land blessed and divinely protected, a force of good, battling enemies who must therefore be the forces of evil. Once, he had believed that there were such things as just wars and righteous causes. Once.

Sebastian opened his eyes, his breath coming short and fast, his clenched hands clammy with sweat. The gloom of his velvet-shrouded bedchamber gave no indication of time, and it was a moment before he remembered where he was, and why. He hadn't meant to sleep, had only intended to rest. Slowly, he squeezed his eyes shut, then opened them again. But the memory of the images remained, dark and haunting and indelible.

Sir Henry Lovejoy decided to take Senior Constable
Edward Maitland with him to Brook Street, along with
another, younger constable named Simplot, whom
Maitland suggested. It wasn't that Lovejoy expected a
man of Devlin's position in Society to resist arrest. But
Lovejoy had to admit to a certain, secret fear that,
minus the two constables' weighty presence, the Viscount might not take Lovejoy seriously. One heard tales
of this viscount, of his irreverent, unconventional ways.
Lovejoy could imagine such a man simply laughing in
the face of an arresting magistrate. Perhaps if Lovejoy
had stood taller than four-foot-eleven in his boots, he'd
have felt more confident. At any rate, he was quietly
pleased to discover that Simplot was even taller than
Maitland, and satisfyingly broad shouldered.

"Wait for us," Lovejoy told the driver of their hackney as they drew up before Devlin's Mayfair residence.
The townhouse was an elegant structure with a neat bay
window and beautifully proportioned ionic portico, but
it couldn't begin to compare with St. Cyr House, that
massive granite pile on Grosvenor Square that would
someday belong to Devlin along with his father's titles,
the estates in Cornwall and Devon and Lincolnshire,
the interests in mining and shipping and banking. Lovejoy stared up at the townhouse's neat, stuccoed façade,
and wondered what it said about relations between the
Earl of Hendon and his only son and heir, that Devlin
chose to reside here, in Brook Street, rather than beneath that palatial paternal roof.

"His lordship'll be finding the lodgings at Newgate a
far cry from this," Maitland said in a quiet aside as a
stony-faced majordomo bowed them into the hall. "A
far cry indeed," he added, his handsome blond head
craning this way and that in an attempt to glimpse more
of that gleaming expanse of black and white marble, the

procession of gilt-framed paintings marching up the sweeping staircase that curved out of sight to the first floor.

"You move ahead of the courts, Constable," hissed Lovejoy as the majordomo's discreet knock upon the library door elicited the Viscount's permission to enter.

"My lord," said the majordomo. "The persons who were here to see you this morning have returned. With another."

Viscount Devlin stood with one buckskin-clad hip resting on the edge of his desk, a shade of annoyance crossing his finely chiseled features as he glanced up from the sheaf of papers he held in his hands. He was built long and lean, with dark hair and a high forehead across which something—or someone—had recently left a nasty gash. "Yes?" he said. "What is it?"

Lovejoy waited for the majordomo to withdraw, then executed a neat bow and said, "I am Sir Henry Lovejoy, chief magistrate at Queen Square. A warrant has been issued in your name, my lord. For the murder of Rachel York."

Lovejoy couldn't have said what sort of reaction he'd been expecting: a flush of guilt, perhaps, or a passionate protestation of innocence. At the very least one might have anticipated expressions of shock and sorrow over the death of a beautiful woman Devlin must surely have admired. But the young man's face remained impassive, unmoved by any emotion except for a faint quiver of what looked very much like boredom.

He set aside the papers. "What is this? Some sort of jest?"

"No jest, my lord. You have been implicated both by evidence found at the scene of Miss York's death and by the testimony of witnesses."

The Viscount crossed his arms at his chest and shifted

his weight so that he could thrust his long legs out in front of him. "Really? That's interesting. What evidence? And who are these witnesses?"

Lovejoy returned the younger man's stare. He had uncanny eyes, as hard and yellow as a noonday sun. It was with effort that Lovejoy kept his voice steady. "I must ask you, first of all, if you can account for your whereabouts between the hours of five and eight yesterday evening?"

The Viscount blinked. "I was out."

"Out?" said Edward Maitland, his jaw thrust aggressively forward. "Out? Out where?"

The Viscount swung his head to subject the senior constable to a long, cool stare. "Out . . . walking."

An angry flush darkened Maitland's cheeks. It had been a miscalculation after all, Lovejoy now realized, to bring the constables. Maitland was far too pugnacious and aggressive, too abrasive and hotheaded, to deal well with a man of Devlin's ilk. Lovejoy cast his subordinate a warning look and said quietly, "You forget yourself, Constable." To Devlin he said, "Can anyone vouch for you, my lord?"

The Viscount brought his gaze back to Lovejoy. They were inhuman, really, those eyes. Wild and feral, like something one might see gleaming out of the darkness of a wolves' den. "No."

Lovejoy knew a flicker of disappointment. How much simpler it would have been for them all if the Viscount had spent those fatal hours dining with friends, or at a pugilistic match. "Then I fear I must request you to accompany us to Queen Square, my lord."

Those disconcerting yellow eyes narrowed. "I wonder, am I allowed to send a servant to fetch a greatcoat and other foul-weather accouterments? I understand it can be rather chilly this time of year in"—he swung to fix

Edward Maitland with a bland, ironic gaze—"Newgate, didn't you say?"

Lovejoy felt a quick shiver run up his spine. There was no way the Viscount could have heard the senior constable's whispered remark, earlier, in the hall. It was impossible. And yet . . . Lovejoy remembered hearing tales, near-legendary accounts he had always dismissed, of this young man's disconcertingly acute eyesight and hearing, of lethal reflexes and a catlike ability to see in the dark. Invaluable abilities he'd exercised to such deadly effect against the French in the Peninsula before he'd come home for reasons shrouded in rumor and innuendo.

"You may, of course, fortify yourself against the cold with whatever vestments you require," Lovejoy said hastily.

An unexpected gleam of amusement flared in those terrible yellow eyes, then died. "Thank you," said Viscount Devlin. And for the second time that day, Sir Henry Lovejoy was left with the perplexing impression that, beneath the surface, all was not precisely as it seemed.

Chapter 7

A half hour later, Sebastian paused at the top of his front steps, one hand resting lightly on the rail. The temperature was falling rapidly with the approach of evening, the fog thinning down to dirty wisps that hugged the pavement and curled around the unlit lampposts. He drew a cold, acrid breath of air deep into his lungs and let it out slowly.

He wasn't particularly worried. His acquaintance with Rachel York had been both casual and decidedly noncarnal in nature. Whatever evidence might seem to implicate him in her death would surely be quickly discredited—even if he did have no intention of telling anyone where, precisely, he had been between the hours of five and eight the previous evening.

And yet as he started down the steps, Sebastian felt an odd sense of heightened awareness, a prickle of premonition. He was acutely conscious of the slow, ponderous movements of the big young constable behind him and the queer, high-pitched voice of the magistrate, Lovejoy, as he hesitated beside the open door of the waiting hackney and said something to the jarvey.

The hackney was an old one, an ancient landau with a low, rounded roof and sagging leather straps and a musty, stale odor. The senior constable, the one named

Maitland, swung around suddenly to catch Sebastian's arm in a rough grip and lean in close. "I daresay it's quite a comedown from your usual mode of transportation," said Maitland, his lips pulled back in a smile, his eyes hard. "Isn't that right?" The man's smile widened enough to show his clenched teeth, his fingers digging in hard. "*My lord.*"

Sebastian met the constable's challenging blue stare with a tight smile of his own. "You'll wrinkle my coat," he said, one hand coming up to close around the constable's wrist. It was a simple maneuver he'd learned in the mountains of Portugal, a trick of pressure applied at precisely the proper points. The constable sucked in a painful breath, his hand losing its hold on the coat as he took an unwary step back.

Days of stinking fog had left the stone steps slippery with a combination of coal soot and freezing condensation. One foot shooting off the edge of the first step, the constable spun around, his back slamming against the iron handrail as he scrambled to catch himself, missed, and went down on one knee on the second step. His top hat landed beside him.

He had pretensions to dandyism, this constable, with his artfully tousled blond curls and high shirt points and intricately arranged cravat. Clapping the hat back on his head, he straightened slowly, a dirty tear running down one leg of his expensive buff-colored breeches.

"*Why, you bloody bastard.*" Maitland's jaw tightened, his nostrils flaring. But it was his hands Sebastian was watching. London constables didn't usually carry knives, although some of the more aggressive ones did. Maitland's knife was a small, wicked thing, with a honed blade that shone even in the faint light of a dull afternoon. The constable smiled. "Try something like that again and you won't live long enough to hang. *My lord.*"

It was all for bluster and effect; Sebastian knew that. But the younger constable—the one with the open face and big, oxlike body—threw a quick, worried glance toward the street, where Lovejoy stood with his back turned and one foot on the hackney step. "Good God, Maitland. Put that thing away before Sir Henry sees."

He lurched forward, intending perhaps to shield the knife from the magistrate's view. But he was big and clumsy, the wet granite steps treacherous. His feet slid out from beneath him in turn. With a startled cry, he pitched forward, straight into Maitland's blade.

Sebastian watched the young man's eyes widen with surprise, his face go slack.

"*Jesus Christ.*" Maitland let go of the knife's hilt, his own features twisting with horror.

The young constable wavered on his feet, his gaze caught by the knife still protruding from his chest. A thin trickle of blood spilled from his mouth. "You've killed me," he whispered, his gaze lifting to Maitland's, his legs buckling beneath him.

Sebastian caught the young man as he fell. Blood spilled over Sebastian's hands, down the front of his greatcoat. Lowering the gasping constable to the footpath, Sebastian ripped off his own neckcloth, pressed it to the bubbling wound in the constable's chest. The fine linen turned red and sodden in his hand.

"Good God," whispered Maitland, staggering down the last step, his face ashen.

"Get a doctor. Quickly," snapped Sebastian.

Maitland stood with one arm wrapped around the area railing as if for support, his eyes wide and staring.

"*Bloody hell.* Sir Henry, if you would—"

Sebastian pivoted on one knee to find Lovejoy standing on the hackney's steps, his little face pinched with shock. "My lord," said the magistrate. "What have you done?"

"What have *I* done?" said Sebastian.

Still grasping the railing, Constable Maitland's wide-eyed gaze lifted from Simplot to the magistrate. "He stabbed him," Maitland suddenly shouted. "He stabbed Simplot!"

Sebastian stared down at the man in his arms. A cold, misty rain had begun to fall, bringing a dark sheen to the paving stones and dampening the graying face of the dying man. Sebastian had seen enough death, from Italy and the West Indies, to Portugal, to recognize the signs when he saw them. The man would die, and Sebastian would be blamed for this death, just as he was already being blamed for the murder of a West End actress he had barely known.

He had considered that a misunderstanding, an inconvenience simply dealt with. Not so simple now, he thought. Easing his hands from beneath the constable's shoulders, Sebastian rose to his feet.

Brook Street, once empty, now resounded with the tramp of approaching footsteps as two Inns of Court Volunteers, dressed in scarlet with yellow facings, white waistcoats and breeches, and black gaiters, appeared around the corner from Davies Street. "You men," shouted Sir Henry Lovejoy from the carriage's open doorway, one trembling hand extended to point, damningly, at Sebastian. "Seize that gentleman. *Constable Maitland.* Snap out of it."

Shaking his head as if to clear it, Maitland pushed away from the railing in a clumsy rush. Sebastian stopped him with a right hook that caught the constable under the chin and sent him reeling back to slam against the stucco wall.

The rain was falling harder now. Someone shouted. The footsteps broke into a run. Sebastian spun around. Calculating the distance to the hackney's box, he leapt, landing beside the startled jarvey with a force that set the old landau rocking on its sagging straps.

" 'Ere, 'ere!" said the jarvey, his bloodshot eyes opening wide in a gnarled, gray-whiskered face. "You ain't allowed up 'ere with me."

"Then I suggest you get down." Seizing the reins, Sebastian tweaked the whip from the man's slack grip and snapped the leather thong over the bays' ears. The ancient carriage jerked forward.

" 'Oly 'ell," gasped the jarvey, and dived for the footpath.

Sebastian threw a quick glance behind him. The Inns of Court men had stopped to kneel beside the wounded constable. But Maitland was running in the carriage's wake, his arms and legs pumping, his face twisted with determination. "Stop that hackney! The man's a murderer."

"Shit," said Sebastian, and spanked the reins hard against the bays' flanks.

Without checking at the corner, he swung onto New Bond Street, cutting between a wide-wheeled freight wagon and a high-wheeled gig driven by a fat man in a yellow coat. The yellow-coated man jerked on his reins, his chestnut rearing up.

"You there!" Sebastian heard Maitland shout. Looking back, Sebastian saw the constable leap onto the gig's high seat. "Give me those reins."

"I say, I say," bleated Yellow Coat.

"Get down," snarled Maitland, bringing the snorting horse under control and pushing Yellow Coat off his perch.

Up ahead, a crush of vehicles jammed the street. Sebastian collected his reins, his eyes narrowing against the steady downpour as he judged the distance between a stalled dowager's barouche and the donkey cart making its slow, ponderous way up the street.

"My lord!" shouted Sir Henry Lovejoy, his rain-lashed head and half his upper body protruding from the landau's open window, his fist pounding against the ancient panels. "In the King's name, I demand you stop this carriage *at once*."

Bloody hell, thought Sebastian. He'd forgotten about the magistrate. "Keep your head in," he shouted, sparing Sir Henry one swift glance.

"I said, I demand you—" Sir Henry broke off, his eyes widening as Sebastian swung around the barouche, nipping in so close that one of the carriage's dangling lamps caught the brim of the magistrate's hat.

"*Good God*," said the magistrate, jerking his bald head back inside the hackney.

Hauling on the reins, Sebastian brought the landau careening in a sharp left onto Maddox Street. Behind them, the donkey brayed and kicked, upending its cart to spill a load of squawking, feather-ruffled chickens across the wet pavement.

"Get that bloody donkey cart out of my way!" screamed Maitland, the gig at a standstill, the blowsy chestnut snorting and tossing its head as the constable jabbed at the ribbons.

The bays were stretched full out now. Sebastian gave them their heads, plowing up Maddox Street past the dignified stone pile of St. George's. A gentle tolling of church bells cut through the crisp evening air. Fashionable ladies in gaily colored gowns and gentlemen holding aloft umbrellas scattered before the charging hackney.

"Stop this hackney," shouted Lovejoy, banging his fist again as Sebastian swerved around the back of the church and onto Mill Street, "in the name of the King!"

Sebastian threw a quick glance behind them, but the street was empty except for a lamplighter and his boy. Sebastian swung back around just as the bays erupted into the rain-washed expanse of Conduit Street and a big-boned black hack, ridden by a young lady struggling to bring her mount under control, reared up before them.

He hauled on the reins, wrenching the bays sideways. The horses plunged, snorting, hooves striking sparks from the edge of the footpath. The joints of the old landau squealed. Wood snapped. The coach body crashed to the pavement, the box skewing sideways.

"*Devlin*," screamed Sir Henry, struggling to push open the hackney's door.

"Shit," whispered Sebastian. Rain sluiced down his face; at some point, he realized, he'd lost his hat. Sliding off the box, he skidded on the wet paving blocks and dodged the young lady's groom as the man scrambled off his own mount to grab the bridle of his mistress's squealing, wide-eyed black.

Well mannered and patient, the groom's mount stood with its big-boned, gray head down, its reins trailing loose in the swirling gutter. Snatching up the wet leather, Sebastian vaulted into the saddle.

"Hey! You there! Stop!" The white-faced groom swung around, his hands full with his mistress's still-skittish hack. "*Stop! Horse thief!*"

Sebastian kneed the gray into a flat-out gallop that carried them down the rain darkened street, toward Covent Garden and the shadowy underworld of St. Giles beyond.

Chapter 8

*C*harles, Lord Jarvis, couldn't remember precisely when he'd become aware of the level of incredible stupidity that characterized the vast majority of his fellow beings. He supposed the realization must have come upon him gradually over the years as he observed the behavior and thought processes of the housemaids and grooms, solicitors and physicians and country squires who populated his childhood world. But Jarvis knew exactly when he'd understood the strength of his own intellect, and the power it gave him.

He'd been ten years old at the time and suffering under one of that long line of tutors his mother had insisted on hiring to teach her dead husband's only son and heir, rather than expose his fragile health (and her own position as the heir's mother) to the potentially deadly rigors of Eton. Mr. Hammer, this particular vicar had been called, and he'd considered himself quite a scholar. Only vulgar necessity had induced Mr. Hammer to accept such an inferior position as tutor to a young boy, and he lost no opportunity to impress upon his pupil the magnitude of Jarvis's relative ignorance and mental incompetence. And then one day he set for Jarvis what was intended to be an impossible task: a mathematical problem that had taken Hammer himself, as an undergraduate at Oxford, a month to decipher.

Jarvis completed the assignment in two hours.

Jarvis's success so enraged his tutor that the man soon found an excuse to punish the boy with a severe beating. But it had been worth it, because in that moment of sweet triumph, Jarvis had understood. He'd understood that most men, even those who were gently born and well educated, had minds that limped and plodded and tied themselves into knots. And that his own ability to think clearly and quickly, to analyze and discern patterns, and to devise intricate strategies and solutions was not only rare. It was also, potentially, a very powerful tool.

At first he had expected things in London to be different. But it hadn't taken Jarvis long to learn that essentially the same degrees of imbecility and incompetence existed at the highest echelons of society and government as were to be found, say, at a meeting of the hounds in Middlesex.

The man Jarvis was dealing with now, Lord Frederick Fairchild, was typical. He was a Duke's son, Lord Frederick, but only a younger son, which meant he'd had to make his own way in life. He'd succeeded fairly well by his society's standards, although a stubborn adherence to Whiggish principles had limited his access to power under the old King George III. Now, with the Prince of Wales about to be named Regent, Lord Frederick had expectations that his years of loyal adherence to Prinny were finally to be rewarded. He'd come here, to the chambers the Prince kept set aside for Jarvis's use at Carlton House, in a rather transparent attempt to ferret out which position, exactly, would be his. That he had aspirations of perhaps even being named Prime Minister was an open secret known to everyone in London.

"The representatives from the Lords and Commons are to have a conference next Tuesday," Lord Frederick was saying, his gentle gray eyes wide and watchful. "If a compromise on the wording can be reached, I see no reason the swearing in of the Prince as Regent should not take place on the sixth." He paused and looked at Jarvis expectantly.

Despite his two-score-and-ten years, he was still considered a handsome man, Lord Frederick: tall and broad shouldered, with a trim waist and an enviably thick, wavy mass of silver hair. A widower, he was quite a favorite with the ladies. He could always be counted on to squire an unescorted matron down to supper, or to solicitously turn the pages of her music when she played. His amiability and social skills kept him amply supplied with invitations to country house parties and the usual whirls of the London Season. But Lord Frederick had expensive habits—dangerously expensive habits, which added a hint of urgency to his voice as he cleared his throat and asked with studied casualness, "Has the Prince made any decisions yet on the disposition of offices for the new government he'll be forming?"

The question was delicately phrased. Everyone knew the Prince of Wales made few decisions on his own outside such pressing matters as choosing the color of the new silk hangings for his drawing rooms, or selecting an architect to undertake his latest renovation project. From his position near the window, Jarvis simply smiled. "No. Not yet."

A spasm of disappointment, quickly veiled, passed over Lord Frederick's features. The man was atypically nervous today. He even jumped when one of Jarvis's secretaries knocked softly at the door and announced, "A Sir Henry Lovejoy to see you, my lord. He says it's important."

"Show him in," said Jarvis, very much aware of Lord Frederick's presence. It would be interesting to see if the man had heard of Rachel York's death. Interesting, indeed. "Well, what is it?" Jarvis asked, his voice gravelly with a deliberate show of impatience when the magistrate appeared.

Sir Henry cast an inquiring glance toward Lord Frederick and hesitated.

"You may speak frankly," said Jarvis, waving a vague hand in Lord Frederick's direction. "I assume this is about Lord Devlin?"

"Yes, my lord." The magistrate paused again, and something about his manner told Jarvis he wasn't going to like what he was about to hear. "He's escaped."

Jarvis never allowed himself the luxury of losing his temper, although he did at times express anger for effect, to inspire fear and to spur men on in their determination to please him. Now he allowed several calculated heartbeats to pass, then said, his tone icy with a nice mingling of incredulity and righteous indignation, "Escaped, Sir Henry? Did you say *escaped*?"

"Yes, my lord. He stabbed one of my constables and stole a hackney carriage, which he then—"

Jarvis pressed the thumb and index finger of one hand to the bridge of his nose and momentarily closed his eyes. "Spare me the details." Jarvis sighed, and let his hand fall. "I trust you've discovered Devlin's destination?"

A faint flush colored the little man's cheeks. There was nothing like a subtle hint of incompetence to make a man feel, well, incompetent. "Not yet, my lord."

From his seat near the fireplace, Lord Frederick rose to stare at them. "Do I understand you to say you've attempted to arrest the son of the Earl of Hendon? On what charges?"

"Murder," said Jarvis blandly.

"Murder? Good God. But . . . I thought Talbot's wound more embarrassing than life threatening. Has he indeed died?"

It was Sir Henry who answered, with another of those bobbing little bows he affected. "Lord Devlin's most recent affair of honor was not, as I understand it, fatal. However, he has been implicated in the death of a young woman whose body was discovered this morning in St. Matthew of the Fields, near the Abbey. An actress by the name of Rachel York."

Jarvis watched with interest as Lord Frederick's jaw went slack. The man was usually better at maintaining his composure. "You've arrested *Viscount Devlin* for Rachel's murder?"

Sir Henry blinked. "You knew her, my lord?"

"I wouldn't say I *knew* her, exactly. I mean, I've *seen* her, of course, at Covent Garden. And I'd heard she'd been killed, of course. But I had no idea that *Devlin* . . . " Drawing a handkerchief from his pocket, Lord Frederick pressed the delicate linen to his lips. "Excuse me," he said, and hurried from the room.

A faint frown deepening a line between his eyes, Sir Henry's gaze followed Lord Frederick's retreating figure.

"I want every available man put on Devlin's capture," Jarvis said, recalling the magistrate's attention.

Sir Henry bowed. "Yes, my lord."

"You've sent to have the ports watched, of course?"

Another bow. "Yes, my lord. Although the Viscount wouldn't exactly be welcome on the Continent these days."

"There's always America."

"Yes, my lord."

The little man was beginning to bore him. Jarvis reached for his snuffbox. "I trust I'll receive a more satisfactory report on this matter in the morning."

"Let us hope, my lord," said Sir Henry Lovejoy, and bowed himself out.

Yet after he left, Jarvis stood for a time at the rain-splattered window, his snuffbox held forgotten in his hand as he stared out at the darkness. The fog had finally cleared so that from here he could see the Mall, its wet pavement shining in the flickering golden light thrown by the streetlamps and the lanterns of the passing carriages.

He hadn't cared, before, whether Devlin was responsible for the death of that actress or not. He still didn't care. All that mattered was that official inquiries into Rachel York's murder be ended as quickly as possible and that the young Viscount's notoriety be prevented from damaging the government at such a critical juncture. If necessary, the Viscount's father, the Earl of Hendon, could be eased out of the government.

In fact, the more he considered it, the more Jarvis thought that some good might come of this tangle after all. While his staunch Tory sentiments made Hendon more palatable to Jarvis than a man of, say, Fairchild's stripe, the fact remained that Hendon had never been one of Jarvis's supporters. The old fool actually believed that politics could be conducted by the same rules of sportsmanship and fair play as a cricket match on the fields of Eton. If Jarvis could finally get rid of Hendon, managing the Prince would be that much easier.

Besides, Devlin's precipitous flight from justice and his presumably fatal attack upon an officer of the law certainly suggested an unexpected degree of guilt. The young man needed to be caught soon. Or killed. Jarvis flicked open his snuffbox, lifted a pinch to one nostril, and inhaled deeply. Yes, he rather thought it would be better if Devlin were killed.

Chapter 9

$\mathcal{T}$he sounds of pursuit had long since faded into the distance.

Sebastian slowed the gray to a walk. Darkness was falling fast, the rain easing to a fine mist as the wind rose. Turning up the collar of his greatcoat against the cold and the wet, Sebastian had time to regret the loss of his hat and to consider his future course of action.

Even here, away from the more fashionable neighborhoods of Mayfair, heads swiveled to follow his passing, and fingers pointed. Sebastian was acutely aware of his missing neckcloth, his mud-splattered boots, the bloodstains on his greatcoat and gloves. His immediate need, he decided, was to remove himself to an area in which his disheveled appearance would occasion less remark. In the back alleys and byways of someplace like Covent Garden or St. Giles, no one would look twice at a hatless man with a torn greatcoat and blood on his gloves.

Beneath the folds of his greatcoat Sebastian felt the weight of his pocketbook and knew a moment of thankfulness for the forethought that had led him to slip the purse into his pocket before leaving the house. He would find an inn, he decided; someplace humble, but warm and dry. And then he would set about contacting those who could—

Sebastian's head came up, his attention caught by a faint sound, barely discernable above the racket of wooden wheels rattling over ruts and the interminable patter of the rain.

He was in a poorer quarter now, a neighborhood of narrow streets with aging houses and small shops, their dirty windows protected by iron grates. There were no fine carriages here, only heavy lumbering wagons and dogcarts winding their way through a growing throng of sturdy working folk, coopers and ferriers, laundresses and piemen, their voices raised in a singsong chorus of *Pies. Rare hot pies.* But he could hear it now, quite plainly: the steady thunder of hooves coming up fast and a boy's voice, shouting, "If'n yer lookin' for that rum cove on a gray, he went that way!"

"Bloody hell," whispered Sebastian, and urged his purloined mount forward into the night.

He abandoned the gray in a warm stall on the edges of St. Giles. It was a notorious district, St. Giles, into which pursuing constables had been known simply to disappear forever. London's authorities avoided it.

The Black Hart Inn lay at the end of a mean little lane known as Pudding Row, in an area of crooked streets and rickety old medieval buildings that seemed to lean against one another for support, their upper floors jutting out over unpaved passages running foul with open gutters. A low, half-timbered relic, the inn had leaded front windows through which only a faint glow of light spilled out into the night. Sebastian paused in the shadow of the doorway, his head turning as he listened.

The rain had stopped, but with the coming of darkness the temperature had plummeted, sending most of

London's residents scurrying indoors. He could hear the distant screech of iron-rimmed wheels and the dull monotony of a church bell sounding someone's death knell, and nothing more. Pushing open the door, he went inside.

A heavy medley of smells washed over him, of ale and tobacco, of bitter coal smoke and hot grease and rank, stale sweat. The common room was dark, the guttering dips casting only a dim light that flickered over walls and low beamed ceilings blackened with age. Men in fustian and corduroy stood with elbows propped on the counter or lounged about scarred tables and benches. They looked up as Sebastian entered, the roar of their talk and laughter ebbing, their sunken eyes suspicious, watchful. He was a stranger here, and strangers in such places were never welcome.

Pushing his way to the counter, he bought a tankard of ale and ordered dinner. The bread would be adulterated with chalk and alum, the beef rancid and gristly, but he would find little better in this district and he'd eaten nothing since the breakfast he'd shared that morning with Christopher at a public house not far from the Heath.

There was a fire at one end of the room. Sebastian made his way toward it, his tankard in hand. The general swirl of noise had resumed, although he was aware of resentful eyes following him, of an air of tense wariness. Furtive shadows moved across the walls as two or three men sidled quietly from the room.

Sebastian was halfway across the sawdust-covered floor, winding his way between packed, unwashed bodies, when a boy of perhaps eight or ten brushed against him.

"A natty lad," said Sebastian, his voice dangerously cheerful as he deftly retrieved his purse from the boy's fist. The unexpected loss of his prize caused the young thief to hesitate so that, dropping the purse into an inner pocket, Sebastian managed to collar the lad and haul him back around, all without setting down the tankard or spilling a drop of ale. "But not a particularly skilled one, I'm afraid."

Every eye in the room was trained upon them and Sebastian knew it. Yet the atmosphere was more one of watchful expectation than of hostility. A market beadle from Covent Garden, a big, ponderous man with a stained waistcoat and three chins, stood up from a nearby table to wipe the back of one meaty hand across his wet lips. "Aye, he's an anabaptist, that one." A low ripple of laughter traveled around the room, for it was a name given to young pickpockets who'd been caught in the act and subjected to the rough-and-ready punishment of being dumped in the nearest pond. "Want we should rechristen him?"

The lad kept his chin firm and his gaze steady, but Sebastian felt a shudder travel up the boy's thin frame. For a homeless child, a dunking in a freezing pond on a night like this could mean death.

"I've no doubt he could use the ablution," said Sebastian, his words greeted by more laughter. "But the boy's done no real harm." Opening his fist, Sebastian let the thin, ragged cloth of the urchin's shirt slide through his fingers. "Go on," he added, jerking his head toward the door when the boy hesitated. "Get out of here."

Instead of running, the boy stood his ground, his dark, unexpectedly bright eyes traveling over Sebastian in open, thoughtful assessment. "On the lam, are you?"

Sebastian paused with his tankard halfway to his mouth. "I beg your pardon?"

The boy was older than Sebastian had first taken him to be—probably more like ten or twelve—and obviously observant enough to notice that beneath the mud and blood, Sebastian's greatcoat was exquisitely tailored, and of a fine cloth that had been new just hours ago. "What'd you do? Lose all your blunt and bolt afore they could shut you up in the Never-Wag? Or did you kill a man in a duel?" One small, bony hand reached out to finger the dark, telltale stain on Sebastian's chest. "Me, I think you killed somebody."

Sebastian took a long, deep swallow of his ale. "Don't be ridiculous."

"Ho. And why else would such a swell cove be stopping at a dive like the Black 'Art? You answer me that."

A prepubescent young girl with thin shoulders and a shank of straight, colorless hair appeared from the back rooms to dump the contents of her tray on the table in front of Sebastian. He stared at the small loaf of suspiciously white bread, the plate of unidentifiable meat awash in ladlefuls of congealing fat, and felt his appetite ebb.

"You should tuck that purse of yers somewhere out o' sight and out o' reach," said the urchin as Sebastian seated himself at the table. "You know that, don't you? It's like an open invitation, bulgin' out yer coat all obvious-like. In fact, it's criminal, I'd say, to be temptin' honest lads into mischief like that."

Sebastian glanced up, his fork halted halfway to his mouth. "And when were you ever an honest lad?"

The boy laughed out loud. "I like you," he said, his gaze drifting to the plate of food before Sebastian. A quiver passed over his features, a spasm of desperate want quickly hidden. "I tell you what: got a proposition for you, I do. If'n you're agreeable, I could 'ire meself out to you for, say, ten pence a day? Show you the ropes o' this part of town, I could. Be your general factotum. A fine gentleman like yerself shouldn't be without a servant."

"True." Sebastian chewed a mouthful, swallowed. "But I'm the strangest creature. I have a decided aversion to being fleeced by those in my employ."

The boy sniffed. "Well, if'n yer dead set on holdin' that against me," he said, his voice dripping reproach, his feet dragging as he turned away.

"Wait a minute."

The boy swung back around.

"Here." Picking up the hunk of bread, Sebastian tossed it to the boy, who caught the small loaf deftly with one hand. Sebastian grunted. "You're a better catch than a foist. Now get going."

Chapter 10

Kat Boleyn had first met Rachel York on the banks of the Thames, on a snowy December night just over three years ago. Rachel had been fifteen then, heartbreakingly young and full of despair. Kat had been all of twenty, but already the toast of London's stage for several years, her own secrets and painful past hidden beneath fine jewels and practiced smiles.

And so it was to the Thames that Kat Boleyn went that Wednesday night, to toss a bunch of yellow roses from the center of London Bridge and watch dry-eyed as they drifted apart and slowly sank beneath the river's black waves. Then she turned purposefully away.

The clouds still hung low over the city, but with the coming of night, the rain had eased off into a fine mist. When she was a little girl, Kat had loved the mist. She'd lived in Dublin then, in a whitewashed house facing an open green edged with chestnuts and giant oaks. One of the oaks, older than all the others, had great spreading branches that reached nearly down to the ground. Even before she started school, Kat's father had taught her to climb that tree.

She always thought of him as her father, even though he wasn't. But he was the only father she'd ever known, and he encouraged her to do things that sometimes frightened her mother.

"Life is full of scary things," he used to tell Kat. "The trick is not to let your fears get in the way of your *living*. Whatever else you do, Katherine, don't settle for a life half-lived."

Kat had tried to tell herself that, the day the English soldiers came. The mist had been thick that morning, and heavy with the acrid scent of burning. She'd stood in the dim morning light and repeated her father's words to herself over and over again as they dragged her mother kicking and screaming from that pretty little white house. They'd made Kat watch what they did to her mother that day, and they'd made Kat's father watch, too. And then they'd hanged them, side by side, Kat's mother and father both, from the oak at the edge of the green.

Those days belonged to a different lifetime, to a different person. The woman who now drove her phaeton and pair at a smart clip through London's lamp-lit streets called herself Kat Boleyn, and she was one of the most acclaimed actresses of the London stage. The velvet pelisse she wore that evening was a bright cherry red, not a smoke-smudged gray, and she wore a string of pearls at her throat, rather than a black band of mourning.

But she still hated the mist.

Reining in before the townhouse of Monsieur Léon Pierrepont, Kat handed the ribbons to her groom and stepped down, easily, from her high-perch seat. "Walk them, George."

"Yes, miss."

She paused on the footpath to stare up at the classical façade before her, lit softly by the gleam of flickering oil lamps. Like so much else about Leo Pierrepont, this house on Half Moon Street was carefully calculated to create just the right impression: large, but not too large, elegant, and with a touch of the faded grandeur to be expected from a proud nobleman now forced to live in exile. When one lived a life that was, essentially, a lie, appearances were everything.

She found him alone, in his dining room, just sitting down to a table laid for one with fine china and gleaming silver and the sparkle of old crystal. He was a slim, delicately built man upon whom the passing years, however difficult they might have been, nevertheless seemed to have rested easily. His face was largely unlined, his light brown hair barely touched with gray. Kat had never known his precise age, but given that he'd been almost thirty when driven from Paris by the Reign of Terror, she knew he must be in his late forties by now.

"You shouldn't have come," Leo said, his attention seemingly all for his soup.

Kat jerked off her gloves and tossed them with reticule, pelisse, and hat onto a nearby chair. "Whose reputation are you afraid will be compromised, Leo? Mine, or yours?"

He glanced up, gray eyes gleaming with a faint smile. "Mine, of course. You have no reputation left to lose." He signaled for the servants to leave them, then sat back. The smile faded. "You've heard what happened to Rachel, I suppose?"

Kat pressed her flattened palms against the tabletop and leaned into them. Beneath the silk bodice of her gown, her heart thudded hard and fast, but she managed to keep her voice calm, steady. "Did you do it?"

If he had, he wouldn't admit it; Kat knew that. But she wanted to watch his face while he denied it.

Leo dipped his spoon into his soup and brought it carefully to his lips. "Come now, *ma petite*. Even if I had wanted Rachel dead, do you seriously think I would have killed her in such a spectacular fashion? In a *church*? From what I understand, the walls were practically painted with her blood."

Kat watched his long, slim hands reach for a piece of bread. "One of your minions could have got carried away."

"I choose my minions more carefully than that."

"So who killed her?"

A shadow touched the Frenchman's features, a brief ghost of concern that Kat almost—*almost*—believed might be genuine. "I wish I knew."

Kat turned away, her quick, long-legged stride carrying her across the room and back again.

Leo shifted his weight in his chair and watched her. "Ring for another glass," he said after a moment. "Have some wine."

"No, thank you."

"Then at least stop pacing up and down the room in that fatiguing way. It's not good for my digestion."

She hesitated beside the table, but she did not sit. "Who was Rachel scheduled to meet last night?"

Picking up a knife, Leo calmly spread his bread with butter. "No one that I'm aware of."

"What would you have me believe then, Leo? That she went there *to pray*?"

"It's what people generally do in a church."

"Not people like Rachel." Kat went to stand before the hearth and stare unseeingly at the glowing coals. There was always danger in this game they played; they all knew that. But whoever had met Rachel last night was more than dangerous; he was evil. And what he'd done could threaten them all. "They'll be looking into her death—the authorities, I mean. They could stumble across something."

"Careful, *ma petite*," said Leo, reaching for his glass.

"The walls have ears." He took a slow swallow of his wine, then frowned. "But no, I don't think the authorities will learn anything that need concern us. I went past her lodgings this morning as soon as I heard what had happened, but the constables were there. I'll go back tonight and make certain she left nothing that could be incriminating."

"You could be too late. They might have found something already."

Leo huffed a soft laugh. "You can't be serious. This is London, not Paris. They're fools, these Englishmen. So afraid of the danger to their liberties posed by a standing army that they'd rather see their cities overrun with thieves and murderers than establish a proper police force. Those constables won't have found anything. Besides"—he thrust another piece of bread in his mouth, chewed, and swallowed—"they think they already know who did it."

Kat swung to face him. "You said you didn't know who killed her."

"I don't know who killed her. But the London authorities think they do. He's doubtless under arrest even as we speak. Some viscount with a reputed propensity for slaughtering his fellow men. He has a strange name. Something like Diablo, or Devil, or—"

"Devlin?" Her breath coming uncharacteristically shallow and fast, Kat left the fireplace and walked up to Leo, her gaze searching his face.

"That's it." He gave her a wide-eyed look and she knew he was playing with her, had recalled Sebastian's name all along. "Ah. I remember now," he said, his head tipping to one side as he smiled up at her. "Devlin was one of your protectors, once. Is that not so? Before he went off to the wars to fight for king and country against the forces of evil and the Emperor Napoleon."

"It was a long time ago." Kat swung away and reached for her pelisse. She felt a sudden need to get away. To be alone.

Pushing back his chair, Leo came to his feet in one smooth motion, his hand reaching out to close on her upper arm, stopping her, forcing her back around so that he could look searchingly into her face. He was so languid, so slender and effete-looking, that one sometimes forgot both how swiftly he could move and what strength those long, thin fingers possessed.

She stared blandly back at him, calling upon all her training as an actress to keep her features inscrutable and willing the rapid, betraying beat of her heart to calm.

But he knew her well, Leo. He knew her talents and he knew, too, this one weakness she refused to admit, even to herself. A wry smile twitched one corner of his lips, then stilled. "When you're only twenty-three," he whispered, his hand coming up to touch her cheek in a movement that was not quite a caress, "nothing in your life was so long ago."

Chapter 11

Sebastian spent what was left of the night in a small chamber above the Black Hart's rear court. After one glance at the bed, he took off his boots, spread his greatcoat on a narrow wooden bench, and lay down upon it. He'd known worse, in the war: watchful nights spent on a cold, stony ground or listening to the scuttling of cockroaches across a dirt floor.

He did not sleep.

When dawn came, he rose from his makeshift bed and crossed to the window overlooking the rubbish-strewn yard below. The morning was raw and bitter cold, but he swung the casement open wide and drew the acrid air deep into his lungs, his thoughts on the events of the evening before.

It had always seemed to Sebastian that such moments came in every man's life; pivotal instants when a chance occurrence or seemingly trifling decision could wrench a man away from what had appeared to be an inevitable future and send him hurtling in a different direction entirely. Yet it was difficult now to determine precisely when that moment in Sebastian's life had come. With his own flash of quick anger and the constable's misstep? Or had it come before that, the night before, with a promise given to a frantic, fearful woman?

Sebastian pursed his lips and blew out a long sigh. Despite everything that had happened, he couldn't regret that promise, nor could he betray the woman to whom it had been made.

Drawing a small notebook from his pocket, he tore out a sheet of paper and scrawled quickly, *Please give Melanie my assurances I shan't betray her. No matter what happens, she mustn't say anything to give herself away. Her life depends upon it. D.* Folding the page once, twice, he wrote the name and address of Melanie's sister on the outside, then thrust the note deep into a pocket.

He had calmly considered, during the long night, the options now open to him and decided these came down to three. He could surrender himself to Sir Henry Lovejoy at Queen Square and place his faith in a system better known for delivering summary judgments than for ferreting out the truth. He could flee abroad, hoping someone might clear his name in his absence but resigning himself to a life in exile if that failed to happen.

Or he could lose himself in the shadows of the city and set to work discovering, on his own, who had killed Rachel York.

She'd been an unusually attractive woman, Rachel. He'd seen her often at the city's various theaters—both on stage and at those select gatherings attended exclusively by such women and the wealthy, high-born men they sought to attract. He'd seen her and, he had to admit, admired her. But he'd never taken her as his mistress, never even sampled what she had, on several occasions, made more than obvious she was willing to give.

He couldn't begin to fathom why or how he had come to be named as her murderer. Yet he could place no reliance on the authorities bothering to discover the truth behind what had happened. When a city's detectives were paid a forty-pound reward for each conviction, true justice was more often than not a victim of avarice.

And so at some point during the long night Sebastian had decided that he would not escape abroad, nor would he surrender himself, trustingly, foolishly, to the dubious expedience of British justice. Out there, somewhere, was the man who had killed Rachel York; Sebastian's only hope lay in discovering precisely who that killer was.

Five years in army intelligence had taught Sebastian that the first thing he needed was information. He needed to talk to someone who'd known Rachel; someone who could identify her enemies, someone who might know why she had gone on a cold winter's night, alone, to meet her death in a small, out-of-the-way Westminster church.

He'd already decided against making any attempt to contact either his own family or friends; they would undoubtedly be watched, and he would do nothing that might endanger them. But no one would think to set a watch upon the actress who'd been playing Rosalind to Rachel's Celia in the Covent Garden production of *As You Like It.* The woman who'd broken Sebastian's heart six long years ago. . . .

The sun was rising higher in the sky, but only a faint hint of lightness showed through the inevitable mantle of dirty fog. He could hear the rumble of wagons and market carts on their way to Covent Garden, and the whirl of a knife grinder's wheel in the yard below.

And, nearer at hand, the sound of quick footsteps in the corridor outside his room.

Flattening himself against the wall beside the door, Sebastian stood tense, waiting. Then he heard a furtive scratching and a boy's whisper. "Oi, gov'nor. 'Tis me, Tom."

It was the urchin from last night. "Tom?" said Sebastian with malicious amusement. "I don't believe I'm acquainted with a Tom."

From the far side of the panel came an impatient oath. "The figger what tried to prig your purse last night."

"Ah. And you expect me to open the door to you, do you, my larcenous friend?"

"Lord love you, gov'nor. Now's no time to be funnin'. There's Bow Street men downstairs right this weery minute. Asking for you, they are—leastways, if'n you're the cove what knifed a constable over Mayfair way and—"

Sebastian opened the door so fast that Tom, who'd been leaning against it, half fell into the room. In the pale light, the boy looked thinner, and dirtier, than Sebastian remembered him. He fixed Sebastian with dark, assessing eyes. "They also say you cut up some mort in a church off Great Peter Street." There was a pause. "Did you?"

Sebastian met the boy's hard gaze. "No."

Tom nodded his head in quick, silent affirmation. "Thought I smelled a rum 'un. But there's two beaks in the common room right this weery minute, askin' about you, and another forty-pounder out the front."

Perching on the edge of the bench, Sebastian pulled on first one boot, then the other. "I take it you're suggesting I might find it advisable to depart through the window?"

"Aye, gov'nor. And pretty soon, too, if'n you're not anxious to dance the Newgate hornpipe."

Sweeping up his greatcoat, Sebastian crossed to the open window and surveyed the yard below. The casement opened above a low, lean-to roof of what he thought might be the kitchen. But the only exit from the yard was through the front arch. He would have to make his way along the slant of the lean-to roof to where it abutted a jutting brick extension of the inn's second story, and somehow climb from there up onto the main roof.

"Why, precisely, did you come to warn me?" Sebastian asked, pausing with one leg over the windowsill to look back at the boy.

"Gor. If ever a cove needed help, it's you, gov'nor."

"Huh. Your altruism, while inspiring, is somehow less than convincing," Sebastian said, and dropped to the sloping roof below.

Light and agile as a cat, Tom landed beside him. "I don't know what you means by that, exactly. But my offer still stands: for a shilling a day, I'm your man. I know these parts weery well, I do. If'n you're set on 'idin' out around 'ere, you couldn't find a better snapper."

"I thought the price was ten pence?" Sebastian said, running along the lean-to roof in a low crouch.

"It was. Only, now that I know the China Street pigs is after you, the price 'as gone up."

Sebastian laughed—just as a shout went up from the yard below.

Chapter 12

Sebastian cast a swift glance toward the yard, where a burly, black-bearded man in a voluminous greatcoat stood with his head tipped back and one extended finger pointing damningly toward the roof.

"Look! That's 'im, fer sure. Stop, I say. *Stop in the King's name*."

"Bloody hell," swore Sebastian. Straightening, he sprinted across the slope of the lean-to, the leather soles of his boots sliding dangerously on the wet slates, the boy two paces behind him.

At the intersection of the kitchen roof and the brick wall of the inn's ell-shaped wing, Sebastian swung around. "Here," he said, reaching down to bracket Tom's slim, bony frame with his hands and lift the boy high. "Grab the edge of the roof and pull yourself up."

Tom's bare, cold-numbed fingers fumbled for a hold, found one. "How you gonna get up?" he panted, heaving his legs up in a grunting rush that rolled him onto his stomach, then his back.

The brickwork of the wall was uneven, offering a handhold here, a foothold there. Sebastian scrambled up beside the boy and held out a hand to help Tom to his feet.

"Gor." Tom let out his breath in a rush of wide-eyed

admiration. "You'd make a first-rate second-story dancer, you would."

Sebastian laughed, his gaze narrowing as he surveyed the tumbledown roofscape spread out around them. A freezing rain had begun to fall, mist-fine and bone-chilling. Blackbeard had disappeared from the court-yard. They could hear more shouts, and the muffled sound of running feet on uncarpeted stairs.

Sebastian glanced down at the boy beside him. In coming to warn Sebastian, Tom had placed himself squarely on the wrong side of the law. Sebastian nodded toward the span of three or four feet separating the Black Hart's rain-slicked roof from the crumbling tene-ment beside it. "Can you jump that?"

To Sebastian's surprise, the boy's dirty face split into a toothy grin. "Aye. You jist watch."

His fists clenched with determination, Tom took off at a dead run toward the edge of the roof, launching at only the last possible instant into a leap that carried him easily across the gaping distance. He landed lightly, his body wavering, his feet slipping for only a moment be-fore he caught his balance on the steep wet tiles.

"I think you must have some training as a second-story dancer yourself," said Sebastian, springing after him. Tom crowed with delight.

Together, they crossed from one sagging rooftop to the next, skirting crumbling chimney pots and dodging broken eaves, their breath little puffs of steam in the cold air. At the end of the block, they found a drainpipe festooned with a tangle of bare wet wisteria branches down which they slithered. They were off and running before the first of the Bow Street men, wheezing and swearing, had emerged onto the Black Hart's mossy roof.

An early morning crowd of market women and milkmaids, piemen and butchers' boys filled the narrow lanes. Rounding the corner onto Great Leicester Street, Tom and Sebastian slowed to a walk, heading toward Charing Cross.

"Where we goin' now?" asked Tom, skipping a little to keep up with Sebastian's long-legged stride.

Sebastian hesitated, then drew from his pocket the folded note he'd written to Melanie's sister that morning. "I have a message I'd like you to deliver to a lady. Cecilia Wainwright, in Berkeley Square." Reaching for his purse, Sebastian counted out a handful of coins. "Here's a shilling for the letter, and a week's wages, besides." There was no way to guarantee that the boy would actually deliver the message, of course. It was a chance Sebastian was going to have to take.

Tom's unsmiling gaze dropped to the money in Sebastian's hand, then lifted. He made no move to take the coins. "You givin' me the heave-ho?"

Sebastian met the boy's dark, inscrutable gaze. "I don't think you understand. Continued association with me could very well get you hanged."

"Naw," said Tom with a negligent sniff. "Transported, more like. I'm scrawny enough I could let on I'm only nine and they'd believe me. They don't send little 'uns to the nubbing cheat." His face darkened as if clouded by a sudden, unpleasant memory. "Leastways, not usually."

"You've a fancy to visit Botany Bay, do you?"

Tom shrugged. "It's where they sent me mum."

It was probably the complete lack of emotion in the boy's voice that got to Sebastian more than anything else. He blew out a long, slow breath. It was an ugly practice, this business of transporting mothers and leaving their children behind to starve on the streets of London. Sebastian held out the money. "Take it."

For an instant longer, the boy wavered, his jaw held

tight. Then he took the coins and slipped the letter inside his shirt. "Where you off to?"

"There's someone I need to see."

Tom nodded and turned without another word, his feet dragging, his head bowed. But at the corner he paused, his head lifting as he swung back around. "What's 'er name, then? This lady what yer so all fired anxious to meet?"

Sebastian huffed a low, startled laugh. "What makes you think it's a lady?"

Tom grinned. "I saw it in yer face. She must be a rare looker." He paused, his head tilting sideways. "So what's 'er name?"

Sebastian hesitated, then shrugged. "Kat. Her name is Kat."

"Kat? That's no name fer a lady."

"I never said she was a lady."

Chapter 13

*L*ord Stoneleigh slept facedown in her bed, his eyes closed, his breathing heavy and even.

At some point during the night he'd shoved down the fine linen of her bedcovers in a fit of restlessness. Kat Boleyn propped herself up on her elbow and let her gaze travel over the broad, naked back and tight buttocks of the man beside her. He'd be a handsome man, if it weren't for that hint of weakness about the chin. They weren't usually so young, the men she took to her bed.

Kat rested her cheek on one palm. She'd been playing the part of this man's mistress for four months now. At first she'd found his youthful ardor and the presents he showered upon her mildly diverting. But he was beginning to bore her. And with the Prince soon to be made Regent, staunch Tories such as Stoneleigh wouldn't be of much use any longer. She was considering setting her sights on Samuel Whitbread, widely expected to be given an important portfolio once the passage of the Regency Bill allowed the Prince to form a new Whig government.

Yawning softly, Kat slid from Stoneleigh's side. At least the older ones rarely stayed the night. She didn't like it when they stayed. Now she'd have to play the part of the lover again when he awoke—at least until she could get him out of the house. Morning performances were not her best.

She slipped her bare arms into a silk wrapper and cast another glance at the tousled blond head on her pillow. She supposed he thought he had the right, since he paid the rent on the house. What he didn't know was that the agent to whom he sent the rent money every month actually worked for Kat. In the past five years, she'd managed to buy up the mortgage not only on this house, but on three other such properties. Men were such fools. Especially the ones with proud old family names, and old money.

Quietly letting herself out of the bedroom, she padded down the stairs. The drawing room was dim, the fire on the hearth unlit, the peach-colored satin drapes still drawn at the windows. The upper housemaid, Gwen, had obviously expected her mistress to sleep until noon or later. Kat went to throw open the heavy drapes and heard a voice from out of the past say, "You're awake early."

She spun about, one hand flying up, ridiculously, to clutch together the gaping neck of her wrap. As if her naked body hadn't once been as familiar to this man as his was to her. As if he hadn't touched every inch of her with his lips, and his tongue, and his incredibly gentle, clever hands.

Sebastian St. Cyr, Viscount Devlin, stood beside the empty hearth, one shoulder propped against the mantel, a boot heel hooked over the cold grate. He'd taken off his greatcoat and thrown it onto the back of a nearby chair. In the misty light of another dreary winter morning, he looked unkempt and dissolute and dangerous. A day's growth of beard shadowed his cheeks, and he had a nasty gash across one side of his forehead.

She'd seen him, of course, in the ten or so months since he'd been back in England—seen him in the crowd at the theater and, once, in New Bond Street. But always from a distance. They'd both been careful to keep a distance between them.

"How did you get in?"

He pushed away from the mantel and came at her, the lines bracketing his unsmiling lips deepening, although not with amusement. Cynical lines that hadn't been there before. "You don't ask why I'm here."

Once, he'd been her heart, her soul, her reason for living. Once, she'd have given up anything for him. Anything. But that was six years ago, and she was as different from that love-obsessed young girl as she was from the laughing child who'd once climbed an oak tree on the edge of a sun-filled Irish green.

He stopped before her, close enough that she could see the shadow of his day's growth of beard and the exhaustion that pulled his features taut. Close, but not too close. Still it seemed there was to be a distance kept between them.

"Do you need money?" she asked. "Or simply an introduction to a trustworthy band of smugglers who aren't particular about the identity of the passengers they carry across the Channel?"

He shook his head. "Do you really think I would run?"

No, he wouldn't run. She might not know all that had happened to this man during those brutal years he was away. But she still knew this about him.

He appeared to have slept in his clothes. His cravat was gone, and what looked like dried blood stained the white cuffs of his shirt. "You look terrible," she said.

The Sebastian she'd known, once, would have

laughed at that. He didn't. His gaze sought hers, captured it. "Tell me about Rachel York."

His eyes were as frighteningly animalistic as she had remembered. She swung away to settle down beside the cold hearth and set to work lighting a fire. She told herself it was natural that he had come here, to ask about Rachel. She and Rachel had been starring together in the Covent Garden production of *As You Like It*. He would know that. There was no reason to worry that he knew anything else.

"According to word on the streets, Rachel's maid is saying she went to St. Matthew's last night to meet you." Kat glanced back at him. "Did she?"

He shook his head.

"They say they found your pistol on her body."

"Really?" His eyes opened a fraction wider, but that was the only reaction he betrayed. "How curious."

When had he become so adept, she wondered, at hiding his feelings? "They also say the constable you stabbed still lives, although he won't for long. Did you know?"

"I didn't stab him."

"Just like you didn't kill Rachel?"

A corner of his mouth twitched. "If you really believed I'd killed Rachel York, you'd be swinging that poker at my head."

Kat sat back on her heels, the poker idle in her hands, her gaze on the man beside the window. "Why do you want to know about Rachel?"

"Because it seems to me that the only hope I have of working my way out of this wretched tangle is to discover who the hell did kill her." He went to the table where she kept a brandy decanter, poured himself a drink, and knocked it back in one long pull. "Any ideas as to who might have wanted to see Rachel York dead?"

She'd thought about it, of course. Thought about who, besides Leo and his associates, could have been responsible. Rachel hadn't been particularly well liked amongst the theatrical community; she'd been too focused and driven—and too successful—not to stir up petty resentments and rivalries. But Kat could think of only one man angry enough, and violent-tempered enough, to attack a woman so brutally, so passionately.

"There is someone. . . ." Kat paused, then said the name in a rush. "Hugh Gordon."

Devlin looked around in surprise. "Hugh Gordon?" A tall, darkly handsome man with a deep voice and the ability to move an audience to tears with a simple gesture, Hugh Gordon was London's most popular male actor since John Kemble.

"Rachel caught his eye her first day at the theater. She was flattered, of course. He helped her career enormously when she was starting out. She may even have fallen in love with him, for all I know. There was talk at one point of marriage. But then he became more possessive. Controlling. More . . . violent."

"You mean, he hit her."

Kat nodded. "She left him after about a year."

Devlin reached for the decanter. "I don't imagine a man with Hugh Gordon's amour propre would take kindly to that."

"He threatened to kill her."

"You think he could do a thing like this?"

"I honestly don't know."

He poured another drink, then simply stood there, regarding it thoughtfully. "What about the men in her life since Gordon?"

Beside her, the coals glowed red hot with warmth.

Kat kept her gaze trained on the fire. "She's had flirta-tions with a number of men, from Lord Grimes to Ad-miral Worth. But I don't think any man has had her in his keeping."

She was aware of his assessing gaze upon her. "Do you know what part of the country she was originally from?"

"Some village in Worcestershire. I don't remember the name. Her father was the vicar there, but he died when she was about thirteen, and she was thrown onto the parish. They apprenticed her as a housemaid to a local merchant."

Kat paused. It was one of the things the two women had in common, the similarity of their pasts. The shared memory of wheals left by a whip on bare, tender young flesh. Of rough hands bruising struggling, frantic wrists. The sharp thrust of pain, and the dull, endless ache of a humiliation and degradation that went on and on.

Kat set aside the fireplace tools with a clatter and stood up. "When she was fifteen, she ran away."

He was watching Kat closely. He knew some of what had happened to her, after her mother and father had been killed. More than she'd ever told anyone else. "That's when she came to London?"

"Of course," said Kat, keeping her voice steady. "Like all young girls hoping to start a new life."

It was an old story, of young women—sometimes girls as young as eight or nine—tricked into the flesh trade by the legion of procuresses who preyed on the innocent and vulnerable. Rachel had fallen into one's clutches before she'd even left the stagecoach.

"You met her when she started at the theater?"

Kat shook her head, a soft, sad smile tugging at her lips. "We met on London Bridge. It was December, if I remember correctly. A few days before Christmas. I talked her out of jumping."

"And found her work as an actress?"

Kat shrugged. "She was bright, with a good accent and exactly the kind of face and body men like. She was a natural."

"So what was she doing at St. Matthew of the Fields on Tuesday night? Do you know?"

Kat shook her head. "I wouldn't have said she was religious."

He came toward her, those strange amber eyes fixed, uncomfortably, on her face. "What aren't you telling me?"

Kat gave a soft, practiced laugh. "I can't think what you mean."

He reached out, his fingertips hovering just above her cheek, as if he'd meant to touch her, then thought better of it. "You're afraid of something. What?"

She forced herself to stand very, very still. "Of course I'm afraid. Rachel and I share many of the same friends and associates."

She watched his lips move as he spoke. "The Kat Boleyn I knew didn't scare so easily."

"Maybe you didn't know her as well as you thought you did."

"Obviously not," he said dryly, and turned away. "How well did you know Rachel?"

"I was probably closer to her than anyone, but even I didn't know her all that well." Kat paused, struggling to put some of what he needed to know into words. "Rachel might have been only eighteen, but life had scarred her. Toughened her. There was a calculating side to her. She could be cold—ruthless even, if she had to be."

"You two had much in common, did you not?"

The stab of hurt his words brought was so swift and unexpected, it nearly stole Kat's breath. She hadn't thought he still possessed the power to touch her heart—hadn't thought that anyone did. She glanced toward the hall. The house was silent, the hush broken only by the clatter of a horse's hooves on the street outside and the mingling cries of the street vendors: *Chairs to mend*, and, *Buy my trap. Buy a rattrap.* "You shouldn't be here," she said.

He smiled then, a faint narrowing gleam of the eyes that she remembered only too well. "What's the matter? Afraid Lord Stoneleigh will awaken and find you gone? I shouldn't think he'll stir for another hour or more."

"How did you know—"

"That he's here? I saw his walking stick and top hat in the entry."

The walking stick and top hat might have told Devlin she had company, but it wouldn't have given him the name of the man in her bed. That information, she knew, he must have acquired beforehand. It shouldn't have mattered. She told herself she didn't care. And yet, disconcertingly, she did.

"So you came via the entry, did you?" she said, keeping her voice light.

He had a habit, she was noticing, of answering her questions with one of his own. "Where did Rachel keep her rooms?"

"Dorset Court. But you can't go there," she added quickly, "if that's what you're thinking."

"Why not? If this maid is saying Rachel went to St. Matthew's to meet me, I need to know why."

"The authorities are watching the house."

He tilted his head, his puzzled gaze searching her face. "How do you know that?"

She knew that because Leo had come to the theater last night, after the performance, and told her. Under the circumstances it wouldn't be prudent, he'd said, for him to be seen there. And so he had come to Kat with a request, framed as a suggestion: that Kat might have her own reasons for making certain that Rachel had left behind nothing incriminating.

"It's known." She paused, then said with studied casualness, "I could go there myself. Talk to the maid. Perhaps even look around and see what I can find. Rachel kept an appointment book. That might tell us something."

He came to stand before her. "You?"

She lifted her head to meet his gaze. It had occurred to Kat that in Devlin she just might have found a potentially valuable ally, someone who had even more interest than she in tracking down the man who had met Rachel in that church. The trick would be in seeing that he learned what was needed to catch Rachel's killer, but nothing more. "You know I can do it," she said.

He knew. He knew about the years she had spent as a young girl in one of London's most notorious rookeries, training as a pickpocket and a thief. And a whore.

She thought he might refuse. Instead he said, "All right. Although I can't help but wonder why."

"For auld lang syne?" she suggested.

"Maybe. And maybe because you're scared. Even if you won't say why."

She thought for a moment that this time he would touch her. Then a faint thump from overhead drew her gaze toward the hall. "You must go," she said quickly. "Come by tomorrow morning, early. I'll tell you then what I've learned."

"Uh-uh." A hint of amusement deepened the lines beside his mouth. "I'll find you."

She let a slow smile spread across her face. "Why? Don't you trust me?"

"Would you?"

Kat's smile faded. Once, she had told him she loved him more than life itself and would never, ever let him go.

And then she'd told him it was all a lie, and hurt him so badly it had torn a hole in her own heart.

"No," she said, and turned toward the stairs, leaving him standing alone in the cold morning light.

Chapter 14

Sir Henry Lovejoy took his position as chief magistrate of Queen Square very, very seriously. He often came into the Public Office early, to go over his case notes, and to study reprints of the decisions of his fellow magistrates.

It was a product of his upbringing, he supposed. That, and the habit of industry. Born of solidly respectable tradesman stock, Lovejoy had decided in midlife to become a magistrate only after having amassed a tidy independence as a merchant. Not a fortune, but a comfortable independence.

It was a shift in direction he hadn't undertaken lightly, for Lovejoy was a methodical man who never did anything without prolonged and careful thought. He'd a number of reasons for this change in vocation, not the least of which was his conviction that a childless man ought to leave something worthwhile behind him, some contribution to society. And Sir Henry Lovejoy was, now, a childless man.

He was sitting at his desk, a muffler wrapped around his neck to ward off the morning chill, when Edward Maitland appeared in the open doorway and said, "Three Bow Street Runners had Devlin trapped at an old inn on Pudding Row, near St. Giles."

"And?" said Lovejoy, looking up from his notes.

"He went out a window and escaped over the roof."

Lovejoy sat back in his chair and peeled his eye-glasses off his nose.

"I've sent some of the lads over there to have a look around," said Maitland. "Although I daresay there's not much point."

"Interesting." Lovejoy chewed the earpiece of his spectacles. "Why do you suppose he's still in London?"

"No place else to bolt, I expect."

"A man of Devlin's resources?" Lovejoy shook his head. "Hardly. How is Constable Simplot?"

"Still alive, sir. But he won't last much longer, not with a sucking wound."

Lovejoy nodded. The knife had punctured the young man's lung. It would be only a matter of time now. Tipping his chair forward, Lovejoy searched amongst the litter on his desk. "What, precisely, have you discovered about this Rachel York?"

"What is there to find out?"

Lovejoy pressed his lips together and refrained from pointing out that if he'd known the answer to that question, they wouldn't have needed to *discover* it. "You searched her rooms, of course?"

"First thing yesterday morning. When we spoke to the maid." Maitland shrugged. "There was nothing of interest. I left one of the lads there, like you ordered, to watch the place overnight." A waste of time and resources, his tone said clearly, although he would never voice such a thought aloud.

Lovejoy gave up looking for his schedule. "When am I due in court this morning?"

"At ten, sir."

"Not enough time," muttered Lovejoy. "I'll have to clear my docket for this afternoon then."

"Sir?" said Maitland.

"There are certain aspects of this case which disturb me, Constable. It warrants looking into further, and I intend to begin by viewing that unfortunate young woman's rooms myself. Something is going on here. I might not know what it is yet, but there's one thing I do know." Lovejoy stuck his spectacles back on his nose. "I know I don't like it."

Chapter 15

$\mathcal{L}$ady Amanda Wilcox didn't discover that her brother Sebastian was wanted for the murder of an actress named Rachel York until the day after his infamous flight across London.

With the Season not yet properly under way, she had opted for a quiet evening at home in the company of her sixteen-year-old daughter, Stephanie. Neither her son, Bayard, nor his father—both of whom had presumably heard the news, having spent the night on the town—bothered to inform her of the scandal. And so it wasn't until Thursday morning, when she came down for breakfast and found the *Morning Post* folded beside her place, as per her staff's standing instructions, that Amanda learned of the social disaster looming over her family.

She was still at the breakfast table, drinking a cup of tea and staring at the *Post*, when her father, the Earl of Hendon, was announced.

He hurried into the breakfast parlor, still wrapped in his street coat and hat and bringing with him an unpleasant medley of smells, of freezing rain and coal smoke-choked fog. His fleshy face was haggard, his mouth slack, his eyes red-rimmed and puffy. He fixed her with a desperate stare and demanded without preamble, "Has he contacted you? *Has he?*"

"If you mean Sebastian," said Amanda, pausing to take a calm sip of her tea, "I should rather think not."

Hendon swung away, one hand coming up to shield his eyes, such a great sigh rumbling from his chest that she was embarrassed for him. "*My God*. Where is he? Why hasn't he sought help from any of his friends or family?"

Amanda folded the paper and set it to one side. "Presumably because he knows his family."

He turned to face her again, his hand falling slowly to his side. "I would do anything within my power to help him."

"Then you're a fool."

His fierce blue gaze met hers, and held it. "He is my son."

Amanda was the first to look away. "Of course," she said dryly. "There is that." She pushed back her chair and stood up. "The only redeeming feature I can see to all of this is that since he was bound to disgrace us eventually, at least he had the courtesy to do it this year. Hopefully the worst of the scandal will have died down by next Season, when Stephanie makes her come out."

"Is that all you can think of?"

"Stephanie is my daughter. What else should I be thinking of?"

He regarded her thoughtfully for a long, intense moment. "I always knew you and Sebastian weren't close. I suppose that was inevitable, given the number of years between you. But I don't think I realized until now just how much you hate him."

"You know why," she said, her voice a harsh tear.

"Yes. But if I can see my way to forget it, then why in the name of God can't you?" He turned away. "Give my best to my grandchildren," he said over his shoulder, and left.

Amanda waited until she heard the front door close behind her father. Then she picked up the morning's edition of the *Post* and went upstairs to her husband's dressing room.

The Wilcox family was an ancient one, older even than the St. Cyrs, and long known for their staid respectability. Far from squandering his wealth on the turf or at cards in the manner of so many of his peers, Martin, the twelfth Baron Wilcox, had taken what had once been merely a comfortable, land-based inheritance and, by judicial investments in a trading company and various other profitable wartime speculations, turned it into a sizable fortune.

Some women might have been appalled by their noble husband's dabbling in commerce; not Amanda. The Earl of Hendon's daughter understood well that while one's claim to gentility would always come from land, financial security and the future of wealth lay elsewhere. Amanda had married Lord Wilcox at the end of her second Season. She'd rarely had cause to regret her decision.

She found him seated before his dressing table, engaged in the very serious business of tying his cravat. Martin Wilcox might be just shy of fifty, with gray threading his receding brown hair, and heavy jowls framing his thin lips, but like most members of the Prince's set, he was a very careful dresser. After one look at his wife's face, he dismissed his valet with a curt nod.

She tossed the opened *Post* onto the dressing table before him. "You might have told me."

Wilcox kept his gaze on his reflection in the glass. "You had retired for the evening," he said, as if that were the only explanation required, and indeed it was, for it had been some fifteen years since Amanda had allowed Wilcox past the door to her bedchamber. Not that he could complain that she hadn't done her duty by him. In the first six years of their marriage she had presented him with first Bayard, then a daughter and a second son. It was only then, having produced the requisite heir and a spare, that Amanda had barred her husband from her bed.

The youngest child had died in its seventh year, but Amanda hadn't been inclined to reverse her decision, and Wilcox—never one to make excessive demands upon his wife—had forborne to press her. Bayard was healthy enough . . . in body, at least, if not in mind.

"My father was here this morning," she said, going to stand in the center of the room, her arms crossed at her chest.

"And?" Leaning forward to study his image in the mirror, Wilcox began to make careful adjustments to the folds of his neckcloth with his fingers. "Does he know where Devlin is?"

"No. He thought I might."

Wilcox grunted. "If your brother has any sense, he's fled the country by now. Nasty piece of work, this, from the sounds of it. I always knew Devlin could be violent, but"—he paused, tilting his head this way and that as he studied his reflection—"I must say, I never expected something like this. The scandals he's forced us to endure in the past were nothing compared to this."

Amanda let out a scornful huff. "Don't be ridiculous. Sebastian didn't murder that woman."

He glanced up, his gaze meeting hers in the mirror, his habitual faint smile curving his lips. "So certain, my dear?"

"You do realize who this dead actress was, don't you?"

Opening a Chinese lacquered jewel box, Wilcox considered its contents, then selected a diamond and two gold fobs. Martin always wore too much jewelry. "Should I?" he said, hanging one of the fobs from his watch chain.

"You might, if you paid more attention to your son and heir. Rachel York is the woman Bayard has been making such an exhibition of himself over since before Christmas."

Wilcox slipped the ring on his finger. "So?"

"So, what if the case against Sebastian falls apart and the authorities start investigating this woman's death? What then?"

"So?" he said again. "There's no harm in a healthy young man admiring a beautiful woman—especially when the woman in question trades on that beauty, and uses it to entice, and to entrap. If the authorities are going to suspect every London buck who ever lusted after that woman, believe me, they'll have a very long list."

Amanda started to say something, then didn't.

"Besides," he continued, "if anyone asks, I have only to tell them that Bayard was with me Tuesday night."

Amanda stared at her husband's bland, untroubled face. "And if he really did do it, Martin? You're worried about the scandal my brother has caused; what if it turns out to be Bayard?"

Wilcox stood up, his jowly face slowly darkening. "What precisely are you saying? That you think your own twenty-one-year-old son capable of a crime you don't believe your rakehell of a brother could have committed?"

Amanda met his angry gaze, her own jaw tight. "You and I both know what Bayard is like."

"I told you," said Wilcox, with more force than usual. "Bayard was with me."

"Well. What a relief. We've nothing to worry about, then," she said dryly, and left the room.

Chapter 16

*H*e possessed a knack, Sebastian had discovered during his years in the army, for playacting, for accents and mimicry and all the subtle nuances of behavior and attitude that could be used to impersonate and deceive. He also knew that, in general, people saw what they expected to see, that men looking for an absconding nobleman would not peer too closely at a humble vicar, or an honest shopkeeper in cheap linen and a poorly cut, drab coat.

And so, after leaving Kat Boleyn's elegant little townhouse, he made his way to the Rag Fair in Rosemary Lane, where he bought a set of secondhand clothes, a drab topcoat, and a rusty black round hat. He stopped at several small shops, where he made an assortment of other purchases. Then, wrapped in his new topcoat, with the round hat pulled low to hide his tawny eyes, he took a room at a respectable but simple inn called the Rose and Crown, and set about transforming himself into someone else entirely.

Sebastian tipped his head first one way, then the other, surveying his reflection in the small mirror above the washstand. Mr. Simon Taylor, he thought he'd be called. He had little sense of style, Mr. Taylor, with his badly cut hair, old-fashioned coat, and poorly tied cravat.

With practiced care, Sebastian used chalk dust to add a few streaks of gray to his dark, newly chopped hair. After months of drifting aimlessly, of living a life at once privileged and predictable and always, inevitably, unbearably boring, he was conscious of a faint stirring of interest, of excitement such as he hadn't known since he'd left the army ten months before.

He found Hugh Gordon in a corner booth of the crumbling old redbrick pub known as The Green Man that had been popular with the theatrical crowd since the days when Elizabeth was queen.

The actor was alone; a tall, elegant man drinking a pint of ale and eating a simple plowman's lunch. His entire posture spoke of self possession and arrogance and a pronounced desire to be left alone.

Shuffling up to the table, Sebastian pulled off his hat and held it, awkwardly, humbly even, before his breast. "Mr. Hugh Gordon?"

Gordon looked up, his dark brows drawing together into a frown. Even offstage, his manner was theatrical, his voice stentorian. "Yes?"

Sebastian tightened his hold on his hat brim. "Pardon me for being so bold as to introduce myself, but I am Taylor. Mr. Simon Taylor?" Sebastian brought the inflection of his voice up at the end, in the manner of one so unsure of himself that even simple sentences come out sounding like questions. "From Worcestershire? They said at the theater I might find you here."

Reaching out, Gordon took a slow sip of his ale. "So?"

Sebastian swallowed, working his Adam's apple visibly up and down. "I'm endeavoring to locate a young relative of my mother's, a Miss Rachel York. I was hoping you might be able to provide me with her direction."

"Do you mean to say you haven't heard?" The timbre of his voice was deep and rich, the intonation flawless. If Gordon hadn't been born a gentleman, he'd certainly done a good job of cultivating both the image and accent.

Sebastian looked confused. "I beg your pardon?"

"She's dead."

"Dead?" Sebastian staggered as if reeling beneath the shock, and sat down on the bench opposite the actor. "Good heavens. I had no idea. When did this happen?"

"They found her in an old church off Great Peter Street, near the Abbey. Yesterday morning. Someone'd slit her pretty little throat."

There was no sorrow in the statement, only a faint lingering of animosity that Sebastian noted with interest, although he was careful to keep all trace of the observation off his face. "But this is dreadful. Any idea who did it?"

"Some nob." Gordon stuffed a forkful of beef in his mouth, and spoke around it. "Or so they say."

"I am so sorry. This must be very hard for you."

Gordon paused with another forkful halfway to his face. "For me? What's that supposed to mean?"

"I was under the impression that you and Rachel were . . ." Sebastian cleared his throat. "Well, you know."

Gordon grunted. "Your information is out of date, my friend. There've been any number of gentlemen who've visited her pleasure palace since me, I can tell you that."

It was a crude and decidedly unloverlike expression.

Sebastian drew a deep breath, his chest lifting in a soulful sigh. "My mother always feared the girl would end up as common Haymarket ware."

Gordon snorted. "Nothing common about Rachel. Hell, a man would need to be a lord, or a bloody nabob at least, to get past her ivory gates these days."

And there, thought Sebastian, lay the source of at least some of this man's resentment toward his former mistress. When she'd been young and just starting out in the theatrical world, Gordon's status as one of the titans of the stage must have made him seem powerful, even godlike to her. But once Rachel had established a reputation of her own and attracted the attention of some of London's wealthiest noblemen, she'd obviously decided she could do better than a common actor. Especially one with a tendency to use his fists on her.

Gordon took a long, deep drink from his tankard. "She used to talk about the day their noble heads would end up on pikes, and how London's gutters were going to run with their precious blue blood." He gave a low, mirthless laugh. "She changed her tune quick enough, didn't she, when they started buying her silks and pearls?"

So Rachel York had sympathized with the aims of the French Revolution. Interesting, thought Sebastian. He shook his head soulfully. "And now one of these noblemen has murdered her?"

"So they say. Although if you ask me, the authorities ought to be taking a closer look at that bloody Frenchman."

"She had a French lover?"

"Lover?" Gordon shoved the last of his bread in his mouth, chewed once or twice, and swallowed hard. "I don't know if I'd call him that. Although the man was paying the rent on her rooms, all right."

"What man is this?"

"One of those bloody émigrés. Claims to be the son of a count or some such nonsense." The flawless accent slipped for a moment, allowing a hint of Geordie to peek through. Pushing away his plate, the actor leaned back and dusted the crumbs off his fingers. "Man by the name of Pierrepont. Leo Pierrepont."

Chapter 17

Sir Henry Lovejoy had two passions left in his life. One was for justice and the law. The other was for science.

Whenever he could, he attended the public lectures given at the Royal Scientific Society; he read the *Scientific Quarterly*, and he tried very, very hard to apply the *scientific method* to his investigations and legal deliberations. But every once in a while, Lovejoy went with his instincts, and played a hunch.

It was his instincts that kept nagging at him over this latest killing, whispering to him that there had to be more to Rachel York's murder in the Lady Chapel of St. Matthew of the Fields than Constable Edward Maitland had so far discovered. And so late that Thursday afternoon, Lovejoy sought out Viscount Devlin's friend and erstwhile second, Sir Christopher Farrell, in Brooks's Club on St. James's and set about finding out more about the Earl of Hendon's infamous, rakehell son, Sebastian.

"Tell me about yesterday morning's duel between Lord Devlin and Captain John Talbot," said Lovejoy when Sir Christopher joined him in the discreet little room tucked away at the top of the stairs that the club had provided for them.

He was an unexpectedly open-faced man, Sir Christopher, with clear gray eyes and an easy manner. Nothing at all like what Lovejoy would have expected in a friend of someone as dark and saturnine as Devlin. At Lovejoy's question, he opened his eyes wide in a studied parody of innocence. "Duel? What duel?"

The room contained a large mahogany table surrounded by some half-dozen chairs upholstered in the same blue brocade as the walls. Lovejoy stood with the table between them, his gaze fixed on the other man's face. "You do your friend no favor, Sir Christopher. I have little interest at the moment in enforcing the codes against dueling. But two days ago, a young woman named Rachel York was brutally assaulted and murdered, and certain evidence combined with accounts from a witness have implicated Lord Devlin. Therefore, the more we know about his lordship's movements these last few days, the closer we will be to understanding the truth of this matter. If you have any information which is pertinent, it would behoove you to provide it. So I ask you again, who was the challenger? Lord Devlin?"

Sir Christopher hesitated a moment, then shook his head. "No. Talbot."

"When and where precisely was this challenge issued?"

Farrell went to look out the window, his hands clasped behind his back. It was a moment before he answered, his words coming out jerkily, as if he begrudged the magistrate each and every one. "Tuesday afternoon. At White's. Sebastian was standing near the entrance to the gaming room, holding a glass of wine. Talbot jostled him in such a way that wine from Sebastian's glass splashed onto Talbot's boots. He demanded satisfaction."

Lovejoy nodded in understanding. "That was the public justification for the duel. Now tell me the real reason."

Farrell swung around, one eyebrow arching in aristocratic affront. "I beg your pardon?"

Lovejoy returned only a tight, bland smile. "There are those who say Lord Devlin was having an affair with Captain Talbot's wife."

Sir Christopher met Lovejoy's questioning gaze. And Lovejoy thought, the man must be hopeless at the gaming tables. Everything he considered, everything he felt, showed on his face. Lovejoy knew the precise moment when Farrell decided to let go of his resistance. Blowing out his breath in a long sigh, he came to sit in one of the chairs ringing the center table. "Talbot certainly thought so," he said, propping his elbows on the table and sinking his chin into his hands. "But it wasn't true. Devlin's relationship with Melanie Talbot never went beyond friendship."

"You believe that?"

Sir Christopher nodded glumly. "Last spring, at a ball at Devonshire House, Sebastian heard someone crying in the garden. He's got the damnedest hearing a body could ever imagine, you know. Anyway, he went to investigate and found Talbot's wife. The bastard had taken exception to the way she was looking at one of the violin players and worked her over pretty bad before storming off in a fit. Sebastian took her home."

"But that wasn't the end of it."

Farrell dropped his hands into his lap and sat back. "No. She needed a friend, and Devlin became one. I always thought she was more than half in love with him, but Devlin's not the kind of man to take advantage of another person's vulnerability."

Lovejoy eyed the other man consideringly. "How well do you know him?"

A slow, unexpectedly boyish smile spread across Sir Christopher's face. "Better than I know either of my own two brothers. Sebastian and I were at Eton together. And Oxford after that."

"But you didn't join the army with him?"

Sir Christopher's smile faded. "No. I didn't even know what he'd done until the day before he was set to leave England."

"A bit of a start, that. Was it not?"

Sir Christopher fell into a troubled silence, as if considering his next words. Then he said, "About a year after we came down from Oxford, Sebastian fell in love with a woman the Earl considered unsuitable. He threatened to cut Sebastian off without a penny, if he married the chit."

"Lord Hendon objected to the lady's birth?"

Farrell rubbed his nose. "She was a Cyprian."

"Ah," said Lovejoy. It was difficult to imagine the proud, arrogant young man he'd first met in the library at Brook Street doing anything so improper or foolish as to fall in love with an Incognita. But then, it must have all happened long ago. One wondered how much, if any, of that impetuous, romantic youth could still be found in the cool, hard man Lord Devlin was today.

"Sebastian swore he'd marry the girl anyway. Only, the lady in question had no interest in marrying a pauper. Once she realized Hendon meant what he'd said, she broke it off."

"So Devlin went to war to get himself killed."

"I'm not sure it was as dramatic as all that. Let's just say he was anxious to get away from England for a spell."

"Understandable," said Lovejoy smoothly. "Yet I

gather he volunteered for some rather dangerous assignments."

"He was in intelligence, if that's what you mean. He was good at it."

Lovejoy made a noncommittal humming sound. "So I've heard. Yet I understand he left the service last year under something of a cloud. What was that about, I wonder?"

Sir Christopher returned Lovejoy's questioning look with a mulish stare. "I don't know anything about that," he said, and on this, it seemed, Sir Christopher would not be drawn.

Lovejoy shifted his approach. "Did you see Lord Devlin this last Tuesday evening?"

"Of course." Sir Christopher's eyes remained narrowed. The man might be easygoing, Lovejoy thought, but he was no fool. He knew to what end Lovejoy was circling back around. "We were at Watier's all night—until dawn the next morning, when we drove out to Chalk Heath."

Lovejoy gave a tight smile. "Yes. But you see, it's his lordship's movements earlier in the evening we're interested in. According to our information, Lord Devlin didn't arrive at Watier's until shortly after nine o'clock, although he left his house some four hours earlier, at approximately five. His lordship claims he spent the intervening four hours simply walking the streets of London. But unfortunately, he says he was alone."

Sir Christopher set his jaw and glared back at Lovejoy. "If Devlin says he was out walking, then that's where he was."

The man had too open a face and too natural a disposition toward honesty, Lovejoy thought, to ever be anything other than a terrible liar. The magistrate spent the next ten minutes pressing Sir Christopher for the truth. But in the end, Lovejoy gave it up.

He'd have better luck, he decided, with the unhappily married Melanie Talbot.

Chapter 18

$\mathcal{R}$achel York had kept rooms on the first floor of a neat little lodging house in Dorset Court, not far from Kat's own townhouse. But it was midafternoon by the time Kat was able to get rid of Lord Stoneleigh and make her way there. Already, the light was fading from the day. As she climbed the long flight of stairs from the ground floor, a hard sleet began to fall, striking the window at the end of the wide hall like a flurry of small pebbles.

"You won't find anyone there, I can tell you that," said a querulous female voice floating down from the second floor just as Kat raised her hand to knock.

Crossing the hall, Kat stuck her head over the banister and looked up. "Excuse me?"

She found a small face, deeply wrinkled by time and surrounded by a halo of white hair, peering down at her from the gloom of the second floor. "She's dead. Murdered in a church, God rest her soul."

"Actually, it was her maid, Mary Grant, I was interested in seeing. I thought I might like to hire her, if she's in need of a new position."

"Huh. She's long gone, that one. Cleaned the place out first thing this morning, she did."

Kat was starting to get a crick in her neck. She shifted

around to a more comfortable position. She could see the woman better now, so small she had to stand on tip-toe to rest her arms on the top of the upper banister. Her purple satin gown was of a style one might have seen in the previous century, although it looked new. Just like the ropes of pearls and emeralds and rubies draping her neck and thin wrists looked real—at least in this light, and from this angle. "Cleaned it out?"

"Took everything," said the elderly woman, her in-flection betraying lingering traces of a Highland accent. "Carried it right off. Easy enough to do, I suppose, see-ing as how her mistress already had most everything packed."

"Rachel was moving to new lodgings?" It was news to Kat.

"Huh. Leaving London, more like, if you ask me."

"Leaving?"

"That's what I thought, although she wasn't exactly what I'd call forthcoming, that girl. All atwitter this week, she was—up in the trees one minute, scared of her shadow the next. She'd found some way to get her hands on some money, was what I thought." The old woman expelled her breath in a little *hmm*. "Lot of good it did her, in the end."

"But . . . I thought there was a constable here. How could Mary Grant have taken anything without his knowing?"

The old woman didn't seem to find Kat's interest in details in any way unusual. She gave another of her lit-tle *hmms*. "That one? He left at first light, he did. And good riddance to him, too. Let me tell you, the number of people we've had, tramping up and down these stairs! Why, it's worse than what it was when that girl was alive."

"I suppose you've had the authorities here. . . ." Kat allowed her voice to trail off encouragingly.

"Aye, three times. At least, I assume that's who they were. And then there was that young man who had a key."

Kat felt a quickening of interest. A young man with a key? None of Rachel's men, as far as Kat knew, had been young. And Rachel never gave any of them keys. "One of her . . . cousins, I suppose?"

The elderly woman laughed, a ribald cackle that echoed eerily down the darkening stairwell. "One of her lovers, you mean. No need to pull your punches with me, young woman. I cut my eyeteeth long ago."

Kat smiled up at her. "Come here regularly, did he?"

The woman sniffed. "Not him. Never seen him before."

This time, Kat kept her smile to herself. She had no doubt the old woman kept a very, very close watch on the stairwell's comings and goings.

"If you ask me," said the woman, "he was here looking for something—something he didn't find."

"Really?"

"Aye. Heard him down there a good five minutes, going from room to room. And I says to myself, he must be searching that place. And then what does he do but come up here and knock at my door, bold as brass, wanting to know if I had any idea where that maid had taken herself off to. As if I would." The old woman fixed Kat with a speculative look. "You're an actress, too, I suppose."

"Well," said Kat hastily, "if Mary Grant is indeed gone, then I suppose I'm wasting my time looking for her here. Thank you for your help."

Kat was aware of that bright, curious gaze fixed upon

her as she walked back down the stairs, her steps slow and deliberate. It wasn't until she had almost reached the ground floor that she finally heard the click of the old woman's door closing above.

Slipping off her half-boots and hugging the wall so that the treads wouldn't creak, Kat darted back up the steps. The lock on Rachel's door was a simple mechanism, easy enough to pick when one has had the right training. Kat let herself in and closed the door quietly behind her.

Rachel had done well for herself in the three short years she'd trodden the boards. The rooms were well proportioned and richly paneled, the hangings at the windows of draped velvet. But the old woman was right: where once had stood gleaming polished tables and satin settees were now only small piles of rubbish and other litter strewn here and there.

Her bare toes curling away from the cold floor-boards, Kat crept softly through the empty, echoing drawing room and interconnecting dining room. Rachel's maid had left very little. At the back of the house lay the chamber Rachel had used as her bedroom, its walls covered in a flattering, pink silk. It was to this room that Kat now went. Crossing the bare floor, she carefully drew back the heavy drapes and let the fading light of the dying day into the room. Then, her arms at her chest, hugging herself against the cold, she went to stand before the fireplace.

The mantel had been cleverly worked, of carved wood painted to resemble marble. Kat studied the fluted pilasters, the scroll-like capitals. She touched first one decorative segment, then the other, pushing, twisting. *It has to be here somewhere*, she thought, just as a small section of the architrave pulled away from the others.

Thrusting her hand into the gaping blackness of the secret nook, she drew out a small book, its gilt-edged pages bound in red leather and tied up with a thong. Rachel's appointment book. Kat checked the compartment again, but it was empty.

Untying the leather thong, Kat leafed quickly through the book. She would need to tear out some of the pages, she realized, before she gave the book to Sebastian. It would be too dangerous to let him see anything that might somehow link Rachel back to Leo. Kat could only hope enough would be left to provide Sebastian with some clue to the identity of Rachel's killer.

The distant sound of the door from the hall opening brought Kat's head up with a jerk. "Mother Mary," she whispered beneath her breath and thrust the small book into her reticule.

A man's voice came to her, high-pitched and sharp with angry incredulity. "What in the name of God has happened here? I ordered a watch set on this place."

Shoving the secret compartment closed, Kat darted through a side door to the back cupboard, off which opened the steep, narrow flight of service steps.

"We left a man here overnight, sir," said another voice, a younger man's voice, at once defensive and conciliatory. "You said nothing about continuing the watch after that."

Hopping inelegantly on one foot, Kat slipped on first one boot, then the other, her elbow thumping the stair door back against the wall as she momentarily lost her balance and wavered.

"What was that?"

Kat's head jerked around as the urgent, high-pitched words echoed through the empty rooms.

"What? I didn't hear anything."

The first voice was moving. "There's someone here. In the back. Quick."

Kat didn't wait to hear more. Her half-boots clattering on the bare steps, her reticule clutched in her hand, she fled.

Chapter 19

$\mathcal{T}$he ruse of simple Mr. Simon Taylor from Worcestershire wasn't going to work with a man such as Leo Pierrepont. Sebastian and Pierrepont didn't exactly move in the same circles, but the émigré knew Lord Devlin on sight, and a poorly cut coat and a few streaks of gray at the temples would be unlikely to prove an adequate disguise. Pierrepont had a reputation amongst the *ton* for shrewdness.

So Sebastian visited a discreet shop on the Strand, where he provided himself with a neat little French Cassaignard flintlock pistol with a cannon muzzle and stepped breech, which fit snugly into the front pocket of his greatcoat. Then, as an early dusk fell over the city and the lamplighters struggled against a steady rain and sharp January wind, he set off for Half Moon Street.

Leo Pierrepont hurried down his front steps, his coat collar turned up and hat brim pulled low against the wind-driven rain. "Cavendish Square," he told the hackney driver, shutting the door behind him with a snap.

"There are more reasons than one might suppose," said Sebastian, lounging at his ease in the far corner, "for the Beau's assertion that gentlemen should avoid riding in hackney carriages."

The Frenchman's start of surprise was almost instantly controlled. "I beg your pardon," he said, his glance darting, betrayingly, to the door. "I didn't realize the jarvey already had a customer."

He had quite a reputation as a swordsman, this Frenchman, his slim body still energetic and agile despite his forty or fifty years. Sebastian slipped his hand from his pocket and calmly aimed the flintlock at the Frenchman's chest. "I think you understand."

Leo Pierrepont stretched out his legs, settled deeper into the seat, and smiled. "Then I fear you overestimate my powers of imagination."

"Yet you know who I am."

"Of course." His eyebrows rose in a very Gallic expression of disdain. "Wherever did you find that appalling coat?"

Sebastian smiled. "The Rag Fair in Rosemary Lane."

"It looks like it. An effective disguise, I suppose, in its way. But only so long as the authorities fail to realize they should be seeking their missing viscount amongst the ill-dressed, hmm?"

"I'm not worried. I suspect you have your own reasons for avoiding the authorities. At least when the topic of conversation is Rachel York."

"And if your suspicions are incorrect?"

"There is that, of course. Still, it's interesting, don't you think, that you were the man paying the rent on her rooms?"

A carriage rattled past, the glow from the torches carried by its linkboys slanting in through the hackney window to highlight the Frenchman's sharp, hawkish features. "Who told you that?"

Sebastian lifted one shoulder in a careless shrug. "Information is easy enough to come by . . . when one uses the right means of persuasion."

The Frenchman regarded him dispassionately for a moment. "Am I to guess why you've chosen to approach me on this matter?"

"I should think the reason obvious."

Pierrepont opened his eyes wide. "Good God. What are you suggesting? That I killed Rachel? What do you imagine to be my motive, I wonder? Not lust, surely. Given the details you've discovered about our arrangement, it's obvious I could have had the girl anytime I chose. Why rape her in a church?"

Sebastian studied the other man's carefully composed features. *Had* Rachel been raped? "Yet you seem to have shared her with others," said Sebastian, keeping his voice deliberately bland. "Was that generosity willing, I wonder? Or not?"

"What do you think? That I killed Rachel in a fit of jealous passion?" Pierrepont waved one long, delicate hand through the air in a dismissive gesture. "Such a fatiguing emotion, jealousy—apart from being rather primitive and plebian. You see, I am not a possessive man, my lord. The arrangement Rachel and I had suited us both—however strange some might find it."

"There are other reasons to kill."

A gust of wind caught the carriage and rattled the glass in the window frame as they turned onto New Bond Street. "There are reasons, yes. But to slit a woman's throat—viciously, repeatedly, until her head is virtually severed from her body? What manner of man does that, hmm?"

"You tell me."

Pierrepont sat silent for a moment, his chin sunk onto his chest, his thoughts seemingly elsewhere. "When I was a young man, I watched my father's head roll in the Place de la Concorde. Did you know that a decapitated head remains conscious for some twenty seconds after it is separated from its body? Twenty seconds. Think about that. It's a long time, no? Do you think Rachel knew that? That horror?"

Sebastian listened to the rattle of the carriage wheels over the cobbles, the jingle of the harness. He hadn't known that about Rachel's death, either. He thought about that vibrant, beautiful young woman, thought about her alone and afraid in that church, her life's blood ebbing away.

"You don't ask, but I'll tell you anyway," said Pierre-pont, his lips drawing back in a cold, hard smile. "Tuesday night, I hosted at a dinner party attended by some half-dozen highly respectable people who can swear I was at home the entire evening. So you see, my friend, you need to seek elsewhere for Rachel's murderer—if you are not, in fact, he."

The hackney slowed, swinging wide into Henrietta Place. Sebastian reached for the door handle. He didn't doubt the Frenchman knew more than he'd been willing to admit, but they were almost to Cavendish Square and Sebastian had no desire to be seen there.

He was beginning to realize how little he really knew about either Rachel York or her death. He knew she'd been murdered in the Lady Chapel of a small parish church near Westminster Abbey after telling her maid she was going to meet him, and that one of his pistols had been found tangled in her clothes. But he had only Pierrepont's word for it that she'd been raped, and that her throat had been repeatedly, savagely slashed. He didn't even know who had found her or at what time, precisely, she had died. These were things he needed to learn, if he were to have any hope of tracking down the real killer.

And it occurred to him that he knew someone who just might be able to tell him.

Chapter 20

By the time he reached the narrow, medieval lane that wound its way around the base of Tower Hill, the wind was blowing in sharp, angry gusts that flapped the wooden signs overhead and sent the rain slashing sideways. In the lee of the deep, crumbling arch of a doorway, his eyes narrowed against the wind-driven rain, Sebastian studied the huddle of old stone buildings opposite. The surgery was dark, but he could see a light burning in the small house beyond it.

He cast a quick glance up and down the street. The freezing rain had driven most people indoors. There was no one to see him as he crossed the lane and knocked on the house's weathered front door.

A dog barked in the distance. Sebastian heard the thump of uneven footsteps coming down the hall. Then there was silence, and Sebastian knew he was being watched. A wise man did not open his door to strangers at night, even when that man was a surgeon.

A bolt slid open and the door swung inward. The man who stood just inside the narrow, low-ceilinged hall was young still, no more than thirty, a dark-haired Irishman with a ready smile that crinkled the corners of his eyes and brought a roguish dimple to one lean cheek. "Ah. It is you," said Paul Gibson, opening the door wider and stepping back. "I was hoping you might come to me."

Sebastian stood where he was. "You've heard what they're saying?"

"Sure then, but you don't expect me to be believing everything I hear, now do you?"

Sebastian laughed and stepped inside.

Paul Gibson bolted the door, then led the way back down the passage, the smoothness of his gait marred at each step by a peculiar little half hitch. He'd been an army surgeon, once—even after a cannon ball took off the lower part of his left leg. "Come into the kitchen. It's warmer there, and closer to the food."

Sebastian had bought a paper-wrapped sausage midway through the morning. But he hadn't stopped for lunch and it was now past dinnertime. The fragrant warmth of the kitchen folded itself around him and he smiled. "Food does sound uncommonly good at the moment."

~

"There are some gentlemen of my acquaintance," said Paul Gibson later, when they were seated at a table before the kitchen fire with a joint of cold ham, a crusty loaf of bread, and a bottle of wine. "They're in the brandy trade, if you know what I mean, and I've no doubt but what they'd be agreeable to—"

"No," said Sebastian, reaching for another slice of ham.

Paul Gibson paused with his wineglass halfway to his mouth. "No?"

"No. Why does everyone keep trying to introduce me to their friendly neighborhood smuggler?" Sebastian met his friend's arrested gaze. "I'm not running, Paul."

Paul Gibson took a deep breath and let it out through pursed lips. "All right. So how can I help?"

"You can tell me what you know about Rachel York's death. Are you the one who did the postmortem?"

In the two years since he'd left the army, Paul Gibson had set up a small practice here, in the City. But he focused a considerable portion of his time and energy on research and writing, and the teaching of medical students, as well as providing the authorities with his expert opinion in criminal cases.

"There was no postmortem."

"What?"

He shrugged and emptied the last of the wine into Sebastian's glass. "They're not automatically done, you know. And in this instance, there wasn't much of a reason for one, really. It was fairly obvious how she'd died."

"You saw the body?"

"No. A colleague of mine was called in." Lurching to his feet, the Irishman limped across the kitchen to fetch another bottle of wine. "It was a brutal attack, from the sounds of it. She'd been beaten as well as raped, her throat slashed not once, but many times."

It fit with what Pierrepont had told him, but Sebastian had been hoping for more. "Would it be possible for you to arrange to see her?"

Gibson shook his head. "Too late. The body's already been turned over for burial. The theater is arranging it."

Sebastian swirled his wine thoughtfully in his glass.

"What do you think you're going to do? Hmm?" Gibson swung his wooden leg over the opposite bench to sit down again with an awkward lurch. "Find the man who killed her yourself?"

"If I don't, who will?"

"It's not an easy thing, solving a murder."

Sebastian looked up to meet his friend's narrowed, worried eyes. "You know what I did in the army."

"Yes. But there's a difference, I should think, between being a spy and finding a killer."

"Not as much as one might imagine."

A hint of a dimple appeared in the Irishman's cheek. "So. Have any suspects yet?"

Sebastian smiled. "Two, as a matter of fact. There's an actor by the name of Hugh Gordon—"

"Ah. I saw him just last month. A very effective Hector."

"That's him. Seems Rachel York was his mistress when she first started at the theater. He took it badly when she left him."

Paul Gibson frowned. "How long ago was this?"

"Some two years ago."

The Irishman shook his head. "Too long. If she'd just left him, I could see it. But passions cool with time."

"One might think so. Except that he still sounds surprisingly bitter to me. I get the impression Mr. Gordon nourishes republican sentiments that he believes Rachel York once shared. I'd say he's as bothered by the blue blood of her recent lovers as anything else."

The Irishman drained his glass. "So, who is her current lover?"

Sebastian reached for the bottle and poured his friend some more wine. "She seems to have been involved with an extraordinary number of gentlemen, at least on a superficial level. But the only one of any significance I've discovered so far is a Frenchman who was paying the rent on her rooms. An émigré by the name of Leo Pierrepont."

"A Frenchman? That's interesting. What do you know about him?"

"Not a lot. He's a man in his late forties, I'd say. Came here back in 'ninety-two. He's known as a good swordsman, but I've never heard anything to his discredit."

"I put my money on the Frenchman."

Sebastian laughed. "That's because it's the French who shot away the bottom half of your leg. Besides, he has an alibi: on the night Rachel was killed, he was giving a dinner party—or so he says. He could be making it up, of course, but it should be easy enough to check."

"Unfortunate." Gibson shifted in his seat, a grimace of pain flashing momentarily across his face as he moved his leg. "Neither sounds like a very promising suspect to me. Is that the best you can come up with?"

"So far. I was hoping Rachel's body might give me some idea of what direction to look in next."

Outside, the wind gusted up, buffeting the back of the house and eddying the flames on the hearth. Paul Gibson turned toward the fire, the flickering light playing over the thoughtful planes of his face. After a moment, he opened his mouth to say something, closed it, then finally said in a rush, "You know, there might be a way.... "

Sebastian studied his friend's averted profile. "A way to do what?"

"A way that I could get a look at Rachel York's body. Do a thorough autopsy."

"How's that?"

"We could hire someone to steal the corpse tomorrow night, after it's been buried."

"No," said Sebastian.

Gibson swung to face him. "I know some men who'd be willing to do it without—"

"No," said Sebastian again.

His friend's lips thinned with exasperation. "It's done all the time."

"Ah, yes. Twenty pounds for a long, fifteen for a half-long, and eight for a short—a long being a man, a half-long a woman, and a short a child. But just because it happens all the time doesn't mean that I have to do it."

The Irishman fixed him with a steady stare. "If she were given a choice, which do you think Rachel York would prefer? That her body be left to rot in its grave, or that the man who put her there be brought to justice?"

"Well, we can hardly ask her, now can we?"

Paul Gibson sat forward, his hands coming up, palms pressed together. "Sebastian, think about this: whoever this man was, he could kill again—in fact, he almost surely will kill again. You know that, don't you? But as long as the authorities are looking for you, they're not going to be doing anything to find him."

Sebastian didn't say a word.

Gibson flattened his hands on the scarred wooden tabletop and leaned into them. "She's dead, Sebastian. The woman who was Rachel York is long gone. What's left is just a shell, a husk, that once held her. In a month's time, it'll be rotting pulp."

"That's simple justification and you know it."

"Is it? What we would do to her is no worse than what time will do to her. And there's nothing you can do to stop that."

Sebastian took a deep, bitter swallow of his wine. He told himself Paul was right, that catching Rachel's killer was more important than preserving the inviability of her grave. He told himself her killer could, if free, kill again. But it was still wrong. He raised his gaze to his friend's. "How soon can you set it up?"

Paul Gibson let his breath out in a quick huff. "The sooner the better. I'll send a message to Jumpin' Jack first thing in the morning."

"Jumpin' Jack?"

The Irishman's dimple flashed, then was gone.

"Jumpin' Jack Cochran. A gentleman in the resurrection trade I have reason to know."

"I won't ask how you know him."

Gibson laughed. "He got his name when one of the stiffs he was sliding out of its coffin suddenly sat up and started talking to him. Old Jack jumped out of that grave real fast."

"You're making that up," said Sebastian.

"Not a bit of it. The lads he had with him were all for swinging a shovel at the man's head and finishing him off right then and there, but Jack would have none of it. Hauled the fellow off to an apothecary, and even paid the bill when the unlucky devil died anyway."

"I am filled with admiration for the man's character," Sebastian said with a grin, and rose to leave.

The Irishman's face fell. "You're staying, aren't you?"

Sebastian shook his head. "I've put you in enough danger as it is, coming here. I've a room at the Rose and Crown, near Tothill Fields. They know me there as Mr. Simon Taylor. From Worcestershire."

Gibson walked with him to the front door. "I'll let you know when everything's arranged." He paused, his face thoughtful as he watched Sebastian button his scruffy topcoat up under his chin. "You do realize, of course, that we could go through all of this, and still not learn anything useful?"

"I know it."

"You're only assuming that the man who killed that poor girl was someone she knew. It might not be, you know. She could simply have been in the wrong place at the wrong time. You might never find who did it."

Reaching out, Sebastian paused with his hand on the edge of the door and looked back at his friend. "No. But at least I'll have tried."

Gibson met his gaze, his face unsmiling and drawn with worry. "You could still leave."

"And spend the rest of my life running?" Sebastian shook his head. "No. I'm going to clear my name, Paul. Even if I have to die trying."

"You could die trying, and still not succeed."

Sebastian settled his hat lower on his forehead and turned into the icy blast of the night. "It's a chance I'm just going to have to take."

Chapter 21

Sebastian stood alone in the shadows and watched as Kat Boleyn separated herself from the knot of laughing, pretty women and hot-blooded, predatory males clustered around the stage door.

Golden lamplight pooled on gleaming wet pavement. The wind gusted up, sharp and bitter, and brought with it a rush of smells, of fresh paint and sweat-dampened wool and the thick grease of cosmetics: theater scents evocative of a time long past, when he'd believed—really *believed*—in so many things, like truth and justice. And love.

He'd been twenty-one that summer, not long down from Oxford and still drunk on the wonders of Plato and Aquinas and Descartes. She'd been barely seventeen, yet in her own way so much older and wiser than he. He'd fallen hopelessly, wildly in love with her. And he had believed, truly believed, that she loved him.

Ah, how he had believed. She'd told him she'd love him until the end of time, and he had believed. Believed her and asked her to marry him. And she had said yes.

It was still raining, but softly now. He watched her walk quickly toward him, the hood of her cloak raised against the drizzle, her gaze turned toward the hackney stand at the end of the street.

"You should be more careful," said Sebastian, falling into step beside her. "Now is not a good time to be out alone at night."

She gave no start of surprise, only glancing up at him from beneath the shadow of her hood. "I refuse to live my life in fear," she said. "I should think you'd remember that about me. Besides"—a soft smile touched her lips—"do you think I didn't know you were there?"

He thought she probably had. He remembered that about her, too—that while most people were hopelessly, cripplingly blind in the dark, Kat's night vision was unusually sharp. Not as good as Sebastian's own, but sharp.

She made a move toward the nearest hackney. He caught her arm, drawing her on up the street. "Let's walk."

They turned their steps toward the West End, part of a crowd of playgoers straggling home through the lamplit darkness. Snatches of light and laughter tumbled from the quickly closed doors of taverns and coffeehouses, music halls and brothels. From a darkened, urine-drenched doorway, a streetwalker hissed at him, her eyes bold, desperate. Haunting. Sebastian looked away.

"What can you tell me about Leo Pierrepont?" he asked.

"Pierrepont?" The rain had stopped now. Kat pushed back her hood. "What has he to do with anything?"

"He was paying the rent on Rachel's rooms."

She was silent for a moment, and he remembered this about her, too, the way she carefully thought things through before speaking. "Who told you that?"

"Hugh Gordon. Pierrepont didn't deny it."

"You've spoken with him?"

"We shared a hackney ride," said Sebastian, and smiled softly at the familiar way her brows drew together in thought. "It's a curious arrangement, don't you think, for one man to be paying the rent on a woman's rooms while knowing she continues to receive other male visitors? Unless, of course, he's acting as her pimp."

Again that pause, as she thought through what he had said and considered her response. "Some men like to watch."

Sebastian knew a surge of unexpected and unpleasant emotions. He wanted to ask how she knew this about Pierrepont—if she, too, had entertained the Frenchman by allowing him to watch her make love to other men. Instead, he said, "Well, that's certainly one alternative that hadn't occurred to me. Your experience in such matters is more valuable than one might realize."

She halted abruptly, her chin jerking up, her eyes flashing. She would have swung away, back toward the theater, if he hadn't caught her arm.

"I'm sorry. That was an unforgivable thing to say."

She met his gaze. He couldn't begin to interpret the dark shift of emotions he could see in her eyes. "Yes. It was." She removed her arm from his unresisting grip and walked on again. A silence fell between them, filled only with the soft swish of the soles of her half-boots gliding over wet pavement and the whisper of old, old memories.

He let his gaze travel over the achingly familiar line of her profile, the arch of her neck. Her nose was small and turned up at the end like a child's, her mouth wide, too wide, her lips full and sensuous. A seductive combination of innocence and sin.

There had been other women in his life since Kat Boleyn; beautiful, intelligent women, including one in Portugal he might even have fallen in love with if Kat

Boleyn hadn't always been there, like a shadow across his heart. And he wondered suddenly if he'd approached her this morning because she'd known Rachel York and could give him the information he needed, or if he had turned to her now for some other reason entirely, a reason his mind sheered away from.

She said, "You haven't asked if I had a chance to speak with Rachel's maid."

A carriage dashed past, the coronet on its panels glistening with wet, the air filling with the scent of hot pitch from the linkboys' torches. Sebastian watched it disappear into the distance, flames wavering against a black sky. "Did you?"

"No. She's gone. Vanished—along with virtually everything in Rachel's rooms that was movable."

He brought his gaze back to her face. "I thought you said the constables were watching the house?"

"Only through the night, according to the elderly Scotswoman who lives upstairs. She also told me a young man came to Rachel's rooms the morning after she was killed."

"A young man?"

"A young man with a key. Looking for something, or so it seems. He went through Rachel's rooms, then popped upstairs to ask our inquisitive neighbor if she knew where Mary Grant had gone."

"Searching for what, I wonder?"

"This, perhaps." Pausing beneath the flickering light of a streetlamp, she drew something from her reticule and held it out to him.

It was a small book, bound in red calfskin and tied up with a leather thong. "I thought her rooms had been emptied," he said, taking the book and loosening the knot in the leather.

"She kept it in a secret compartment in the mantelpiece."

She didn't say how she'd known about that compartment. He glanced up at her, then down at the book. It was fairly new, less than a fifth of its pages having been used.

And most of those first pages were now missing.

"The front pages have been cut out," he said, running one finger along the ragged edges.

The clouds overhead shifted fitfully with the wind. The rain had cleared away the city's nearly perpetual blanket of yellow fog, allowing rare glimpses of a distant full moon. In the shimmer of moonlight, her face appeared pale and faintly troubled. "It's almost as if she knew something might happen to her."

"Assuming it was Rachel who did it." Sebastian thumbed through the dozen or so pages that were left. They covered little more than the previous week. "You think she was protecting someone?"

"I don't know. It seems a reasonable explanation, doesn't it?"

There was another explanation, of course: that Kat Boleyn had cut the pages out herself. Only, if there'd been something here she hadn't wanted Sebastian to know about, why bother to give him the book at all? Why not simply destroy the thing and claim it had never been found? Why even offer to go to Rachel York's rooms in the first place? To keep him from discovering whatever secret had been written on those missing pages? But why? *Why?*

"Have you looked at what's left?" he asked.

She nodded. "I've put notations beside the names I recognized. Most of them are people connected in some way with the play."

"Any of them have a reason to wish Rachel harm?"

"Not that I'm aware of. Besides, we had a performance the night she died. We were all at the theater."

Here was an aspect of Rachel York's murder that hadn't occurred to him. "All of you except for Rachel. Why wasn't she there?"

"Her understudy went on in her place. Rachel sent word at the last minute, saying she was ill."

"Did she do that often?"

"No. I can't think of another instance. Rachel was never ill."

Sebastian glanced quickly through the remaining pages. They mainly contained notations for meetings with the likes of hairdressers and seamstresses. But one name appeared on virtually every day. "Who's Giorgio?"

"I think it might be Giorgio Donatelli. He helped design and paint the scenery when we did *The School for Scandal* last year. But he's become increasingly popular as a portrait painter since then. He's had commissions from the Lord Mayor and several members of the Prince of Wales's inner circle. I don't know why Rachel would be seeing him."

"What do you know of him?"

"Not much, except that he's young, and rather romantic-looking. He's Italian."

"Our young man with the key?"

"I don't know. It's not like Rachel to give any man the key to her rooms."

Sebastian started to put the book in his pocket, but she reached out and touched his arm, stopping him.

"You didn't look to see if she'd written down her Tuesday night appointment at St. Matthew of the Fields."

Somewhere in the night, a tomcat howled, a deep

throaty caterwaul of primal beastiality. Sebastian met the gaze of the woman beside him. "Did she?"

"Yes."

There was a ribbon, stitched into the binding for use as a place marker. The book opened easily to its last entry.

At the top of the left-hand page, in a neat, well-schooled copperplate, Rachel York had written *Tuesday, 29 January 1811*. Sebastian scanned that day's entries. She'd had a lesson with a dancing master at eleven that morning, another appointment near the theater at three. Then he saw the words *St. Matthew's* and, beside that, a name.

St. Cyr.

Chapter 22

Later that night, alone in his small chamber at the Rose and Crown, Sebastian lit a candle, slipped the leather-bound book from his pocket, and settled down in the room's single, straight-backed wooden chair to read.

All the pages containing Rachel's entries prior to the afternoon of Friday, January 18, had been cut from the book. Sebastian stared at the date at the top of the first surviving page. It had been bitterly cold that week, he remembered, as he followed Rachel York's fine copperplate through the mundane passage of the last days of her life, through the rehearsals and performances, the lessons and appointments with tradesmen. He leafed through each successive day, scanning the entries, not realizing until he reached the morning of Thursday the twenty-fourth that another page was missing, the page for Thursday evening—along with the following morning, which must have been on the overleaf of the same page.

Thoughtful, Sebastian thumbed back to the beginning. Was there a significance, he wondered, in the pattern of missing pages? What had happened in her life on those two successive Friday mornings or Thursday nights that Rachel hadn't wanted anyone to know about?

Or that someone else hadn't wanted Sebastian to know?

Sebastian returned to the afternoon of Friday, the twenty-fifth. After that, the pages continued without interruption up to Tuesday, the twenty-ninth, the evening Rachel died. The evening she had planned to meet someone named St. Cyr in St. Matthew of the Fields.

He went back again to that first page, paying more attention this time to each individual entry and to the notations Kat had made beside them, in pencil. There was little out of the ordinary: singing lessons and meetings with wardrobe; a reminder to pick up a pair of dancing slippers from the shoe repair man. Each appointment with each individual would need to be checked out, of course. But Sebastian found his attention focusing on two names.

The painter, Giorgio Donatelli, appeared frequently, each time with only the brief notation, *Giorgio*, and a time. But even more intriguing was an individual referred to simply as "F." Kat had circled each appearance of the initial, along with a question mark.

Once more, Sebastian went back to the beginning and ran through the entries. Whoever "F" was, he—or she—appeared in the twelve days covered by the book's surviving pages twice: on the evening of Wednesday, the twenty-third, and again on Monday, the twenty-eighth. In other words, Rachel had met with "F" the evening before the missing Thursday, and again the night before she died. A coincidence, Sebastian wondered, or not?

"F" could be a lover, of course—someone so familiar, so dear, that a simple initial sufficed. But he could also be a person whose involvement in her life Rachel had wanted to keep secret. Why? For the same reason she had kept her appointment book hidden?

Conspicuously absent from Rachel's days was the

name of the man who had been paying the rent on her rooms, Leo Pierrepont. If neither Pierrepont nor "F" had been Rachel York's lover, then who had been? Sebastian found it difficult to believe that such a woman had not had one. Except, then, why didn't the lover's name appear in her book? Because she took his regular appearances for granted? Or because his visits were so erratic, she never knew when he might appear?

A wind had come up, rattling the shutters on the window and causing the flame of the candle to flare, then almost die in a sudden, cold draft. A distant burst of laughter sounded, muffled, from the common room below. Out in the hall, a board creaked.

Rising quietly from his chair, Sebastian snuffed the candle flame between thumb and forefinger, plunging the room into darkness. Slipping the small French pistol he'd bought that afternoon in the Strand from his great-coat pocket, he flattened himself against the wall, then reached out to turn the handle and throw open the door to the hall.

" 'Oly 'ell!" yelped Tom, looking up, wide-eyed, from where he sat cross-legged on the bare floorboards opposite Sebastian's door. "Don't shoot me."

Sebastian lowered the pistol. "What the devil are you doing here?"

In the dim light cast by the oil lamp dangling from a chain at the top of the stairs, the boy's face looked pinched, cold. "Fer such a sharp cove, you can be mortal wet, at times. It's watchin' yer back, I am."

"My back," said Sebastian.

Tom shrugged. "Well, yer door, at any rate."

"Why?"

The boy's jaw tightened. "You paid me fer a week, you did. I'm earning me wages."

Sebastian dropped the flintlock into his coat pocket. "Let me get this straight. You don't see a problem in lifting a stranger's purse, but you refuse to be given wages you don't feel you've earned?"

"That's right," said Tom, obviously glad to be understood. "I gots me pride."

"And a highly original set of principles," said Sebastian.

The boy simply looked up at him, puzzled.

A gust of wind slammed against the inn, whistling through the eaves and sending an icy draft sluicing down the corridor. Tom shivered, his thin arms creeping around his legs, hugging them closer to his body.

Sebastian sighed. "It's a bit drafty out here for conversation. You'd best come in."

For a brief instant, Tom hesitated. Then he scrambled to his feet.

"How did you find me, anyway?" Sebastian asked, closing the door against the cold as the boy scooted across the room to the fire.

One bony shoulder lifted in a shrug. " 'Twern't difficult. All's I did was ask around 'til I cottoned on to a young mort named Kat."

"You followed me here from Covent Garden?"

Tom stretched his chilblain-covered hands out to the glowing coals. A residual shiver racked his thin, ragged frame. "Aye."

Sebastian studied the boy's half-averted profile. He was bright and resourceful, and determined, it seemed, to earn his "wages." Sebastian thought about all the names and appointments in that little red book, and an idea began to form in his mind.

Opening the door to the room's ancient wardrobe, he rummaged around and came up with a quilt and an extra pillow. "Here," he said, tossing the bedding toward the boy. "You can sleep by the fire. Tomorrow we'll see about getting you a room over the stables."

Tom caught first the pillow, then the quilt. "You mean yer keeping me on?"

"I've decided I can use an associate of your talents."

A wide, toothy smile broke across the boy's face. "You won't be sorry, gov'nor. There won't be any bung-nappers getting their dibs on yer cly or foggles whilst I'm around, I can tell you that. Nor any tripper-ups nor rampsmen thinkin' yer easy pickin's."

"Get some sleep," said Sebastian, turning away with a smile. "I have an early assignment for you tomorrow. I'd like you to discover the address of a certain Italian gentleman."

"An *Italian*," said Tom, in exactly the same tone of voice he might have used had Sebastian divulged a friendship with a cockroach.

"That's right. An Italian." Sebastian slipped the pistol from his pocket and placed it, along with his pocket-book, beneath his pillow. "A painter, to be exact. A man by the name of Giorgio Donatelli."

~

The dreams are rarely the same. Sleep and time distort memory; events become disjointed. Fleetingly glimpsed faces and haunting images recombine with unrelated incidents to torture and taunt. In a mist-shrouded mountain village, simple stone walls rise up scorched and shattered. Reaching out, Sebastian turns over a woman's flyblown body to find Kat's lifeless blue eyes staring up at him. He cries out, and fresh red blood seeps from her gashed neck. Her lips move. "Aidez-moi," she says: Help me. "Je suis mort." I am dead. But the knife is in his hand

and he is the one slashing, he is the one killing, and the
bloodlust runs hot and sweet through his veins—

"Oie, gov'nor. You right there?"

Sebastian opened his eyes to find the boy, Tom, sitting up, his thin body silhouetted against the glowing
embers of the fire.

"I'm fine. I was just . . . It was just a bad dream." Sebastian rolled onto his back, one bent arm coming up to
cover his eyes. "Go back to sleep."

Chapter 23

The following morning, Sebastian sent the boy off with a full stomach and a suit of warm clothes that included a topcoat and new boots. He half expected the urchin to disappear back into the seething slums from which he'd come. But less than three hours later, Tom was back at the Rose and Crown with information that an Italian painter by the name of Giorgio Donatelli could be found at Number Thirty-two, Almonry Terrace, Westminster.

"What's this, then?" said Tom, eyeing Sebastian as he wound a roll of padding around and around his torso.

Sebastian, who had made another visit that morning to Rosemary Lane and a variety of small shops, pinned the end of the padding and reached for his new, considerably larger shirt. "Today, I am Mr. Silas Beaumont, a plump, prosperous, but not particularly well-bred merchant from Hans Town who is interested in having his daughter's portrait painted. While I am discussing the possibility of engaging Mr. Donatelli for this all-important task, you will poke around the area and discover what his neighbors have to say about our friend Giorgio." He balanced a set of spectacles on the end of his nose, and affected an earnest, if somewhat vapid, look. "All in the most discreet fashion possible, of course."

Tom sniffed. "Take me for a flat, do you?"

"Hardly." By winding two cravats around his neck, Sebastian managed to make his neck look twice its normal size. His hair was as gray as an old man's, and the judicious application of theatrical cosmetics had deepened the lines of age on his face. "While you're at it, you might see what you can find out about a woman who used to visit Mr. Donatelli fairly regularly. A young, attractive woman with golden hair. Her name was Rachel York."

Tom regarded him through narrowed, thoughtful eyes. "You mean, the mort what was cut up in St. Matthew's Church a few nights back?"

Sebastian glanced over at the boy in surprise. "That's right."

"She the one the bolly dogs think you pushed off?"

"If by that impenetrable sentence you're asking if she's the woman the authorities have accused me of killing, then the answer is yes." Sebastian shrugged into his new, very large coat.

"You think this Italian cove is the one what did for 'er?"

"I don't know. He might be. Or he might be able to give me some idea as to where else to look."

"That's yer lay, is it? You figure if you cotton on to the one what *did* do for this Rachel, then the beaks'll quit 'oundin' you?"

"Essentially, yes."

"So who else you thinkin' mighta done for her?"

Sebastian, who was rapidly developing a healthy respect for Tom's abilities and powers of perception, gave him a quick rundown of his conversations with Leo Pierrepont and Hugh Gordon.

"Huh," said Tom, when Sebastian had finished. "Me, I'd put me money on one of them foreigners."

"You might be right," said Sebastian, reaching for his new walking stick. "But I think it best to keep an open mind."

~

The neat, two-story brick building at Number Thirty-two, Almonry Terrace, didn't fit Sebastian's image of a struggling artist's garret. The living quarters occupied the ground floor, while a small hand-lettered sign beside an external stair pointed upward to the studio. Donatelli was doing well indeed for a man who had been painting theatrical scenes just the year before.

Sebastian took the stairs with the ponderous effort one might expect of a fat, self-indulgent merchant. At the top of the steps, a door set with uncurtained small panes of glass showed him a large room lit with an unexpected flood of light by an abundance of large windows all, likewise, uncurtained. In the center of the room stood a young man, palette and brush in hand, his posture one of studied thought as he stared at a large canvas on an easel before him.

Sebastian knocked, then knocked again when the young man continued to stare at his canvas. After a third knock, Sebastian simply opened the door and walked into a blast of warm, turpentine- and oil-scented air.

"Hallooo there," he said with hearty vulgarity, clapping his hands together in the manner of men coming in from the cold. "I did knock, but nobody answered."

The young man swung around, a lock of dark hair falling across his brow as he looked up, distracted. "Yes?"

Romantic, Kat had called him. Sebastian had thought it an odd description at the time, but he understood it now. Tall and broad shouldered, the Italian was like a handsome shepherd or troubadour from a Venetian painting of two centuries before. Curly chestnut-colored hair framed a face with large, velvet brown eyes, a classical nose, and the full, bowed lips of a Botticelli angel.

"I'm looking for a Mr. Giorgio Donatelli," said Sebastian. There were not one, but three braziers burning in the room, he realized. Donatelli obviously missed the warmth of Italy. Already Sebastian was beginning to regret the second neckcloth and the padding around his middle.

Reaching out, the painter rested his brush and palette on a nearby table. "I'm Donatelli."

"Name is Beaumont." Sebastian puffed out his exaggerated chest and struck a self-important pose. "Silas Beaumont. Of the Beaumont Transatlantic Shipping Company." He fixed the artist with an expectant stare. "You've heard of us, of course."

"I believe so," said Donatelli slowly, obviously not willing to risk offending a potential patron with an affront to the man's image of self-importance. "How may I help you?"

The artist's English was good, Sebastian noticed; very good, with just enough of an accent to increase that air of romance. He'd obviously been in England a very long time. "Well, it's this way, you see. I was talking to the Lord Mayor the other day, about how I was wanting to find someone to paint my daughter Sukie's portrait— she's sixteen now, my Sukie—and, anyway, he suggested you."

"You needn't have put yourself to the trouble of coming here," said Donatelli, casting an anxious glance around the studio, like a housewife flustered to have been caught behind on her cleaning.

Sebastian waved away the suggestion with one gloved hand. "I wanted to see some of your work— more than just the one or two pictures you might choose to trot out for my inspection. Never buy a horse without getting a good look at the stable, I always say." He cast an inquiring eye about the room. "You do have more than this, I hope?"

Donatelli reached for a rag to wipe his hands. "Of course. Follow me."

Still wiping his hands, he led the way through an open door to a large back room that was virtually empty except for the dozens and dozens of canvases, large and small, propped against the walls.

"Aha," said Sebastian, rubbing his hands together. "This is more like what I was expecting."

The painter was good, very good, Sebastian decided, making a slow tour of the room. Rather than the sentimental, flattering formality of a Lawrence or a Reynolds, here was vigor and iridescence of color. Sebastian's steps slowed, his respect for the Italian's talent increasing as he studied portraits and sketches, vast dramatic tableaus and small studies. Then he came to a stack of paintings, turned against the wall. Curious, he reached for the top canvas.

"I don't think that's exactly the sort of thing you're looking for," said Donatelli, starting forward.

Sebastian held him off with one outflung hand. He was looking at a painting of Rachel York. Not a portrait of Rachel, the actress, but a depiction of Rachel as Venus, rising naked and utterly desirable from the sea, her flesh flowing and contoured and so realistically depicted that one saw the sensuality of a woman rather than the idealized goddess of the myth.

"No, but I do like this. It's so very . . ." Sebastian paused. *Erotic*, was the word that came to mind. He changed it to, "Evocative."

Donatelli, who'd been watching him with anxious eyes, relaxed.

"Hold on," said Sebastian with a sudden, pronounced start. He leaned forward, as if to study the painting more closely. "Goodness gracious, isn't she that actress—the one who was recently killed?"

"Yes." The word came hissing out on a pained exhalation of air.

"Sad business, that." Sebastian shook his head and tut-tutted in the manner of old Mr. Blackadder, the apothecary his father used to call in whenever one of the servants took ill. "Very sad. One has to wonder what the world is coming to these days." He shifted the canvas to one side and found himself staring, again, at Rachel York, this time as a Turkish odalisque with one toe dipped in a bath, her only covering a wisp of scarlet satin twining in and out of her bare arms.

"I say, here's another painting of her. And another," said Sebastian, shifting more canvases. "And another. She modeled for you frequently, did she?"

"Yes."

"A remarkably beautiful woman," said Sebastian.

Donatelli reached out one hand, his fingers hovering just above that vibrant, painted face, as if he might caress the cheek of the living, breathing woman herself. His hand shook. And Sebastian, watching him, thought, *Ah, so he cared for her.*

But how much? Enough to kill her in a rage of passion?

"She was more than beautiful," whispered Donatelli, his fingers curling into a fist as he let his hand fall to his side.

Sebastian brought his gaze back to the woman on the canvas. This particular painting was different from the others, the colors a swirling golden riot of greens and blues, with something of Tiepolo's use of sharp shadow accents painted with vigorous gaiety against a wide, sunlit sky. Here, she sat upon a hillside bathed in the bright, vibrant light of spring. She had her legs drawn up beneath a flounce of petticoats, her posture almost childlike, her head thrown back, smiling, as if caught in the instant before an outburst of carefree laughter.

Sebastian looked down at the image of that vibrant, vital young woman, and he knew an unexpected stirring that was part sadness, and part outrage. "She was so young," he said. "So young and full of life." His gaze lifted again to the man beside him. "It seems difficult to imagine how anyone could want her dead."

A quiver of emotion, dark and painful to see, passed over the man's handsome, tormented face. "It's an ugly world. An ugly world, with ugly people in it."

"At least the police seem to know who did it. Some earl's son, is it not? A Lord Devlin?"

Donatelli's lips twisted in a savage grimace of hate and bitter, useless rage. "May he rot in hell for all eternity."

"She knew him, did she?"

The painter shook his head. "Not that I was aware of. When I first heard what had happened to her, I thought it was that other one."

"That other one?"

Donatelli sucked in a shuddering breath that lifted his chest and flared his nostrils wide. "He's been following her for weeks—months maybe. Hanging around outside the theater door. Waiting across the street, whenever she came here. Watching her. Everywhere she went, he was there."

"She didn't report him?"

Donatelli shook his head. "I wanted her to go to the authorities, but she said it wouldn't do any good. You know what they're like, these *aristos*. To them, we are little better than animals. Things to be used and thrown away."

The vehemence of his words took Sebastian by surprise. He was remembering what Hugh Gordon had said, about heads on pikes and blood running in the gutters. And he wondered if perhaps Gordon was wrong, that Rachel hadn't abandoned her more radical ideas after all. Ideas Donatelli obviously shared.

"What's his name, this nobleman?" Sebastian asked.

He thought for a moment that the artist wasn't going to answer him. Then Donatelli shrugged, his jaw thrust forward in a determined effort to control his emotions.

And told him.

~

"You're lookin' mortal queer," said Tom when they met up at the local tavern for a pint of ale and steak and kidney pies. "What'd this Italian cove have to tell you, then?"

"It seems Rachel York used to model for him." Sebastian pushed through the crowd around the bar and led the way to an empty table in a quiet corner. "So, how did you go on?"

Slipping into the opposite bench, Tom wrapped his hands around one of the pies and twitched his shoulder in a careless shrug. " 'E's a foreigner. People around 'ere don't seem to 'ave much to do with 'im. Although they noticed the girl, all right. She musta been some looker, that Rachel."

"She was." Sebastian ate silently for a moment, then said, "Any other women visit his studio frequently?"

"Not so's anyone noticed." Tom took a large bite of pie, and spoke around it. "Think 'e was tupping her?"

"Possibly, but I'm not sure. Don't talk with your mouth full."

Tom swallowed, hard, his eyes widening with the effort. "So we didn't learn nothin' from all this?"

"Oh, we learned something." Sebastian took a deep draft of ale and leaned his shoulders back against the wall. "According to our painter friend, a man was following Rachel about for months. A gentleman, to be precise."

Tom polished off the last of his pie and set about licking his fingers clean. "Did he tell you this cove's name?"

"Yes. His name is Bayard Wilcox."

Something in Sebastian's tone caused the boy to stop with his last finger halfway to his mouth. "Know the bloke, do you?"

Sebastian drained his tankard and stood up abruptly. "Quite well, as a matter of fact. Bayard is my nephew."

Chapter 24

Charles, Lord Jarvis, paused in the doorway of the princely dressing room and watched His Royal Highness, George, the Prince of Wales, pivot first one way, then the other as he studied his reflection in the series of ornate, gilt-framed looking glasses that lined the room's silk-covered walls. Several of the Prince's boon companions, Lord Frederick Fairchild among them, lounged at their ease about the cavernous, crimson and gold room, their discussions ranging from the use of champagne in boot polish to the newest opera dancers to catch their fancy. A dozen ruined cravats lay scattered across the chamber's richly hued Turkey carpet, while the Prince's man hovered at the ready with another armload of starched white linen neckcloths, should the Prince's present endeavor be no more successful than the last. Prince George might require the assistance of two footmen to shove his corpulent body into his coat, and a mechanical contrivance to hoist him into the saddle, but he always insisted on tying his own cravats.

"Ah, there you are, Jarvis," said the Prince, looking up.

Jarvis, who had spent the past half hour trying to soothe the wounded dignity of the Russian ambassador, simply bowed and said, "Sir?"

"What's this Lord Frederick is telling me about Spencer Perceval and his damned Tory government pushing for restrictions on our regency?" The Prince's full, petulant mouth puckered into a frown. "Restrictions? What restrictions?"

Jarvis shifted a crumpled shirt and torn satin waistcoat from a gilded chair shaped like a lotus blossom, and sat down. "A temporary restriction only," he said blandly, "to be lifted after one year."

"A year!"

"The doctors insist the King continues to improve," said Lord Frederick, his voice tight with worry. It was the Whigs' greatest fear that mad old King George III might recover before they were able to return to power. "There are those in the Commons who are saying a regency may not be necessary after all."

"What do you think?" said George, whirling to face his friends. It took Jarvis a moment to realize that the question referred not to his father's health, but to the Prince's latest attempt at executing a complicated new knot for his cravat.

Sir John Bethany, an aging roué with full, ruddy cheeks and a girth to rival the Prince's, hauled out his quizzing glass and subjected his friend to a long, thorough inspection while the Prince waited in an agony of suspense. "Brummell himself could do no better," said Bethany at last, letting the quizzing glass fall.

The Prince's face broke into a wide smile that collapsed almost at once. "You're just saying that." With an impatient oath, he ripped off his latest creation and began again, one eye cocking back toward Jarvis. "Our powers will be the same as the King's, of course?"

Jarvis cleared his throat. "Not quite, sir. But you will be allowed to form a government—"

"I should rather think so," interjected the Prince.

"Although it will need to be announced before you are sworn in by the Privy Council."

The Prince so often played the buffoon that one tended to forget that the blood of a host of kings—French and Spanish, English and Scottish, from William the Conqueror and Charlemagne to Henry II and Mary Queen of Scots—flowed through this man's veins. He could strike a decidedly kingly pose, when he so chose. "Don't start, Jarvis," said George, suddenly every inch the prince.

Jarvis inclined his head in a wordless bow.

The regal manner faded almost instantly. George sighed. "If only Fox were still with us. Dashed inconsiderate thing to do, dying like that."

"Just so," said Jarvis. He waited a moment, then added, "Although Perceval thought perhaps—"

"The devil fly away with Perceval," said the Prince in a explosion of warmth. "It's enough to give a man palpitations." He stopped suddenly, the fingers of one hand going anxiously to his opposite wrist. "Our pulse is galloping. The next thing you know, we'll be having abdominal spasms."

Jarvis rather thought the Prince's abdominal spasms could be traced to the mountain of buttered crab he'd consumed the evening before, and the two bottles of port with which it had been washed down, but he kept the observation to himself.

"It's really far too early in the day for such discussions," said the Prince, his hand shifting to the royal belly, a spasm of distress contorting his fleshy features. "It's dangerous for the digestion. I will lie down for a spell."

"And your appointment with the Russian ambassador, sir?"

The Prince looked genuinely puzzled. "What appointment?"

"The one scheduled for half an hour ago. He's still waiting."

"Cancel it," said the Prince, one hand coming up to shade his eyes as if the light had suddenly become too much. He tottered toward a nearby divan shaped like a crocodile padded with crimson satin. "Do close the drapes, someone. And bring my laudanum. Dr. Herberden says I must have a dose whenever I feel anxious, to avoid any danger of agitation of the blood."

His thoughts kept carefully to himself, Jarvis personally went to draw the drapes. Short of the old mad King effecting a miraculous recovery, sometime in the next week the Regency Bill would pass and this indolent, pleasure-loving, spendthrift prince would be sworn in as Regent. But as much as the Prince of Wales might find the image of himself as Regent flattering, his experience with the squabbles and intrigues of politics was as limited as his interest. Jarvis was confident that in the end—and given the right set of circumstances—the Prince would be only too happy to be guided by others' wisdom.

Solicitously turning down the lamps, Jarvis ushered the Prince's companions from the room and quietly closed the door. The Whigs might think their long years of political exile were about to end, but men like Lord Frederick Fairchild were too idealistic to anticipate the lengths to which their opponents were willing to go to keep them out of power, and too mealymouthed to ever be ruthless themselves.

In government, one needed to be ruthless. Ruthless, and very, very clever.

~⌀~

Sir Henry Lovejoy was looking over case reports at his battered old desk when the Earl of Hendon, a polished walnut box tucked under one arm, walked into Love-joy's office at Queen Square.

Behind him came the sweating, bald-headed clerk, his normally squinty little eyes big and round over the spectacles he wore pushed down to the end of his nose. "I tried to announce him, Sir Henry, truly I did—"

Lovejoy waved the man away. "That's all right, Collins." Lovejoy had been expecting an angry confrontation with his fugitive's powerful father. The magistrate had already decided how he would behave: deferential, polite, and respectful, but firm. Standing, he extended one hand toward a nearby chair with worn, brown leather upholstery. "Please have a seat, my lord. What may I do for you?"

"That won't be necessary." Setting the small wooden case on Lovejoy's desk, he stood with his feet planted wide, his hands clasped behind his back. "I've come to turn myself in."

"Turn yourself in, my lord?" Lovejoy shook his head in confusion. "For what?"

Hendon looked at him with withering contempt. "Don't be a bloody idiot. For the murder of that actress, Rachel York, of course. I did it. I killed her."

Chapter 25

"*H*ow old is this nevy of yers?" Tom asked.

They were walking along Haymarket. The air was cold, the kind of damp, penetrating cold that sank bone deep. Wisps of dirty mist drifted across the cobblestones, wrapped around the half-dead plane trees in a small, nearby square. By nightfall, the yellow fog would be back, thick and pungent and bitter.

"Twenty. Maybe twenty-one," said Sebastian. "His mother is my elder sister."

Tom glanced up at him. "You don't like 'im much, do you?"

"He was the kind of little boy who got a kick out of tearing the heads off live turtles." That, and worse. Sebastian shrugged. "I may be prejudiced. He could have grown out of it."

"They'd don't, usually," said Tom, his jaw set tight and hard, as if to ward off memories too savage to be recalled. And Sebastian wondered again at the life the boy must have led, before he'd tried to lift Sebastian's purse in the common room of the Black Hart.

A bath, a change of clothes, a few good nights' sleep, and a consistently full belly had wrought a startling transformation in the boy. From what Sebastian had been able to gather, Tom had been alone on the streets for at least two years. Of his life before that, the boy seldom spoke.

"Why?" Sebastian asked suddenly, his gaze on the boy's sharp-featured, freckled face. "Why in God's name have you decided to throw in your lot with a man in my situation? I can't believe it's for a shilling a day, when you could earn many times that by simply lodging information against me at Bow Street."

"I would never do that!"

"Why not? Many would. Perhaps most."

The boy looked troubled. "There's lots o' bad things 'appen in this world. Lots o' bad things what 'appen, and lots o' folks what do bad things. But there's good, too. Lots o' good. Me mum, before they put her on that ship for Botany Bay, she told me never to forget that. She said that things like 'onor, and justice, and love are the most important things in the world and that it's up to each and every one of us to always try to be the best person we can possibly be." Tom looked up, his nearly lashless eyes wide and earnest. "I don't think there's many what really believes in that. But you do."

"I don't believe in any of that," Sebastian said, his voice harsh, his soul filled with terror by the admiration he saw shining in the young boy's eyes.

"Yes, you do. Only, you thinks you shouldn't. That's all."

"You're wrong," said Sebastian, but the boy simply smiled and walked on.

They turned onto Grange Street, each lost in his own thoughts. Sebastian kept turning over and over in his mind all that he had learned about the woman he stood accused of killing. It seemed to Sebastian that the essence of the woman who had been Rachel York continued to elude him. It was as if each of the men he'd spoken to so far—Gordon, Pierrepont, Donatelli—had

shed light on a facet of her life only. Sebastian had
caught glimpses of Rachel as a new young actress, full
of passionate rhetoric about revolution and the rights of
man; of Rachel as a mistress, seductive, compliant; of
Rachel as an artist's model, beautiful and yet, ultimately, two-dimensional, an image onto which the
viewer could project his own fantasies and illusions.

Only from Kat had Sebastian picked up a sense of
anything beyond that famous face and sensuous body—
the Rachel York who'd once been a young child, alone
and afraid and abused by a society that had no care for
its weaker or less fortunate members. And yet Kat's
rendering, too, had been blurred, incomplete, an image
of Rachel as seen from a distance. He needed to see
Rachel through the dispassionate eyes of someone who
had known, intimately, all the various aspects of her life,
the pattern of her days.

What he needed, Sebastian decided, was to talk to
that maid, Mary Grant.

Stopping abruptly, he swung to face Tom. "I want you
to find someone for me, a woman named Mary Grant.
She used to be Rachel York's maid. But she cleaned the
place out right after her mistress died, so she's probably
living pretty high at the moment."

Tom nodded. "What's she look like, this Mary
Grant?"

"I haven't the slightest idea."

The boy laughed, his eyes gleaming with anticipation.
He wasn't just good at this sort of thing, Sebastian was
beginning to realize; Tom enjoyed it.

"Right then," he said, one hand coming up to anchor
his hat to his head. "I'm off. But you watch yer back," he
called as he dashed away. "You hear?"

Kat drew the folds of her black mantle more closely about her and hastened her step. The air was cold and damp, the gray clouds over the rooftops pressing down heavy and low. She should have called a hackney, she decided, just as a man's darkly coated form loomed up before her. She let out a small gasp of surprise, quickly stifled.

"This isn't like you, Leo," she said, keeping her voice light. "You must be nervous if you've taken to slinking around London."

Leo Pierrepont fell into step beside her. "Did you manage to get into Rachel's rooms?"

"Last night."

"And?"

"As you said, there was nothing incriminating."

A narrow line appeared between the Frenchman's brows. "You checked the compartment in the bedroom mantel?"

"Of course. It contained Rachel's appointment book. Nothing more."

"You're quite certain? You searched everywhere?"

"There was nothing else to search. Rachel's maid cleaned the place out. Down to the walls."

"Her maid?" Something in Leo's tone made Kat look over at him. "What's the woman's name?"

"Mary Grant. Why? What did you think I might find there?"

Instead of answering her, he said, "I had an unpleasant conversation last night with your young viscount. Somehow or other he's found out I was paying for Rachel's rooms."

"Hugh Gordon told him."

"Gordon? How the devil could he have known?"

"One can only assume he heard it from Rachel."

Leo's intense gray eyes narrowed as he searched

Kat's face. "He's been in contact with you, has he? Devlin, I mean."

Kat shrugged and quickened her pace. "One could say he has a vested interest in discovering who killed Rachel."

"And you're helping him?" Leo reached out a hand to touch her shoulder, stopping her. "Be careful, *mon amie*. He might find out some things you'd rather he didn't learn."

Kat swung to look up at him. "I'm always careful."

A smile quirked up one side of the Frenchman's thin, tight lips. "Except with your heart."

Kat stood very still. "*Especially* with my heart."

~∽

There were only so many places a young man of Bayard's crowd could be found in London on a cold, foggy January afternoon.

Sebastian finally ran his nephew to ground at the Leather Bottle, a tavern near Islington that was popular with cutpurses and highwaymen, and the bored, rich young men who liked to rub shoulders with them and learn their thieves' cant and make believe for a few, gin-soaked hours that their lives had, if not meaning, then at least excitement and challenge.

It was early enough that the crowd in the tavern was still thin. A few of the men looked up at Sebastian's entrance, but he had dressed for the part, taking as his model the dashing young gentleman of the highway who had attempted some months back to hold up his carriage one night on Houndslow Heath.

Bayard was at the bar, laughing and talking too loudly with two or three of the gangly, socially maladroit young men with whom he tended to associate.

Bayard was very much his father's son, brown haired and weak chinned and already inclined even at his young age to run to flesh.

Ordering a glass of blue ruin, Sebastian leaned in close to his nephew and poked the muzzle of the Cassaignard between his ribs. Bayard froze.

"That's right," whispered Sebastian, his voice pitched low and rough. "This is a pistol, and it will go off if you do anything—I repeat, *anything*—stupid."

Bayard's eyes rolled frantically sideways.

"No, don't turn around. And stop looking like you just shit your pants or some such thing. We wouldn't want to alarm your friends, now would we? You need to smile."

Bayard gave a sick giggle that came out sounding more like a half-choked hysterical sob. "Who are you? What do you want from me?"

"We're going to walk together, very slowly, to that table over there, near the far corner. You're going to sit down first, and I'm going to sit opposite you, and we're going to have a nice little chat." Sebastian reached for his drink, but the muzzle never left Bayard's side. "Walk, Bayard."

Bayard walked, his legs trembling and unsteady.

"Now sit."

Bayard sat. Sebastian took the rickety, straight-backed chair opposite. The light in the tavern was murky, the few small windows obscured by grime, the tallow dips dim and foul smelling. A heavy odor of sweat and tobacco and spilled gin filled the air.

"Now," said Sebastian, smiling, "you need to try very, very hard not to forget that I have a gun pointed at your crotch."

Bayard nodded, his eyes widening as he got a good

look at Sebastian for the first time. "Good God. It's you. Whatever are you doing in that rig? You look like a bloody bridle cull."

Sebastian smiled. "An appropriate getup, don't you think, for one in danger of cutting a caper upon nothing?"

Sebastian watched, bemused, as Bayard's fear slowly dissipated beneath the onslaught of a deep and powerful fury. "I heard it was you," he said, enunciating the words through clenched teeth, "*you* who killed her."

"You're forgetting the pistol, Bayard," said Sebastian as his nephew half rose from the table.

Bayard sank back into his chair, his gaze locked on his uncle's face. "Did you do it? Did you? Did you kill Rachel?"

"I was going to ask you the same thing."

"*Me*? But I *love* her." The present tense of the verb wasn't lost on Sebastian. "Besides, it's your flintlock they're saying was found on her body."

"And yet it's you who's been preying on the poor woman since before Christmas."

Bayard's eyes widened, that brief flash of anger sliding away as the fear surged again. "*Preying* on her? What are you saying? I never touched her! Why, I never even managed to summon up the courage to *approach* her. The one time I found myself face-to-face with her, I was so overcome I couldn't open my mouth."

"You never actually spoke to her?"

"No! Never."

Sebastian leaned back in his seat. "When was the last time you saw her?"

Bayard worried his lower lip between his teeth. "Monday night, I think. I went to her performance. But that was all! I swear."

"You're sure?"

"Yes, of course."

Sebastian stared across the table at his nephew. As a child, Bayard had been not only spoiled and cruel, but also dangerously, almost pathologically untruthful. He wondered how much, if any, the boy had changed. "Where were you Tuesday night?"

Bayard might be self-indulgent and weak, but he wasn't stupid. His eyes widened. "You mean, the night Rachel was killed?"

"That's right."

"We planned to spend the evening in Cribb's Parlor." He jerked his head toward the two men still leaning on the bar, their attention focused on the mammoth breasts of the woman slinging gin behind the counter. "Robert and Gil and I. We'd been here—at the Leather Bottle—most of the afternoon, so we were pretty well lit by the time we got there."

"You were there all night?"

"Well, actually, no." He scrubbed one hand across his face, as if to wipe away an unpleasant memory. "I started feeling unwell."

"You mean you shot the cat."

A deep stain of mortification and resentment colored the younger man's cheeks. "All right. Yes. Robert and Gil were hauling me out of there when what should we do but run smack up against my father. It was damned embarrassing, I can tell you that. He insisted on taking me home. I must have passed out in the carriage because the next thing I know, I'm in my own bed and he's hauling off my boots and prosing on about how lucky I am that my mother didn't see me."

"What time was that?"

Bayard looked confused. "What time was what?"

"At about what time did you pass out?"

Bayard shrugged one shoulder. "I couldn't say for certain. Early. Around nine, I suppose."

Sebastian studied his nephew's red, sulky face. It would take time, but it should be easy enough to trace Bayard's movements through the course of Rachel York's final day. If he were telling the truth.

"Wait a minute," Bayard said suddenly, sitting forward. "I did see Rachel on Tuesday. It must have been about midway through the afternoon, when I swung by the theater on my way here. I was hoping I might get a glimpse of her, and there she was."

"At the theater?" Sebastian frowned, trying to remember Rachel's schedule for the afternoon before her death. "They were rehearsing?"

"No, no. She wasn't actually at the theater, you see. She was in the goldsmith's across the street. I wouldn't even have noticed her except for the way he was shouting—"

"He?"

"That actor. You know the one? He was doing Richard III at Covent Garden when it burned down."

"You mean Hugh Gordon?"

"Yes, that's him."

"You're certain?" said Sebastian, frowning. What was it Hugh Gordon had said at the Green Man? *I haven't spoken to her for six months or more.*

Bayard nodded vigorously. "I'd have recognized his voice even if I hadn't seen him."

"They were quarreling?"

"I don't know about that. But I could see he had her by the arm and he was leaning into her, all threatening-like. I was about ready to go in there and ask him what the devil he thought he was doing, treating a lady that way, when he gave her a little shake and let her go."

"You didn't hear anything he said?"

"Not so's I remember. Except at the very end, right before he turned away. He said—" Bayard broke off, a strange, arrested expression narrowing his eyes and slackening his jaw.

From somewhere at the back of the room came a sharp breaking of glass, followed by an outburst of laughter. "What?" said Sebastian, his gaze on his nephew's face. "What did Gordon say?"

"He said he'd make her pay."

Chapter 26

Sir Henry Lovejoy stared at the man who stood in the center of the office. The Earl of Hendon was built big and powerful, with a barrel-like torso and a thick head, his nose broad and flat in a slablike, plain-featured face. If there was any resemblance between this man and his son, Lovejoy couldn't see it. "You, my lord? You're confessing to the murder of Rachel York?"

"That's right. She went to that church to meet me." The Earl fixed Lovejoy with a fierce blue stare, as if he could somehow compel the magistrate to believe him. "And I killed her."

Lovejoy sat down so fast, his chair made a little thumping noise. He had been expecting some kind of trouble from Viscount Devlin's influential father, but never in Lovejoy's wildest imaginings could he have anticipated this. He shook his head, his voice coming out even higher pitched than usual. "But . . . why?"

It was a question the Earl didn't seem to have expected. "What do you mean, *why*?"

"Why did she meet you in St. Matthew's?"

Hendon pressed his lips together and sucked in a deep breath that flared his nostrils and expanded his chest. "That is none of your damned business."

"Forgive me, my lord, but if you expect me to accept your confession, it is very much my business."

Hendon swung away to take a quick turn across the room and back. "What the bloody hell do you think I went there to meet her for?" He glowered at Lovejoy, heavy eyebrows furrowed, as if daring Lovejoy to disbelieve him. "A girl like that?"

The implications were as inescapable as they were unbelievable. Lovejoy met the Earl's challenging gaze without flinching. "In a church, my lord?"

"That's right." Hendon rested his hands flat on the desk and leaned into them. "What are you saying? That you don't believe me?"

Lovejoy sat very still. It was obvious what the Earl was trying to do, of course. This was hardly the first time Lovejoy had been confronted by an anxious father willing to do anything, say anything to save a beloved son. When it came to a father's love for his child, Lovejoy supposed it made no difference, after all, whether the father was a blacksmith or a peer of the realm.

A heavy, sad sigh escaped Lovejoy's chest. "There is the matter of Lord Devlin's pistol, which was found on the body."

"That's just it. It's not Sebastian's pistol. It's mine."

Reaching for the wooden box he'd set on the desk, Hendon flipped open the brass clasps and flung back the lid. It was a dueling pistol case, Lovejoy realized. And there, nestled in green baize, lay the mate to the flintlock Constable Maitland had found on Rachel York's body. The molded cradle for the pistol's twin was conspicuously empty.

"They were given to me by my father," said Hendon, "the fourth Earl, shortly before his death. When I was Viscount Devlin."

There was a small engraved brass plate affixed to the front of the box. Lovejoy leaned forward to read it. TO MY SON, ALISTAIR JAMES ST. CYR, VISCOUNT DEVLIN.

Lovejoy knew a moment of deep disquiet. "This proves nothing," he said slowly. "You could have given these pistols to your own son at any time these past ten years or more."

"My son has his own dueling pistols." The Earl's mouth curled up into a hard smile. "As a matter of fact, he was using them the very morning after that girl's murder."

"So I had heard." Standing up, Lovejoy went to stare out the window overlooking the bare branches of the plane trees in Queen Square below. Not for an instant did he believe Lord Hendon's tale. But if the Earl were to stick to this confession, if he were to insist that he and not his son had perpetrated that savage act of carnage in St. Matthew's on Tuesday night . . . Abruptly, Lovejoy swung back to face him. "Describe for me the disposition of the body."

"What?"

"Rachel York's body. You say you killed her. You should be able to describe for me precisely how you left her. Where she was, what she would have looked like when she was found."

Lovejoy watched, fascinated, as the nobleman's face seem to collapse in upon itself, becoming pale and almost slack with horror, as if he were being forced to look again upon that bloodied, savaged body.

"She was in the Lady Chapel," Hendon said, his voice hushed, strained. "On the altar steps, on her . . . on her back. She had her knees bent up, and there was blood. . . ." He swallowed hard, the muscles of his throat working with the effort. "The blood was everywhere."

Reaching out, Lovejoy wrapped his hands around

the wooden back of his desk chair and gripped it hard. "What was she wearing, my lord?"

"A gown. Some satin. I don't remember the color." Hendon paused. "And a pelisse. Velvet, I think. But both were ripped. And stained dark with her blood." His eyes squeezed closed as if to block out a horrific vision, and he brought up one clenched hand to press the knuckles against his lips.

Lovejoy stared at the man standing across from him. They had been very, very careful to keep the more sordid details of Rachel York's murder from the papers. The only way Hendon could have known these things was if he had seen Rachel York's body himself ... or had it described to him by someone who had seen her dead. By the man who had killed her.

Lovejoy pulled out his chair and sat down again. "You say you had an assignation to meet Miss York at St. Matthew's?"

"That's right."

Lovejoy yanked a paper pad toward him and reached for his pen. "And for what time was this meeting scheduled?"

Hendon didn't even hesitate. "Ten."

Lovejoy looked up. "Ten? You're quite certain, my lord?"

"Of course I'm certain. I arrived a few minutes late, but not by much."

Lovejoy set aside his pen and pressed his fingertips together. "So you arrived at St. Matthew's a few minutes after ten? And walked inside to meet her? Is that what you're saying?"

Hendon's heavy brows drew together in a puzzled frown. "That's right."

Lovejoy felt a sad, almost pained smile thin his lips. "I'm afraid that's impossible, my lord. Miss York was killed sometime between five and eight o'clock, which is when St. Matthew of the Fields is locked every evening."

"What are you talking about?" Lord Hendon's fleshy face turned a dark, angry color, his voice booming out so loud that he brought the clerk, Collins, scurrying to the door in alarm. "I arranged to meet that woman in St. Matthew's at ten, and the door in the north transept sure as hell wasn't locked when I got there."

Lovejoy held himself very still. "With all due respect, my lord, I believe you are attempting to protect your son by taking the blame for Rachel York's murder yourself." Reaching across the desk, Lovejoy closed the lid on the dueling pistols case and drew it toward him. "You'll understand our need to keep this, of course. No doubt it shall prove to be a valuable piece of evidence. . . ." Lovejoy hesitated, then said it anyway. "At your son's trial."

Chapter 27

By the time Sebastian reached Kat Boleyn's town-house in Harwick Street, the fog was so thick the street-lamps were little more than murky hints of dim light, and the familiar, bitter stench of soot choked the cold evening air. It would be a dark night, a good night for smugglers and housebreakers.

And grave robbers.

He pushed the thought from his mind. His assignation with Jumpin' Jack Cochran and his crew wasn't until midnight. There was much to do before then.

Sebastian lifted the collar of his coat against the damp and studied the house opposite. It was early enough that Kat hadn't left for the theater yet. He could see her slim, elegant shape, silhouetted against the drawing room drapes, along with the shadow of what looked like a child. Puzzled, Sebastian crossed the street.

"I'll announce myself," he told the thin, mousy-haired maid who answered his knock at the door.

He was already taking the stairs to the first floor two at a time before the woman had recovered enough to say, "But—*sir*! You can't do that!"

He could hear Kat's husky voice, even before he reached the drawing room door.

"There's a saying, that a good foist must have the same talents as a good surgeon: an eagle's eye, a lady's hand, and a lion's heart. An eagle's eye to ascertain a purse's precise location, a lady's hand to slip lightly, nimbly into the man's clothes, and a lion's heart"—she paused, and he could hear the smile in her voice—"to fear not the consequences."

"Gor. How did you do that?" said a voice Sebastian recognized as belonging to his young protégé, Tom.

Sebastian could see them now, standing at the far end of the room with their backs to the door. Kat was wearing a black silk gown made high at the neck, with modest crepe sleeves that told him she must have only recently returned from Rachel York's funeral. He couldn't even begin to guess at the reason for Tom's presence.

"Now let's try it again," she said, handing the boy a small silk purse. "This time, I'll close my eyes while you hide it in one of your pockets. Try to detect the instant I lift it." She squeezed her eyes shut.

Tom tucked the purse deep into his pocket. "Ready."

Leaning against the door frame, Sebastian watched as Kat brushed past the boy once, then again, extricating the purse from his pocket on the second pass with deft, practiced skill. She was good. Very good. But then, before he'd met her, before she'd become one of Covent Garden's most acclaimed actresses, this is what she had done, on the streets of London. This, and other things she rarely talked about.

"When you gonna lift it?" said Tom, still waiting patiently.

Kat laughed and waved the purse under the boy's nose.

Tom's face shone with admiration and delight. "Blimey. You are good."

"One of the best," said Sebastian, and pushed away from the doorway.

Kat swung to face him, an amused smile still curving her full lips. "At least this time you knocked," she said, and he was left wondering if she'd been aware of his presence, of him watching them, all along.

He turned to Tom. "I thought you were planning to spend the evening searching for Mary Grant?"

Tom nodded. "I figured Miss Kat 'ere might be able to put me on to a few places to look."

Sebastian took off his highwayman's jaunty hat and tossed it onto a nearby chair. "I don't think I'll ask how you progressed from that to pickpocket lessons."

The boy ducked his head to hide a grin. "Well, I'll be off, then."

Sebastian watched Tom saunter off whistling a most improper ditty through his teeth. Beside him, Kat said, "Tom tells me you've hired him as a snapper."

Sebastian smiled. "Actually, he's proving useful for a variety of tasks."

She tilted her head, looking up at him. "You trust him?"

Sebastian met her thoughtful gaze and held it. "You know me. I have a foolishly trusting nature."

"I wouldn't have said that. On the contrary, I'd have said you're an extraordinarily perceptive judge of character."

Sebastian lifted one corner of his mouth in an ironic smile and turned away to strip off his greatcoat. "You went to the funeral," he said, tossing the coat and his gloves onto the chair.

Kat walked over to the bellpull and gave it a sharp tug. "Yes."

He could see the strain of the last few days in her face. She might not have been excessively close to

Rachel York, but the young woman's death had obviously shaken Kat, and the funeral had been hard on her. He wondered what she'd say if she knew he had a rendezvous with a group of resurrection men scheduled for midnight.

She ordered tea and cakes from the flustered, mousy-haired maid, who appeared stuttering apologies for her failure to properly guard the door.

"Hugh Gordon was there," said Kat, when the housemaid had taken herself off.

"Was he?" Sebastian stood with his back to the fire, his gaze on the face of the woman he'd once loved to such distraction he'd thought he couldn't live without her. "That's interesting. How about Leo Pierrepont?"

She came to settle on a sofa covered in cream and peach striped silk. "The son of a French comte attend the funeral of a common English actress? Surely you jest."

Sebastian smiled. "And Giorgio Donatelli?"

"He was there, weeping profusely. I hadn't realized he and Rachel were so close. But then, he's Italian. Perhaps he simply cries easily." She leaned her head back against the silk cushions, the flickering light from the candles in their wall sconces shimmering gold over the smooth bare flesh of her throat as she looked up at him. "Did you have an opportunity to speak to Hugh?"

Sebastian wanted to touch her, to run his fingertips down the curve of her neck to her breasts. Instead, he shifted to stare down at the coals glowing on the hearth. The mantel was of white Carrara marble, he noticed, the Sèvres vases exquisite, and the oil painting above them looked like a Watteau. Kat had done very well for herself in the past six years. And he had survived.

"You were right," he said, his voice sounding strained, even to himself. "Hugh Gordon is still furious with Rachel for having left him. Perhaps furious enough to kill."

"You think he did it?"

"I think he's hiding something. He was seen arguing with her near the theater on the afternoon she was killed."

"Do you know what about?"

"No. But he said he'd make her pay." Sebastian swung about as the housemaid reappeared at the door, a tray of tea things in her arms. "I'd like to know where he was later that night."

"He's doing Hamlet at the Stein." Kat reached for the teapot. "But they're not set to open until this Friday."

Sebastian waited until the maid had withdrawn again, then he said, "I also had an opportunity to make the acquaintance of the painter, Giorgio Donatelli. It seems Rachel was modeling for him."

Kat glanced up from pouring the tea. "Nothing ominous there."

"Perhaps. Unless she was sleeping with him, too."

"He is a very beautiful man. And Rachel liked beautiful men."

Sebastian reached to take the cup from her hand. He was very, very careful not to let his fingers brush hers. "According to Donatelli, Bayard Wilcox has been following Rachel around since before Christmas."

"Isn't he your nephew?"

"Yes, he is. Did she never tell you about it?"

"She did mention once or twice that some nobleman was watching her, although she never told me his name. She tried to laugh it off, but I thought she was being less than honest with herself, that he was making her nervous." Kat took her own cup into her hands. "Is he capable of such a thing, do you think? A crime of such passion, such violence?"

Sebastian brought his cup to his lips, and nodded. "Except that he says he was with his friends until just before nine that night, at which point he passed out drunk and had to be carried home by his father."

"But you don't believe him." She said it as a statement, not a question.

"I learned long ago not to trust anything Bayard tells me. But in this case, it should be easy enough to find out if he's telling the truth or not."

Kat sat back, her gaze on the cup she held, idle, in her lap. "You do realize, of course, that it's possible Rachel didn't know her killer? He could be anyone. Anyone at all."

"I don't think so. If she'd been found in the streets, or even in her rooms, then I might believe that. But she went to that church on Tuesday specifically to meet someone. I know it wasn't me. So who was it?"

"It couldn't have been some cousin named St. Cyr?"

Sebastian shook his head. "No." They weren't a family that tended to breed, the St. Cyrs. His father had several cousins he disliked intensely, but they all lived up north, in Yorkshire or some such place. And it was not a common name. "I keep coming back to that appointment book. Whoever removed those pages did it to prevent something from being known. And yet the book was left so that it could be found. Why?"

"But the book was hidden!"

"Yes. Except you knew where to look for it. It's conceivable others could have, as well. Pierrepont, for instance? He was paying the rent on her rooms. He might very well have a key."

She sat silent for a moment, as if considering this. "The woman upstairs described the man she saw the morning after Rachel's death as young. Pierrepont must be almost fifty."

"He could have sent someone."

Kat thrust aside her teacup and stood up. "You think *Pierrepont* killed Rachel?"

Sebastian watched her walk over to straighten one of the drapes at the front windows. It was a fussy thing to do, not at all like her. "Why not? He was involved with her. For some men, that's all the reason they need, if the woman decides to try to walk away from them. Or if she should suddenly become infatuated with a beautiful Italian painter."

Kat turned to face him again. "When I was at Rachel's lodging house, the Scotswoman who lives upstairs told me she thought Rachel was planning to leave London."

"You think it's true?"

"I don't know. Rachel certainly never said anything about it. But this woman seems to have the impression Rachel was about to get her hands on a lot of money."

"Money?" Sebastian set aside his empty cup. "I wonder if she was blackmailing someone."

Hardly had the words left his mouth when a thought occurred to him, a thought at once inevitable and so terrible as to take his breath. And he knew by the way Kat's eyes flared wide that the possibility had come to her at almost exactly the same time. "No," he said, before she could give voice to it.

"But—"

"No," he said again, walking up to her. "You're wrong. I know my father. He might be able to kill, given the right provocation, but not like that. He could never kill like that."

Her head fell back, her wide, beautiful eyes dark and troubled as she looked up into his face.

It wasn't simply something Sebastian was saying; he truly believed Hendon could never have raped Rachel

York on those altar steps, or left her dying in a sea of her own blood. And yet . . .

And yet the name St. Cyr had been there, in the dead woman's small red leather book. And the gentleman who'd been stalking her for so many months wasn't only Sebastian's nephew.

Bayard Wilcox was also the Earl of Hendon's grandson.

Chapter 28

Sebastian met Jumpin' Jack Cochran and his two-man crew in a dark byway just off Highfield Lane. A cold wind had come up, tossing the bare branches of the elm trees and silhouetting against a storm-swirled sky the church's spire just visible above the slate roofs of the nearby row of houses.

"Don't kin why yer so feverish to tag along," said Jumpin' Jack, hawking up a mouthful of spittle that he shot downwind. " 'Tain't as if the good doctor's affeared we cain't be relied on t' deliver the goods."

The grave robber was an incredibly tall, lean man somewhere between forty and sixty, with deep-set, narrowed eyes and rawboned features and a good two weeks' of graying beard grizzling his cheeks and chin. But he was a natty dresser, with a bright red kerchief tied around his neck and striped trousers that showed only a hint of mud around the cuffs. The resurrection business was a lucrative one.

Sebastian simply returned the man's quizzical stare and made no attempt to put his reasons into words. This man made his living stealing dead bodies from churchyards. He would never be able to understand the compulsion that had brought Sebastian here, the belief that his responsibility for the desecration of

Rachel York's grave somehow obligated him to be there to witness it.

They left the resurrection men's cart and horse in the care of one of the lads and set off down a narrowed, darkened alley. They walked softly, their long-handled tools wrapped in sacking to prevent them from clanking together. In a nearby yard, a dog began to bark, deep, throaty howls that blew away with the wind. They kept walking.

Rachel York had been laid to rest in the churchyard of St. Stephen's, an ancient sandstone pile that rose up suddenly before them. Hundreds of years of internments had raised the level of its graveyard so far above the street that the swelling soil had to be contained by a stone wall some three feet high. And still it bulged out, pestilent and seemingly filled to bursting.

Along the top of the wall ran a high iron fence topped with a menacing row of spikes. But at the end of the alley lay a narrow side gate, half-overgrown with ivy, which someone had been paid to leave unlocked. The same person had obviously been compensated for oiling the gate's hinges. No telltale squeak shrieked out into the stillness of the night as they slipped quietly inside.

A foul stench hung in the air, dank and vaguely, sickeningly sweet. The other men moved as if blind, only risking an occasional flash of their shuttered lantern as they crept through the dark, moonless night. But Sebastian could see almost too well the scattered gray headstones and looming arches of tombs, the occasional pale glow of a skull or long bone protruding here and there from the muddy earth. The cold night air filled with sounds, the wind rising through the bare branches of the trees, the stealthy, muffled padding of feet on a muddy path and the hushed, strained breathing of nervous men.

"Here 'tis," whispered Jumpin' Jack, his lantern flashing for an instant on a mound of naked, freshly turned soil. Unwrapping their tools, the two men set to digging, shovels scraping softly as they sank deeper and deeper into the earth.

The stench was stronger here. Lifting his head, Sebastian realized it came from the long, half-filled trench of the poor hole, half-lost in the gloomy shadows of the far corner. In the distance, the dog was still barking. From somewhere nearer at hand came the slow, steady drip, drip of water.

The *thwunk* of metal striking wood echoed around the yard. Jumpin' Jack let out a grunt of satisfaction and said, "Got it."

Sebastian forced himself to look down into that dark hole. The resurrection men were experts at their business. Rather than exhuming the entire coffin, they'd simply dug down to the head. Using one of the shovels as a pry, Jumpin' Jack levered open the top of the casket. Then the young boy with them—a stocky lad of about sixteen named Ben—jumped down into the hole. Wheezing a string of curses under his breath, he slowly eased what was left of Rachel York from the coffin, the still, white-clad body showing ghostly pale against the darkness of the turned earth.

Squatting down beside the corpse, Jumpin' Jack slipped a knife from the sheath at his side and began with swift, practiced strokes to cut away her shroud.

Sebastian's hand reached out to grip the man's arm, stopping him. "What are you doing?"

Jumpin' Jack hawked another mouthful of spittle, his pale eyes glittering in the darkness as he spat into the gaping hole beside them. "Ain't no law agin cartin' a dead body through the streets. But ye can win yerself seven years in Botany Bay, if'n yer caught with a stiff in graveclothes."

Sebastian nodded and took a step back.

They stripped the body of everything except the band wound lengthwise around her head to hold her jaw closed. Then, leaving the naked body lying in the muddy path, they shoved the graveclothes back into the coffin, closed the lid, and quickly shoveled the earth back onto the empty grave.

"You there, Ben," said Jumpin' Jack, squatting down to grasp the body's bare white shoulders. "Grab her feet."

Sebastian collected the shovels and the lantern, while the other two men lifted the body between them, one bare arm flopping down to drag limply in the mud as they set off toward the gate.

From somewhere in the distance came the cry of the watch, *One o'clock and all is well.*

～

They carried Rachel York's body into the small stone outbuilding behind Paul Gibson's surgery and laid her on a flat granite slab with drains cut around the outer edges in a way that reminded Sebastian, uncomfortably, of an ancient sacrificial altar he'd once seen in the mountains of Anatolia.

He paid Jumpin' Jack fifteen pounds, which was the going price for a "half-long" and more than a good housemaid could earn in a year. As the resurrection men's cart rattled off into the night, Paul Gibson thrust home the bolt on the outside door, then limped over to hang his oil lamp from the chain suspended above the table.

Golden light flooded the room, throwing the two men's shadows tall and unnaturally thin across the rough plaster of the wall behind them. "Nasty piece of work, this," he said after a moment.

Sebastian had to force himself to look down at what lay on the slab before them. Rachel York had been a beautiful woman, her body long limbed and gracefully made, slim of waist and hip, with full, ripe breasts. Now her soft flesh was deadly pale, and smeared with the mud from her grave. But he could see other marks, bruises left by hard fingers digging into her wrists. More bruises, on her arms, her cheeks. And ugly slashes across her neck so deep that one might almost imagine her attacker's objective had been to sever her neck. Reaching out, Paul Gibson untied the band around her head and her jaw fell open. Sebastian looked away.

"It would have been better if I could have examined her before she was bathed and laid out and dumped in the mud," Paul said. "Much will have been lost."

Sebastian didn't like the way the small, stone-walled outbuilding smelled. Or the way it felt. He knew a sudden, driving urge to get away. "How long will it take?"

Paul Gibson reached for what looked like a butcher's apron and tied it around his neck and waist. "I might be able to tell you something in the morning, although, of course, the full postmortem will take longer."

Sebastian nodded, the smell of death so thick in his nostrils that each breath became a labor. He realized that Paul Gibson was looking at him strangely. "I don't suppose you've heard?" said the doctor.

"Heard what?"

"This afternoon, your father walked into the Queen Square Public Office and confessed to the murder of Rachel York."

Chapter 29

Sebastian had been about nine years old when he'd begun to realize that there was something different about him, that most people couldn't overhear whispered conversations held in distant rooms, or read the titles of the books on the shelves of the library in the dark of the night, or from across the room.

Sometimes he wondered if most people experienced the world around them a little bit differently from their fellows, if the assumption of commonality was simply an illusion. Once he'd met a man who thought a yellow dog was the same color as the swath of vivid green spring grass in which the dog played, and who swore the gray cloth of his suit was blue. It had been a stray remark made by Sebastian's sister, Amanda, that had first made Sebastian aware of the fact that most people couldn't see colors at night, that for them, darkness reduced the world to a shading of grays through which they moved almost blind.

He'd found his ability to see in the dark particularly useful when he'd undertaken special assignments for the army during the war. He found it useful now as he slipped over the garden wall of St. Cyr House on Grosvenor Square, and crept toward the terrace.

Alistair St. Cyr, the fifth Earl of Hendon, slept in a

massive Tudor tester bed that had once belonged to the first Earl's great-grandfather. He came awake slowly, lips pursing in his sleep, eyelids fluttering open, closed. Open.

He sat up with a rasping gasp, jaw slack, eyes flaring wide as he took in the clusters of candles burning on the bedside table and along the mantel. His gaze lifted to where Sebastian leaned against the bedpost with his arms folded across his chest, and he let out a sigh of relief. "*Sebastian*. Thank God. I've been hoping you'd come to me."

Sebastian shoved away from the bedpost to stand with his arms at his side, anger thrumming through him. "What the bloody *hell* did you think you were about, walking into that Public Office and trying to convince people that you're the one who killed Rachel York?"

The expression on Hendon's face was one Sebastian had never seen before, a strange mingling of grief and worry and what looked very much like guilt. "Because I'm the one she went to meet that night."

Tuesday, St. Matthew's, St. Cyr.

"Oh, Jesus," whispered Sebastian, one hand coming up to shade his eyes.

Hendon thrust aside the bedclothes and stood up, a powerful figure of dignity despite nightshirt and cap. "But I swear to you, she was already dead when I found her."

Sebastian huffed a laugh, his hand falling back, loosely, to his side. "What do you think? That I'm going to believe you've taken to rape and murder in your old age?"

Turning, he went to crouch before the fire and stir up the coals on the hearth. He felt the heat fan his cheeks, lick at the graveyard chill left deep within his being. A whirl of disparate, incomprehensible facts suddenly clicked into place, making perfect, awful sense. "So it was your pistol they found," he said, his gaze on the flames before him.

A cough rumbled deep in the older man's chest. "I took it with me, just in case. I didn't even realize I'd dropped it until I arrived home and found it missing. I thought about going back, looking for it, but . . ." He hesitated. "I couldn't bring myself to do it. I guess I was hoping I'd lost it someplace else."

Sebastian threw another shovelful of coal on the fire and watched it lay there, dark and smoldering. "And why, precisely, were you meeting Rachel York alone in a Westminster church in the dead of the night?"

"I can't tell you that."

Sebastian twisted around, one knee pressing into the hearth rug. "You *what*?"

Wordless, his father stared back at him, that strange mingling of emotions shading his brilliant blue eyes.

"Was she blackmailing you? Is that it?"

"No."

Sebastian thrust aside the coal scuttle and stood up. "What else am I to believe?"

Hendon scrubbed a hand across his face, his jaw working soundlessly back and forth in that way he had when he was thinking, obviously deciding what he was going to tell Sebastian and what he was going to keep to himself. "She contacted me early Tuesday," he said at last. "She had something she thought I might be interested in purchasing."

"So she was blackmailing you."

"No. I told you, she had something to sell. Something I wanted to buy. We agreed upon a price, and she said she'd meet me at St. Matthew's, in the Lady Chapel, at ten o'clock."

"Why St. Matthew's?"

"She said it was quiet. There'd be less chance of our being disturbed or discovered." A round table with a gleaming, well-polished inlaid top stood at the foot of the massive bed, and Hendon went to seat himself in one of the nearby lyre-backed chairs. "That little cross-biting cully of a magistrate, that Lovejoy, he claims the church was locked at eight that night, but it wasn't. The north transept door was open when I arrived there, just as she'd said it would be."

"Did you see anyone else about?"

"No." Hendon's laced fingers tightened until the knuckles showed white. "No one. I thought we were alone. She'd lit all the candles on the chapel's altar. I could see the flames flaring up together, like a warm golden glow as I walked toward the back of the church. Then I saw her."

He rubbed one splayed hand across his eyes as if to wipe away the memory of what he'd seen. "It was ghastly, the way she'd been left lying there, on the altar steps with her legs spread. . . ." His voice trailed away to a whisper. The effort it took him to push the words out was an almost palpable thing. "You could actually see the bloody imprints of his hands on the bare flesh of her thighs. So much blood, everywhere."

Sebastian gazed across the room at his father's ashen, troubled face. No one would ever describe the Earl of Hendon as a sensitive man. He was hard, irascible, phlegmatic; he could be brutal. But he'd never been to war, never seen the blackened, bloated bodies of children lying in the burned ruins of their home. Never seen what artillery—or even a couple of drunken soldiers—could do to the once soft, smooth flesh of a woman.

Sebastian kept his voice steady, dispassionate. "And

this—this whatever it was you went there to buy. Did she have it on her?"

Hendon sucked in a deep breath that lifted his chest, then blew it out again through pursed lips and shook his head. "I looked for it." He pressed a clenched fist against his lips, and Sebastian thought he knew what it must have cost his father to approach that bloodied, ravished body and systematically, ruthlessly search it. "That must have been when I dropped the pistol. I had hoped I'd left it in the pocket of my greatcoat. I threw it away, you know—the greatcoat, I mean. Stuffed it down one of the drains in Great Peter Street. There was so much blood on it I could never have explained it to Copeland. I washed off my boots as best I could, but I still had to invent some faradiddle about stopping to help the victims of a carriage accident." His gaze seemed to come unfocused, as if he were seeing into the past. "So much blood."

Sebastian walked over to stand on the far side of the table, his gaze studying his father's face. "You must tell me what you went there to buy."

Hendon leaned back in his chair, his jaw set hard. "I can't."

Sebastian slammed the open palm of one hand down on the table between them. "Whatever you went to St. Matthew's to buy is very likely the reason Rachel York died. How the bloody hell am I to discover who killed her when you won't even tell me what this is all about?"

"You're wrong. My business with that woman has nothing to do with her murder."

"You can't know that."

"Yes, I can."

Sebastian leaned his weight into the tabletop, then shoved himself away. "*Bloody hell.* Don't you understand what's at stake here?"

Hendon pushed to his feet, his face darkening. "You seem to forget who we are. Who I am. Do you seriously think I will allow a son of mine to be brought up on murder charges like some common criminal?"

Sebastian kept his voice steady. "You can't fix this, Father. A woman is dead."

"An inconsequential whore?" Hendon swiped at the air between them. "Her death I could have dealt with. What I want to know is what the hell you thought you were about, stabbing a constable and leading the authorities on a chase across London?"

"The man slipped and fell against another constable. It wasn't even my knife."

"That's not what they're saying."

"They're lying."

Sebastian met his father's gaze and held it. Hendon let out a long sigh. "The constable's not dead yet, but from what I hear it's only a matter of time. You'll need to leave the country until I can sort all this out."

Sebastian smiled. "And Jarvis? You can't tell me the King's very busy cousin isn't behind the authorities' haste to see me arrested."

Sebastian knew from the way his father's jaw worked that he was right. United the two men might be in their hatred of the French, republicanism, and Catholics, but Hendon was far too much a stickler for the preeminence of rules and propriety to ever find favor with a Machiavellian schemer like Jarvis. "I can take care of Jarvis."

Sebastian pressed his lips together and said nothing.

"I've made arrangements," Hendon said, pushing up from the table. "With the captain of a ship—"

"I'm not running."

Hendon went to jerk open a small drawer in the bureau on the far side of the bed. "There is no shame in temporarily removing yourself from harm's way."

The big old house seemed to stretch out around them, painfully familiar and suddenly, unexpectedly dear in the hushed stillness of the night. "I'm not running," Sebastian said again. "I'm going to stay here and find out who killed that woman. And why."

Hendon turned, a flash of what might have been fear flaring in his eyes. He hesitated, then thrust out his hand. "Here. At least take this."

Sebastian glanced down at the banknotes in his father's big, blunt-fingered, outstretched hand. "I don't need money."

"Don't be a bloody ass. Of course you need money."

It was true. His various purchases at the Rag Fair and in Haymarket had seriously depleted his funds, and he would need more in the days to come.

He took the money and turned toward the window, only to pause as a thought occurred to him. "Leo Pierrepont claims he was hosting a dinner party the night Rachel York was killed. Can you find out if it's true?"

"Pierrepont? The French émigré? What the hell's he to do with this?"

"Maybe nothing. Maybe everything. Can you find out?"

That expression Sebastian could never quite read was back on his father's face. "For God's sake, Sebastian. This is madness. If you won't leave the country, then at least lie low until it all blows over. I'll hire the best Bow Street has to offer. They'll track down the real killer. Just concentrate on keeping yourself safe."

Sebastian gave a soft laugh and turned to fling up the sash. "I'm afraid you'll find that the best of Bow Street is already busy." He threw one leg over the sill, then paused to glance back at his father's tense, troubled face. "They're all out there right now. Looking for me."

The next morning the clouds hung low and heavy, and there was a bite to the air that spoke of snow before nightfall.

Turning up the collar of his greatcoat against the cold, Sebastian set off on foot toward the City, walking briskly to keep warm. At the base of Tower Hill he bought a bag of roasted chestnuts from an old woman, then ended up giving most of them away to the small knot of ragged children who huddled nearby, stamping their feet and rubbing their hands in the bitter cold. He knew they had always been there, these bands of half-starved urchins, just like the desperate mothers clutching their wailing, dying infants, and the homeless, helpless old men and women. Yet it seemed to Sebastian as if he had, somehow, never really noticed them before. Or perhaps it was simply that he had never before walked among them, alone and vulnerable and sharing their fear.

"You don't look as if you went to bed last night," said Paul Gibson, when the surgeon's young maidservant led Sebastian back to the kitchen where the Irishman was just finishing what looked like a quick breakfast of oatmeal and ale.

Sebastian rasped one hand across his unshaven cheek. "I didn't."

Gibson grinned. "Neither did I." He swung his wooden leg awkwardly over the bench and stood up. "Come see. I've a few things that might interest you."

Following his friend along the weedy path, Sebastian took a last, deep breath of cold air and ducked his head to enter the small stone outbuilding that served Gibson as a dissection room. There was a dampness to the room that he didn't remember from before, the dankness accentuating the pungent stench of death and decay.

"I spent a good hour simply washing the mud off

her," said Gibson, limping to the body that lay white and cold on the altarlike slab. Sebastian was glad to see the surgeon hadn't actually started cutting yet. "The slices on her neck were made by a two-edged knife, probably a sword stick, such as a gentleman might carry hidden in his cane or walking stick."

Sebastian nodded. He had such a walking stick himself. As did Hendon.

"It was done like this—" Gibson demonstrated by slashing his arm through the air, first one direction, then the other. "Your killer cut back and forth, over and over again." He let his arm fall. "There must have been a fair amount of blood splattered around that chapel."

"So I hear." Sebastian studied the savagely hacked flesh of Rachel York's neck, and remembered what his father had said, about being so covered in blood he'd had to throw away his greatcoat. Whoever had done this must have walked away from that church drenched in blood. As Leo Pierrepont had said, the attack had half severed the head from the neck. And Sebastian was left thinking, How had the Frenchman known that?

"Because of the way it was done," Gibson was saying, "there are slashes running from both the left and the right. But if you look closely, you'll see that the cuts made from left to right are longer and deeper, which tells us that the man you're looking for is right-handed."

"And fairly strong?"

Gibson shrugged. "She was a small woman. Any reasonably-sized man could have overpowered her, although she did fight him. She wanted desperately to live, this woman." With remarkable gentleness, he picked up one of the hands lying so pale and still against the granite slab. "Look at how the nails are broken and torn here—and there," he said, pointing. "Not only that, but I found traces of skin embedded beneath two of the remaining nails on her right hand."

Sebastian glanced up in surprise. "You mean, she scratched him?"

"I'd say so, yes. But I suspect it was before he pulled the knife on her. There are no cuts on her hands."

Sebastian ran his thoughts back over the men he had spoken to; none had borne signs of having been scratched—at least, not in any place that was visible. "So she probably scratched him while he was raping her."

"I'm afraid not." Paul Gibson laid Rachel's hand back down on the cold stone. "She was raped after she died. Not before."

"*What?* How can you be sure?"

The Irishman leaned over the body. "Look at the bruising around her wrists and on her forearms. You can see where she struggled against him. But there's no sign of bruising on her thighs. There would be, if he'd been forcing her legs apart, holding her down. Nor is there any bruising on her feminine parts; only a slight inner abrasion that could have come after death."

He swung away to pick up a shallow, enameled basin from the long, low table that stood beneath the small paned front window. "But this is the most telling piece of evidence," he said, and Sebastian found himself staring at a torn piece of satin, now so stained with blood it was impossible to guess at its original color.

"Presumably, it's from her dress. I found it *inside* her. He must have shoved it into her when he entered her. The minor abrasions she suffered from the rape couldn't be the source of all this blood. This blood must be from her throat. Which means that by the time he mounted her, he'd already killed her."

The damp cold of the room was starting to penetrate through the cheap wool of Sebastian's coat. He brought his cupped hands up to his mouth and blew on them, his gaze drifting back to the still form lying on that slab. He was remembering what his father had said, about seeing the bloody fingerprints on her bare white thighs. And it hadn't even clicked.

Sebastian let his hands fall to his side. "So he—what? Struggles with her, bruising her arms and wrists, maybe backhanding her across the face when she scratches him. He pulls a sword from his walking stick, slashes her throat, over and over again, killing her. And *then* he rapes her?"

Gibson nodded. "And picture this: the way he had hacked at her throat, she would have been wet with blood. They both would have been."

Sebastian breathed a harsh sigh. "My God. What manner of man does such a thing?"

"A very dangerous one." Gibson set aside the basin with a clatter that rang loudly in the cold room. "There's a name for this particular form of depravity. It's called necrophilia."

Sebastian brought his gaze back to the savaged, naked body of the woman before them. He'd heard of it, of course. There were places in London that specialized in catering to every sort of vile perversion a man could imagine—sodomy, sadomasochism, pederasty. And this.

"So he killed her in order to rape her?" Sebastian said. And he thought, *What if Kat was right? What if Rachel York was killed by someone who didn't even know her? What if her death had nothing at all to do with who she was, with the men who had moved through her life, or even with the mysterious rendezvous she had scheduled that night with the Earl of Hendon?* How could Sebastian hope to find her killer, then?

"Perhaps," said Paul Gibson. "Then again, some men

are sexually stimulated by the act of killing." His soft gray eyes grew troubled with the shadow of old, ugly memories, his voice dropping to a pained, torn whisper. "As we both know."

Sebastian nodded, not meeting his gaze. It was something they'd both seen too many times during the war, the brutal lust of soldiers, still bloody from battle and turned loose on the hapless women and children of a conquered city, or a farm that simply happened to have the misfortune to lie in the army's path. There was something about the act of killing that could bring out everything primitive and not quite human within a man. Or was that kind of thinking a misconception, Sebastian wondered, born of human arrogance? Because this particular brand of selfishly cruel destructiveness was all too peculiarly human. Many beasts in the wild killed for food, for survival, but there were none who killed for the sadistic, sexual pleasure of it.

"So he could have killed her for some other reason entirely, and found the whole experience so exciting that he felt compelled to ease his lust on her dead body."

The doctor nodded. "The inner abrasions are slight. He must have already been very excited when he entered her." He hesitated, then said, "There is one other thing, which may or may not be pertinent. Did you notice the scars on her wrists?"

Sebastian leaned forward to study the blurred, faded outline of old scars encircling each of her wrists like bracelets. Sebastian had scars like that himself, from his days in Portugal: a legacy of twelve painful, bloody hours spent twisting his wrists against the tight bite of a binding rope.

"And look at this." Reaching beneath one shoulder, Gibson rolled the body so that Sebastian could see the faint lines of white scars crisscrossing her slim, beautiful back. "Someone took a whip to her."

"How long ago, would you say?"

"I'm not sure." Gibson eased the body back down. "At least several years ago, I'd say." He was moving around the room now, assembling instruments on a tray. "I might have more to tell you in a day or two, when I've had a chance to do the actual autopsy."

Sebastian nodded, his gaze caught by the still, beautiful features of the woman before him. Her skin had been pale, even in life; now in the cold morning light she looked nearly blue, her full lips a surprisingly dark purple. "I want to rebury her when you're finished," he said.

Gibson came to stand beside him. He had stopped clattering his surgical tools. "All right."

Sebastian kept his gaze on all that was left of Rachel York. Less than a week ago, she had been nothing to him—a name on a playbill, a pretty face only. Even after he'd been accused of her killing, his thoughts had all been for his own survival, his desire to find her killer driven by his own needs, not hers.

But at some point in the last few days, he realized, that had changed. Rachel York had been less than nineteen years old when she died; a young woman, alone and defenseless, battling to survive in a society that used and discarded its weak and unfortunate as if they were somehow less than human. And yet she had stubbornly refused to allow herself to become a victim. She had struggled against the odds, fought back, brave and determined . . . until someone, some man, had cornered her in the Lady Chapel of an ancient, deserted church and done *this* to her.

The world was full of ugliness, Sebastian knew that; ugliness, and ugly people. But you couldn't let them win, those men who took what they wanted with never a thought or care for the ones who suffered and died as a result. You could never stop fighting them, never let them think that what they did was right or somehow justified. Never let them triumph unchallenged.

"You'll have justice," he whispered, although the woman before him was long past hearing, and he'd lost his belief in an all-knowing, benevolently attentive God long ago, on some battlefield in central Spain. "Whoever did this to you won't get away with it. I swear it."

He was suddenly aware of Paul Gibson standing beside him, a strange expression quirking up one corner of his lips. "And here I thought you'd given up believing in either justice or righteous causes."

"I have," said Sebastian, turning toward the door.

But his friend only smiled.

Chapter 30

The snow began before midday.

Sebastian walked through crooked medieval streets. Ice filmed over the water standing in the open gutters. A ragged woman hurried past him, her shawl-wrapped shoulders hunched against the weather, her breath white in the cold, dank air. He walked until the smell of the river was thick in his nostrils and seagulls cried overhead. Beneath his feet the cobblestones turned slippery with the snow that fell in great wet flakes from out of a yellow-white sky.

Cutting between a boarded-up warehouse and a high stone wall, he climbed down a short flight of ancient steps to where the Thames stretched out before him, thick and brown and wide, the wind strong enough now to kick up little whitecaps and fill the air with the scent of the distant sea. Even with the cold and the snow, the river teemed with boats, lighters and culls, and barges and hoys heading downriver to Gravesend and the open sea beyond. It was the lifeblood of the city, this river, and yet how often had he gone through the movements of his days within scant blocks of it and remained essentially oblivious to its existence for weeks on end.

He'd known it was there, of course, yet because it intruded so little on his life, it was easy to ignore, like the distant wailing of hungry children in the night, or the muffled rumble of the parish carts making their early morning rounds, collecting the endless supply of white-wrapped bundles that fed the poor holes of St. Stephen's and St. Andrew's, St. Pancreas and the Spital-fields Churchyard.

Easy to ignore, too, was the existence of those dark, unassuming houses in Field Lane and Covent Garden, where for a few coins a man could buy the right to un-lock a room and do whatever he liked to the shivering, frightened child or sobbing woman he would find there; houses where whips cracked and bodies twisted in agony, where there was no hope, no God, only en-durance and the ultimate deliverance of death. What-ever perversion a man lusted after, he could buy in this city, for a price.

The snow was falling harder now, and faster. Sebas-tian looked up, letting the small white pellets sting the cold skin of his face. What was becoming a recurrent fear swelled within him, the fear that he was never going to clear himself of this terrible crime of which he'd been accused. And what then? he wondered. What if Rachel York's killing had been nothing more than a random act of violence? What if he could never find the man who had slashed her throat and sated his lust upon her dead, bleeding body? What then of his promise to see justice done, for her and for himself?

He'd told himself her killer must have been someone close to her, someone who knew she would be waiting alone and vulnerable in that church so late at night. And yet Sebastian realized now he'd been wrong, that her killer could simply have seen her in the streets and fol-lowed her, watched as she lit the holy candles on the altar and then come at her out of the darkness, a lethal and intimate stranger.

Sebastian rubbed a hand across his eyes, aching now from lack of sleep. After he'd left his father's house in Grosvenor Square, he'd spent what was left of the night walking the slowly lightening alleys and byways of the city. He kept turning what his father had told him over and over again in his mind, trying to figure out what Rachel York could have been selling that his father would be so desperate to buy that he agreed to meet her in a deserted church in the dark of the night.

He'd sworn it wasn't blackmail, but Sebastian had to acknowledge that that could be mere quibbling, a question of semantics only. Whatever it was, Hendon wanted it badly enough that he'd forced himself to overcome his horror and search Rachel York's bloody, mutilated body in hopes of finding it.

Yet he hadn't found it. Which could mean either that her killer now had it, or that Rachel York had never brought it to St. Matthew's in the first place.

Then again, Sebastian couldn't discount the possibility that his father was lying, that Hendon had found it and taken it, after all.

An unexpected chill shook him. Sebastian turned up his collar against the cold. Hendon's refusal to talk baffled him. After all these hours of walking the streets, of turning over one possibility after another in his mind, Sebastian was still no closer to understanding. It was only now, as he watched the snowflakes falling thick and fast from a lowering sky, that he was able to admit to himself that beneath the confusion and rage coursing through him every time he thought about his interview with his father, what he felt most powerfully was a deep and abiding sense of hurt. For try as he might, he found it impossible to imagine a secret so important that a father would place its preservation above the life and freedom of his only surviving son.

~♥~

That afternoon, Sebastian paid an interesting visit to the small goldsmith's shop across the street from Covent Garden Theater. He was just turning away when he spotted Tom, whittling on a block of wood with a small pocketknife as he waited in the protective lee of the theater's wide porch.

"What are you doing here?" said Sebastian, walking up to him.

"Waitin' for Miss Kat. She knows someone she reckons might be able to put me onto this Mary Grant's whereabouts, but she figures it'd be better if'n she were to introduce me to the cove 'erself."

"Ah," said Sebastian, who knew something of the kind of "friends" Kat had from her early days in London. Leaning forward, he peered at the quadruped taking shape beneath the boy's nimble fingers. "What is it?"

"A 'orse," said the boy, proudly holding it aloft.

"Like horses, do you?"

Tom nodded. "I always thought it'd be just grand to be one o' them tigers, sittin' up behind some sportin' gentleman in 'is curricle, watchin' 'im tool a pair of prime 'igh steppers."

Sebastian personally had little use for the current vogue for employing children as grooms. But as he looked down into the boy's shining eyes, he found himself saying, "Once I fight my way clear of this wretched mess I'm in, I could take you on as a tiger. If you're interested."

Tom's eyes narrowed. His face was wary and guarded against disappointment, but his breathing had quickened, his jaw going slack with awe. "You got a curricle?"

Sebastian laughed and stepped out into the street. "That I do."

"Got a tiger?"

"Not yet."

The boy nodded, struggling to contain a grin. "Where you off to, then?"

Sebastian turned up his collar against the snow. "To have another talk with Hamlet."

Chapter 31

Darkness came early that day, settling over the city with a heavy fall of snow.

Across the street from the lodging house where Hugh Gordon had rooms, Sebastian stomped his numb feet and watched the stocky, gray-haired woman who came in daily to "do" for the actor close the street door behind her and set off toward the Strand, the snow blanketing her head and shoulders with white as she hurried through the gathering gloom.

Sebastian waited while a coal cart trundled by, followed by a brewer's wagon. Then he crossed the street, with each step easing himself into the persona of Cousin Simon Taylor from Worcestershire. By the time he stood outside Gordon's door, his shoulders had slumped and he was twisting his hat anxiously in his hands as he waited for Gordon to answer his knock.

"Oh, it's you, is it?" said the actor, his lips pressing together in annoyance as he cast a distracted glance toward the ornate ormolu clock on his sitting room mantel. He kept the door open no more than a foot. "I don't have a great deal of time at the moment—"

"It won't take long," said Sebastian, smiling hopefully.

Gordon hesitated, then pushed his breath out in a sigh and opened the door wider. "Very well. What is it?"

"I was wondering if perhaps you could clear up something for me," said Sebastian, scooting through the door. "The thing is, you see, I was speaking with the very kind gentleman who owns the jewelry store across the street from Covent Garden Theater—you know the place, don't you? The one with the new gaslights? Well, Mr. Touro was telling me—that's the proprietor's name, Mr. Jacob Touro?—he was telling me how Rachel was in his shop on the very afternoon she died. But what I find confusing, you see, is that while you told me that you hadn't seen Rachel for the better part of six months, Mr. Touro says that you came in his shop that same afternoon and confronted Rachel." Sebastian fixed the actor with an anxious gaze. "Actually, *accosted* is the word he used."

Hugh Gordon returned Sebastian's stare with a bland look. "Obviously, the man is mistaken."

"Well, one might think so. Except, he's a particular fan of yours, is Mr. Touro," Sebastian continued, smiling amicably as he seated himself—without invitation—on a high-backed settee covered in burgundy brocade. "He says he hasn't missed a one of your performances in the past five years. And I gather that Cousin Rachel was one of his best customers, if you know what I mean? So, of course, when he read the next day about what had happened to Rachel, he remembered the incident. Although I must assure you that he has no intention of telling the authorities about the argument, or the way you seized Rachel's arm and threatened to kill her."

Gordon stood in the middle of his ornate, burgundy, and lace-draped sitting room, his eyes narrowing thoughtfully, as if he were beginning to reassess his attitude toward Rachel's Cousin Simon. "I never did any such thing."

"You're right: I exaggerate. According to Mr. Touro,

the precise phrase you used was 'Beat you within an inch of your life.' "

The actor was silent for a moment, as if considering whether to continue denying the meeting or to provide Sebastian with some abbreviated, distorted version of the truth. Abbreviated distortion won.

"Rachel owed me money," he said, swinging away to pour himself a brandy from an ornate tray of heavy gold-rimmed glasses that looked as if it might have been part of the stage props for a production of the *Arabian Nights*. "She has owed it to me ever since she first started at the theater. She wasn't making much in those days, so I provided her with everything she needed in the way of dresses and such. She always knew it was no gift."

"I'm sure you were more than generous with her," said Sebastian, his smile hard.

Gordon's brows drew together in an exaggerated frown. Everything about the man was exaggerated, Sebastian decided, from the opulent, plush burgundy and gold trappings of his sitting room to his stentorian speech and theatrical gestures. One of the hazards, one might suppose, of always playing to a large, distant audience. "She used those dresses to sink her avaricious little talons into another man and leave me," said the actor, his brandy-clutching hand waving expansively through the air. "What would you expect me to do? Just forget it?"

"You seem to have forgotten it for the better part of two years."

Gordon shrugged. "A man has expenses."

Sebastian studied the actor's gaunt cheeks and shadowed, preoccupied eyes. It was a look one saw often these days in the gaming hells and clubs of London— the haunted look of a man who was badly dipped. "What's your poison? Faro?"

A wry smile curved the actor's full lips. "Actually, I've chosen hazard as my own particular road to perdition."

Sebastian regarded the other man thoughtfully. Debt had a way of making people desperate. And a desperate man could be a dangerous man. "There are those who say you've a ready fist," said Sebastian, "when it comes to women."

Gordon drained his drink with one practiced flick of the wrist, then pointed a finger at Sebastian over the rim of the empty glass. "Women like a strong man, a man who knows how to keep them in their place. Don't ever let anyone tell you different."

Sebastian nodded, as if in agreement. "I can see how a man with a heavy hand might get carried away, sometimes. Maybe set out to teach a woman a lesson and end up going too far."

Gordon slammed the empty glass down on a nearby table, his nostrils flaring wide with a quickly indrawn breath. "What are you suggesting? That I killed Rachel? What kind of a bloody fool do you take me for? Rachel owed me *money*. When I saw her on Tuesday afternoon, she swore she'd have it to me by Wednesday noon." He ran one hand through his dark hair, his fingers splaying wide, gripping, his voice dropping suddenly to almost a whisper. "You can't get money out of a dead woman."

Sebastian was remembering what Kat had told him, about the young man who'd been seen letting himself into Rachel's rooms early Wednesday morning. Hugh Gordon was in his mid-thirties, but a woman in her eighties would surely describe him as young. "I'm not so sure about that," said Sebastian. "If you know a woman has money and she's refusing to pay what she owes, you can always go to her rooms and collect the debt yourself. If she's dead."

Gordon let his hand fall. "Good God. Now I'm a thief, as well as a murderer?"

Sebastian kept his gaze on the other man's face. "Where were you Tuesday night?"

"I was here. At home. Studying my lines."

"Alone?"

"I work best alone." He glanced again at the ormolu clock on the ornate mantel. "Look, I have a performance that starts at seven. We just opened last night and I need to—"

"Relax." Sebastian gave the man a slow, mean smile. "You've plenty of time."

Gordon met Sebastian's steady gaze. "You're not Rachel's cousin, are you?" His brows twitched together. "What are you? Some sort of Bow Street Runner?"

Sebastian smiled. "Something like that." It was even, in a sense, true, he thought; he was certainly running *from* Bow Street.

Gordon swung away to jerk the burgundy velvet drapes closed against the growing cold. "She was an unusual woman, Rachel," he said suddenly, one hand still gripping the heavy cloth as if he were struggling to put his thoughts into words. "There wasn't much she was afraid of. She told me once that fear made a person vulnerable and she refused to ever be vulnerable again. But I'd noticed lately that she was nervous, jumpy—as if she'd suddenly found herself over her head in something and wasn't quite certain how she was going to get out of it."

Sebastian watched the other man turn away from the window. "Something like—what?"

"Actually, I'm beginning to wonder if Rachel wasn't passing information to the French."

"The *French*?" It was the last thing Sebastian had expected. "What makes you say that?"

"Look at the men she chose." Hugh Gordon brought his hands up together in a gesture reminiscent of Moses Preaching to the Masses, and Sebastian knew then that the affectation of a confidence suddenly shared was an act, that whether it was true or not, this was information Hugh Gordon had deliberately decided to impart—probably with the specific intention of deflecting suspicion from himself. "Usually there's a pattern with women. One will go after men with money, another likes the pretty boys, the dandies and pinks, while another is mad about any man with a title. Not Rachel. The men she selected tended to work in the Foreign Office, like Sir Albert. Or they were close to the King, like Lord Grimes. Once she even had an admiral in tow."

Admiral Worth. Sebastian had heard his name along with that of Sir Albert and Lord Grimes and others whispered in the streets. As he ran through the names, he realized it was true, that Rachel York's noble lovers shared this one, common trait: all were privy to information which could prove very useful if it were to fall into the wrong hands.

"You make no secret of having shared Rachel's republican principles," said Sebastian. "Have the French ever approached you?"

He expected angry denials and heated, patriotic rhetoric. Instead, Gordon met Sebastian's questioning gaze and said simply, "However much I might wish to see changes here, I'm still an Englishman. I would never betray my own country."

"But you think Rachel could?"

Gordon lifted one shoulder in a shrug. "Rachel had a lot of anger in her, a lot of hate—both because of the things that had been done to her in her own life, and because of what she saw happening to others around her. She spent one afternoon a week working as a volunteer at St. Jude's Foundling Home. Did you know that? She used to say that Napoleon might have betrayed the Revolution, but what the French had was still better than what most people have here."

Sebastian studied the other man's high-browed, aesthetic face. Hugh Gordon was an actor, a man who made a living out of making people believe a lie. Not for an instant would Sebastian ever trust him. But for all his posturing, his words had a ring of sincerity to them, and that terrible weight of plausibility that can come with an unlooked-for truth.

Outside, the wind gusted up, driving a flurry of snow against the windowpanes with a violence that sounded unnaturally loud in the sudden silence. He realized Gordon was watching him with narrowed, assessing eyes. "You don't believe me, do you? Yet you have by now surely verified that what I told you before was true, that Leo Pierrepont was paying the rent on Rachel's rooms."

"What would you have me believe? That *Leo Pierrepont* acts as Napoleon's agent?"

"Nothing as simple as that. Leo Pierrepont is what I think they call a spy master."

Sebastian pushed to his feet. "Leo Pierrepont's family lost everything they owned fleeing the Revolution twenty years ago."

Gordon gave a tight little smile. "Pierrepont fled the Revolution and the Republic. But France is no longer a republic, now is it?"

The point was well made. The bloody, fervent days of the Republic and the Year II belonged to the past. Lately, more and more émigré families had been making their peace with France's new emperor, swearing allegiance to the new government of France and reclaiming old estates. Sebastian eyed the other man, assessing. "It's an easy enough accusation to make. Where's your proof?"

"Men as good as Pierrepont don't leave proof."

"Indeed. Yet the last time I spoke to you, you would have me believe Leo Pierrepont was Rachel's lover."

Hugh Gordon's smile widened into something at once genuine and vaguely scornful. "Actually, I believe I said the authorities would do well to look into Rachel's association with him. I don't recollect calling him her lover. That was your own assumption."

Chapter 32

$\mathcal{T}$he Earl of Hendon's visit had done much to overcome Sir Henry Lovejoy's lingering doubts about the guilt of Viscount Devlin. But Lovejoy was a methodical man, and so on Saturday afternoon he decided to devote a few hours to setting to rest the question of Captain and Mrs. John Talbot.

The captain, Lovejoy discovered, was a tall, handsome man in his early thirties, the youngest son of a small Devonshire landowner. With a commission in the Horse Guards, he'd had a promising future ahead of him until he'd made the mistake of running away with an heiress named Melanie Peregrin. His superiors hadn't looked kindly upon this romantic adventure. Captain Talbot's career had languished, while Melanie's father had been so infuriated by what he termed his daughter's perfidy that he cut her off without a penny and refused to allow her to cross his threshold again.

It was snowing heavily by the time Lovejoy reached the Talbots' narrow brick townhouse off Upper Union Street in Chelsea. The house was small and undoubtedly hired, but the front door had been painted a cheery red, the knocker polished until it shone, and someone with an artistic eye had placed two potted rosemaries on either side of the entrance. Lovejoy noted these details

and stowed them away for future analysis. They didn't
sit well with the image of the weeping, battered wife Sir
Christopher had painted for him.

Nor did the calm, self-possessed young woman who
introduced herself as Melanie Talbot.

He was fortunate enough to find her at home, and
alone. Lovejoy apologized for the lateness of his call;
Mrs. Talbot apologized for the dishevelment in which he
found her.

"I'm afraid I'm somewhat of a messy painter," she
said, her smile sweet and almost impish as she rubbed
her thumb against the splotch of paint that showed dark
blue against a pale inner wrist. Lovejoy might have been
misled into believing she'd been indulging a genteel,
feminine interest in watercolors, except that when he'd
first arrived he'd caught a glimpse of her up on a ladder,
painting the walls of her dining room.

"I am grateful you've consented to see me on such
short notice," said Lovejoy, taking the seat she indi-
cated in the small, pleasant sitting room overlooking
the snow-filled street. The furniture in the room was
old-fashioned and battered, he noticed, but tasteful,
with good clean lines—the kind of thing one might find
tucked away in the attics of some ancient country estate, or for sale, cheap, in the markets of Hatfield
Street. If Melanie Talbot's love match had proved to be
an unhappy one, it certainly wasn't preventing her from
working hard to make her home pleasant and comfortable, whatever her reduced financial circumstances.

She sank into the chair opposite him, a lithe, unusually attractive young woman with very fair hair and
large blue eyes set wide in a delicately molded face. Exactly the kind of female to inspire any young buck—and
more than a few old ones—with the desire to cast himself in the role of her knight in shining armor.

She gave Lovejoy a broad, beautiful smile. "And how, precisely, may I help you, Sir Henry?"

"I have a few questions I'd like to ask about Lord Devlin."

Lovejoy watched, fascinated, as a gust of fear passed across her lovely features. She threw a quick, nervous glance toward the narrow hall, as if to reassure herself that no one could have overheard. Then her smile broadened again, bright and utterly false. "I'm not sure how much I can help you. Lord Devlin and I are the merest of acquaintances only."

"Indeed, Mrs. Talbot? I have it on excellent information that you and his lordship are considerably more than that. And let me hasten to reassure you that if you fear your husband—"

"And what makes you think I would have reason to fear my husband, Sir Henry?" she asked sharply.

Lovejoy returned her firm, direct gaze. "I know what happened at the Duchess of Devonshire's ball last year."

"Ah." Her chest hitched on a small sigh as she sat silent for a moment, seemingly lost in thought. Then her gaze lifted to his again, her jaw hardening. "Very well. Devlin and I are friends, good friends. But nothing more."

Lovejoy kept his expression impassive. "It's my understanding that your husband and Lord Devlin fought a duel last Wednesday morning."

Her smile, this time, was neither impish nor sweet. "Surely, Sir Henry, you are aware that we wives are never told of such things?"

"But you knew."

She stood abruptly, going to stand before the painted mantel where a small fire burned feebly on the hearth, providing little warmth. "You must understand, Sir

Henry," she said, her gaze on the fire. "I promised my husband I would sever all contact with Lord Devlin."

Lovejoy studied the slim, taut line of her back. "And when did you make this promise?"

"On Monday last."

"You didn't see Lord Devlin on Tuesday?"

"No. Of course not. I am a good and obedient wife. That's what's expected of a woman, isn't it?" she said, the sneer in her voice as much for herself as for the society in which she lived.

"So you wouldn't be able to tell me where his lordship spent that evening?"

"No." She swung to face him, and he was shocked by the strength of the emotion he could see in her face. "But I can tell you how he *did not* spend Tuesday evening. He didn't spend it murdering that poor woman you found in St. Matthew of the Fields."

"So sure, Mrs. Talbot?"

She pushed out a harsh breath, her eyebrows twitching together in thought. "Who told you about the Duchess of Devonshire's ball?"

"I'm afraid I can't say."

"But you know—you know what brought Sebastian and me together?"

Lovejoy nodded, noting her unconscious use of the Viscount's first name.

"He'd just come back from the war." She paused. "We both had demons we needed to deal with. I like to think that I helped him at least half as much as he helped me."

"The demons a man brings home from war can sometimes drive him to do terrible things."

She shook her head. "The kind of demons that haunt Lord Devlin aren't the sort that drive a man to rape and murder." She paused, then pushed on resolutely, her head held high. "I would actually have given myself to him, if he'd have had me. Does that shock you, Sir Henry? There was a time I would have been shocked by it. Only . . ." She swallowed, then shook her head and left the rest of the sentence unsaid. "But he wouldn't. So tell me, Sir Henry; is that the kind of man who rapes a woman in front of an altar?"

"I don't know," said Lovejoy, meeting her tortured gaze. "I don't know what kind of men do such things. But they do exist." He nodded toward the snowy darkness. "One of them is out there right now, walking around. Perhaps it's Lord Devlin. Perhaps it's someone else—some man buying a sausage at his local pub, or perhaps sitting down to dinner with his wife and family. And no one—*no one*—who knows him thinks he's capable of such a terrible thing. But he is. He is."

Lovejoy removed his hat and hung it on the hook beside his office door, then simply stood there for a moment, lost in thought, his gaze focused on nothing.

They were back again, all those niggling little doubts about Lord Devlin's guilt, that feeling that there was more going on in the death of Rachel York than any of them had yet grasped. He knew it was unscientific, unempirical, maybe even irrational. But his intuition had been right too many times in the past for him to ignore it now.

With a shrug, he jerked his mind away from the sad-eyed woman he'd just met and set to work unwinding his scarf. He had his coat half-unbuttoned when his clerk, Collins, stuck his head around the corner.

"What is it?" asked Lovejoy, looking up.

"It's about the Cyprian who got herself killed in that church, sir—that Rachel York. Constable Maitland thought you might like to know."

Lovejoy paused with his coat half on, half off. "Know what?"

"We've just heard from the sexton of St. Stephen's, sir. They've had grave robbers. Last night. And it was *her* grave what they hit."

"Are you telling me someone has stolen Rachel York's body?"

"Yes, sir. Constable Maitland, he thinks it's just a coincidence, but—"

Collins let his voice trail away into nothing, for Sir Henry, his coat gripped distractedly in one hand, was already gone, leaving his hat and scarf still swaying on their hooks beside the door.

Chapter 33

By the time Sebastian neared Half Moon Street, the darkness was complete, the snow a heavy, dirty white blanket that seemed to smother the city. But at the French émigré's elegant townhouse, golden light blazed from every window. Thick straw buried the granite setts that paved the street, and a red carpet stretched down the entry steps to the footpath. It was just past six, but already a crowd had begun to gather, ragged men and women and children huddled together against the cold. Some murmured darkly, but most were laughing and joking in excited anticipation. They were something of a spectacle, these grand galas put on by the *ton*; not quite as entertaining as a hanging, but considerably more magnificent than a balloon ascension.

"Monsieur Pierrepont's having a ball tonight, is he?" asked Sebastian, snagging a half-grown lad in livery who came rushing past, his face flushed with self-importance.

"Aye. A masquerade," said the boy, his eyes bright with as much excitement as if he were to be one of the guests.

Sebastian watched the boy dash off, then stood for a moment as a part of the crowd, his gaze drifting from one blazing window to the next.

He kept turning over in his mind what Hugh Gordon had told him, that Rachel York might have been passing information to the French through Leo Pierrepont. If it was true, if Rachel York *had* been involved in some kind of underhanded game with the French, then it cast her killing in a different light entirely.

And if it was true, then what was Sebastian's father doing meeting with her, in secret, in the dark, deserted Lady Chapel of an out-of-the-way Westminster church?

~

It was just minutes to curtain time. Kat was hurrying down a backstage corridor when a strong hand closed around her arm from behind, drawing her back into the shadows.

"*Sebastian.*" Kat cast an anxious glance up the hall. "Why are you here? Someone might see you."

"I need a costume."

In the dim light of the oil lamp at the end of the corridor, she could see the rough cut of his coat, the touches of gray he'd added to his dark hair. "I'd have said you were already fairly effectively disguised."

"I had something a bit more elegant in mind. Something in silk or satin."

"Satin? Going to a ball, are you?"

"Something like that."

~

He waited until just before midnight, when the crowd of costumed revelers would be at its thickest and a stray pirate wearing a loo-mask and a black domino over a black and gold satin doublet might pass unnoticed.

Creeping quietly through the snow blanketed back garden, Sebastian mingled for a moment amongst the couples braving the cold on the terrace, then slipped in-

side through one of the long French doors that opened
to the ballroom.

He walked into a blast of warm air scented with
beeswax and delicate French perfume and the pungent
odor of hundreds of hot, damp bodies pressed together
in a confined place. Above the roar of voices and genteel laughter, the sweet strains of a quadrille could be
faintly heard coming from a small ensemble set up on a
dais at the end of the room, where a few brave couples
were attempting to dance through the crowd. Leo Pierrepont's masquerade would undoubtedly be deemed a
"sad crush," which was a way of calling it a resounding
success.

Weaving his way through Valkyries and Romeos,
Arab princes and Renaissance ladies, Sebastian found
himself in the hall, where a teasing conversation with a
dimpled young housemaid provided him with the information that Monsieur Pierrepont's library could be
found at the foot of the stairs on the ground floor, near
the back of the house.

The door to the library was closed. When he opened
it, Sebastian could see why, for much of the furniture
which had been cleared from the house's reception
rooms was obviously being stored in here. Shutting the
door behind him, Sebastian threaded his way through
looming piles of settees and rolled carpets and end tables to jerk back the heavy velvet drapes at the
windows.

The lamps from the nearby terrace shone on the
snow outside to suffuse the library with a pale, white
glow. Turning, Sebastian cast an expert's appraising eye
around the room. About half the library's walls were
taken up by floor-to-ceiling mahogany bookcases, while
the open panels in between were covered with Pierrepont's collection of broadswords and dueling rapiers,

daggers and cutlasses, their carefully maintained blades gleaming in the night.

Sebastian searched the room quickly but methodically, looking for anything that might associate Leo Pierrepont with Napoleon's government and the dirty, underhanded game of spying. He checked behind pictures and along the backs of the bookcases. He rifled expertly through desk drawers, and found nothing. Stymied, he perched on the edge of the desk.

His gaze fell on a small, carved wooden box, sitting on the desk's green leather top. *If you want to hide something*, went the adage, *display it in plain sight*. Sebastian flipped open the box's wooden lid, and smiled.

To the uninitiated, it was a simple if somewhat curious cylinder about six inches long and composed of a row of disks of white wood revolving on a central iron spindle. But to those who knew, it was a wheeled cipher, invented by an ingenious American named Thomas Jefferson. Each of the cylinder's thirty-six disks contained the letters of the alphabet arranged randomly. If identical cylinders were used by two parties to encrypt and decipher their correspondence, the resulting code was virtually impossible to break.

Sebastian held the cylinder between his hands, thoughtfully twirling the disks with his thumbs as he considered its implications. The Americans themselves had, curiously enough, recently abandoned the Jefferson cipher in favor of a far less secure device, while the English preferred, stubbornly, to rely upon their Black Chamber with its invisible inks to safeguard their secret correspondence. But the former American president's clever little invention remained in favor with the Americans' old ally, France.

Sebastian turned his head, his attention caught suddenly by a faint sound. He had been aware all the while of footsteps rushing past in the hall outside as servants hurried to and fro. But he heard now a different stride, firmer and more deliberate; a tread that stopped abruptly before the library's door.

Sebastian dropped the cylinder into an inner pocket just as the door opened abruptly to flood the darkened room with light.

Chapter 34

A slender musketeer stood in the doorway, an oil lamp in one hand, his gaze shifting from Sebastian to the open box on the desk, then back again. He eased the door shut behind him with a soft click.

"You have strayed far from the party, monsieur," said Leo Pierrepont, setting the oil lamp he carried on a nearby table.

"My apologies." Sebastian pushed away from the desk. "I shall rejoin the other guests at once."

"I think not." With a sideways lunge, the Frenchman snatched one of the rapiers from the library wall and brought it around, the sharp blade singing through the air to bring Sebastian to an abrupt halt some ten feet shy of the door. "I think, monsieur," said Pierrepont, the tip of his blade executing a neat pattern through the air, "that you and I must have a little talk. No?"

"A talk would be interesting"—Sebastian leapt back, levering his weight on one outflung arm so that he vaulted over the desk to land lightly behind it. Pierrepont came after him in a rush, sword flashing, just as Sebastian seized a gleaming Spanish rapier from the wall near the casement window and brought it up to catch the Frenchman's descending blade with a clanging ring of metal—"all other things being equal," said Sebastian, smiling.

Pierrepont leapt back, panting lightly, his pale eyes bright with a strange glow of exhilaration. "It is you, isn't it? Devlin? I've heard you're a good swordsman— for an Englishman."

Sebastian laughed.

Pierrepont lunged, the long blades clanging together as Sebastian parried easily.

"Why did you kill Rachel York?" Sebastian asked almost conversationally, sliding away from the Frenchman's flashing sword only to close again, his booted feet moving softly across the Oriental carpet. "What did you think? That she intended to lodge information against you?"

"Information? Against me?" Pierrepont's lips drew back in a smile as their swords came together again. "And what sort of information would that be, monsieur?"

"Information about your little spy ring."

Pierrepont parried Sebastian's lunge. "Your experiences in the war obviously overset your imagination, *monsieur le vicomte.*"

"Perhaps. But I have enough of my wits left to reason that if what I've heard is true—if Rachel *was* feeding you tidbits of information gleaned from her noble lovers—then her death might suggest that at least some of the details of your activities have become known."

"And who has encouraged you in this fantasy? Hmm?"

"What's the matter, monsieur? Scared?" said Sebastian, just as Pierrepont launched a swift and brutal attack.

The Frenchman was at the end of his thrust when Sebastian circled his blade and danced sideways to slide in, his own blade flashing. The tip of his rapier sliced neatly through the musketeer's silk to the flesh beneath.

Pierrepont leapt back, a thin line of bright red blood seeping through the white front of his shirt, his lips tightening into a grim smile. "We must fence together some other time, monsieur. If you don't hang, that is." Turning his head, he raised his voice to shout, "Arnaud. Robert. *Aidez-moi.*" The men were obviously close. The library door burst open, spilling two of Pierrepont's burly footmen into the room.

Sebastian tightened his grip on his rapier, his breath coming in pants. With his path to the door blocked, the only possible way out of the room was through one of the long casements overlooking the rear garden. He hesitated for the briefest instant, then ran straight at the nearest window, one domino-wrapped arm flung up before his face to catch the worst of the impact as he crashed through in a shower of breaking glass and splintered wood.

It was a drop of some six or eight feet to the snow below. Sebastian hit the ground hard, broken glass crunching beneath him as he scrambled to his feet and took off running across the snow-filled garden. From somewhere above came a woman's scream. A man shouted; then Sebastian heard a yelp of pain as one of Pierrepont's henchmen swung his leg over the jagged window glass and made as if to follow.

"No. Let him go," said Pierrepont, standing before the broken window, the palm of one hand pressed to his bleeding chest. "Let him go. . . .

"For now."

~

The Earl of Hendon was in a big overstuffed armchair beside his library fire, a well-worn, leather-covered volume of Cicero lying open on his lap, when Sebastian walked in, the black loo-mask dangling from one finger.

"Good heavens," said the Earl after only the briefest of hesitations. "You look as if you've just fought the battle of the Spanish Main. And lost."

Sebastian swiped at a trickle of blood running down his cheek and laughed. Hendon was a master of the British art of unemotional calm. Only his tense lower jaw and subtly increased breathing betrayed any hint of shock or anxiety.

Crossing to the brandy decanter warming on a small table near the fire, Sebastian eased out the cut-crystal stopper and soaked his handkerchief with the neat alcohol. "I've just had a rather interesting encounter with Monsieur Léon Pierrepont."

"Ah, yes. I'd heard he was to have a masquerade tonight."

"I found this in his library." Reaching his left hand into his pocket, Sebastian produced the small cylinder and tossed it to his father.

Hendon caught it neatly. "What is it?"

Sebastian dabbed the alcohol-sodden cloth against first one, then the next of his various cuts, the breath hissing out through his clenched teeth. "It's a Jefferson cipher. I think the man is spying for the French." Sebastian watched his father's broad, plain-featured face for some flicker of surprise. There was none. "You don't strike me as being particularly shocked by the possibility."

Setting aside the cylinder, Hendon folded his hands, calmly, on the swell of his stomach. "About a year ago, a certain gentleman whose name is irrelevant allowed Monsieur Pierrepont to catch him in a potentially embarrassing escapade."

"Exactly what kind of escapade?"

"A sexual one. The gentleman involved—let's call him Mr. Smith, shall we—has somewhat unusual tastes. Tastes he'd prefer not be made public."

Sebastian pressed the handkerchief against the cut on his cheek and held it there. "And?"

"He wisely realized the need to confess the entire sordid tale and ask for guidance. I discussed the matter with Lord Jarvis, and between the two of us, we decided we could use Mr. Smith."

"You mean as a double agent, feeding selected information to the French via Pierrepont?" Sebastian tossed the blood-soaked cloth aside and poured himself a drink.

"Yes." The Earl shoved up from his chair and went to stand before the fire. "The French will always have spies and their spy masters in London. It's better for us if at least some of the players are known. That way, they can be watched and the flow of potentially damaging information can be managed . . . to some extent."

"And Rachel York? Was she passing information to Pierrepont?"

Hendon's face went suddenly ashen. "Good God. Who told you that?"

"The same person who told me about Pierrepont. Is it true? Was Rachel one of Pierrepont's spies?"

"I don't know."

Sebastian fixed his father with a hard stare. "Are you sure? She wasn't blackmailing you into passing government secrets to the French?"

Hendon's blue eyes flashed dangerously, his fists clenching at his sides. "My God. If you were anyone but my son, I'd call you out for that."

Sebastian slammed down his drink. "What else am I to think?"

The Earl stood very still, his jaw working back and

forth in thought. He let out a strained sigh, then said, "That morning, the Tuesday she died, Rachel York came to me. She said she had in her possession a certain document that she was willing to sell."

"What sort of document?"

Hendon hesitated.

"What was it, *damn* it?"

The Earl's face had taken on an odd, ashen quality. "An affidavit, providing detailed proof of an indiscretion committed by your mother."

"My mother?"

Sebastian knew an odd sense of dislocation. His mother had died long ago, in a yachting accident off the coast of Brighton the summer he was eleven. A kaleidoscope of memories from that time swirled around him, of sun-sparkled sea and a woman's sweet laughter and a deep, profound sense of loss. He pushed them away. "Were you able to obtain this document?"

"No. I told you, the girl was dead by the time I reached the chapel. I looked for it but she didn't have it on her."

The coals on the hearth hissed, the sound seeming unnaturally loud in the sudden, strained silence. "You do realize, don't you," said Sebastian, "that this document was very likely the motive for the killing?"

"Don't be ridiculous." Hendon fumbled in the pockets of his dressing gown and came up with his pipe and a pouch of tobacco. "The disclosure of its contents would embarrass me, but no more."

"How much were you willing to pay for it?"

"Five thousand pounds."

Sebastian let out a low, soundless whistle. "There are those who would consider five thousand pounds more than sufficient motive for murder."

Hendon didn't say anything, just set about the business of filling his pipe. Sebastian watched him tamp down the tobacco, his features set in hard, uncompromising lines. And it came to Sebastian how little, in some ways, he really knew his own father. "And if the man who killed Rachel York has this document now? What then?"

Hendon shook his head. "I don't think she brought it with her to the chapel. More likely than not she was planning to try to hold out for a higher price."

Sebastian supposed it possible, but it wasn't particularly likely, given what he'd heard about Rachel's nervousness and her plans to flee London. A deep disquiet bloomed within him. There was too much going on here that he didn't understand, that he needed to understand if he were to have any hope of catching Rachel's killer. "Did she tell you how she got her hands on this affidavit?"

"No."

"You didn't ask?"

"Of course I asked. She refused to say." Hendon swiped one of his big, beefy hands across his lower face. "Good God. If she was working for Pierrepont, then in all likelihood she got the document from him."

"But you don't know."

"No."

"She could have had another purpose, you know. If it were to become known that you were buying incriminating documents from a French spy, you'd be ruined."

Hendon stuck the stem of his pipe in his mouth and bit down on it hard. "It won't become known." Lighting a taper, he held it to the pipe's bowl, his cheeks hollowing as he sucked hard, then blew out a stream of thin blue smoke. "You asked me to look into Pierrepont's activities last Tuesday night."

"And?"

"He did have a dinner party at his house that night. It was arranged hastily, for he'd only just returned from the country that morning."

"So he couldn't have killed Rachel."

"Not necessarily. According to one of the guests, Pierrepont excused himself and was absent for a considerable period of time somewhere around nine or ten."

"Long enough to get to Westminster and back?"

"Perhaps."

Sebastian swore softly and crudely. "Why the hell didn't you tell me about this affidavit from the very beginning?"

"I thought it irrelevant. I still think it irrelevant. What does it matter why Rachel York was in that church? Some brute simply happened upon her there, alone, and took advantage of it. He raped her and then he killed her. It happens all too frequently these days."

"Except that she was raped after she was killed."

Hendon's mouth went slack around the stem of his pipe. "Good heavens. What manner of man would do such a thing?"

"Someone who enjoys killing," said Sebastian.

~⌾

He made his way back to the Rose and Crown through crooked byways filled with sparkling white snow that scrunched audibly beneath each step. A few stray flakes still floated down, lazy and peaceful in the night. It was as if, between them, the darkness and the snow hid all that was ugly, all that was horrible and dangerous about the city, so that he was aware suddenly of the beauty of the row of ancient stone arches fronting a nearby shop, and the intricate fretwork of the old timber-framed Tudor house beside it. And he wondered, which was more real, the ugliness or the beauty?

He let out a soft sigh, his breath white in the cold air as he turned over and over in his mind what he'd learned that night, about his father, and about Leo Pierrepont and Rachel York. He wondered why a woman like Rachel York would have allowed herself to be drawn into the dangerous shadow world occupied by men such as Leo Pierrepont. What had driven her? Political convictions? Greed? Or had she somehow been coerced into acting against her will?

Whatever her original motive, something had obviously gone badly wrong in Rachel York's life. According to her neighbor, Rachel had been packing to leave London. The money she had hinted at, obviously, was to have come from Hendon. But it wouldn't have been enough to lure away a woman on the threshold of a promising stage career. There was obviously something in Rachel's life Sebastian was missing. Something important.

He had nearly reached the Rose and Crown. As he had done so many times in the past, during the war, Sebastian paused just down the street, every sense alert to the subtle differences that could tell him his hiding place had been discovered. But all lay peaceful and quiet in the gently falling snow.

He entered the inn's public room, warm with the piney scent of fire and the murmur of sleepy voices, and made his way to the back of the inn and up the stairs to his chamber. What he needed, he decided, was to come to a better understanding of Rachel York's life. In the morning, he would visit the foundling hospital where she'd volunteered once a week. And if Tom could find that maid, Mary Grant . . .

Sebastian paused in the dim, drafty hall outside his door. He couldn't say what had warned him. Some faint, lingering scent, perhaps. Or perhaps it was simply a vestige of the primitive instinct that alerts an animal returning to its lair that all is not entirely as he left it. Whatever it was, something told Sebastian even before he fit the key into the lock of his door that she was there.

He hesitated for the briefest instant. Then he pushed open the door and walked into his past.

Chapter 35

She sat in the battered old chair beside the hearth, her head tipped back so that the firelight played over the elegant curve of her long, graceful neck and brought out the hint of auburn in her dark hair. She had worn a cherry red velvet opera cloak that now lay discarded on a nearby table, but she had come to him still dressed in the costume of her character, Rosalind.

"You picked the lock, I suppose." Sebastian closed the door behind him and leaned back against it.

"It's a very old lock," said Kat Boleyn, the barest hint of a smile touching the edges of her lips.

He pushed away from the door and walked toward her. "Why did you come?"

"You left your clothes at the theater. I brought them."

He didn't bother to ask how she had found him here, at the Rose and Crown. She would have her ways, as he had his. It was a danger he had both acknowledged and accepted when he first decided to approach her.

"You're hurt," she said when he came to stand before her, close enough that his legs almost touched hers, but not quite.

"I went through a window."

"Leo found you, did he?"

"What makes you think I went to see Pierrepont?"

"There weren't that many masquerades in Mayfair tonight." She shifted subtly in her seat, so that her thigh just brushed his. "What sent you there?"

"According to Hugh Gordon, Pierrepont is a French spy master."

She sat very still and quiet for a moment, then said, "And do you believe him?"

Sebastian shrugged. "Gordon had no proof, of course. But I found a code cipher in Pierrepont's library." What Hendon had told Sebastian, he would keep to himself.

"What has any of this to do with Rachel?"

Sebastian turned away to swing off his cloak and hang it on a hook beside the bed. "I think she might have been passing Pierrepont information. She seems to have shared her favors with an interesting collection of men. Men in positions to know tidbits they might easily let slip, things like troop movements and shifting alliances and the thinking of those close to the King."

"They say someone stole Rachel's body from the churchyard," she said. "Was it you?"

"Yes."

Any other woman would have felt the need to affect a feminine display of shock and horror. Not Kat. She watched him strip off his doublet and shirt, then go splash cold water from the basin over his blood-encrusted face and neck. "What do you expect to learn from it?"

The room's towel was coarse and stiff, and he dabbed gently around his cuts. "I don't know. But I've already learned one interesting little fact: whoever killed Rachel York slit her throat first. Then he sexually assaulted her."

"That's a nasty little perversion."

Sebastian tossed aside the towel. "What kind of man likes to have sex with a dead woman?"

"A man who hates women, I should think."

Sebastian looked down at the bloodstains he'd left on the old towel. He hadn't thought of it that way, that Rachel's rape was an act of hate rather than lust, but he suspected Kat was right. Whoever killed Rachel York had taken joy in her destruction, had been sexually aroused by the act of slitting her pale throat and watching the life ebb slowly from her pretty brown eyes. Most men felt the need for at least some measure of response in the women with whom they copulated—it was, after all, the reason behind a prostitute's little moans and gasps of simulated pleasure. But Rachel York's killer was the kind of man who could find his release in the unresponsive, empty shell of what had once been a living, breathing woman.

Sebastian thought about the significant men in Rachel's life, about Hugh Gordon and Giorgio Donatelli and Leo Pierrepont. Were any of them that twisted, that consumed by hatred for women? Or how about the others, that continually shifting parade of well-placed men such as Admiral Worth and Lord Grimes from whom she had, perhaps, coaxed sensitive information? Suspicion of all things feminine—one could easily label it a basic dislike of women—was so common as to be almost a tradition amongst the gentlemen of England, with their elite boys' schools and stuffy men's clubs and addiction to such masculine sports as boxing and cockfighting and hunting. But it didn't lead most of them into murder and mutilation. What kind of man crossed that line? When did mistrust and dislike shade into something darker, something dangerous and evil?

Sebastian listened to the flutter of the wind beneath the eaves. He knew it again, that fear that he was never going to find Rachel York's killer, that the man who had slit her throat and indulged his lust on her dead, bloodied body was some chance stranger, a random shadow from the night that Sebastian was never, ever going to track down.

He heard a whisper of movement, a rustle of cloth. Kat came to stand before him, her touch gentle as she cradled his face between her hands. "You'll find him," she said softly, as if he had spoken his fears out loud. "You'll find him." And even though he knew she spoke out of a need to reassure rather than from conviction, he found comfort in her words. Comfort, and the echo of an old but never forgotten desire in her touch.

He caught her to him, his fingers twisting in the dusky fall of her hair. His mouth sought and found hers, her breath coming now as rapid and shallow as his. He kissed her eyes and touched the smooth, warm flesh of her neck, and felt his body quicken with a need that was more than physical.

With increased urgency, his lips captured hers again. A shower of hot coals settled with a murmur on the hearth beside them as he bore her down on the bed, her arms wrapping around his neck, her body rising up to meet his touch.

Fevered hands tore away cloth, found the pleasures of smooth warm flesh beneath sliding fingers. And in that moment, he didn't care about the nature of her association with Leo Pierrepont. He didn't even care about the things she had said on that dark day six years before. He needed her.

With a soft sigh, Sebastian buried himself inside her. They moved as one, slowly at first, the tempo rising as he felt the coldness and the fear inside him fade away into the gentle rhythms of her body and the warmth of her keening breath mingling with his.

Afterward, he lay on his back in the firelit softness of the night. He held her nestled close, kissed her hair, listened to the sounds of the city settling to sleep around them, the distant rumble of a lone carriage and, nearer, the slamming of a shutter. He let his hand drift down her side, over the naked swell of her hip, and breathed in the unforgettably warm and heady fragrance of this woman.

After a time, she shifted her weight, rising up on her elbow so she could look down at him. She said, "What would an angel fear?"

He laughed softly, running his hand up her bare arm to her shoulder. "What kind of question is that?"

She traced an invisible pattern across his naked chest with her fingertip. "I was thinking of that line from Pope—you know the one? 'Fools rush in where angels fear to tread.' What would an angel have to fear?"

"Falling from grace, I suppose. I don't know. I don't believe in angels."

"An immortal being, then. What could an immortal being possibly fear?"

He thought about it for a while. "Making a wrong decision, I would think; choosing badly. Imagine having to live with that for an eternity." He turned his head to look at her profile, beautiful and unexpectedly serious in the firelight. "Why? What do you think an angel would fear?"

She was silent for a moment. Then she said, "Love. I think an angel would fear falling in love with a mortal—someone who could be theirs for only a short time and then would slip away forever."

He caught her to him, his elbow hooking behind her neck to bring her down to his kiss. This time when they came together, there was an edge to her lovemaking, a quiet kind of desperation that he noted, even if he could not understand it.

Sometime before dawn he awoke to the gentle patter of her footsteps on the worn floorboards, the rustle of cloth as she moved about, dressing. He could have said something, could have reached for her, stopped her.

He let her go, the door easing closed behind her on a breath of cold air.

Then he simply lay there, staring into nothingness and waiting for the coming of dawn.

~

By the next morning the snow had turned into a dirty brown slush that dripped off eaves and ran in wide rivulets down the center of unpaved streets.

Avoiding the steady rush of water sluicing from broken gutters and sagging awnings, Sebastian made his way to St. Jude's Foundling Home, on the south bank of the Thames, near Lambeth. The Home turned out to be a large, gloomy structure built some two centuries before of the same red Tudor brick and in the same forbidding, fortresslike style as Hampton Court. Except that the Foundling Home was, of course, considerably less well kept than Hampton Court.

"I don't know how much I can help you," said the prune-faced matron when Sebastian presented himself to her in the guise of Cousin Simon Taylor from Worcestershire. "Miss York always came in on Mondays, which is my day off."

The pursing of the mouth with which Matron Snyder spat out the name *Miss York* said much about the nature of the two women's dealings with one another. She was a hard-faced woman, Matron Snyder, with a solid build and a massive, shelflike bosom. If she had ever been young or pretty, her disposition had long ago stamped out all traces of such earlier failings.

"Had it been up to me, of course," said the matron, "*her* kind would never have been allowed through the Home's doors."

Sebastian pursed his own lips and nodded in sympathetic agreement.

"I suppose the Reverend Finley might be able to tell you something," said Matron Snyder, unbending a shade. "Miss York was quite a favorite of his."

"Reverend Finley?" Sebastian felt a quickening of interest. Until now, he'd found no trace of the mysterious "F" who appeared twice in the pages of Rachel's appointment book. But if Rachel had developed a romantic interest in the Home's young spiritual counselor, it did much to explain her continued visits to the place.

Mrs. Snyder's mouth pursed again. Obviously, she didn't approve of Reverend Finley, either. "If you hurry, you might find him in the courtyard. He often visits with the children there on Sunday mornings, before services."

The courtyard was a cheerless, windswept place of cracked walks and patchy grass showing brown beneath the dirty remnants of last night's snow. Turning up his collar against the cold, Sebastian walked across the neglected quadrangle, toward the group of pinch-faced children he could see clustered at the far end in a rare slice of thin winter sunshine. As he neared the group, he realized they were gathered around a man who was telling them a story about a lion and a rabbit; a thin, stoop-shouldered old man, his balding pink pate fringed with white hair, a pair of thick spectacles perched on the end of his long, thin nose.

Sebastian hung back, his hands thrust deep into the

pockets of his cheap greatcoat, a smile tugging at his lips as he watched the old reverend hold that band of ragged charity children enthralled with the simple power of his words. Whatever had been the nature of Rachel's relationship with this man, it obviously wasn't romantic.

"Terrible business, what happened to Rachel," said Reverend Finley when, his story ended, he hurried the children toward the chapel and turned to listen to Sebastian's introduction. "Such a tragedy."

"Had she volunteered here for long?" Sebastian asked as the two men turned to walk together.

The old reverend peeled the wire-rimmed glasses off his face and rubbed his reddened eyes. "Nearly three years. Which is more than most women can take around here. They always start out full of such determination and good intentions, but it gets to them after a while. So many of the wee ones die, you see. I've never quite been able to understand it myself. But Rachel, she had this theory, that they died from a lack of love. And so she'd come every Monday afternoon and spend time holding each of the poor babes in turn. Just hold them. Sing to them."

Sebastian stared off across the snowy courtyard to where the Matron Snyder was bustling about, getting the children lined up two by two at the chapel doors. "An unusual activity for such a woman, surely?"

"You mean, for a successful actress?" The old reverend lifted one thin shoulder in a shrug. "Rachel was an unusual woman. Most people, when they have the good fortune to pull themselves up from a bad situation, they soon forget where they came from. Rachel didn't."

"But Rachel was never a foundling."

"No. But she knew what it was like to be a child alone and friendless in this world." The reverend paused, his features pinched and troubled. "I sometimes wonder . . ."

"Wonder what?"

At the end of the quadrangle, the chapel's lone bell began to ring, a solemn, steady toll. The old man's eyes narrowed as he stared up at the small spire above them. "This past month or so, Rachel seemed different somehow. Preoccupied. It was almost as if she were afraid of something. But I never said anything to her about it. These last few days, after what happened . . . Well, I can't help but wonder if I made a mistake. If perhaps I could have helped her in some way, if I had only asked."

"You don't have any idea what she was afraid of?"

Finley shook his head. "No. I wish she had confided in me, but she didn't."

"Did you know she was planning to leave London?"

The old man glanced around in surprise. "No. I'd no notion."

"Any thoughts as to where she might have been planning to go?"

He considered this for a moment, but shook his head. "No. I could hardly see her going back to Worcestershire."

No, Sebastian thought; she wouldn't have gone back to Worcestershire. "Was there a man in her life, do you think? A man she maybe was afraid of?"

Most of the children were in the chapel now. Only three or four stragglers remained, hurried along by Matron Snyder, who cast a quick, disapproving glance at the two men.

The Reverend Finley turned toward the open chapel doors. "We never spoke of such things, of course, but I'd have said yes, Rachel was in love with someone—although I don't think it was anyone she was afraid of. She had that look a woman gets when she's happy in love." A sad, almost wistful smile touched the old man's lips. "You might think I'm too old to recognize that look, but we were all young once, you know."

~~~

Sebastian walked through the cold, windblown streets of Lambeth to the banks of the Thames, where he took a scull that carried him across the river to the steps just below Tower Hill. From there it was but a short distance to Paul Gibson's surgery.

He found his friend wrapped in a tattered quilt and sitting in a cracked leather armchair beside the parlor fire, his staring gaze fixed on the glowing coals.

"Leg bad, is it?" said Sebastian, sinking onto the ragged chair opposite.

"A wee bit." Gibson looked up, his eyes bright with the unholy fires of the opium eater. It was an addiction far too many wounded men carried home with them from the war. Normally the Irishman could keep his compulsion under control, but there were times when memories of what he'd seen in the war would loom unbearable or the remnants of shrapnel in his leg would twist and bleed, and he would disappear for days into a drug-induced fog. "But I've finished your postmortem, never fear."

"And?"

Gibson shook his head. "Nothing more, I'm afraid. If she'd been brought to me directly, there might have been some sort of evidence. But as it is . . ."

Sebastian nodded, swallowing his disappointment. He'd known it was a long shot. "I was wondering if you could get in touch with Jumpin' Jack for me."

"Cochran?" Gibson huffed a soft laugh. "Looking to steal another body, are you?"

Sebastian grinned and shook his head. "It's information I'm interested in this time. I'm wondering if those in the resurrection trade have heard of anyone expressing a specific interest in female corpses."

Paul Gibson nodded thoughtfully. "Think to come at your man from that angle, do you?"

"It's worth a try." Sebastian pushed to his feet, his hand grasping his friend's shoulder for a moment before he turned toward the door. "I'll drop by again in a few days. See how you're getting on."

He was reaching for the knob when Gibson stopped him by saying, "There is one thing my more complete examination of the body did reveal. It may or may not have a bearing on your investigation."

Sebastian swung back around. "What was that?"

"Rachel York was in what the ladies refer to as a *delicate situation.*"

Sebastian felt a sudden twist, deep down in his gut. He thought about what the Reverend Finley had told him, about Rachel York coming to St. Jude's Foundling Home every Monday afternoon to hold the babies and sing to them, so that they wouldn't die from lack of love. Had she known? And if she had known, what must her last thoughts have been, when she felt her killer's knife slash across her throat, again and again?

"How far along was she?" Sebastian asked, his voice oddly hoarse.

"Almost three months, I'd say. Enough that she would surely have known she was carrying a child."

Chapter 36

$\mathcal{S}$ebastian was nursing a tankard of ale in the public room at the Rose and Crown when Tom burst in from the street, bringing with him a blast of icy air scented with coal smoke.

"I found 'er," he said, his voice high and tight with exaltation. "I found yer Mary Grant. And she musta done weery well with that stuff she lifted from her old mistress, weery well indeed, 'cause she's livin' as high as you please—in Bloomsbury, no less."

Rachel York's erstwhile maid had taken rooms in a lodging house facing a respectable street just south of Russell Square. By the time Sebastian got there, the sky was a flat white that promised more snow before nightfall.

Conscious of a surge of anticipation and hope he tried to damp down, Sebastian climbed the neat staircase to the first floor. The door was to his left, as Tom had said it would be. But when Sebastian rapped sharply on the freshly painted panels, it creaked open beneath his touch.

"Miss Grant?" he called, his voice echoing in the stillness. He pushed the door open wider and stepped inside.

He was standing in a parlor filled with the cherry-wood furniture and gilt-framed mirrors and expensive oddities that had once belonged to Rachel York. All had been thoroughly, savagely ransacked.

Mirrors and pictures had been torn from the walls and smashed; chairs lay overturned, their stuffing spilled out across the rumpled rug. Drawers had been pulled from bureaus, their contents strewn about in what appeared to have been a wild, frantic search.

Sebastian closed the door behind him with a snap that sounded unnaturally loud in the early afternoon hush. He walked from one room to the next. Impossible to know what the intruder had been searching for, or if he had found it. But when Sebastian entered the bedroom, he thought he knew at least part of the answer to that question. For here, only half the room lay in disarray; the rest had not been touched.

Sebastian walked to the chest of drawers that stood on the far side of the room, its bottom four drawers still intact. Lacy, feminine things spilled from the top drawer where it lay broken on the carpet. It was the logical place to have begun a search of this kind; women were always tucking secret things away amongst their undergarments. Whoever Mary Grant's intruder was, he was obviously new to this game.

Sebastian hunkered down beside the broken drawer, his attention caught by the corner of what looked like a piece of blue paper that had fallen or been kicked so that it lay almost completely hidden beneath the chest's frame. Easing the edge of the paper from beneath the wood, Sebastian found himself holding a blue envelope across which someone had written in a bold, masculine-looking scrawl, *Lord Frederick Fairchild*.

He was one of the most prominent, articulate Whigs in the House, Lord Frederick, urbane and witty and—

unlike most of the Prince of Wales's set—remarkably temperate. When the Prince was sworn in as Regent in a few days' time, it was commonly assumed that Fairchild would be selected to help form the new Whig government.

Sebastian stared thoughtfully at the blue envelope in his hands. Here, surely, was the "F" referred to in Rachel York's red leather-covered book. Could Lord Frederick even be the father of her unborn child? And maybe her murderer?

The room was cold, the fire on the hearth having been allowed to burn itself out. The sweet scent of lilac water hung heavy in the air, but beneath it Sebastian caught a hint of another odor, a sharp, metallic stench only too familiar to any man who'd ever gone to war.

With a sense of profound foreboding, he tucked the envelope into an inner pocket and stood up. The door to the dressing room stood half ajar. One hand on the pistol in his greatcoat pocket, Sebastian crossed the room to push the door open wider....

And found himself looking at what was left of Mary Grant.

Chapter 37

She lay sprawled on her back, her eyes wide and sight-less, her torn, bloodied clothes shoved up to reveal flesh gleaming pale and naked in the fading light. Her throat had been hacked so savagely that her head had nearly come off.

Sebastian stood just inside the doorway, his gaze traveling around the small, wainscoted room. He hadn't seen the Lady Chapel at St. Matthew of the Fields after Rachel York's killer had left her there, but he imagined it must have looked much like this, the blood splattered high and wide across the surrounding walls until it ran down the paneling in thin rivulets, the killer's bloody handprints standing out stark and damning on the bare white flesh of the dead woman's spread thighs.

There was nothing Sebastian could do for this woman now, but he crouched beside her anyway and touched his fingertips to her bloodstained cheek. She was still faintly warm.

He sat back on his heels, his hands gripping his knees as he gazed down into those pale, unseeing eyes. She was younger than he'd expected her to be, probably no more than twenty-five or thirty, with flaxen hair and a sallow complexion and the kind of sharp, small features one saw often on the streets of London. She must have thought she was a downy one, awake on every suit. She'd seen a chance to take everything that had once belonged to her mistress—the fine furniture, the expensive clothes and jewels—and she'd seized it. She must have thought she'd hit upon a way to set herself up for a good long while.

Except that all she'd really done was set herself up for murder.

Sebastian stared at the bloody handprints on Mary Grant's thighs. The pattern was the same for both women: first the kill, then the sexual assault. It spoke of a man driven to murder by a desire to slake a peculiar, sick kind of lust. Except that the link between the two women could only mean that their killings weren't random: whoever had killed Rachel York had not come upon her simply by chance in the Lady Chapel of St. Matthew of the Fields. He had sought her out. And then he had tracked down her maid, Mary Grant, and killed her, too.

But why? *Why?*

What if the sexual use of the women's bodies had been not the reason for the killing, but an effect, a release of the excitement and bloodlust generated by the act of killing? Mary Grant could have been killed because she surprised her murderer in the act of searching her rooms, or because she had known something that might have identified him as Rachel York's killer.

Or had the killer marked both women for death for some other reason entirely?

Sebastian fingered the envelope in his pocket. Whether it had been dropped by mistake or been left, deliberately, so that it might be found, the involvement of a man such as Lord Frederick Fairchild in this affair was ominous. The two women had been linked to a French spy ring, while Lord Frederick was the man most likely to be named the next prime minister of England when his dear friend, the Prince of Wales, took over as Regent. . . .

A whisper of movement brought Sebastian's head jerking around, but it was only the heavy satin drapes at the window, shifting in a sudden draft. He could hear the wind outside, picking up now. It would be dark soon.

He pushed to his feet. He knew the urge to cover Mary Grant's bloody, abused body, to shield her from the staring, assessing eyes that would in time find her, but he forced himself to turn away and leave her rooms essentially the way he had found them.

He was letting himself out the street door when he brushed past a stout matron who paused to look straight up into his face. And in that brief instant before he turned away to hurry down the front steps, he recognized her, and saw, in turn, the flicker of recognition in her eyes.

"My lord!" she called after him. "That is you, isn't it? Lord Devlin?"

Sebastian kept walking, his hat pulled low, his shoulders hunched against the cold. But his heart had begun to pound, and he was cursing silently to himself.

Her name was Mrs. Charles Lavery, and she was the widow of a colonel who'd served with Sebastian in the Peninsula. She would think, for now, that she had been mistaken, that she'd simply seen a stranger who happened to remind her in some vague way of the young viscount she'd once known. She'd tell herself she was silly not to have noticed sooner the shabbiness of his clothing, the touches of gray where his hair showed beneath his hat. But when they found Mary Grant's body, as they surely would, Mrs. Lavery would recall this chance encounter.

And tighten the noose around Sebastian's neck.

~◯

"I don't get it," said Tom, his small face pinched with the effort of assembling his thoughts. They were in a hackney carriage, the light from the streetlamps flickering over the worn leather upholstery as they turned down Pall Mall, heading toward St. James's.

"Lord Frederick is a Whig," said Sebastian, struggling to explain early nineteenth-century English politics in a way that might make sense to a child of the streets. "But for the last twenty years or so, the Tories have dominated the government."

Tom shoved his fists deep into the pockets of the warm coat Sebastian had bought him and made a rude noise through his nose. "Not much to choose between the lot of them, if'n you was to ask me."

Sebastian smiled. "In many ways, you're right. But in general, the Tories see themselves as staunch defenders of the country's established institutions, such as the monarchy and Church of England, which means they're against any kind of change, especially things like religious toleration and parliamentary reform—"

"Things the Whigs is for?"

"Basically. And unlike the Tories, the Whigs are against continuing the war with Napoleon."

Tom looked up in surprise. "You mean, they like the *French*?"

"Hardly. But they question the Tories' motives for continuing the war. War is costly. It leads to high taxes and government loans taken out at high interest, which is good for the large landowners and merchants who are lending to the government, but not so good for the common people, like farmers and tradesmen and day workers. If the Whigs come to power, we'll very likely see a peace treaty with France."

Tom nodded, his eyes bright with understanding. "So what you thinkin'? That this Lord Frederick's been playin' some underhanded game with the French, and 'e offed them two women because they threatened to squeal on 'im?"

"Perhaps. Or perhaps it's simply in someone's best interest to make it appear that way."

"Meanin' the Tories," said Tom.

The boy was surprisingly quick. Sebastian nodded. "That's right."

"Your da's a Tory, ain't 'e? Chancellor o' the Somethingeranother?"

Sebastian glanced sideways at his young friend. "Who told you that?"

"Miss Kat."

"Ah."

They were nearing the Recital Rooms on Ryder Street. Faint strains of a violin could be heard, barely discernible above the rattle of carriage wheels and the clip-clop of horses' hooves. Leaning forward, Sebastian rapped on the front panel, then settled his hat low over his eyes and wound his scarf carefully about his lower face as the jarvey cut in close to the curb and pulled up in the shadowy netherworld between two streetlamps.

～

Sebastian stood in the shadows and watched the bejeweled, perfumed crowd of men and women descend the front steps of Compton's Recital Rooms.

Even in this rarified collection of expensively dressed gentlefolk, Lord Frederick stood out, a handsome, urbane figure in flawless white linen and an inimitably cut coat. Laughing and talking amongst themselves, the small, self-absorbed group had just reached the footpath and turned toward the Mall, probably intending to sup at Richard's, when Sebastian stepped forward, a dark figure half-hidden in shadow. "Lord Frederick?"

Lord Frederick turned. "Yes?"

"I was wondering if'n I might have a word with you, my lord?"

A shade of annoyance passed over the other man's amicable features. "Not now, my good man. But you may come see me tomorrow, if you like."

"If'n that's the way you wants it," said Sebastian, settling his hat even lower. "I was thinkin' maybe you'd prefer a more private conversation, considering what I got to say. But I could come by your house in the mornin', if'n you don't mind your family findin' out about your dealings with Rachel Y—"

Lord Frederick took a quick step forward, his breath hissing out a warning as he threw a glance back over his shoulder, as if to make certain his friends hadn't heard. "For God's sake, keep your voice down."

Sebastian simply stared back at the man expectantly.

Lord Frederick hesitated, then said curtly, "Excuse me one moment." Turning toward his friends, he said with a wide smile, "Go on without me. I'll catch up with you later." His smile faded the instant he swung back to Sebastian. "Who are you? What do you want?"

Sebastian shoved his hands deep into the pockets of his greatcoat, and rocked back and forth on his heels. "Well, you see, we found your name in Miss York's appointment book—you do know Miss Rachel York, the one who was murdered Tuesday last in Westminster? We were wondering if you could tell us what it was doing there."

Lord Frederick had an admirable control over his features. Not a flicker of either surprise or consternation showed in his smooth, amiable face. "You're from Bow Street, I assume? I'm sorry, but my acquaintance with Miss York was entirely superficial. I really don't see how I could possibly be of assistance to you."

Sebastian sighed. "I was afraid you'd say somethin' like that. The thing is, you can talk with me straight here and now, all nice and friendly. Or we can have our little chat down at Bow Street."

"You're bluffing. You wouldn't dare."

Sebastian met the other man's gaze, and held it.

Lord Frederick looked away first. Pursing his lips, he blew out his breath in a long sigh, then gave a shaky laugh. "Very well. Miss York and I were having a little liaison. You know how these things are."

"You mean, you was having sex with her."

Lord Frederick laughed again, weakly. "Crudely put, but essentially accurate, yes."

"And that's all there was to it?"

"What more is there to such affairs?"

"Well, the answer to that might surprise you—least-ways when the lady in question appears to have been working for the French."

Fairchild might have control of his features, but he couldn't stop the blood from draining from his face, leaving him looking pale and frightened.

Sebastian studied the other man with interest. "I'm guessing you'd have me believe you didn't know about that?"

"No. Of course not. Are you quite certain of that?" Lord Frederick jerked out his handkerchief and pressed the fine folds of silk to his upper lip. "This is dreadful," he said, his voice muffled by the handkerchief. "Just dreadful. There must be some mistake."

The man was in obvious distress. But it was also true that he was no longer meeting Sebastian's gaze.

"Where exactly were you last Tuesday night?"

"I spent the evening with the Prince, of course.

Why?" Lord Frederick's jaw went slack with sudden comprehension. "Good God. Surely you aren't suggesting that I killed her?"

"You do have a motive. My lord."

An unexpectedly powerful blaze of anger flared in the other man's eyes. "You dare? You *dare* take that tone with *me*? What is your name? Hmm?" He stepped forward, his gaze narrowing as he tried to peer into Sebastian's shadowy, muffled face. "Speak up, man. Who's your superior at Bow Street? I swear to God, I'll have your job over this."

Sebastian smiled. "I never said I was with Bow Street."

"*What?* Then who are you working for?" Fairchild demanded. But he spoke only to darkness and a scattering of dry leaves carried along by the night wind, for Sebastian had gone.

~

"He's hiding something," said Sebastian.

From the shelter of a columned portico, he and Tom watched as Lord Frederick strode briskly away, the *tap-tap* of his boot heels echoing eerily in the thickening fog. He had obviously changed his mind about rejoining his friends at supper; he was headed away from Richard's in the Mall and toward Piccadilly instead.

Tom fidgeted with impatience. "Think he's our man?"

"I'm not sure," said Sebastian, one hand closing over Tom's shoulder to hold him back when he would have moved. "But it'll be interesting to see where he goes." They waited until their quarry was almost out of sight. Then Sebastian squeezed the boy's shoulder and let him go.

"*Now*," said Sebastian.

With the grace and noiseless gait of an alley cat, Tom slipped from behind the column and darted forward, a shadow following a shadow through the mist-filled night.

Chapter 38

Sir Henry Lovejoy paused in the dressing room doorway and stared down at what was left of Mary Grant. They hadn't covered the body yet, and the smell of her blood hung thick in the air. He was glad he hadn't had a chance to eat his supper yet.

"There's no doubt this time as to who did it," said Edward Maitland.

Lovejoy glanced back at his constable. "There's not?"

"We have a witness." Maitland flipped open his notebook and turned it toward the golden pool of light cast by one of the oil lamps they'd lit. "A Mrs. Charles Lavery. She saw Lord Devlin leaving the building this afternoon."

"She's sure it was Devlin?"

"Said she knows the Viscount. Her husband served with Devlin in Spain." Maitland closed his notebook with a snap. "No doubt he's our man, sir."

Lovejoy crouched down beside the dead woman and studied her face. She was young, but not particularly attractive. Nothing like Rachel York. "Why this woman? Why go through all the bother of tracking her down?"

"She knew Rachel York had gone to St. Matthew's that night to meet him." Maitland shrugged his expensively tailored shoulders. "So he kills her to shut her up."

"But she'd already told us about that." Lovejoy's gaze drifted around the disordered room. "What else did she know, I wonder? And what do you suppose he was looking for?"

"Money," Maitland suggested. "Or something to sell. Jewelry perhaps."

"We're dealing with the heir to an earldom here. Not some petty thief."

"Still, he must be getting short of the ready by now, for all that. A man's gotta eat."

"Hmm. Perhaps. Yet Rachel York's reticule had also been searched, if you'll remember." Lovejoy pushed to his feet, his knees creaking. "I wonder," he said, half to himself. "I wonder . . ."

There was something peculiarly soothing about the sight and sound of a fire. Kat Boleyn sat with her feet curled up beneath her, her head tipped back against the silk upholstery of her drawing room sofa, her gaze on the flickering flames before her as she listened to the voice of the man she'd once loved telling her about his visit to St. Jude's Foundling Home.

And about Mary Grant.

"It's not your fault," Kat said when Devlin had finished and fell silent beside her. "It's not your fault that he got to her first."

"No. I know it's not," he said, his gaze on the fire.

"In a way, you're this killer's victim, too."

"I know it's not my fault," he said again.

"But you're still feeling guilty."

He looked up to meet her gaze. A hint of a wry smile touched his lips, then faded as he sucked in a deep breath. "I suppose because in some way I can't begin to understand, this all has to do with me. I keep circling around it, catching glimpses of it, but I can't seem to grasp it. And in the meantime, these women are dying."

She touched his shoulder and he turned toward her, his fingers digging into her arm as he buried his face against her breasts. She felt a shudder rip through him, then he lay still.

Disturbed by the tumult of her own feelings, she touched her hand, lightly, to his hair, just above the nape of his neck. "It's odd, isn't it?" she said quietly. "All those years Rachel went every Monday afternoon to St. Jude's, and I never knew about it."

He shifted so that his cheek lay against the bare flesh of her chest where it showed above the bodice of her gown, and his hand rested high on her stomach. "She was with child. Did you know?"

Kat's fingers stilled in his hair. "No. I didn't know. It happens sometimes. Even when one is careful."

The tip of his finger traced a delicate pattern against the thin silk of her gown, spreading a warm glow that seemed to start from deep within her. And she marveled at the effect this man's touch could have on her. Even when she didn't want it to. Even when she tried to steel herself against it.

He said, "The Reverend Finley seems to think she was in love with someone."

Kat's hand closed over his, stopping that slow, seductive motion. "You think she was killed because of the baby?"

"Perhaps. But it doesn't explain the rape. Or what was done to Mary Grant." He lifted his head to look at her. "How well do you know Lord Frederick?"

As a friend of the Prince of Wales, Lord Frederick was a frequent guest at the kind of functions to which

women like Kat were invited. She supposed she probably knew the man better than Devlin, who wasn't of that
set and had spent so many years out of the country besides. She linked her fingers with Sebastian's, although
even that simple touch filled her with a confusion of
feelings she didn't want and didn't need.

"I wouldn't have said he's capable of that kind of violence," she said after a moment's thought. "In fact, I'd
say he's one of those rare men who actually *likes*
women, if you know what I mean? The kind who enjoys
women's company, who likes talking to them about
things such as fashion and music and art. He has a
daughter, Elizabeth, who married the Earl of South-
wick's eldest son just last month. You can tell by the
look on his face whenever he talks about her how much
he adores her."

"She's his only child, isn't she?"

Kat nodded. "His wife died almost fifteen years ago,
but in all that time, he's never remarried, never set up a
mistress."

"And yet he suddenly drifts into a casual liaison with
a woman who just might be passing information to the
French? It doesn't make sense." He propped himself up
on one elbow so that he could draw a heavy paper from
the inner pocket of his coat and hand it to her. "Is this
Rachel York's handwriting?"

Kat found herself holding an envelope, a blue envelope with the words *Lord Frederick Fairchild* written
across it in Leo Pierrepont's bold scrawl.

"No," she said, handing the envelope back to Sebastian and meeting his gaze squarely. "At least, I don't
think so. I don't recognize it."

He tucked the envelope away.

"Where did you get it?" she asked.

"I found it in Mary Grant's rooms."

"Empty?"

"Yes."

He ducked his head, his lips brushing the tender flesh just below her collarbone, his hands going aroving to all the secret places that made her heart race and her breath catch. All the places he had discovered so long ago and apparently not forgotten.

She'd thought she could hold her heart aloof. She'd meant to hold her heart aloof. But an unexpected, unwanted flood of tender emotions and deep, unacknowledged wants brought the sting of tears to her eyes and lent an urgency to the hunger with which her body rose up to meet his.

~

The next morning, Sebastian received a message from Paul Gibson, to the effect that a certain gentleman of their acquaintance had some information Sebastian might find interesting. This gentleman had agreed to meet Sebastian in Green Park at ten that morning, at the southeast corner.

Wary of a possible trap, Sebastian arrived at the rendezvous early, only to find the park's open fields populated by nothing more than a dozen dairy cows and their attendants. Not until half past ten did the tall, cadaverously thin man appear, wearing striped trousers and a jaunty red kerchief, and bringing with him a faint, indefinable odor of decay that seemed to emanate from him with each step.

Jumpin' Jack Cochran hawked up a mouthful of phlegm, spat, then wiped his mouth with the back of his hand. "I 'ear tell you's lookin' for some nonmedical gent what's interested in buyin' half-longs."

"That's right," said Sebastian. He counted out five pounds, folded them into a roll, and handed it over.

Jumpin' Jack licked his lips, jammed the money deep into his coat pocket, and rubbed his mouth again. "I had me just such a request about a month or so ago, from a feller claimin' he was an artist, although I thought at the time he was a queer 'un."

"Do you remember his name?"

Jumpin' Jack let out a laugh that turned, quickly, into a cough. "You don't go askin' folks' names in this business. But I'd know the feller agin if'n I was to see him. Young, he was, with a head o' dark curly hair, just like a girl's. My Sarah, she was moonin' about the place for days after she saw him. Said he was like the angels in them paintings hangin' over the side altars in Trinity Church." Cochran spat again. "You'd think the girl'd have more discretion, her being a proper English-woman and him some heathen foreigner."

Sebastian felt his pulse quicken in anticipation. "He was a foreigner?"

"Aye. From Italy or some such place. Or so he said. They all sound pretty much the same to me."

"Where did you deliver the goods? Do you remember?"

"Aye. Almonry Terrace, it was. In Westminster."

Chapter 39

*D*onatelli was in his studio when Sebastian came through the door.

The artist half turned, his slack mouth agape with shock, the breath whooshing out of him when Sebastian's shoulder caught him in the gut and brought him down.

"What are you doing? What do you want from me?" the Italian managed to gasp, before Sebastian shoved his forearm up beneath the man's chin, cutting off his air.

"I understand you've been buying yourself some half-longs," said Sebastian through gritted teeth. "Is that the way you like your women, hmm? You like it when they don't move, don't talk back, don't even *breathe*?"

Donatelli's angelic brown eyes went wide. He tried to speak, but all he could get out was a gurgle.

Sebastian eased the pressure on the man's throat just enough to let him gasp, "No! It's nothing like that. I do medical illustrations."

Sebastian made as if to increase his pressure on the man's throat again. "Gammon."

"No! I swear it's true. My last commission was for the female torso." He made as if to push up from the floor, then went limp again, his features twitching with fear, when Sebastian brought up the small flintlock and laid the muzzle against the man's temple.

Donatelli licked his lips, his eyes rolling sideways in an effort to watch Sebastian's finger on that trigger. "If you let me go, I'll show you. They're in the back room."

Sebastian hesitated, then let the man up.

Donatelli's hand crept to his throat. "Mother of God, you could have killed me."

Sebastian leveled the flintlock at the artist's chest. "The illustrations."

Donatelli nodded. "They're back here." He staggered toward the other room. "See?" They were a series of perhaps a dozen, rendering in meticulous detail the torso of a woman in various stages of dismemberment, from a variety of angles.

"I work with a medical student from St. Thomas's," said Donatelli, his voice still hoarse, strained. "He does the dissections while I sketch."

"Now why would a painter who's suddenly become Society's newest discovery need to be hawking anatomy sketches to medical journals?"

Donatelli twitched one shoulder in a very Mediterranean shrug. "I began doing it for extra money when I was painting scenes at the theater. I keep it up because it improves my ability to realistically render the human form. I'm not the only painter who studies cadavers. Look at Fragonard."

Sebastian turned away from the bloody renderings. "Where were you the night Rachel York was killed?" The illustrations might provide the artist with a plausible excuse for buying female human cadavers, but that was all.

The Italian's eyes went wide. "*Me*? But ... surely you don't believe that I killed Rachel?"

Sebastian kept his gaze steady on the other man's face. "Where were you?"

"Why, here, of course. Painting."

"Anyone with you?"

The Italian tightened his jaw. "No."

Sebastian paused, his attention caught by a nearby small canvas. It looked like a study for a larger painting, a family portrait. The grouping was of a man and three women, each at a different stage in her life. The matriarch of the family sat in the center. She was thin and wrinkled and stooped with age, but her eyes still shone with such determination and pride that she completely overshadowed the woman to her left, a pale, vacant-faced lady of middle years who was undoubtedly the man's wife. On the other side, the family's brown-haired, plain-faced daughter, who looked to be in her early twenties, stared at something just out of sight, as if to disassociate herself from the others. And towering above them all, his arms spread as if both to protect the women and to dominate them, stood a large, jowly man with a florid complexion and fiercely staring eyes that Sebastian recognized as Charles, Lord Jarvis.

Sebastian glanced up to find the artist watching him nervously. "You're doing a portrait of Lord Jarvis's family?"

"That's the study. The portrait itself was finished last spring."

"When you were still painting theatrical scenery?"

A muscle ticked along the side of Donatelli's jaw. "Lord Jarvis is known for his generous encouragement of new artists. He's the man responsible for bringing me to the attention of the *ton*."

Sebastian looked back at the family grouping. He

was aware of a shadow of a thought flitting about the edges of his consciousness. But when he tried to reach for it, it simply floated away, a pale, mocking chimera that was there, and then gone.

The small flintlock still in hand, Sebastian continued about the room, studying the various canvases propped against the walls, looking for something that would tie all the strange, disparate threads of Rachel's life and death together.

He stopped suddenly before a haunting painting of a young girl, her wrists tied together over her head, her naked body twisted in agony, her eyes cast heavenward as if to beseech her god for mercy. As he looked closer, Sebastian realized that the girl was Rachel, only younger. Much younger. "That's Rachel York, isn't it? As a child."

Giorgio Donatelli was looking, not at the painting, but at him. "You're the merchant who was here on Friday. You look different, but the features are the same." His brows drew together in a troubled frown. "You asked about Rachel then, too. Why?"

There were probably half a dozen things Sebastian could have said. He decided to use the truth. "Because I'm trying to find out who killed her."

"They say they know who did it. A viscount named Devlin."

"I am Devlin."

Sebastian wasn't sure how he expected the other man to react. Donatelli glanced down at the pistol Sebastian still held in his hand, then away, and nodded once, as if he'd somehow come to this conclusion himself.

"Rachel used to talk to me sometimes," he said, jerking his chin toward the canvas, "when I was painting her. She'd tell me about her life, about when she first came to London. And before. It's what gave me the idea for this painting."

"Her life in Worcestershire?"

Donatelli's eyes shone dark and fierce. "She was only thirteen when her father died. Her mother was already dead and she had no relatives willing to take her in, so she was thrown on the parish. They sold her as a house-maid." He sucked in a deep breath that flared his nostrils and expanded his chest. "They do that here, you know. You English, you talk so fine, looking down your noses at the Americans and prosing on about the sin and inhumanity of their African trade. And yet you sell your own children into slavery."

He paused. "They sold her to a fat old merchant and his wife. She was mad, that woman. Sick in her head. She used to tie Rachel to a post in the cellar and lay her bare back open with a whip."

Sebastian stared down at the naked, frightened girl in the painting. He was remembering the thin, crisscross-ing bands of white lines Paul Gibson had found on Rachel's back, and the scars on her wrists.

"But what the merchant did to her was even worse." Donatelli's voice trembled with emotion. "He used Rachel as his whore. A thirteen-year-old girl child, and he bent her over his desk and took her from behind like a dog."

"A woman who's been through something like that, I wouldn't think she'd have much use for men," said Sebastian softly.

"She learned to do what she needed to survive."

"Did you know she was planning to leave London?"

Donatelli's gaze shifted away. "No. She never mentioned it."

"But you knew she was with child."

It was said as a statement, not a question. To Sebas-

tian's surprise, Donatelli's eyes went wide, his lips part-
ing as if on a sudden gasp of fear. "How do you know
that?"

"I know. Who was the father? You?"

"No!"

"Who then? Lord Frederick?"

"Lord Frederick?" Donatelli gave a short, sharp
laugh. "Hardly. The man's a *Bulgarus*."

It was an old term, *Bulgarus*; an old term for a man
with certain tendencies that were as old as time. Sebastian's first inclination was to reject the accusation out of
hand. Except that Donatelli was too passionate, too
transparent to be much of a liar. And it didn't sound like
a lie. "If that's true, then why was he involved with
Rachel?"

"He wasn't. She was his—how do you say it? His
cover. He paid her for the use of her rooms so that he
could meet his lover there. A young clerk."

It was a common enough ruse, especially amongst
those in espionage and government: cover up one secret by disguising it as another, a secret so spicy and
naughty that if anyone should happen to discover it,
they'd never think to look beyond it to the real, more
dangerous truth it was intended to disguise. Thus, if
Lord Frederick's visits to Rachel York's rooms were to
become known, people would automatically assume
that he'd set up the young actress as his mistress.
Shocking, of course, but a common enough activity for
a man of his age and wealth. Society would titter and
gossip about it, but no one would ever think to look beyond it to the real secret that would destroy him, if it
were to become known.

The problem with those kinds of arrangements, however, was that they left one vulnerable to blackmail. And
blackmail was often a motive for murder. Except . . .

Except that it was hard to imagine a man whose tastes ran to young male lovers being so physically aroused by the act of killing as to rape the dead bodies of his female victims.

Sebastian's gaze fell on another of Donatelli's paintings, the one of Rachel as an odalisque, preparing for her bath. For the first time he noticed that the painting also contained the figure of a man, peering out at her from behind a nearby planting of pleached orange trees.

"Tell me again about Bayard Wilcox," said Sebastian suddenly. "You said he used to watch Rachel, follow her around. But he never actually approached her?"

"Not until last Saturday."

Sebastian looked up in surprise. "Saturday?"

"At Steven's in Bond Street. We went there after the play—a group of mainly theater people. At about half past eleven, Bayard arrived with some of his fellow *aristos*." Donatelli's angelic features quivered with remembered revulsion and disgust. "They were falling down drunk. Propping each other up. Laughing like idiots. Then Bayard, he saw Rachel. He went quiet all of a sudden and left the others to come lean against a nearby column and stare at her in that way he had. His friends tried to pry him away, but he wouldn't budge. So they started teasing him. Said he must be some kind of a eunuch, to stand around simply looking at a woman the way he did. They said that if he had any balls, he'd walk up to her and tell her how he felt about her."

"So he did?"

Donatelli nodded. "Walked right up and told her he wanted to fuck her. In those exact words. She threw her punch in his face."

"What did Bayard do?"

"I've never seen anything like it. One minute he was blubbering all over himself, saying she was like a goddess to him, and how he couldn't think of anything but what it would be like to have her naked and beneath him. Then she threw the punch in his face and it was as if he turned into someone else. I mean, his face actually changed—his eyes scrunched together and his lips curled back and his skin grew dark. It was as if he were possessed by someone else. Someone evil."

Sebastian nodded. He knew what Donatelli was talking about. He'd seen that kind of a change come over Bayard, even when he was a boy.

"If we hadn't been there," Donatelli was saying, "I think he'd have killed her on the spot with his bare hands. We had to physically hold him back until his friends finally dragged him away. You could still hear him screaming when he was outside, spewing the most vile obscenities. Saying he was going to kill her."

"He said that? That he wanted to kill her?"

Donatelli nodded, his face ashen and strained. "He said he'd rip her head off."

Chapter 40

*N*ormally, Sunday was the only day of the week when Charles, Lord Jarvis, spent any time at home. He would shepherd his mother, wife, and daughter to church in the morning, and then he'd sit down with them for a traditional English Sunday dinner before retreating to one of his clubs, or to the chambers set aside for his use in Carlton House or St. James's Palace.

But a condition his doctors called inflammation of the heart—which Jarvis himself considered little more than heartburn—had kept him in bed that Monday under the care of his caustic, sharp-tongued mother, who ran his household while his wife retreated farther and farther into her own misty dream worlds and his daughter was off tilting at windmills and meddling in things she refused to believe were none of her affair.

It was one of the ironies of Jarvis's existence, that his life was filled with women. In addition to his mother, wife, and daughter, who lived with him, Jarvis was far more involved than he would have liked in the lives of his two sisters: weepy, harebrained Agnes, forever needing his help to tow her useless husband and son out of dun territory; and Phyllis, who, while no more intelligent than her sister, had at least had the wit to marry well.

Women, in Jarvis's opinion, were generally even

more profoundly brainless and foolish than most men. True, there were some exceptions—females with astonishingly rational, quick minds who tended to be either embittered and sour, or sarcastic and irreverent, and who irritated him even more than their empty-headed sisters. His deep and abiding hatred of the French notwithstanding, Jarvis had to agree with Napoleon in this, if nothing else: the only two things women were good for were recreation and reproduction.

Which was a thought that brought him back, as it often did, to Annabelle, his wife.

She'd been a fey, pretty little thing when he'd married her, a thin slip of a girl with sparkling blue eyes and a merry laugh and a handsome dowry. But she'd proved a severe disappointment. She'd managed to produce only one living daughter and a sickly, weak son before succumbing to a series of yearly miscarriages and stillbirths that the doctors claimed had ruined her health and overset the balance of her delicate mind. Jarvis knew better. Annabelle's mind had never been balanced. But whatever hopes he might have had that her precarious health would soon carry her off proved misplaced. She lived on, year after year, forbidden by her doctors from providing him with the release his body still occasionally craved and unable to produce the son he needed to replace David, lying now in a watery, unknown grave.

Yet of all the women in his life, it was his daughter, Hero, who tended to cause Jarvis the most grief. A stubborn, wrongheaded creature, she had dedicated her life, nauseatingly, to good works, while spouting any number of alarming sentiments gleaned from her reading of the likes of Mary Wollstonecraft and the Marquis of Condorcet. Worse, having stubbornly resisted his efforts to contract for her any number of advantageous matches, she was now nearly twenty-five, and well on her way to becoming a spinster for life. Never the pretty, taking little thing her mother had been, whatever good looks she might once have had were in danger of fading fast.

She was off right now, inspecting a workhouse, of all things. Just the thought of it brought a sour burn to his chest so that he was in no good humor when, midway through the afternoon, that fool magistrate, Lovejoy, was finally ushered into his presence.

"You wished to see me, my lord?" said the little man, bowing.

"It's about time," groused Jarvis from the sofa beside the fire, where he had set up a kind of temporary office. "I hear Devlin has killed again."

"We don't actually know—"

"He was seen there, wasn't he?"

The little man pressed his lips together and sighed. "Yes, my lord."

"The Prince is greatly displeased by this entire affair. There are whispers on the streets. Alarming talk. They're saying it's reached the point that noblemen in this country can kill with impunity, that common folks' women are no longer safe even in their own homes. It's the last thing the Prince needs, with his installation as Regent just two days away."

"Yes, my lord."

"The Prince wants Devlin brought in—or dead—within forty-eight hours. Or Queen Square will be looking for a new magistrate. Do I make myself clear?"

"Yes, my lord," said Lovejoy, and bowed himself out.

Chapter 41

*I*t was just past noon when Sebastian reached his sister's townhouse on St. James's Square.

"*My lord*," said Amanda's butler, his eyes widening in surprise and fear when he answered the door to Sebastian's preemptory knock.

"Bayard's still at home, I presume?" said Sebastian, brushing past the man and heading for the stairs.

"I believe Mr. Wilcox is in his dressing room, my lord. If you care to wait in the— *My lord*," bleated the butler, but Sebastian was already taking the stairs two at a time.

Sebastian flung open the dressing room door without warning to find Bayard in his shirtsleeves, his neck craning back at an awkward angle as he struggled with one of the monstrously wide cravats he affected. He spun about, his jaw going slack, his eyes opening wide. "*Devlin.*"

Sebastian caught him in an angry rush that sent a chair flying and took the two men across the room to slam Bayard's back up against the wall, hard enough to drive the air out of him in a painful huff.

"You lied to me," said Sebastian, pulling his nephew away from the wall, then slamming him back against it a second time. "You said you'd never gone near Rachel

York. Now I hear you threatened to kill her at Steven's in Bond Street."

Bayard's voice wheezed, his chest jerking with the effort to draw breath. "I was foxed! I didn't know what I was doing, let alone what I was saying."

"You were foxed the night she died, too. How do you know what you did then?"

"I would never hurt her! I *loved* her."

"You said you were going to rip her head off, Bayard. Then a few days later, someone comes bloody close to doing exactly that. I still remember the turtles, Bayard."

Bayard's mouth sagged, his eyes opening wide with horror. "Is that what happened to her? How do you know that? Oh, God, it's not true, is it?"

Sebastian tightened his hold on his nephew's arms, lifting him up until his feet barely touched the floor, and holding him there. "What about the other one, Bayard? Mary Grant. Why did you go after her, too?"

The mystification on Bayard's face was so complete that Sebastian knew a moment of misgivings. "Other one? Who the devil is Mary Grant?"

A woman's voice cut through the sudden, thick silence. "Let him go," said Amanda. "Let him go or I swear to God, Sebastian, I'll bring the constables down on you."

Sebastian swung his head to stare at his sister. She stood in the doorway, a tall, middle-aged woman with the inescapably proud bearing of an Earl's daughter. She had their mother's coloring and slim, graceful stature, but enough of their father's blunt, heavy features that, by the age of forty, she resembled the Earl far more than the beautiful, ethereal woman who had once been the Countess of Hendon.

Sebastian hesitated, then eased his grip on Bayard's arms to let the boy slump against the wall.

Bayard stayed where he was, his shoulders pressed against the paneling, his mouth slack, his breath coming hard and fast.

"You knew, didn't you," said Sebastian. "You knew he killed that girl."

Bayard wiped a shaky hand across his loose, wet lips. "I didn't! Why won't you believe me?"

Sebastian kept his gaze on his sister's face. "You knew, and yet you kept quiet about it. And now he's killed again."

"I tell you, I didn't kill her," said Bayard. "I didn't kill anyone."

Amanda's gaze shifted to her son, her face set so cold and hard that for a moment, Sebastian knew a stirring of sympathy for his nephew. She had always looked at him this way, even when he was a little boy, pathetic in his hunger for her love. "Leave us."

"But I swear to you, I didn't kill anyone!"

"Leave us now, Bayard."

Bayard's throat bulged with the effort of swallowing. He hesitated a moment, his mouth working as if he were trying to say something. Then he ducked his head and pushed away from the wall, brushing past his mother in an awkward, ungainly rush from the room.

Amanda watched him stumble toward the stairs, then brought her gaze back to Sebastian. "The incident in Bond Street means nothing," she said. "A boy's wild talk, that's all."

"Is that all it was? You know what he's like, Amanda. You've always known, even if you didn't want to admit it."

"You make too much of a schoolboy's wild ways."

"A *schoolboy*?"

Amanda walked over to right the chair that had been knocked sideways in the struggle. "Know this, Sebastian: I will not allow my son to be destroyed as a result of the inconsequential death of some worthless little bit of muslin who deserved everything she was given."

"My God, Amanda. We're talking about a human life."

Amanda's lip curled in disdain. "We don't all have such a mewling weakness for the dregs of society. One would think you'd have learned your lesson after your experience with that light-skirt who used you for such a fool six years ago. What was her name? Anne Boleyn? No wait, that was another man's whore. Yours was named—"

"Don't," said Sebastian, taking a hasty step toward his sister before drawing himself up short. "Don't start on Kat."

"Good heavens." Amanda's eyes widened with wonder as she searched her brother's face. "You're still in love with her."

Sebastian simply stared back at her, a faint, betraying line of color heating his cheeks.

"You're seeing her again, are you?" She gave a shrill laugh. "You never learn. What does she think is in it for her this time, I wonder? A chance to play the grieving widow at your hanging?"

"I won't die for your son, Amanda."

The amusement faded from Amanda's face. "I tell you, Bayard had nothing to do with that light-skirt's death. He was with his friends until nine o'clock, when Wilcox picked him up and brought him home. He never went out again."

"That lie might satisfy the authorities this time. But he'll do it again, Amanda. And then what? For how long do you think you can protect him?"

An angry flush darkened her cheeks and deepened the sparkle of animosity in the brilliant blue eyes that were so much like their father's. "Get out of my house."

The sound of loud knocking, followed by excited voices and a rough shout, echoed up the stairs. Sebastian turned toward the commotion, his lips pulling back into a hard smile. "You might not have called the constables, my dear sister, but it appears that Bayard did."

Chapter 42

There were only two constables, both on the wrong side of forty, one tall and bone lean, the other slow and fleshy.

The first was halfway up the stairs when Sebastian's fist caught him under the jaw with an audible *smack* that closed the man's mouth and sent him arm-wheeling backward.

"I say," blustered the second, just before Sebastian buried his fist in the man's soft gut. His eyes widened, and he doubled over with a wheezing *whooph*.

Bayard was standing at the base of the stairs, his derisory, self-satisfied smile fading fast. "You little bastard," said Sebastian, and punched him, too, just for the bloody hell of it, on his way out the door.

After that, Sebastian spent the next several hours attempting to disprove Bayard's alibi, only to discover that Bayard and his two companions had indeed spent the afternoon and evening of the previous Tuesday getting conspicuously and roaringly drunk at the Leather Bottle in Islington. Their subsequent arrival at Cribb's Parlor, followed by their hasty departure, had been equally spectacular and memorable. In fact, the doorman distinctly remembered helping to load the insensible young gentleman into his father's carriage. He even remembered the time, for the city's church bells had begun to toll nine o'clock just as the carriage pulled away.

~

Tom found Sebastian in a coffeehouse near the Rose and Crown, a tankard of ale cradled in his left hand, a bloodstained handkerchief wrapped around the knuckles of his right.

"What'd you do to yer hand?"

"I hit something."

"A bone box, you mean?" Tom said with a grin, and slid onto the opposite bench, a paper-wrapped Cornish pasty clutched in one fist. "Find out something on yer nevy?"

Sebastian took a long, slow swallow of ale. "That he has an ironclad alibi."

Tom looked up from tearing the paper off his pasty. "A what?"

"An alibi. Verifiable proof that he was somewhere else at the time of the crime. In this instance, passed out insensible in his father's arms." Sebastian stretched back on the bench. "My pool of suspects is rapidly diminishing. Bayard had the motive and means but not, apparently, the opportunity to commit murder. Giorgio Donatelli had the opportunity but no motive that I can see—apart from the fact that nothing we've learned about the man suggests he's capable of such extreme violence. Lord Frederick claims he was with the Prince of Wales at the time of the killings, and while I haven't had a chance to verify that, I would assume at any rate that a man of his inclinations would be unlikely to indulge in our killer's particular form of necrophilia."

"Necro-what?"

Sebastian glanced over at the boy's open, inquisitive face. "Never mind that one."

"There's still the Frenchman," said Tom. He paused to take a bite of his pasty, but swallowed quickly before continuing. "And that actor, Hugh Gordon. All you got is 'is word for it that 'e was 'ome studyin' his lines that night."

"A love affair that went bad two years ago seems an unlikely motive for murder, but you're right, it wouldn't hurt to look into his movements that night. Why don't you ask around, see if any of his neighbors remember seeing him that night."

Tom nodded and swallowed the last of his pasty. "I got somethin' interesting on yer Lord Frederick. 'E went to see a friend last night. A young friend what 'as rooms in Stratton Street, over Marylebone way."

Sebastian drained his tankard and pushed it aside. "Who is he?"

"Folks around there didn't seem to know—I take it 'e 'asna lived there long. So I followed 'im this morning."

"And?"

" 'Is name is Davis. Wesley Davis. Turns out 'e's a clerk. At the Foreign Office."

~

It was the hour of the fashionable promenade in Hyde Park, the hour when everyone with pretensions to being anyone was careful to be seen there, walking, trotting sedately along the Row on a showy hack, or bowling up the avenue in a suitably stylish curricle, phaeton, or barouche. The weather hadn't been particularly favorable lately, but that morning's bleak sunshine had melted what was left of the snow, helped along by a stiff wind that was still blowing hard enough to keep away the stinking, yellow London fog. Society's finest were out in droves, bundled up to their stiff upper lips against the cold.

Sebastian kept his hat pulled low and his scarf wrapped about his lower face, but his scruffy appearance still attracted more attention than he would have liked as he waited patiently beside the footpath, some twenty yards away from where Lord Frederick had paused to speak to a fawning matron and her blushing young daughter.

He might be nearly fifty and a younger son, but Lord Frederick was still considered quite a catch, for all that. His first wife had, unfortunately, left most of her considerable fortune tied up in trust for their daughter, but everyone knew that the chances were more than even that the man would be made prime minister in just a few days' time. True, he'd shown no disposition to remarry in all the years since his wife's tragic death, but the recent marriage of his dearly loved only daughter had raised hopes in the bosoms of the Metropolis's mamas—as well as among more than a few of Society's more attractive widows. Surely, they reasoned, the need for female companionship would at long last inspire Lord Frederick to look about him for a wife—especially when one considered the pressing need for someone to play the part of his political hostess.

Of course, they didn't know about the existence of one Mr. Wesley Davis of Stratton Street.

Smiling smoothly, Lord Frederick extricated himself from the clutches of the two ambitious ladies, tipped his hat, bowed, and continued up the footpath. He wore buff-colored doeskin breeches and a many-caped Garrick, and carried an ivory-handled ebony walking stick that swung idly in one hand as he headed toward Park Lane.

Sebastian fell into step beside him. "I've a flintlock in me pocket big enough to blow a hole in yer gut the size o' a dinner plate, so don't ye be getting any fancy ideas about hollerin' out, or tryin' to skewer me with the fancy little sword ye got hidden in that cane o' yers," Sebastian added when the man's fist tightened around his walking stick.

Fairchild relaxed his hold on the stick's ivory handle, but his expression remained calm and defiant. "Surely you don't expect to get away with armed robbery in broad daylight in the middle of Hyde Park?"

"I don't want yer boung and geegaws. All's I wants is for us to have us a little chat. Over there." Sebastian nodded toward a wooden bench set back amongst the shrubbery. "Beneath that chestnut tree."

Lord Frederick hesitated a moment, then stepped off the footpath into the long wet grass.

"Sit down real easy-like," said Sebastian, when Fairchild reached the bench and turned to look back expectantly. "And drop that walking stick. That's right. Now kick it over here."

Keeping a watchful eye on the man on the bench, Sebastian reached for the cane at his feet. The mechanism that released the ivory handle from the ebony shaft was easy enough to find. The shaft fell away with a well-oiled hiss, revealing a gleaming, two-edged blade. "Nasty little piece of work, this," he said, in his own voice and diction.

Lord Frederick set his handsome, square jaw. "The streets are dangerous places these days."

Sebastian laughed and loosed the scarf from about his lower face. "You've no idea how dangerous."

A mingling of recognition and shock sagged the other man's face. "Oh, God. You're Devlin, aren't you?" He swallowed, a new kind of wariness narrowing his eyes, replacing the initial slackness of surprise. "What do you want from me?"

"The truth would be nice. For a change." Sebastian played with the sword stick in his hand, learning the weight of it, testing the balance. "I'll save us some time, shall I, by telling you what I already know? For instance, I know that whatever else you were doing with Rachel York, you weren't tupping her."

Lord Frederick gave a sharp laugh. "Don't be absurd. What do you think I was doing in her rooms twice a week?"

"Pleasuring a young clerk from the Foreign Office named Wesley Davis."

Fairchild sat silent. He managed to keep his features composed, but the fear was there, like a shadow darkening his soft gray eyes.

"It's the reason you never remarried, isn't it?" said Sebastian. "Because while you might enjoy chatting with the ladies about gardens and furniture design and the latest sonata, you've never had the least interest in taking any of them to bed."

For a moment, Sebastian thought the man meant to continue denying it. Then his shoulders sagged, the skin around his eyes tightening as if in a wince, and he said softly, "Who else knows?"

"That's what I'm wondering." Sebastian considered the sword. It was double edged and very, very sharp. "Rachel was blackmailing you, was she? Her silence, in exchange for whatever little secrets the French might be interested in getting their hands on."

Fairchild's head jerked back. "What? Good God. I would never do such a thing." He sucked in a deep, angry breath that flared his nostrils. "What do you think? That because I favor peace with the French that makes me a traitor? I'm against this war because it is

destroying our country, not because I sympathize with
Napoleon." He flung out one arm in an expansive sweep
that encompassed the East End of London, his voice
taking on the stentorian tones of a speaker in Parliament. "Look around you. Children are dying of starva-
tion in our streets. Men by the tens of thousands have
been thrown off the land their families worked for gen-
erations, while women who once made a decent living are
now reduced to selling themselves in alleyways and
under bridges. The price of a pound of bread has doubled
in the last twenty years, while a typical working man's
wages have fallen to almost half what they once were.
And for what? So that a handful of industrialists and
merchants can grow rich by lending their money to the
government and equipping the armies that will be used
to put the old crowned tyrants of Europe back on their
thrones?"

It could have been an act, a performance intended to
deceive, but Sebastian didn't think so. The man's entire
being was practically throbbing with indignation and
the fierce determination of the hopeless idealist. "Are
you telling me Rachel York never asked you to pass her
sensitive information?"

Fairchild stared back at him, eyes widening with a
horrified kind of revelation. "Good God. What is it you
think? That I killed her? That she was threatening to
blackmail me, so I shut her up?"

"I might," said Sebastian, still playing with the sword,
"except for one thing."

"What's that?"

"Whoever killed her, raped her."

"Heavens." Fairchild clasped his hands together between his knees, and stared down at them for a moment.
"I didn't know. Poor Rachel."

He said it as if she had been his friend. And it came

to Sebastian that, in some strange way, they probably were friends, this gentle, troubled nobleman and the woman who had gone every Monday afternoon to sing to the babies in St. Jude's Foundling Home.

After a moment, Fairchild looked up and said, "Are you quite certain she was working for the French?"

"No. But everything I've found seems to point in that direction."

Fairchild pursed his lips and pushed out a long, troubled breath. "A few weeks ago, Wesley's rooms were broken into. He had these letters I'd written him—probably something like half a dozen of them. " A faint hint of color tinged his cheeks. "It was a foolish thing to have done, I know that now."

"The letters were taken?" said Sebastian, wondering if this Wesley Davis had also played a part in setting up Lord Frederick for blackmail.

Fairchild nodded. "I was sick with worry. Rachel and I talked about it. She promised she'd deny everything if someone tried to use the letters against me, although we both knew it would do precious little good if it did come to that. Then last Friday, she came to me. She said she'd discovered who had the letters and she knew someone who could get them back for me. Steal them, actually."

"For how much?"

"Three thousand pounds."

It was less than what she'd demanded from Hendon. And it came to Sebastian that there might very well have been others she'd approached; other rich, powerful men, one of whom might have decided to kill rather than pay for the secrets she had to offer.

He studied the man who sat slumped on the bench, lost in his own thoughts. "Do you think she's the one who took the letters from Davis's rooms in the first place?"

"Rachel?" Lord Frederick considered this a moment, then shook his head. "I don't think so. Although the last few weeks, she seemed afraid of something. I don't know what. She talked about going away, starting over someplace else."

It fit with what the others had told him, Hugh Gordon and the Reverend Finley at St. Jude's. "When were you supposed to meet her? Tuesday?"

Fairchild's chest lifted with a weighty sigh. "I only wish I had. It's what she wanted, but it wasn't easy for me to raise that kind of money. I asked her to give me until Wednesday." He scrubbed one hand across his face, rubbing his eyes with his thumb and forefinger. "I was still getting the money together when I heard she'd been killed."

"So who has the letters now?"

His hand fell back to his side. He looked haggard. Frightened. "I wish I knew. As soon as I heard what had happened to Rachel, I went past the lodging house where she kept her rooms. I had some notion of going up and looking for them, but the constables were there. I didn't dare stop."

Sebastian nodded. So Fairchild had gone to Dorset Court that day. But if he hadn't gone up to search Rachel's rooms, then who had?

Fairchild jerked up from the bench and took an agitated step away before whirling back around. "If those letters are made public, I'll be ruined. Absolutely ruined."

Sebastian studied him dispassionately. "Did Rachel tell you who had the letters?"

A faint flush touched the man's high, aristocratic cheekbones. "Yes. Leo Pierrepont."

"Of course," said Sebastian. "I should have known."

At the far end of the Row, a young blade on a showy,

white-marked chestnut sent his mount cavorting. Sebastian lifted his head and watched the chestnut's four white stockings flash in the thin winter sunlight. And he knew it again, that tantalizing sensation of a thought hovering somewhere on the edges of consciousness, just beyond his grasp.

"Exactly who had she found to steal the letters from Pierrepont? Did she say?"

The other man shook his head. "All I knew was that it had to be done while Pierrepont was out of town for the week, at Lord Edgeworth's country house down in Hampshire. She was hoping to be gone by Thursday, before Pierrepont had a chance to come back and find the letters missing. I could be wrong, but had the impression . . ."

"Yes?"

"He's the one she was afraid of. The one she was running away from."

Sebastian glanced down at the gleaming blade in his hands. The sword stick was a common enough weapon amongst London's noblemen. Sebastian's own father carried one, while Leo Pierrepont was known to have an extensive collection.

Sebastian slid the blade back into its sheath with a quiet hiss. Lord Edgeworth had hosted a party at his Hampshire estate the week before, Sebastian knew; as a part of that set, Pierrepont had undoubtedly been invited. But if he'd been planning to spend the week, something must have changed his mind, for he'd come back in time to host a dinner party on Tuesday night.

The night Rachel York was killed.

Chapter 43

Sir Henry Lovejoy sat in the empty pit of the Stein and watched Hugh Gordon, decked out as Hamlet, rehearse his climatic sword fight with a significantly overweight Laertes.

The discovery of Mary Grant's ravaged body should have removed whatever lingering doubts the magistrate might have had about Lord Devlin's guilt. Lovejoy himself had interviewed their witness, Mrs. Charles Lavery, and he'd found her a solid, no-nonsense woman. If Mrs. Lavery said she'd seen Lord Devlin leaving the lodging house, then Lovejoy was inclined to believe the man had been there. And yet . . .

And yet, the doctor who examined Mary Grant's body had given it as his opinion that she'd been killed earlier in the day, perhaps before noon. And while most people didn't put much stock in such things, Lovejoy had too much respect for the scientific method to ignore the doctor's report. Except that if Devlin hadn't killed Mary Grant, then what was he doing there at her rooms? Why was he still in London at all?

Lovejoy shifted uncomfortably in his seat, remembering his interview with Charles, Lord Jarvis. If Henry's wife, Julia, were still alive, she'd tell him he was being a stubborn fool, trying to understand Sebastian St. Cyr rather than simply concentrating on capturing him. And Henry, he'd tell her that he was doing everything in his power to bring the Viscount in. He just needed to tie up one or two loose ends, for his own satisfaction.

And then Lovejoy realized what he was doing, and heaved a soft sigh. His Julia had been gone from him for almost ten years now, but he still had these little conversations with her, imagining what she would say, what he would say in response.

A thump followed by a bustle of movement and laughing chatter drew his attention back to the stage. The scene had ended. Still wiping his hot face with a towel, Hugh Gordon ran lightly down the steps, to the pit.

"You wanted to speak with me?" he said. He was smiling, but Lovejoy noticed the wariness in his dark eyes, that cautious kind of watchfulness one saw often in the face of a man confronting a magistrate.

"That's right." Stiff with the cold, Lovejoy pushed to his feet. "I understand you and Rachel York were once . . ." He hesitated, searching for an expression that wouldn't offend his moral sensibilities. But any irregular sexual liaison of that sort outraged Lovejoy's strict Evangelical principles. He finally settled on the word, "involved."

Gordon's nostrils flared with a quickly indrawn breath. "Everyone knows who killed her. It's that viscount, Lord Devlin. He did Rachel, and yesterday he got that other one over in Bloomsbury. So why are you here talking to me?"

The aggressiveness of the man's tone took Lovejoy by surprise. "We've been doing some checking into your background, Mr. Gordon, and we've discovered a few things which disturbed us."

"Such as?"

"Does the name Adelaide Hunt mean anything to you?"

The man hesitated, his jaw clenched as he considered his response. "You obviously know it does. I haven't seen the woman in years. What's she to do with anything?"

"I understand you cut her up once, quite badly. In fact, you almost killed her."

"She tell you that?"

Lovejoy said nothing, just looked at the man expectantly.

A muscle bunched along the actor's jaw. "I was defending myself. The bloody woman came at me with a bed warmer. Did she tell you that?"

"As I understand it, you flew into a rage when she attempted to break off the relationship. She wielded the bed warmer to defend herself."

"No charges were ever pressed, now were they?"

Lovejoy drew in a deep breath scented with greasepaint and the faint, lingering tang of orange peels. "Some men make it a habit of cutting up women who try to break off with them. I understand you were particularly angry with Rachel York when she left you for another man."

A faint flush darkened the actor's lean, handsome face. "So? That was almost two years ago now. What is it with you people? I explained all this to that other fellow."

"What other fellow?"

"The one who came around a couple of times, asking questions about Rachel. First he claimed to be her

Cousin Simon Taylor from Worcestershire, then he said
he was a Bow Street Runner."

"What? What did this man look like?"

Gordon shrugged. "Tall, lean, dark. Younger than he
was trying to make himself look. Dressed rather
scruffy."

Lovejoy felt a quickening of interest verging on excitement. *See, Julia,* he thought. *This stubborn fool is
onto something after all.*

For the description fit almost perfectly with that of
the man seen leaving Mary Grant's lodgings. The man
identified by Mrs. Charles Lavery as Viscount Devlin.

~

Edward Maitland was coming down the Public Office's
front steps when Sir Henry Lovejoy made it back to
Queen Square.

"I want you to set a couple of men to watching Hugh
Gordon. Both at the theater, and at home," said
Lovejoy.

The constable drew up in surprise. "What? You don't
seriously think Gordon is our man?"

Lovejoy hadn't entirely discounted the possibility,
but he wasn't about to go into all that with Maitland.
"No, I don't. But Devlin seems to have developed an interest in him. He's already approached Gordon twice,
and he may try to do so again. I want us to be ready for
him."

Chapter 44

That evening, Lady Amanda attended a soirée given at the home of the Duchess of Carlyle.

The signs of looming social disaster were subtle, but there—in the furtive looks cast in Amanda's direction, the whispered conversations that broke off abruptly when she drew too near. Amanda felt a cold anger hardening her heart as she moved with easy determination amidst the steely-eyed matrons and turbaned dowagers. She was Lady Amanda, wife of the Prince's boon companion Lord Wilcox and daughter of the Earl of Hendon, Chancellor of the Exchequer. They would offend her at their peril.

Midway through the evening, she was surprised to see her own husband approaching her through the throng. Having no taste for the whirl of social functions or visits to the theater and opera that occupied his wife's time, Wilcox normally retreated after dinner either to an evening session of the House of Lords or to one of his clubs.

"Something wrong, dear?" she said in a smiling aside as she lifted a glass of champagne from a passing servant's silver tray. "Has Sebastian's latest exploit resulted in your being blackballed from White's? Or has Boney landed at Dover?"

Wilcox's habitual placid smile was firmly in place, but his eyes were grave. "Bayard tells me his uncle paid you a visit this afternoon." Even as he spoke, he kept his gaze moving casually over the glittering crowd. "Is that wise, my dear?"

"Really, Martin. Do you seriously think I had extended Devlin an invitation? Suggested he might want to hide out in the carriage house, or perhaps pose as one of our footmen?"

"No. I suppose not." For one telling moment, Wilcox's smile slipped. "Where the devil *is* he hiding, anyway?"

"He didn't happen to mention it. But unless I miss my guess, he's taken refuge with that light skirt he made such a fool of himself over when he first came down from Oxford."

Wilcox swung his head to stare at her. "You can't be serious."

"Oh, but I am." Amanda set aside her glass. "Ah, there's Lady Bainbridge. Do excuse me, dear." And she left him then, to make use of the information or not, as he chose.

~

Sebastian watched Leo Pierrepont rein in before the open door of his carriage house. Night came early to the streets of London in February; by four, the mews and the gardens leading up to the house were already dark. "Giles!" the Frenchman shouted, his voice echoing hollowly in the cold stillness. "Giles? *Où est tu*?" He waited expectantly. "Charles?"

Swearing to himself, he swung from the saddle to lead the tired chestnut into the stables. He lit the lamp suspended from the rafters, glanced around the softly lit area, then said, "Merde," under his breath and reached to unbuckle his cinch.

From the shadows of an empty stall at the end of the row, Sebastian waited, listening to the muttered grunts of a man unused to the task of unsaddling and grooming his own horse. The smell of warming oil mingled with the scents of hay and oats and horseflesh. In a nearby stall, one of Pierrepont's carriage horses moved restlessly.

Slipping the flintlock pistol from his pocket, Sebastian crept to where the Frenchman, still grumbling, crouched to run a currycomb over his chestnut's wet belly. Sebastian held out the pistol until the muzzle was scant inches from Pierrepont's ear. At the sound of the hammer being pulled back, Pierrepont froze.

"Move very carefully, Monsieur Pierrepont."

Pierrepont turned his head, his gaze focusing on the pistol before lifting to Sebastian's face. "Where are my groom and coachman?"

"Someplace where we don't need to worry about them disturbing us."

The Frenchman straightened slowly. "What do you want?"

"I thought I'd tell you a story."

Pierrepont's eyebrows lifted. "A story."

"A story." Sebastian settled back against the edge of a bale of hay, the pistol still held, loosely, in his hand. "It goes something like this: Once upon a time, in a place we'll call Windsor Castle, there lived a mad old King."

"How original."

"Yes, isn't it? Anyway, while our King slips deeper and deeper into his own mad world, his houses of Parliament in nearby Londontown are busy negotiating the details of a bill that will make the King's eldest son Regent, meaning he will rule in his father's place."

"This is fascinating." Pierrepont leaned against a nearby wooden post and crossed his arms at his chest. "I do hope there's a point to it."

"I'm getting there. The story has a villain, you see. A man named Napoleon."

"Of course. The villain is always a Frenchman."

Sebastian smiled. "Napoleon's country has been fighting a war against our old mad King for close onto twenty years, so naturally Napoleon takes an interest in these negotiations. He realizes this Regency might be a good thing for France."

"And how's that?"

"Well, you see, the King has always aligned himself with a group of men in Parliament we'll call the Tories. Like the old King, the Tories don't like change. They think the way to keep their country strong is to keep the old institutions such as the monarchy and the church strong. And because they're making a tidy profit out of the war, the last thing they want is any kind of peace treaty with our villain, Napoleon."

"War can be quite lucrative."

"For some. But our future Regent, the Prince, has surrounded himself with men who adhere to another party. Let's call them the Whigs, shall we? Now these Whigs, they tend to look to the future, rather than the past. They believe that if their country is to prosper and remain strong, there must be changes. They see that while this long, costly war has made some men very, very rich, the common people of the country have suffered. Terribly. So they say, 'Why are we fighting this war? Napoleon is over there in his country, we're over here in ours. We're the ones who declared war on him. Why don't we simply end this madness and have peace?'"

"Why not, indeed," said Pierrepont with a tight smile.

"Now our villain, Napoleon, he's not particularly anxious to continue this war, either. He's looking forward to negotiating a peace treaty with the Whigs when they come to power. But because he's a clever man, he decides it would be a good idea to increase his bargaining position. It occurs to him that one way to do that would be to have some kind of leverage with the gentleman everyone assumes will become Prime Minister when our Prince forms his new government." Sebastian paused. "Let's call this Whiggish gentleman Lord F, shall we?"

The faintest hint of surprise flickered across the Frenchman's face. "Go on."

"Now Napoleon, he has a secret supporter in Londontown, an individual we'll call the Lion."

Pierrepont huffed a laugh. "Surely you can do better than that, monsieur?"

"Sorry. Anyway, Napoleon instructs the Lion to discover Lord F's weakness. All men have weaknesses, and it doesn't take the Lion long to discover that Lord F has a preference for handsome young men. So the Lion comes up with a plan. He lures Lord F into an affair with a handsome young clerk in a sensitive position— let's say the Foreign Office, shall we? And he arranges it so that the compromising rendezvous take place at the rooms of one of the Lion's assistants, a passionate young revolutionary we'll call . . ." Sebastian hesitated. "Let's call her Rachel, shall we?"

"It's your story."

"So it is. The way I see it, the handsome young clerk entices Lord F to write some very compromising love letters, which find their way into the Lion's possession. The trap is now set. All our villains need do is wait for Lord F to become Prime Minister."

"You are going someplace with this, I trust."

"Almost there," said Sebastian, shifting his weight. "You see, as clever as this plan is, something goes wrong. Something frightens Rachel, and she decides to flee Londontown. She gets the bright idea that if she steals Lord Frederick's incriminating letters—along with a few other valuable documents which the Lion has collected—and sells them to the interested parties, she can make a tidy sum with which to start a new life. She waits until the Lion is out of town, steals the documents, and sets about selling them."

Pierrepont kept his face blank. "Go on."

"Unfortunately for Rachel, the Lion has a change of plans. He comes home early from his country house party. He finds the documents missing, and it doesn't take him long to figure out who has them. He follows Rachel to a meeting she has set up at St. Matthew of the Fields, and he kills her there in a very, very nasty way—as a warning, perhaps, to his other assistants, lest they be inclined to get similar bright ideas in the future."

Pierrepont let his arms dangle loosely at his sides. "It's an entertaining story, *monsieur le vicomte*. You ought to consider writing for the stage. Or for children. But a story is all you have. You've no proof. And no idea at all of what you're really caught up in. You're a fool. You should have left London days ago, while you still could."

Sebastian's lips pulled back into a hard smile. "There's just one thing I don't understand. My mother's affidavit—which I gather Rachel also stole from you; why did you have it? To put pressure on my father?"

Pierrepont assumed an exaggerated expression of consternation. "*Alors.* Is there something in your father's past that would make him vulnerable to pressure?"

"Now who's being the fool?" Sebastian raised the pistol and leveled it at the other man's chest. "What was it for?"

Pierrepont shrugged. "Evidence of dirty little secrets

in the lives of important men are always useful." He glanced toward the darkness beyond the open carriage house doors. But Sebastian had heard it long before—the sound of stealthy footfalls, coming through the garden. Fast.

He slid off the bale, moving behind the Frenchman to catch him around the neck with one forearm and press the pistol's muzzle against his temple.

"Tell them to pull back," Sebastian whispered. Then added, "Now!" when Pierrepont hesitated.

"*Restez-en là*," called Pierrepont. The footsteps stopped.

"It might be a good idea to let them know we're coming out. And don't even think of trying anything," Sebastian added, as Pierrepont called out again.

"You're wrong, you know," said Pierrepont over his shoulder as Sebastian dragged him toward the entrance.

"About what?"

To his surprise, Pierrepont laughed. "About the rest of it, I won't say. But you're wrong in this," he said, as Sebastian let him go and stepped back into the night. "I didn't kill Rachel York."

Chapter 45

$\mathcal{A}$ day of relative inactivity had left Jarvis feeling restless. Restless and impatient for the events to come. In less than thirty-six hours, the Prince of Wales would be sworn in as Regent. Tomorrow would be an entertaining day. Most entertaining.

Some time after midnight, he set aside the report he'd been reading and stretched to his feet. The house lay empty and silent around him, all the troublesome women of his life having long ago retired to their respective rooms.

Making his way down to the library, he poured himself a glass of brandy, then went to unlock the upper right-hand drawer of his desk and ease it open. It wasn't often that Jarvis allowed himself the luxury of gloating, but he indulged himself now, sliding the paper out to hold it for a moment in his hands.

Smiling softly to himself, he was just closing the drawer again when he heard his daughter's voice. "Is something wrong?"

He looked up to find her standing in the doorway, one hand cupped around the flickering flame of her chamberstick to shield it from drafts. She was a tall woman, Hero. Too tall, in Jarvis's way of thinking, and far too thin, with narrow hips and no bosom. She had mousy brown hair she wore unstylishly long and straight, and lately she'd taken to pulling it back in a severe style more suited to some Evangelical missionary than to a young lady of fashion. But she'd let it down tonight, and in the golden glow of the candlelight it struck him suddenly that his daughter might actually be passably pretty, if she'd only try.

He frowned and said, "What's wrong is the way you've taken to doing your hair. You ought to wear it down more often. Get the front cut in curls the way they're doing these days."

She gave a startled trill of laughter. "I'd look ridiculous in curls and you know it. And I wasn't talking about me." Her smile faded into a look of concern. "Are you certain you're all right?"

Jarvis had been blessed with a particularly winning smile. He'd learned long ago to use it, to reward and cajole and mislead. He used it now, and saw the lines of worry on his daughter's face ease as she smiled back at him.

"I'm fine, child," he said, and turned the lock on the desk drawer.

Chapter 46

$\mathcal{K}$at closed her eyes, and smiled. The years of artifice and practiced calculation, of determinedly holding herself aloof, had slowly obliterated the memories. She'd forgotten what it could be like, forgotten the warm, inner glow of joy that could come from palms sliding over beloved, sweat-slicked skin. Forgotten, too, the stomach-clenching thrill of seeing familiar dark shoulders rise above her, the breath-catching delight of strong fingers capturing her hand to hold her a willing prisoner while soft lips went aroving. She'd forgotten that beyond mere physical sensation and release, far beyond it, lay rapture and a union so spiritual in essence as to reach the sublime.

The night around them lay quiet and dark, filled only with the ragged twining of their breath and the crackle of the fire on Kat's bedroom hearth. Hands trembling, she clutched Sebastian's tensing body to her, her legs tightening around his waist as she felt the shudders start to rip through him, heard him say her name in a tortured cry, felt his body pulsing so deep within her own.

Afterward, he smoothed her hair from the dampness of her forehead, nestled her into the curve of his arm as he eased himself down beside her and kissed her softly below her ear. His smile was tender in the night. But already his

eyelids were fluttering closed. She felt the strain and wor-
ries of the long day drain out of him, felt his arms go limp
around her, and knew he slept.

Sometimes, she'd learned, he had nightmares, memories of the war that could jerk him awake wide-eyed and
sweating. But for now his sleep was undisturbed. Lying
quietly beside him, she listened to him breathe, watched
the play of firelight over the strong bones of his face.
But when the emotions surging within her threatened to
become overwhelming, she slipped away from him carefully so as not to wake him. Catching up a cashmere
shawl from the back of a nearby chair, she went to stand
looking out over the mist-shrouded parterres of the garden below.

She had never stopped loving him. She supposed
that in some secret, unacknowledged corner of her
heart she'd always known the truth. She knew now, too,
that beneath all the throbbing anger and hurt of the
last six years, Sebastian's love for her still burned, a
warm and beautiful thing. But the hardest part of all
was facing the stark realization that she was never
going to stop loving him, that this pain of loving him
would go on and on, stretching into all the bleak and
lonely years to come.

Letting the drapes settle back into place across the
cold-frosted window, she turned again to the man who
still lay gently sleeping in her bed. Her gaze roved over
him, over the proud, aristocratic line of nose and jaw.
For one weak moment she allowed herself to fall into a
dangerous reverie, a seductive fantasy in which she
imagined the future that could be theirs together if Sebastian were never to clear himself of this terrible crime
of which he'd been accused; if rather than someday taking his place as the Earl of Hendon, he were to remain
a fugitive forever.

But she stopped short of actually *wishing* it might be, although a sigh stretched her chest and tears she would never let fall stung her eyes. For it was because Kat loved Sebastian so much that she had driven him from her six years ago. And she knew well this man she loved. She knew that as long as there was breath within him, Sebastian would keep fighting to clear his name.

Or die trying.

～◯～

The next morning, the sun was little more than a faint promise on a misty horizon when Sebastian returned to the Rose and Crown. He was in his room having breakfast when Tom came in, bringing with him the smells of London, of snow and coal smoke and the roasting meats sold by the sidewalk vendors. "Gor, it's colder than a witch's tit out there," he said, stomping his feet and blowing on his stiff red hands before holding them out to Sebastian's fire.

Sebastian looked up from buttering his toast. "Where are your gloves?"

"I give 'em to Paddy."

"Paddy?"

"Aye. Paddy O'Neal. He's a neighbor of that actor cove, Hugh Gordon. And get this: accordin' to Paddy, Gordon pinched the 'ackney Paddy'd sent one o' the neighborhood lads to fetch for 'im last Tuesday night. 'E even threatened to plant Paddy a facer when the old codger give him what for."

Sebastian pushed back his chair and stood up. "Are you certain it was Tuesday night? This—er, old codger could have his days mixed up."

"Not that old bugger. Every Tuesday for the past fifteen years, 'e's been takin' part in a Perpetual Devotion on Lower Weymouth Street. His slot is from nine to ten, and that's where 'e was goin' when Gordon pinched the carriage."

Sebastian looked at the boy in surprise. "And how did you come to know about such things as Perpetual Devotions?"

A faint line of color touched the boy's cheeks, but all he said was, "I knows."

Sebastian let that pass. "So Gordon went out before nine?"

Tom nodded. "That's right. And get this—our Paddy even knows where the cove went—'eard 'im giving orders to the jarvey."

"And?"

"He told the 'ackney driver to take 'im to Westminster."

Chapter 47

Kat was in her dressing room, attending to her correspondence some hours after Sebastian had left, when her flustered maid showed Leo Pierrepont to the room. Kat looked up from her writing desk in surprise. "Is this wise, Leo?"

Pierrepont tossed his hat onto a nearby table and went to stand before a window overlooking the street. "He was here last night, was he?"

"Sebastian, you mean? Dear Leo. What have you been doing? Peeking through my curtains?"

He kept his gaze on the scene outside the window. "And Lord Stoneleigh?"

Kat set aside her pen and leaned back in her chair. "I've grown tired of his lordship. I've no doubt he'll recover from the heartbreak in"—she hesitated, a cynical smile touching her lips—"a fortnight, shall we say?"

Leo said nothing. Their association had always been like this. Kat had made it clear from the beginning that she would choose her own lovers—or victims, as Leo liked to refer to them. For while Kat frequently cooperated with Leo, she had never precisely worked for him. He might make requests, but he knew better than to try to give her orders.

He swung suddenly away from the window, his face unexpectedly drawn in the pale morning light. "This involvement of yours with Devlin is dangerous. You realize that, don't you? He suspects that my relationship with Paris is not precisely as I would have people believe it to be."

Kat pushed away from her writing desk and stood up. "As long as it's only a suspicion—"

"He also knows about the missing documents."

Kat stood perfectly still. "What missing documents, Leo?"

His thin nostrils flared on a suddenly indrawn breath. "Last week while I was in Hampshire someone took some papers from the hidden compartment in my library's mantel. A man and a woman, working together."

"Who do you suspect? Me?"

Leo shook his head. "This was the work of amateurs." He hesitated, then said, "I think it was probably Rachel."

Kat felt a shiver of apprehension run up her spine. "What sort of documents are we talking about here, Leo?"

One of his shoulders twitched in a typically Gallic gesture. "Love letters from Lord Frederick to a handsome young clerk in the Foreign Office. The birth certificate of a child born on the Continent some years ago to Princess Caroline. That sort of thing."

"What else?"

Amusement suddenly lightened his intense gray eyes. "You don't really expect me to tell you, now do you, *mon amie*?"

Kat did not smile. "Anything that implicates me?"

He shook his head. "No. You should be safe enough—unless you do something foolish. I, on the other hand, might find it prudent to leave London precipitously. If so, I'll try to send you word. You know where to go?"

"Yes." It had all been arranged before, including the name of the out-of-the-way inn south of town where she would try to meet with him, if possible, should he be forced to flee England.

Kat watched him reach for his hat. This theft of what must have been a valuable cache of documents cast Rachel's death in a new, sinister light. "Tell me something, Leo. Why did you return early from Lord Edgeworth's country house party last Tuesday?"

He swung to look back at her. "I received word that an emissary from Paris would be contacting me. Why?"

"So you were meeting with him during the hour or so that you neglected your guests?"

"Yes. He arrived earlier than I expected." Leo cocked his head, his assessing gaze studying her face. "Are you back to thinking that I killed Rachel, hmm?"

"It would appear you had reason."

Pierrepont settled his hat on his head. "So did your young viscount."

"Did he? And how's that?"

The Frenchman smiled. "Ask him."

~

Sebastian was just leaving the Rose and Crown and heading toward Covent Garden when a scruffy boy of about eight came running after him with a note from Paul Gibson.

Come see me when you get the chance, the Irishman had written in a hasty scrawl. *I'll be at the Chalks Street Almshouse until noon.*

Tossing the boy a penny, Sebastian hesitated, then turned his steps toward the East End.

Housed in a soot-blackened cluster of ancient stone

buildings that had once been a Franciscan monastery, the Chalks Street Almshouse lay on the edge of Spitalfields, not far from Shepherds' Place. Run by a private benevolent society as a humane alternative to the city's public workhouses and poorhouses, the almshouse provided clothing and food and limited shelter to the area's poor. Paul Gibson could often be found there at odd hours, bandaging workingmen's wounds, examining infants that refused to thrive, and surreptitiously dispensing preventatives to the district's growing population of prostitutes.

"They get younger and younger every year," said Gibson with a sigh, as he drew Sebastian into the small, unheated alcove allotted to him by the almshouse directors. "I don't think I've seen one over the age of sixteen today."

Through the room's single, grime-incrusted leaded window, Sebastian watched the doctor's last patient dart furtively across the street. The girl looked all of twelve. "It's not a vocation conducive to longevity."

"Unfortunately, no," said Gibson, his eyes blessedly clear and bright this morning. "It occurred to me the area's *filles de joie* might be a good source of information about gentlemen with certain vile tastes, but I haven't turned up anything of use in that respect so far." Gibson wiped his hands on a towel and went to close the door to the cabinet where he kept a few meager supplies. "There is one thing I thought you should know about, though. I've had this nagging feeling ever since I finished Rachel York's autopsy—this feeling that I was overlooking something. For the longest time I couldn't figure out what it was, but then last night when I was giving my lecture at St. Thomas's on musculature, it came to me."

Sebastian swung away from the window, his gaze searching his friend's face. "What's that?"

"One of the first things I noticed when I was bathing Rachel York's body was that her hand had been broken. From the nature of the break, it was obvious it had occurred after rigor mortis had set in, which is why I didn't attach much importance to it at first. I simply assumed it was done by the woman hired to lay out the body—it's often necessary, you know. But last night, I got to thinking . . ."

"Yes?"

"If the laying-out woman had to break Rachel's hand to get it open, then it must have been clenched. Like this." Gibson held up his fist. "But we know Rachel was scratching at her attacker." He uncurled his fingers into a clawing position. "Like this." He relaxed his hand. "If she'd been raped before death, then I'd say perhaps she clenched her fists at the end, the way a person tends to do when they're trying to endure something painful. But we know that's not the case."

"So what are you saying? That she died clasping something in her hand?"

Gibson nodded. "I suspect so. Of course it could have been something as innocuous as a clump of hair she'd torn from her attacker."

"Or it could have been something considerably more significant. There's no way we'll ever know now."

"Maybe. Maybe not. I'm trying to locate the woman who laid out the body. If I can convince her I don't mean to prosecute her for theft, she might tell me."

Sebastian went to stand again beside the window overlooking the narrow, refuse-filled street. Dark gray clouds hung low over the city, promising rain. After a moment, the Irishman came to stand beside him, his gaze, like Sebastian's, on the lowering sky. "Have you given any more thought to taking a little vacation in America?"

Sebastian gave a soft laugh. "I'm not likely to have much luck finding Rachel York's killer in some place like Baltimore or Philadelphia, now am I?"

"It's not Rachel York I'm thinking about. She's dead. It's Sebastian St. Cyr who's worrying me."

Sebastian shook his head. "I can't leave, Paul. There's more involved in this than I realized at first. Far more."

Paul Gibson perched on a nearby stool while Sebastian outlined Rachel's involvement with Leo Pierrepont. "So what do you think?" said the Irishman when Sebastian had finished. "That Pierrepont found out she'd taken the papers from him and killed her?"

"Either him, or one of the men against whom the French were collecting damaging information. I doubt Lord Frederick and my father are the only men Rachel approached. Any one of them could have killed her."

The doctor nodded. "She was involved in dark doings, that girl. Dark doings with dangerous men."

"I suspect the pages torn from her appointment book are linked to Lord Frederick and Pierrepont, but I'm beginning to wonder if I'm ever going to know for sure." He blew out a harsh breath. "It's even possible Pierrepont's documents have nothing to do with her death at all, beyond explaining why she was at that church so late at night."

Gibson studied him through narrowed eyes. "You've found something else, have you?"

Sebastian met his friend's gaze, and nodded. "My nephew, Bayard. He seems to have been infatuated with the woman. Followed her everywhere."

"A common enough occurrence, surely, when one is dealing with beautiful actresses and opera dancers, and callow young men newly on the town?"

"Perhaps. Except that the Saturday before Rachel

died, Bayard flew into a rage at Steven's and threatened to kill her. Said he was going to rip her head off."

"Ah. Not so common. Is he capable of such a thing, do you think?"

"I never liked him as a child. He could be cruel. Vicious even . . ." Sebastian let his voice trail off. "Yet it doesn't seem possible that he could have done it, given that he spent the evening in a very public display of riotous excess before passing out in front of Cribb's Parlor. His own father took him home."

Gibson sat silent for a moment, lost in thought. "No, it doesn't seem possible, does it? And there's that other woman, Mary Grant. Why would Bayard track her down and kill her?"

Sebastian shook his head. "No reason I can think of. Although for that matter, the same could be said of Hugh Gordon. Rachel owed him money, and he's badly dipped enough that he might well have killed her in a fit of temper if she refused to pay. But why the maid? It doesn't make any sense. Unless—" Sebastian broke off suddenly.

"Unless . . . what?"

Sebastian sat forward. "Unless Gordon hunted Mary Grant down because he was looking for the papers Rachel had taken. Think about it: Gordon knew Rachel was involved with Pierrepont and the French. What if he also knew she'd stolen the documents and was planning to sell them? He might well have decided to get his hands on them and sell them himself."

"And where does Mr. Gordon say he was last Tuesday night?"

Sebastian pushed away from the stool. "He says he was at home, studying his lines. But according to a cranky old Irishman named Paddy O'Neal, Gordon went off in a hackney just before nine o'clock."

"Any idea where he went?"

Sebastian smiled. "Westminster."

~

Sebastian found Hugh Gordon in a cloth warehouse in the Haymarket, where the actor was inspecting an array of Bath superfine on a shelf against the side wall.

"Oh, God. It's you again," he said, when Sebastian came to stand beside him. "What the devil do you want now?"

"How about the truth for a change?" Sebastian leaned against the nearby dark-paneled wall and smiled. "You followed Rachel to St. Matthew's last Tuesday night. Didn't you?"

"What?" Gordon glanced nervously over his shoulder. "Of course not. I told you, I was home last Tuesday night, studying lines."

"That's not what Paddy O'Neal says."

"Paddy? What the hell has that dotty old Irishman to do with this?"

"He says you pinched the hackney he'd called that night. And took it to Westminster."

"He's lying."

"Is he? You needed money—lots of money, more even than Rachel owed you. I think you found out about the documents Rachel took from Pierrepont and came up with the bright idea of scaring her into giving them to you. Only, she refused." Sebastian leaned in close and lowered his voice. "That's when you grabbed her, wasn't it? Maybe even gave her a shake, just like you used to do. Only, this time Rachel fought back. Tried to claw your eyes out. So you backhanded her—"

"This is crazy," Gordon began.

"—across the face," continued Sebastian without pause. "And when she came at you again, you pulled the blade from your walking stick and slit her throat. And then, because fighting with women always makes you hard, you raped her—"

"*What?*" The word came out in a low-voiced explosion of shock. "What are you saying? That Rachel was raped *after* she was killed?"

"That's right," said Sebastian. "I suppose it takes something out of a man, giving in to that kind of bloodlust and passion. Maybe that's why it wasn't until the next day that you finally made it around to Rachel's rooms, hoping to find the papers there. Only, her maid had cleaned the place out by then, hadn't she? So you had to track *her* down. And when you found her, you killed her, too. Why, I wonder. Because she didn't want to let you take the papers? Or was it because by then you'd realized you'd acquired a taste for dead women?"

Gordon's Adam's apple moved painfully up and down as he swallowed, hard. "I swear to God, it's not what you think."

Sebastian pushed away from the wall, his hands hanging loose at his sides.

Gordon took a quick step back and licked dry lips with a nervous dart of his tongue. "You're right. I did go to Westminster that night. But I wasn't anywhere near St. Matthew's." He hesitated, then said in a rush, "There's this woman. Her . . . her family wouldn't approve, if they knew she was seeing me, so we meet at an inn. A place near the Abbey. The Three Feathers, it's called. We were there half the night. You can check with the innkeeper if you want."

Sebastian nodded. It would be easy enough, as the man said, to check. A flicker of movement in the street drew Sebastian's attention to the shop's bowed front window. It had begun to rain, a fine mist slowly turning the pavement dark and wet. He glanced back at the actor. Hugh Gordon, too, was watching the street.

Sebastian studied the man's suddenly heightened color. It occurred to him that while Gordon had expressed shock at the idea that Rachel had been raped after death, he had shown no surprise when Sebastian mentioned the documents taken from Pierrepont. "And yet you did know about the papers Rachel took from Pierrepont."

Gordon jerked. "All right. Yes. I did know. Rachel let it slip when I was pressing her for the money. But I swear to God, *I didn't kill her.*"

Sebastian shifted so that the actor was between him and the shop's front door. "Who else knew Rachel had those papers?"

"I don't know. How could I? Why don't you ask her lover?" The actor's lower lip protruded in a pronounced sneer. "He ought to know. After all, he helped her steal them."

A man hovered just outside the shop door. He had his head turned so that Sebastian could see little of his face. But there was something familiar about the set of his shoulders, the angle of his jaw. "Her lover?" said Sebastian sharply. "Who? What's the man's name?"

"Donatelli. Giorgio Donatelli," said the actor just as Edward Maitland, followed by another constable, came hurtling through the shop's front door.

Chapter 48

Sebastian sprinted toward the back of the shop, the leather soles of his Hessians slipping on the highly polished wooden floorboards.

"Halt!" shouted Edward Maitland from behind him. "Halt in the King's name!"

A trestle table piled high with bolts of silks and satins reared up before them. Sebastian careened into it, the board flying from its trestles to knock both constables off their feet behind him.

"Stop him!" shouted Maitland, scrambling up onto his hands and knees in a shimmering sea of unfurling cloth.

Someone grabbed a handful of Sebastian's coat. Twisting around, Sebastian heaved a small case of notions into the ponderous gut of a middle-aged, red-faced man whose mouth opened, bleating air. He let go Sebastian's coat.

He could see the rear door through a workshop at the back. Praying the damn thing was unlocked, Sebastian raced toward it and smiled as he felt the latch give beneath his hand.

He cleared the small back stoop in one leap to land in a narrow alleyway, his boots sending up sprays of muddy water as he fled past a pile of smashed wooden crates and barrels rimmed with rusting iron. He rounded the corner onto Panton Street just as Edward Maitland erupted out of the shop's back door with a shout lost in a sudden, thundering downpour of rain.

Sebastian fled west through Leicester Square, dodging between a high-perch phaeton and a scarlet-bodied barouche. The thong of a whip snapped close; wood splintered as horses drew up to a snorting, head-tossing stand. A woman screamed.

Sebastian ran on, the wind whipping at his coat, the rain driving hard in his face. Shaking his head to clear the water from his eyes, he threw a quick glance over his shoulder to find Edward Maitland holding steady at about a hundred yards behind him, arms and knees pumping. The second constable had fallen away.

They were in that part of town where the fashionable streets of Piccadilly and Pall Mall fell away quickly to the narrow byways and seedy alleys of Covent Garden. The paving beneath Sebastian's boots grew rough, the streets increasingly crowded. A huddle of ragged urchins cheered as Maitland slipped on a pile of manure and almost went down; an old woman in a tattered shawl called out, "God save you, young man!" as Sebastian sprinted past.

Then he heard Maitland shout, "Stop that man! He's a murderer!" Looking up, Sebastian saw the top of the street blocked by a troop of Bow Street Horse Patrol on their way back from the city's outskirts: three men in blue and red, mounted astride big bay hacks.

They spurred their mounts forward, hooves thundering in the narrow space between the two rows of old half-timbered houses. A side street opened up beside him and Sebastian pelted down it, only to find himself caught up in an eddy of ragged paupers, bird-chested men with stooped shoulders, and dirty-faced women in tattered gowns, their bone-thin hands clutching squalling infants wrapped in shawls. There were children, too: mat-haired toddlers and half-grown youngsters dressed in rags, their bare arms and legs covered with running sores. Here were the poor and desperate of the city, who had descended on St. Martin's Workhouse in search of outdoor assistance and been turned away.

Sebastian fought to push his way through as the crowd swirled around the workhouse. Then a man at the end of the street seized an apple seller's barrel and tossed it through the window of a nearby bakery. Shattered glass flew, setting off a roar that wavered through that pushing, seething sea of pinched faces and sunken eyes. "Bread! Free bread!"

The mob surged forward, a starving tide that swelled around Sebastian, carrying him into Flemming's Row. And there at the top of the Row stood Edward Maitland, the three riders in the familiar blue and red of the Bow Street House Patrol ranged behind him. The horses stood with feet braced, heads jerking, nostrils flaring as the Bow Street men held their mounts steady, forming a virtual sieve of horseflesh through which the crowd streamed, surging ever forward, carrying Sebastian with them.

Twisting around, Sebastian fought to turn back, but the momentum of the mob was too great. He could see the flush of triumph in Maitland's fair, handsome face, the wild exultation in his eyes as he and the Bow Street men simply waited for the crowd to drag Sebastian to them.

He was reminded of the riptide in the cove where he often swam as a boy. It could be a deadly thing, that cold tide, pulling the unwary inexorably out to sea. They'd learned early, he and his brothers, that the only way to fight the tide was to go with it. And so Sebastian quit fighting now and simply allowed the mob to take him, only using his height and weight to inch his way deliberately to one side, first to the curb, then up onto the narrow footpath fronting the row of houses opposite St. Martin's.

Once the houses here had been grand, of three and more stories. But they had long since deteriorated into poor lodging houses, their sagging gutters sluicing rainwater, their broken windows stuffed with rags, their street doors either unlatched or missing entirely. He was careful to keep his gaze fixed on the men at the top of the street, lest some furtive glance betray his intent. And so Sebastian knew the instant it dawned upon Maitland what was about to happen.

With a quickly shouted warning to the Bow Street men, Maitland started forward, just as Sebastian ducked through the dark doorway that opened up beside him.

He found himself in a dimly lit hall stinking of urine and damp and rot. Once the walls had been covered in figured scarlet silk, which now hung in curling brown tatters from stained plaster fallen away in great patches to show the bare wood of the lath beneath. In an open doorway on his left stood a dark-haired little girl of about five, holding what looked like a newborn baby. The room behind her was empty.

She just stood there, silent and wide-eyed, and watched as Sebastian sprinted down the hall, past the broken banisters and bare, sagging steps of what had once been a grand sweeping staircase. The back door stood half ajar and Sebastian slammed through it on a run. Leaping off the broken stoop, he crossed a small yard bordered on two sides by looming, high brick walls and strewn with broken tiles and staved-in barrels and molding, stinking piles of refuse. What had once been a coach house lay at the bottom of the yard, but when Sebastian pushed against its iron-bound oak door, he found it locked.

"*Bloody hell*," he swore, pounding one fist against the stout panels. From the street on the far side of the house came shouts and the sudden, insistent ringing of the alarm bell. "Bloody hell," he said again, swinging around, his shoulders pressing back against the door.

Beside him, a set of outside steps curled up to the loft. Pushing off, he bolted up the stairs. The hutch door at the top was locked, too. Sebastian kicked out once, twice. Wood splintered beneath his boot and the door swung inward on creaking hinges.

The loft was a crudely partitioned space. He crossed the room. Moldering piles of old hay crunched beneath his boots and sent up dust clouds to dance in the dim shaft of light filtering through the grime-and-cobweb-choked casement opposite. Throwing open the window, Sebastian swung first one leg, then the other over the sill and eased himself through the narrow space. The rain was coming down harder again, striking his bare face with cold, needlelike stabs. Lowering the weight of his body on his stretched arms, Sebastian sucked in a deep breath and let himself drop.

He hit the slimy pavement below in a roll and came up at a run, his feet slipping and sliding on a sour-smelling sludge of rotten cabbage leaves and old straw and unidentifiable muck. Ahead, the broken arch of the old mews opened up onto a side lane, the crowd thin enough here that he could push his way through, heading away from the workhouse and Maitland and the Bow Street Horse Patrol. From somewhere behind him came a shout, then another, and the renewed ringing of the alarm bell. Sebastian ducked his head against the rain and walked on, just another ragged, wet, grime-smeared man, unremarkable except for his height and the lean good health of his frame.

Chapter 49

*G*iorgio Donatelli hurried home through the early afternoon rain, a loaf of bread under one arm. Ducking beneath his front door's shallow overhang, he was fumbling with his keys when Sebastian moved up behind him.

"Here. Allow me," said Sebastian, reaching past the stiffening Italian to push open the door.

"Mother of God," whispered Donatelli, his face paling as the bread started to slip from his grasp. "Not you again."

Sebastian caught the bread just before it hit the stoop, and gave the artist a wide smile. "Let's have a little chat, shall we?"

~

"You didn't tell me you and Rachel were lovers," said Sebastian.

Donatelli sat in a worn, tapestry-covered armchair beside the parlor fire, his elbows on his knees, his dark curly head sunk into his hands. He lifted his head slowly, his jaw hardening. "I know this country of yours, the way you English are about foreigners."

Sebastian stood on the far side of the room, his shoulders against the wall, his arms crossed at his chest.

He knew his nation, too, knew its arrogance and its fears and its willingness to blame anyone foreign, without due process or anything even vaguely approaching rational thought. Donatelli was right; if the authorities had known the Italian was Rachel's lover, it would have been Donatelli they'd have moved to arrest, however much the evidence might have pointed to Sebastian.

"I've heard Rachel was planning to leave London," said Sebastian. "Did you know?"

Donatelli surged to his feet, his dark eyes flashing. "What are you suggesting? That she was planning to leave *me*? That I flew into a jealous rage when I found out and killed her? Mother of God, of course I knew. She was carrying my baby!"

Sebastian held himself very still. "So you were both planning to leave? Is that it? Why? After years of struggling you're finally being offered more commissions than you can handle, while Rachel had a promising career ahead of her on the London stage. Why would either of you want to throw all that away?"

Donatelli went to stand beside the hearth, one hand resting on the mantel, his gaze on the fire. After a moment, he let his breath out in a long sigh, and it was as if he let go all his rage with it. "We were going to Italy. To Rome. Rachel . . . Rachel was afraid of something. I don't know what. She wouldn't tell me what it was. She said it was better I didn't know."

"But you knew she was passing whatever information she picked up from her lovers to the French via Pierrepont."

Donatelli nodded, his lip curling in disdain. "It's amazing the things men will let slip in an effort to impress a beautiful woman."

Sebastian studied the other man's strong profile. He wondered at the sanguinity with which the painter could discuss the woman he loved flirting with other men, perhaps even coaxing them into her bed in her quest for information. "Did you know she stole a collection of documents from Pierrepont?"

Donatelli nodded, his gaze still fixed on the glowing coals. "God forgive me, I even helped her. Last Sunday, while Pierrepont was in the country, I distracted the butler while she slipped into Pierrepont's library. She knew right where he kept them, in a secret compartment in the mantelpiece. He'd had just such a hiding place contrived for her, you see, in her rooms in Dorset Court."

"Exactly how many documents did she take?"

Donatelli shrugged. "I know there was an envelope containing some half dozen of Lord Frederick's letters, but that wasn't all. I think she was planning to contact three or four different people. I don't know for sure. I didn't want any part of it. I told her it was dangerous, what she was doing, that it was like blackmail. But she said it wasn't, that the people she was selling those papers to would be glad to get them." His voice trailed away into a tortured whisper. "I was afraid something like this would happen."

"And yet you went looking for the papers yourself, when you knew she was dead," said Sebastian. He was remembering what Kat had told him, about the young man who'd searched Rachel's rooms the morning after her death. The young man with a key.

Donatelli glanced around, dark color staining his high cheekbones. "I was afraid—afraid that whoever had killed Rachel would come after me, too. I thought maybe if I had the documents, if I could give them to him . . ."

"Give them to whom?" said Sebastian sharply. "Pierrepont? Do you think he knew it was Rachel who took the papers from his house?"

"Perhaps. I wouldn't be surprised if he'd noticed something was wrong these last few weeks. She wasn't herself."

"Because of what she was doing for Pierrepont?"

"I don't think so. She was proud of what she did, of the part she was playing in the fight to bring republicanism and social justice to this country. But then . . ."

"Then what?"

"I don't know. It was as if someone was making her do something she didn't want to do, something that frightened her. When she found out about the baby . . ." His voice broke and he had to swallow. "She decided we needed to leave. That's when she came up with the idea of taking the documents from Pierrepont and selling them, so we'd have money to start over in Rome."

"Do you think someone discovered she was passing secrets to the French?"

Donatelli swung away from the fireplace, his clenched hands coming up to press against his lips. "I'm not sure. Perhaps. It might have had something to do with that Whig—the one they were saying would be named Prime Minister when the Prince becomes Regent tomorrow."

"You mean Lord Frederick?"

"Yes, that's the one," said Donatelli. "Lord Frederick Fairchild. Pierrepont was using Rachel in a scheme to try to control him." He let his hands fall to his sides. "You have heard, haven't you? About Pierrepont?"

Sebastian shook his head, aware of a deep tremor of disquiet. "What about Pierrepont?"

"The government has moved against him. He's been denounced as a spy, his house raided."

Sebastian shoved away from the wall. "And Pierrepont himself? Is he under arrest?"

"No. Either he's very lucky, or someone warned him

in advance, because he fled. They say he's already left London." Donatelli's lips twisted into a wry smile. "It's ironic, isn't it? All that scheming to entrap a man who won't even be Prime Minister."

"What? What do you mean?"

"You are very poorly informed, are you not? It was announced this morning. The Prince has decided not to ask the Whigs to form a government. The Tories will remain in power."

⁓

By the time Sebastian reached Lord Frederick's townhouse on George Street, the rain had slowed to a light drizzle.

A pattern was beginning to emerge, he thought, a tangled web of plot and counterplot. The key features might still be blurred and indistinct, but they were coming more and more into focus.

Raising his hand, Sebastian beat a sharp tattoo on the townhouse door. "A Mr. Simon Taylor," he said when the door swung inward to reveal a somber butler with ruddy cheeks, an impressive girth, and the requisite expression of haughty disdain, "to see Lord Frederick."

The man's features remained admirably bland as he took in the full insult of Sebastian's Rosemary Lane breeches and coat, now soaking wet from the rain, and smeared here and there with malodorous muck from his run through the back alleys and stews of the city. The butler's first instinct, obviously, was to send such a visitor to the service entrance. But there must have been something about Sebastian's demeanor and calm self-confidence that gave the butler pause. He hesitated, then said, "Is his lordship expecting you?"

"He should be. I am Rachel York's cousin."

The man gave a rarified sniff. "Wait here," he said, and turned toward the hall. . . .

Just as the sharp *boom* of a pistol shot reverberated on the far side of the closed library door.

Chapter 50

Sir Henry Lovejoy was at his desk, dozing lightly after a pleasant meal of steak and kidney pie at the corner tavern, when he was jerked awake by his clerk's apologetic hiss.

"Sir Henry?" said Collins, his bald head appearing around the door frame. "There's a lady here to see you. A lady who refuses to give her name."

Lovejoy could see her now, a delicately built young woman fashionably dressed in a redingote of soft blue with a matching, heavily veiled round hat. She waited until the clerk had reluctantly withdrawn, then lifted her veil to reveal the pale, troubled features of Melanie Talbot.

"Mrs. Talbot." Lovejoy pushed hastily to his feet. "You need not have put yourself to the trouble of coming here. If you'd sent a message—"

"No," she said with more force than he would have expected. She looked fragile, this woman, with her fine bone structure and slight frame and sad eyes, but she was not. "I've waited too long as it is. I should have told the truth from the very beginning." She sucked in a deep breath, then said in a rush, "Devlin was with me the night that girl was killed."

Lovejoy came around his desk, one hand outstretched to usher his visitor toward a chair. "Mrs. Talbot, I understand your desire to help the Viscount, but believe me when I say that this is entirely unnecessary—"

"Unnecessary?" She jerked away from him, her blue eyes flashing with unexpected fire. "What do you think? That I'm making this up? John swore he'd kill me if he ever found out I'd seen Sebastian again. Do you think I would risk that? For a lie?"

Lovejoy stopped, his hand falling to his side, all the old doubts about this case blooming anew within him. "What are you saying? That you met Lord Devlin last Tuesday evening despite your husband's prohibition?"

She went to stand before the window overlooking the square. "John told me about the duel—bragged about it, about how he was going to kill Sebastian."

"So you . . . what? Thought to warn his lordship that your husband intended to shoot to kill? Surely his lordship was aware of that?"

She shook her head, her lips curling up unexpectedly into a wry smile. "John could never have bested Sebastian. I went to Sebastian to secure his promise that he would not kill my husband."

She swung away from the window. "That surprises you, does it?" she said when Lovejoy only stared at her. "You think that if I were truly miserable with my husband I would have been glad to be rid of him in whatever way possible. You don't understand what it's like for a woman. As difficult as my life is, John is all I have. My father would never take me back. If anything happens to my husband, I'll be left destitute. On the streets. I couldn't face that."

"Where did you meet with Lord Devlin?"

"In a quiet corner of the park. I don't think anyone saw us. I swear, all we did was talk. But even if John could be brought to believe that, it wouldn't matter. He'd—" Her voice cracked and she broke off.

Lovejoy watched her slim throat work as she swallowed. There were bruises there, he realized, nearly hidden by the lace edging of her dress. Four bruises in the shape of a man's fingerprints. "What time was this?"

"From half past five until just before eight."

It must have taken a considerable effort, Lovejoy thought, for Captain John Talbot's beautiful young wife to convince Lord Devlin not to kill her abusive husband. But if she were telling the truth, it would have been virtually impossible for Devlin to have made it to the Lady Chapel of St. Matthew of the Fields in Westminster in time to kill Rachel York either before or after his meeting with Mrs. Talbot.

If she were telling the truth.

Lovejoy fixed her with a hard stare. "What made you decide to come forward with this now?"

A hint of color touched her pale cheeks. "I should have told you the truth before. But Sebastian had sent me a note, through my sister." Opening her reticule, she drew forth a torn, creased piece of paper and handed it to Lovejoy. "He warned me to keep silent. I kept hoping you'd realize that it was all a mistake, your thinking Sebastian was somehow involved in that woman's death, that I wouldn't need to say anything. That John need never know. . . ."

Lovejoy stared down at the hastily written words on the scrap of paper. The ink was smudged, as if with tears. "There is no need for you to say anything."

"What?" She shook her head, her eyes wide, not comprehending. "What are you saying?"

"I'm saying that there is no point for you to put yourself at risk by coming forward with this information. Thanks to the duel, your association with Lord Devlin is

well known and the worst possible implications have
been read into it. It will simply be assumed that you've
made this story up, that you are lying to protect the man
you love."

"But it's the truth." Her narrowed eyes searched his
face. "You believe me, don't you?"

"As a man, here and now, I would probably say yes.
But as a judge, weighing your testimony against the
other evidence in court?" He shrugged. "I think not."

"But that's absurd."

Lovejoy tucked the Viscount's note into his pocket.
"That's the law."

Chapter 51

*L*ord Frederick's butler seized the brass handle of the library door, his eyes going wide. "It's locked."

Sebastian thrust the man aside and kicked out hard. The wood splintered beneath his boot heel and the door slammed open against the wall with a shattering crash.

The room beyond lay in semidarkness. The fire in the grate had been allowed to burn low, and someone had drawn the heavy brocade drapes across the windows. The only light came from a flickering brass oil lamp on the desk, the frosted glass shade casting a soft glow over what was left of Lord Frederick Fairchild.

He lay sprawled back at an unnatural angle in his desk chair, one hand dangling limply toward the carpet. Blood was everywhere—on the polished wooden desktop, on the tufted leather chair, the bookcases and paneled walls beyond. Sebastian thought, at first, that the man who had killed Rachel York and Mary Grant must somehow have made it here to this house before him. Then his gaze fell on the neat little ivory-handled pistol still gripped in Lord Frederick's clenched hand, and he understood.

Swiping a trickle of mingling rainwater and sweat from his face, Sebastian crossed the room's Oriental carpet to jerk open the drapes at the windows overlooking the rear garden. The pale light of a rainy winter's afternoon suffused the room. Fairchild had held the pistol's muzzle against his temple, shattering the right side of his head into a bloody, pulpy mess. Sebastian was just turning from the window when the man's chest jerked, his mouth opening as he sucked in air and breathed. He'd blown away the better part of the side of his skull, so that Sebastian could see the shiver of the man's brain beneath the white bone of his skull and the torn, bloody flesh of his scalp. But he wasn't dead yet.

"*Merciful heavens*," said the butler with a startled gasp, one fist pressing against his lips as he fled the room. From the hall came the sound of someone violently retching.

Lord Frederick took another labored breath. "Should have put the damned muzzle in my mouth," he whispered.

Sebastian hunkered down beside him. "Do you know who I am?"

A flicker of recognition showed in the man's eyes. "He had one of my letters. One of my letters to Wesley."

"Who? Who has the letters?"

"Jarvis." The man's shattered head moved restlessly against the bloody leather of his chair. "Showed it to the Prince. Said it had been found amongst Leo Pierrepont's papers ... that I was working with Pierrepont to go behind the Prince's back and make peace with France." His next breath rattled in his throat. "Not true. Never betrayed my country. Never would ..."

"But the Prince believed it?"

The man's eyes squeezed shut as if in a spasm of pain, his voice fading. "Jarvis ... Jarvis said if I didn't go quietly, he'd see the letter was made public. Couldn't let Elizabeth ... my little girl ... ruin her."

Sebastian leaned forward, one hand wrapping

around the chair's leather-padded arm. "The letter—
how did Jarvis get it?"

Fairchild's eyes stared back at him, wide and
sightless.

Sebastian sat back on his heels, his hand still gripping
the chair's arm. He became aware, suddenly, of the insistent shrill of a constable's whistle and the butler's
voice shouting, "There. He's in there. In the library."

Sebastian was on his feet, tossing up one of the rear
windows, when he heard the sound of running footsteps
crossing the marbled hall. He threw one leg over the
windowsill.

"You there! Stop! Stop, I say!"

Slipping through the window, Sebastian landed
lightly in a bed of wet, freeze-browned foliage and
darkly sodden earth, and broke into a run.

~⌐

Charles, Lord Jarvis, startled his valet by returning to
Berkeley Square shortly before four that afternoon. He
wasn't a physically vain man, Jarvis, but the events at
Carlton House that evening would be particularly mo-
mentous. And in an age that placed inordinate importance upon appearance, a wise man attended to such
things.

Donning knee breeches and silk stockings with a
swallow-tailed coat, he resisted his valet's efforts to
lighten his florid complexion with a hint of powder, and
made his way downstairs to his library. Jarvis might
keep chambers in St. James's Palace and Carlton House,
but his most important papers were here, in Berkeley
Square.

He had to admit that he'd been mildly worried at one
point, that the sensational manner of that girl's death
might create difficulties. But in the end all had gone off

essentially as planned. The looming danger of a Whig
government had been averted; Perceval and the Tories
would remain in power and the war against atheism, republicanism, and the forces of evil would continue.

Pausing at the base of the stairs, Jarvis lifted a pinch
of snuff to his nostrils and breathed in deeply, sighing
with satisfaction. There were those, he knew, who
couldn't understand why he resisted the Prince's stren-
uous efforts to convince Jarvis himself to form a government. But Jarvis understood what most did not: that
men who align themselves openly with one party or pol-
icy thereby lose any semblance of objectivity, and that
those who seek to exercise their power through office
all too often find themselves *out* of office and therefore
out of power. Jarvis's allegiance was to Britain and her
king, not to any party or ideology, and he had no need
for the petty flattery and pomp of a premiership. His
dominance rested not on some fleeting government position, but on the supremacy of his intellect and the
strength of his personality and the selfless wisdom of his
unswerving devotion to his country and its monarchy.

Tucking the snuffbox back into his coat pocket, Jarvis
opened his library door, surprised to find the heavy
drapes at the window still open to the cold, darkening
afternoon. A whisper of movement jerked his gaze to
his desk, where a young man stood, a roughly-dressed
young man with a mud-smeared, rain soaked coat and a
neat little Cassaignard pistol.

"Unexpected, but fortuitous," said Viscount Devlin,
his strange amber eyes gleaming as he leveled the pistol
at Jarvis's chest. "Please, do come in."

Chapter 52

The yellow fog was coming back.

He couldn't see it yet, but Sir Henry Lovejoy could smell it in the cold, moist air as he paid off the hackney and hurried through the churchyard. A raw bitterness pinched at his nostrils and burned his throat and tore at his lungs. Soon, it would be upon them again, like a thick, stinking blanket of death.

Pausing, he stared up at the squat western towers and plain façade of St. Matthew of the Fields, the golden sandstone blackened by centuries of coal smoke and grime. The yellow fog had been upon them last Tuesday night, he remembered.

He kept thinking about what the Earl of Hendon had told him, how his lordship had come here at ten o'clock that night to meet Rachel York and found the north transept door unlocked, as she had said it would be. At the time Lovejoy had dismissed his lordship's statements, had thought them the inventions of a father desperate to save his only son and heir from the hangman's noose. Now Lovejoy wasn't so certain.

He followed the sound of a spade striking dirt around to the back of the church, where he found the sexton, Jem Cummings, digging a grave.

"Mr. Cummings," said Lovejoy, being careful not to

venture too close to the new grave's muddy edge. "I was
wanting to ask you if there was any way Rachel York
could have entered St. Matthew's church after eight
o'clock last Tuesday night?"

The sexton's rhythm broke, earth sliding back into
the grave from his shovel as he faltered. He hesitated,
then sank the metal tip deep into the earth with a loud
thwunk. "I been lockin' that north transept door every
night since 'ninety-two," he said, throwing a shovelful of
dirt high and wide, "ever since one o' them heathen Ja-
cobins come in here and—"

"Yes, yes, I know," said Lovejoy hastily, cutting him
off. "But that's not what I'm asking. I'm asking if there's
any way Rachel York—or perhaps someone else—
could have unlocked that door after you left. You must
understand that your answer could be of vital importance to this case. The life of an innocent man may well
depend upon it—and may God have mercy on your soul
if you are being anything less than truthful."

Jem Cummings straightened slowly, his shovel falling
idle in his hands, his toothless gums working back and
forth on his lower lip. He hesitated, then setting aside
the shovel, turned abruptly away to rummage amongst
the assorted effects he had piled up at the edge of the
grave. When he swung back, it was with something
clutched close in his hand. He hesitated again, then held
it up. Stepping gingerly, Lovejoy reached down and
found himself holding a heavy iron key.

"I found it in the Lady Chapel," said Jem, not meeting Lovejoy's gaze. "Last week, when the cleanin' lady
and me was dealing with the blood and all. It was back
under one of them fancy little pews, which is why I
reckon your lads didn't see it. It fits the north transept
door."

Lovejoy sucked in a quick breath that hissed loudly

between his teeth. "Why did you not come forward with this immediately?"

The sexton wiped a splayed hand back and forth across his unshaven face. "I weren't exactly truthful when I told you how it was, last Wednesday mornin'. You see, I coulda sworn I'd locked the north transept door the night afore. But then I come here the next day and there it was, open, with them men's bloody footprints in the transept and that girl left so indecent-like in the Lady Chapel. I thought I musta been misremembering, that I'd forgotten to lock the door after all . . . that it was me own fault, what was done to the church. All that blood . . ."

The old man reached again for his shovel, then simply stood there, gripping the handle, his gaze on the earth beneath his feet. "When I found that key, I knew I'd been right, that I had locked the door after all. She musta unlocked it herself when she come. Only by that time it was too late to say anythin' about it, 'cause I'd already told your constable I'd found the door locked that mornin'."

Lovejoy's hand tightened around the iron key, the toothed end digging into his palm. "You do realize the implications of this, don't you? That it completely changes our estimation of Miss York's time of death?"

Jem Cummings nodded, his head ducking as he thrust his shovel back into the earth.

Lovejoy stepped back. "How many people have a key to this church?"

"I don't rightly know. You'd haveta talk to the Reverend McDermott about that. He oughta be in the Rectory about now."

Lovejoy nodded and turned away, only to swing back as another thought struck him. "Just a moment. Did you say you saw *men's* footprints in the transept that morning?"

"That's right."

"Are you certain?"

"Course I am. I mighta lived in Londontown these past forty years and more, but I grew up in Chester. Me da, he was gamekeeper to Lord Broxton, and he taught all us little ones how to read game tracks. Men's tracks is no different. There was two sets of men's bloody footprints, comin' out o' that chapel. Ain't no doubt about that."

Chapter 53

Sebastian propped a hip on the edge of Lord Jarvis's heavily carved Jacobian desk, one leg swinging back and forth as he leveled the Cassaignard flintlock at the fat man's chest. "Just don't do anything stupid."

"I never do anything stupid," said Jarvis, his glance flicking from Sebastian to the long windows overlooking the rear garden, then back again. "You've tracked mud on my carpet."

"So I have. A legacy of my recent conversation with Lord Frederick Fairchild."

Jarvis leaned his back against the closed door and crossed his arms at his massive chest. "Really? Is that statement meant to be significant?"

"Lord Frederick tells me you presented the Prince of Wales with one of a collection of indiscreet letters written by Lord Frederick to a certain young gentleman in the Foreign Office. Now, as I understand it, you led the Prince to believe this letter was found in the possession of a French agent named Monsieur Léon Pierrepont. Which is curious, don't you think, given that Rachel York stole those letters from M. Pierrepont's townhouse shortly before she was murdered last Tuesday?"

Jarvis's full lips curled up into a smile. "Really?"

"Don't," said Sebastian, pushing away from the desk. "Don't try my patience. I've had a long and very fatiguing day."

Jarvis's gaze passed, derisively, over Sebastian's rain-soaked and muddied Rosemary Lane clothing. "Obviously."

Sebastian plucked a stray wisp of hay from his lapel and let it fall. "How did you find out Rachel York was working for the French?"

"There is very little happens in this town I don't know about."

"So you—what? Offered her protection from arrest if she agreed to cooperate with your scheme to discredit Lord Frederick?"

"Traitors' deaths are such messy, painful affairs. It's amazing what people will agree to do in order to avoid that kind of unpleasantness." Jarvis nodded toward a cut-crystal decanter warming on a table beside the hearth. "I trust you won't shoot me if I should venture to pour myself a glass of brandy?"

A tapestry bellpull hung just to one side of the carved mantel. Sebastian smiled. "Of course not. As long as you remember what I said about Stupid Things."

He watched the big man cross the room. It did much to explain Rachel York's nervousness in the weeks leading up to her death, if Jarvis had discovered her association with the French and used it to coerce her into working for him.

Jarvis reached for the brandy decanter and lifted it from its tray with slow, ponderous movements.

"So Rachel stole the letters from Pierrepont to give them to you," said Sebastian.

"Letter," said Jarvis, correcting him. "Fair Rachel provided me with one letter only."

"And the other documents? Did she take those at

your directive as well? Or was that her own initiative?
Is that why you killed her? Because she'd discovered
something she wasn't meant to know?"

Jarvis huffed a soft laugh. "You don't seriously think
I would stoop to killing some insignificant little bit of
muslin, now do you?"

"As a matter of fact, yes."

"Why would I? She'd delivered the letter I needed. I
admit it wasn't as incriminating as I had hoped, but in
the end it served its purpose. Quite nicely."

"You see, that's one of the things that puzzles me.
Rachel York stole some half a dozen of Lord Frederick's letters from Pierrepont's townhouse, yet you say
she gave you only one. What happened to the others?"

Jarvis's florid, self-confident face gave nothing away.
But Sebastian saw a hint of surprise flicker in the man's
eyes. "I neither know nor care."

"And here I thought little happens in this town that
you don't know about." Sebastian watched Jarvis splash
a generous measure of brandy into a glass. "You did
know, of course, that it wasn't true, what you told the
Prince. Lord Frederick might have been foolishly indiscreet, but he wasn't dealing with the French."

Jarvis eased the crystal stopper back into the decanter and set it aside. "Truth is such an overrated com-
modity. This country could not continue with a mad king
on the throne; everyone knew that. We needed this Regency. But the creation of the Regency threatened to
provide the Whigs with an opportunity to seize power.
And then what? They would have taken the greatest,
happiest nation in history—the admiration of the
world—and ruined it. All in the name of a set of shallow,
presumptuous French principles like 'democracy,' and
'freedom.' The kind of madness that can only lead to
chaos and confusion and the disintegration of all social

order. That's the only truth I'm interested in. The only truth that matters."

"I heard Prinny announced his government. He's decided to retain Spencer Perceval and the Tories."

"That's right. There'll be no Whig government, no peace negotiations with the French, no reform of Parliament, no Catholic emancipation."

"I wouldn't have thought even Prinny could be induced to turn from his friends so easily."

Jarvis let out a sharp laugh. "The Prince's friendship with the Whigs has always stemmed more from a petulant son's desire to spite his father than from any real dedication to Whiggish causes."

Sebastian knew it for the truth. Beneath his veneer of easygoing modernity, the Prince of Wales was essentially the same Catholic-hating, autocratic-minded monarchist as his father, George III.

Jarvis shifted closer to the hearth, as if drawn to the warmth. A large canvas heavily framed in gilded wood hung over the mantel, a group portrait of Lord Jarvis with his wife and mother and daughter. Sebastian had seen this portrait before, as a small study in the studio of Giorgio Donatelli.

"You say you had no reason to want to see Rachel York dead," said Sebastian. "Yet she knew enough to expose all your clever machinations for what they were."

"Not without exposing herself."

Sebastian kept his attention, seemingly, on the dramatically swirling colors of Donatelli's canvas. All the jagged, inconsistent pieces of the puzzle were beginning to fall into place: Leo Pierrepont, patiently spinning a web in which to ensnare the man everyone expected to be the next Whig prime minister, while Lord Jarvis schemed to keep the Whigs from gaining control of the government in the first place. And Rachel York—fiercely passionate, badly frightened—had been caught between them.

"The way I see it," said Sebastian, "whether you killed her yourself, or had her killed, or simply created the set of circumstances that led to her death, you're the one who is ultimately responsible for what happened to Rachel York."

"Am I expected to be overcome with remorse?" Jarvis lifted his brandy glass to his lips. "What difference does the life or death of one stupid little whore make when the future of an empire hangs in the balance?"

Sebastian knew a flash of sheer, potent rage. "It makes a difference to me."

"Only because you've been foolish enough to allow yourself to be saddled with the blame for it."

Sebastian nodded toward the family portrait over the mantel. "And the commission to Giorgio Donatelli? Was that a part of the payment?"

There was a step in the hall, the soft whisper of a woman's slippers over marble tiling. Jarvis's hand inched toward the bell cord. Sebastian drew back the pistol's safety with a click that reverberated loudly around the room. "That would fall under the heading of Stupid Things to Do, my lord."

Jarvis froze, just as the door from the hall swung open.

"Your carriage has been brought round, Papa," said a young woman, stepping into the room. "Do you wish me to tell Coachman John to—"

She was a tall young woman, almost as tall as her father, with ordinary brown hair she wore slung back in an unbecoming bun. One hand still on the knob, she drew up just inside the room with a small gasp that jerked Sebastian's attention away from the man by the hearth for one, disastrous moment.

And in that moment, Jarvis fell on the bell rope and gave it a hard yank.

Chapter 54

Sebastian leapt toward the woman. Catching her by the arm, he spun her around in front of him just as the first footman appeared in the door. His fingers digging into her arm, Sebastian pressed the flintlock's muzzle against the side of the woman's head. "Tell them to back off," he said to Jarvis.

Consternation, fury, and a whisper of what might have been fear chased each other across Jarvis's normally impassive face. His jaws clenched tight, only his lips working as he glared at the wide-eyed men piling up in the open doorway and spat out, "Stay back, you fools."

Arms spread, his gaze fixed on Sebastian, the lead footman took a step back, then another, his fellows falling back with him.

"Miss Jarvis here—" Sebastian glanced questioningly at the woman he held. "That is, I assume you are Miss Jarvis?"

Maintaining awesome composure, she slowly nodded her head.

"I thought so." Sebastian edged through the door and out into the hall, dragging the woman with him. "Miss Jarvis here is going to provide me with an escort to safety. I do trust you will all have the sense not to attempt anything heroic."

The hall seemed suddenly full of servants, white-faced men and women who fell silently back as Sebastian edged Jarvis's daughter toward the front. From the doorway of the library, Jarvis nodded to the stony-faced butler, who rushed to open the door.

An eerie, opaque darkness loomed beyond, what was left of the day having been swallowed by the fog that curled through the open door and drifted into the hall, bringing with it a foul, acrid stench that pinched the nostrils and tore at the throat.

Sebastian glanced down at the woman who held herself so stiff and straight in his grasp. "You did say there's a carriage outside, didn't you?"

"Did I?" she said in an admirably clear, steady voice.

"I rather think you did." He glanced at one of the maids, a big-boned, ruddy-faced woman who stood just inside the front door, her arms wrapped around her head, her eyes squeezed shut so tight, her entire face contorted with the effort.

"You there."

The maid's eyes flew open wide, her mouth going slack.

"Yes, you," he repeated, when she simply stared back at him, the bodice of her gown jerking up and down with each rapid, shallow breath. "Get in the carriage. Now."

"Surely one hostage will be sufficient to guarantee your safety," said Miss Jarvis hastily. "You don't need Alice."

"It's not my safety I'm concerned about." Sebastian shifted the muzzle of the gun toward the maid. "Now, Alice. In the carriage."

With a bleat of terror, Alice scuttled down the front steps and up into the carriage.

Sebastian backed up the carriage steps, hauling Miss Jarvis with him. "It would be detrimental to the ladies' health were anyone to attempt to follow us," he said to the grim men crowding the door behind them. "Drive toward Tothill Fields," he shouted to the coachman. "*Now*."

At the crack of the whip, the horses leapt to the traces, the carriage lurching forward with a jerk that set the lanterns to swinging on their brackets. The maid huddled into a corner of the forward seat, her hands holding her apron over her face as she let out a series of soft little screams.

"Stop that infernal nonsense," said Sebastian after roughly the twentieth scream.

"She's afraid," said Miss Jarvis.

Sebastian transferred his attention to the woman who sat tall and stiff-backed on the seat beside him. "You're not?"

She swung her head to look directly at him. In the swaying light from the outside lanterns, he could see the terror in her eyes. "Of course I am."

"I must say, you control yourself admirably well."

"I see no point in indulging in hysterics." She ran one hand up her other arm briskly, as if to warm it. A brazier of coals spread its slow heat through the carriage, but a damp cold radiated off the glass and her modest muslin gown was not designed for warmth.

Sebastian reached for the carriage robe of wool lined with fur that lay folded up beside him and held it out to her. "I shan't harm you, you know."

After the briefest of hesitations, she took the robe with a politely murmured, "Thank you," and wrapped it around her shoulders.

"Do you know who I am?" he asked.

An earsplitting shriek from the forward seat jerked his attention back to Alice. "Mary, Mother of God!" cried the maid, dropping her apron to show them a wild face. "He's going to ravish us both. Ravish us, and leave us headless and eviscerated like a heathen offering on some pagan altar." Her body went suddenly rigid, her fists digging into the plush upholstery at her side as she began to laugh hysterically.

Leaning forward, Miss Jarvis calmly slapped the maid across the face. Alice sucked in a startled breath, her eyes going wide, then squeezing shut as she collapsed back into her corner and began to cry. Miss Jarvis took one of the maid's hands in her own and said gently, "There, there, Alice; it will be all right. We're quite safe." To Sebastian, she said, "I know who you are."

Sebastian nodded toward the quietly sobbing maid. "So, obviously, does she."

Miss Jarvis paused in the act of chafing the maid's trembling hand between her own large, capable ones. "A humorist, I see. I hadn't expected that."

"And what, precisely, were you expecting? To be ravished and left split like a sacrificial lamb on the altar of Zeus?"

Alice let out a new bleat of terror.

Miss Jarvis threw Sebastian a frowning glance. "Hush. You're frightening her again."

Sebastian studied the woman beside him. She was somewhere in her early twenties, he supposed, brown of hair and unremarkable of feature, if one discounted the unmistakable gleam of intelligence and ready humor in those calm gray eyes. He tried to recollect what he had heard of Jarvis's daughter, and could call little to mind.

"Why did you insist on bringing Alice?" she asked after a moment.

He glanced out the window. They were bowling up Whitehall now, harnesses jangling, the horses' hoofbeats reverberating oddly in the damp, heavy fog. Soon the narrow streets of old Westminster would close in around them. It would be an easy thing, then, to lose any would-be rescuers and make his way to the Three Feathers Inn, where he intended to have a little chat with the landlord.

"Merciful heavens," said Miss Jarvis, her eyes opening wide as the carriage slowed for a turn. "Is *that* why she's here? To safeguard my reputation from the tongues that wag and do love to speculate on all manner of unrighteous things? Do you really think it will help?"

Sebastian opened the door beside him. "One can only hope," he said, and slipped out into the damp night.

Chapter 55

*I*t didn't take him long to locate the Three Feathers, a surprisingly elegant little inn located on a cul-de-sac just off Barton Street. With some persuasion—not all that tactfully applied, for Sebastian was tired—the innkeeper divulged that Hugh Gordon and an unidentified, heavily veiled lady had indeed spent the previous Tuesday night in the inn's best chamber.

But the Three Feathers was a busy establishment; the innkeeper had no way of knowing whether or not the actor had stayed at his lady's side all evening. And Barton Street was just around the corner from Great Peter Street and the ancient church of St. Matthew of the Fields.

Leaving Westminster, Sebastian caught a hackney to Tower Hill. "Ah. There you are," said Paul Gibson when he opened the door to Sebastian's knock half an hour later. "So Tom found you, did he?"

"No," said Sebastian, quickly closing the door against the acrid cold of the coming night. "I haven't seen the boy since this morning. Why? Have you discovered something?"

"Not as much as I might have wished." The doctor led the way down the narrow hall to the parlor, where he poured Sebastian a measure of mulled wine from the bowl warming near the fire. "You're looking decidedly the worse for wear."

Sinking into one of the seats beside the fire, Sebastian grasped the cup in both hands. "So everyone keeps saying." He took a sip of the warm wine, then leaned his head against the back of the chair and closed his eyes. "I feel as if I've been chased across London and back again for the past hundred years."

Gibson smiled. "Which probably explains why Tom didn't find you." He poured himself some of the mulled wine and came to take the other chair. "I tracked down the woman who did Rachel York's laying out. A horse-faced old battle-ax by the name of Molly O'Hara."

Sebastian brought his head forward and opened his eyes. "And?"

"Rachel York had a man's fob clutched in her fist. Unfortunately, by the time I found her, our dear Molly had already sold the trinket. She remembered little about it, beyond the fact that its swivel was broken."

"Rachel must have torn it from her attacker's waistcoat, just as he slit her throat."

"Yes, that's the way I figure it. The goldsmith Molly sold the trinket to used the damage to drive a hard bargain with her." The doctor drew a square of paper from his pocket. "A Mr. Sal Levitz. In Grace Church Street."

"You went to see him?"

"Yes, although I fear I didn't handle it as well as I should have."

"Let me guess. He claims he sold the trinket some fifteen minutes before you walked in his door."

Gibson gave a wry smile. "I'm afraid so. All I managed to get out of him was a rough sketch of the piece." Unfolding the paper, he smoothed it open on the arm of his chair. "Rather than a seal, the fob carried a charm, a Corinthian column worked in eighteen-carat solid gold.

Whoever Rachel York's attacker was, he was obviously a gentleman. Or at least very wealthy."

Sebastian reached for the paper. "You do realize, of course, that your Mr. Levitz probably melted the damn thing down the instant you were out the door." Sebastian gazed at the sketch. "A foppish affectation. Prinny himself started the fad for these columns some months ago. Without the actual piece to trace, it's of no use at all."

"I'm afraid not."

Standing up, Sebastian began to pace the small room. "*Bloody hell*," he said suddenly, his hand tightening to crush the drawing into a tight ball. "I had this incredible conceit, this belief that if I could trace the pattern of Rachel York's life through her last days, if I could understand why she went to that church—what dangerous game she was involved in—then I'd know who killed her. Not simply *know* it, but be able to prove it." He let out a hoarse laugh and tossed the crumpled paper onto a nearby table. "What hubris."

"*Do* you understand what she was involved in?"

"I think so, yes." Coming back to the fire, Sebastian quickly summed up the conversations with Gordon and Donatelli, then the death of Lord Frederick and the meeting with Jarvis.

"I'd still put my money on the Frenchman," said Gibson, when Sebastian had finished. "He could easily have found out Rachel was cooperating with Jarvis, *and* that she was the one responsible for the theft of his documents. Not only that, but he would have had a reason to go looking for the maid, Mary Grant, to get the remaining documents from her."

"So would Hugh Gordon," said Sebastian. "We know he was in Westminster last Tuesday. And while the innkeeper at the Three Feathers confirmed Gordon was there, he could easily have slipped out at some point during the evening."

The doctor pushed up from his chair to go stir the bowl of mulled wine. "I still don't understand the part Lord Jarvis played in all this."

Sebastian smiled and drained his cup. "That's because you don't have Jarvis's devious mind. Lord Jarvis knew Pierrepont was the French spymaster in London—according to my father, it's been known for over a year. Jarvis must have realized Lord Frederick was falling into one of the Frenchman's carefully spun traps. Only instead of warning the man, Jarvis developed a plan of his own, a plan to discredit the Whigs and prevent them from taking over the government when the Regency was proclaimed."

"So he—what? Approached Rachel and threatened her with a traitor's gruesome end if she didn't deliver one of the letters Fairchild wrote to his young lover? I can see how that might discredit Fairchild. What I can't see is how it implicates him and the Whigs with the French."

"Ah. But Jarvis didn't immediately take the letter to the Prince, remember? He waited until today, when the Prince is doubtless in a high fret over tomorrow's installation. Then, acting as if he's only recently discovered Pierrepont's activities, Jarvis ordered the Frenchman's townhouse raided. Only *then* did he produce the letter and tell the Prince it was found in Pierrepont's possession. And because Pierrepont has conveniently disappeared, there's no danger of the Frenchman spilling the truth."

Gibson carefully ladled more steaming wine into Sebastian's cup. "But if Jarvis was planning to expose Pierrepont and raid his townhouse anyway, why pressure Rachel York to produce one of the letters ahead of time? Why not simply seize the letters in the raid?"

"Because there was always the possibility that the letters wouldn't be found, and a man like Jarvis doesn't leave that sort of thing to chance." Sebastian took the warm drink in both hands. "And remember, the letter wasn't the only thing implicating Lord Frederick. The fool was meeting his lover in the rooms of a woman known to be working with the French."

"Poor girl," said Paul Gibson, refilling his own mug. "So Jarvis intended to betray her anyway?"

"I suspect so. Except that Rachel was smart enough to realize she was in danger. She decided she needed to get away and she came up with a plan of her own—to take the rest of Fairchild's letters, and the document about my mother, and God knows what else, and sell them to the interested parties."

"Huh," said the doctor, easing back down in his chair. "If you ask me, the killer could be any one of them— Pierrepont, Gordon, Donatelli—even bloody Jarvis himself."

"You're forgetting Bayard," said Sebastian, going to stand beside the hearth. "He might have been falling down drunk when his father took him home at nine. But we have only Amanda's word for it that he stayed there. It's not beyond belief that he went out again, looking for Rachel. He could have followed her to that church and killed her."

"But why would Bayard go after the maid, Mary Grant? Pierrepont and Gordon both had a good reason to want to get their hands on the rest of those documents. Even Donatelli admits he went looking for them. But Bayard knew nothing of them."

"True," said Sebastian, his gaze on the glowing coals on the hearth. "Yet of them all, Bayard is the one I'd say is unbalanced enough to slake his lust on a woman's dead body."

"How well do you know the others? Mmmm? When it comes right down to it? We know Hugh Gordon is prone to violence against women, while Pierrepont must have witnessed enough horrors during the Revolution in Paris to turn anyone's mind. In fact, of them all, the only one I *can't* see committing such an act of unbridled emotion is Lord Jarvis. He's too damnably cool and calm and in control."

"Rather like his daughter," Sebastian said wryly.

A hint of amusement eased the worried lines on the Irishman's forehead. "You know what they say: the apple doesn't fall very far from the tree."

Sebastian spun around. "Say that again."

"What? Say what?"

"*Apples and trees*," said Sebastian, crossing the room to snatch up the crumpled goldsmith's sketch. "Good God. Why didn't I see it before?"

Chapter 56

The Black Dog stood on the far edge of Walworth, to the south of London. A half-forgotten coaching inn nearly hidden by an encroaching beech forest and the swirl of fog that wrapped around its redbrick walls, it was known for the discreetness of its keeper and the fine French wines that paid no customs on their way into its cellars.

Wearing a warm velvet habit and a heavily veiled hat, Kat reined in her mare beneath the flickering torches in the inn's yard. A coach and four, well loaded and ready for travel, stood waiting near the arch. "Walk the horses," she said to her groom. "I won't be long."

She found Leo in a private parlor on the low-ceilinged first floor, at a small table where he sat hurriedly writing, a pair of silver-rimmed spectacles perched on the end of his nose.

"How did you manage to get away?" Kat said, shoving back her veil and closing the door behind her with a snap.

He looked at her over the rims of his spectacles. "How do you think?"

"You were warned." It was a statement rather than a question. "Why?"

He stood up, then reached to shuffle his papers into

order. "You've heard the whispers, surely? About Lord Frederick's suicide and all sorts of dark plots implicating the Whigs?"

"But none of it's true."

"Of course not. Which is why it is in the best interests of those surrounding the Prince that I not be caught. Hence, the warning." He peeled off his eyeglasses and tucked them into a pocket. It occurred to her that she hadn't realized he wore them.

She watched him walk over to thrust his papers into a small leather case and snap it shut. "How long have they known about you?"

Something in her voice made Leo glance back at her and smile. "Worried they know about you, too, *ma petite*?" He shook his head. "I don't think so. You may still give valuable service to France."

"I don't give a damn about France."

He laughed. "I know you don't. But you do hate England with a commendable—and very useful—passion. In my experience, those with an emotional motivation always make the best agents. A man who betrays his country for money, or because he has been caught in some foolish indiscretion, can all too frequently turn on you." Leo puffed out his cheeks and let go a long, painful breath. "I should have realized it sooner."

Kat shook her head. "Realized what?"

"There were four sets of documents taken from me the Sunday before Rachel was killed," he said, shrugging into his coat. "In addition to Lord Frederick's collection of letters and the royal birth certificate, there was also an affidavit relating to a certain indiscretion committed by your viscount's mother, and a bill of sale for a ship and cargo reported by its owner as lost at sea."

"I don't understand."

Leo adjusted the lapel of his coat. "The latter proved a most useful acquisition, since the perpetrator of that little insurance fraud happens to be a boon companion of the Prince. He hasn't been in a position to provide us with many state secrets himself, but he's been an invaluable source of information on other men's peccadilloes and potential weaknesses—Lord Frederick's unfortunate inclinations being only one of many."

"What are you saying?"

"What I'm saying is that unless the Prince of Wales has recently taken to rape and all sorts of other ungodly occupations, then Rachel's murderer is very likely your young viscount's own brother-in-law, Martin, Lord Wilcox."

Kat let out her breath in a rush. "Are you certain?"

"No. But I'd watch the man, if I were Devlin." Pierrepont reached for his hat, then paused. "I gather Devlin doesn't know you favor the French in this little war to which he devoted—what? Five years of his life?"

"It's Ireland I fight for. Not the French. There is a difference."

"Indeed there is," Leo agreed, walking up to her. "But I suspect it's a difference that would be lost on Devlin." He reached out, his hand unexpectedly gentle as he touched her cheek. "Don't fall in love with him again, *ma petite*. He'll break your heart."

Kat held herself very still. "I can control my own heart."

Leo's eyes crinkled into a smile that faded abruptly as he turned away. "Paris will be sending someone soon to take my place," he said over his shoulder. "Be alert. He will contact you. You know the signal."

Kat followed him, wordless, to the yard. She watched his traveling carriage disappear into the night. Then she lowered the veil over her face, remounted her horse, and rode away.

∼

The fog lay heavy in the streets of London, a thick, throat-burning swirl of noxiousness that turned flickering gaslights into ghostly golden glows lost in the gloom.

Kat drew up before her house and handed the reins to her groom. "Stable them," she said, sliding from the saddle. She stood for a moment, listening to the muffled beat of the horses' hooves disappearing into the thickness of the night. Then she threw the train of her riding skirt over her arm and turned, just as a dark figure materialized from out of the mist. Kat sucked in a startled gasp.

"You ain't seen the gov'nor, 'ave you?" said the boy, Tom.

Feeling vaguely ridiculous, Kat let go her breath in a soft sigh of relief. "I believe he received a note from his friend, Dr. Gibson. Perhaps he could tell you something."

Tom shook his head. "It's Gibson who's wantin' to see 'im. Somethin' about a geegaw what was found in that mort's hand."

Kat paused at the base of her front steps. Someone was walking toward them on the footpath; a man with the flaring cape and measured gait of a gentleman.

"Miss Boleyn?" he said, one hand coming up to touch his hat brim as he paused beside her.

"Yes?" She knew a fission of fear, a precognition of understanding at the sight of his middle-aged, quietly smiling features. "May I help you?"

"I am Lord Wilcox," said the man, his hand dropping ominously from his hat to slip inside his cape. "I must ask you to accompany me to my carriage." He nodded into the mist-swirled darkness. "It's just there, at the end of the street."

Kat was aware of Tom tensing beside her, his eyes wide on the gentleman before them. "And if I refuse?" she said, her voice coming out low and husky.

His hand tightened around something just inside his cape and she realized it was a pistol he held there. A pistol he now lifted to point at her. His gaze noted the direction of her glance, and he smiled. "As you can see, that really is not an option."

Chapter 57

*A*manda was eleven the year her brother Richard told her the truth about their mother.

He'd been home from Eton that summer, ten years old and very full of himself. Amanda might have been a year his senior, but she was only a girl, after all, her world a tightly drawn circle of schoolroom and lessons and walks in the park with Nurse. She listened in shocked silence to Richard's excitedly whispered tales of the revolting thing men did to women, about how they came together in a shameful, naked coupling of bodies. And then, while she was still retching in horror at the thought she might someday be forced to endure just such a vile invasion of her own body, Richard told her of the rumors he'd heard about their mother. About how the Countess of Hendon did *that* with other men besides her husband, Amanda's father.

Amanda hadn't believed Richard, of course. Oh, she'd seen enough activity amongst the estate's farm animals to realize that *that* part of his information, at least, was probably correct. But she refused to believe what he said about their mother, about how the beautiful, laughing Countess did *that* with everyone from royal dukes to common footmen. Amanda hadn't believed a word of it. Not a word.

But suggestions can have an insidious way of worming into a body's soul and eating away at it. As summer stretched into autumn, Amanda found herself watching their mother. Watching the look that crept into the Countess's sparkling blue eyes whenever a handsome man walked into the room. The way she tilted her pretty blond head and laughed when a man spoke to her. The way her lips could part and her breath catch when he took her hand.

And then one rare sunny day in September, when the Countess and her children were rusticating down in Cornwall and the Earl danced attendance, as usual, upon the King, Amanda escaped the schoolroom and went for a walk. The air was crisp and sweet with the earthy scent of plowed fields and sun-warmed pine needles, and she walked farther than she'd meant, farther than she was allowed. A restlessness had been building within her lately, an unsettled yearning that led her to leave the trim terraces of the gardens and the neatly hedged-in fields of the home farm behind, and penetrate deep into the wild tangle of forest that stretched away toward the sea.

It was there that she found them, in a sun-soaked hollow sheltered by a rocky outcropping from the brisk winds blowing off the white-capped water. The man lay on his back, his naked, sweat-slicked body stretched out long and lean, his neck arching in what seemed at first an agony. A woman sat astride him, her soft white lady's hands holding his larger, darker ones cupped over her breasts, her lower lip gripped between her teeth, her eyes squeezing shut in ecstasy as she rode him. *Rode him.*

In the months that had passed since Richard's visit, Amanda had sought to picture this vile thing that he had told her about. But never had she imagined—never could she have imagined anything like this.

Drawn by a sick combination of horror and fascination, she crept closer, her heart pounding painfully within her, her stomach acids backing up hot and sick into her throat. But it wasn't until her fascination had drawn her, trembling and nauseous, ever closer, that Amanda realized the truth. That the woman whose breath came in such harsh, ragged gasps was her own mother, Sophia Hendon. And that the man whose naked pelvis thrust up again and again in a savage, pounding rhythm, who buried his body deeper and deeper inside hers, was her ladyship's groom.

Amanda never told Richard what she had seen that day, although she knew from the bitter remarks her brother occasionally let fall that he blamed their father for the things their mother did, blamed Hendon for devoting all his time to King and country, and neglecting his lonely, lovely wife. But Amanda knew the truth, for she had seen the hunger in their mother's beautiful, sunlit face. The shameful, insatiable hunger.

It had been dark for some time now, the fog swallowing the last glimmers of daylight before sliding away imperceptibly into night. The maid, Emily, had come at one point to draw the drapes and lay fresh coals upon the fire, but Amanda had sent her away.

Shaking off the long-ago memories, Amanda went now to turn up the flame of the oil lamp that filled the dressing room with a sweetly scented glow, and to close the heavy brocade drapes against the cold radiating off the long windows overlooking the square.

Crossing the room to her writing desk, she paused, her head raised as she listened. But the house lay silent around her, and after a moment she slid back the discreet latch that opened the desk's hidden compartment, and drew forth the single piece of parchment from within.

She'd read it perhaps a hundred times already, but now she read it again, drawn by something she didn't care to define, to this strange recital of that long-ago sin, written in Sophia Hendon's own hand. Amanda couldn't begin to guess what had driven her mother to set it all down in such stark, bare sentences, and then swear to it before witnesses. Nor did Amanda know how that harlot, Rachel York, had come by such a curious document, or for what purpose it had been intended. But Amanda had no doubt that the document had come from the actress.

Her blood still stained one corner.

It was Coachman Ned who'd first let slip the truth about that Tuesday night—or at least, the truth as he knew it. It had taken some time—and a few carefully worded threats—but eventually Amanda had drawn from him a curious tale, of how his lordship had been on his way to Westminster when he'd come upon Master Bayard, insensible with drink, on the footpath in front of Cribb's Parlor. They'd taken the boy up into the carriage, of course. Only, they hadn't brought him straight home. On his lordship's orders, Coachman Ned had continued on to Great Peter Street, in Westminster, where his lordship had left the boy in the servant's care.

It was not a servant's place, of course, to question his master's movements, although Coachman Ned admitted he'd been worried, watching Lord Wilcox disappear alone and on foot into that stinking fog. And his worst fears had been confirmed when, some twenty or thirty minutes later, Lord Wilcox had been set upon by thieves. He came staggering back to the carriage, his assailants' blood drenching the front of his overcoat and still dripping from the sword stick he'd used to fight them off. He'd given Coachman Ned strict instructions that her ladyship was not to be told of the incident, lest it overset her nerves. He'd used the same line, Amanda eventually learned, to keep his valet, Downing, mum as well.

Bayard had snored insensible through it all. But Amanda wondered at the two servants, who surely knew her to be impervious to the kind of nervous spasms that troubled so many of the ladies of her station. She wondered, too, how they could have remained so unquestioningly believing when the gory details of what had happened that night in the Lady Chapel of St. Matthew of the Fields were on everyone's lips. But then, perhaps neither Coachman Ned nor Downing had ever noticed the way his lordship's face could draw taut with sexual excitement at the sight of a harlot being whipped through the streets. Perhaps they didn't know about the string of housemaids he'd forced over the years, or the one he'd cut when she tried to refuse him. But Amanda had known, and pondered, and eventually been driven to ferret out the truth.

Refolding the parchment, Amanda carefully tucked it away and slid the secret compartment home. She wondered what Wilcox had thought, when he'd discovered the document missing. It was only by chance that Amanda had come upon it when she went looking for something—anything—that might confirm what in her heart of hearts she already knew to be the truth. The other papers she'd found with the affidavit—love letters from Lord Frederick to someone named Wesley and an interesting royal birth certificate—she left where she had found them, for they were of no significance to her. But her mother's confession Amanda had taken without hesitation. A document of that nature was too volatile, too potentially valuable to be left in the hands of someone such as Martin.

She was so lost in thought that she missed the sound of the door quietly opening. It was only the change in the atmosphere of the room that told her, suddenly, that she was no longer alone. Turning her head, she found Sebastian leaning against the doorjamb.

She knew a moment of consternation at the thought he had seen her with their mother's affidavit. Then she realized he was looking at her, not the writing desk, and she knew he had not.

"Where is he?" Sebastian demanded in a taut, menacing voice. "Where's Wilcox?"

"You seem to make it a habit of entering other people's houses uninvited," she said, ignoring the question.

He pushed away from the door frame and came at her, his terrible amber eyes on her face. "You know, don't you? For how long? How long have you known?"

In spite of herself, Amanda took a step back. "Known what?"

"I thought it was Bayard," he continued, as if she had said nothing. "I was remembering all those nasty little incidents from when he was a boy. The time he set fire to the henhouse at Hendon Hall, just so he could have the fun of watching it burn. All the unmentionable things he used to do to any stray animal unlucky enough to fall into his clutches."

He drew up before her, close enough that she could smell the acrid wet of the fog that had seeped into his rough, workingman's clothes. "I used to wonder where it came from, that utter lack of empathy for the suffering of others, that streak of cruelty bordering on madness. I even wondered if perhaps it ran hidden within me, too. And then one day I saw Wilcox laugh at the sight of a cotter's child being torn apart by a pack of hounds, and I knew. I knew where it came from."

"You're the one who is mad."

"Am I?" He swung away. "You've heard the news, I suppose? About Leo Pierrepont?"

"Pierrepont?" Amanda shook her head. "What has he to do with anything?"

"Dear Amanda. Can it be that you really don't know? Hendon told me something a few days ago, something that should have piqued my curiosity, except that I missed it. He said the government has known about Pierrepont's ties to Napoleon for the better part of a year now, ever since a certain gentleman he called Mr. Smith found himself under pressure from Pierrepont to provide information of value to the French government. It seems Hendon and Lord Jarvis decided between them to simply sit on the revelations about Pierrepont, and use this compromised gentleman as a sort of double agent."

"So?" said Amanda.

"So, the curious thing is that while Father and Jarvis both serve the King, on a personal level the two men can barely tolerate each other. Which tells me that the only reason Jarvis discussed the situation with Hendon is because the compromised gentleman had come to *Hendon* for help. And the only man I can think of who would do that is your husband. Wilcox."

Amanda stood very still, watching her brother prowl restlessly about her dressing room. She hadn't known this about Wilcox, that he'd been careless enough to allow himself to fall into a French trap. She gripped her hands together, shaken by an onrush of cold rage directed not just at Martin but at this man, her brother, who had come here to taunt her with her husband's stupidity.

"What did they have on him, I wonder?" Sebastian said, pausing to fiddle with the quill she'd left lying on the leather-covered writing surface of her desk. "Something more, I suspect, than a mere sexual indiscretion. Whatever it was, Rachel must have found evidence of it when she helped herself to a cache of sensitive documents in Pierrepont's possession. A fatal mistake, poor girl, since she must then have offered to sell the incriminating evidence to Wilcox. She didn't know the kind of man she was dealing with." He swung suddenly to face her. "But you did."

"You're mad," Amanda said again, her hands gripping together tighter and tighter.

"Am I? That day I came here to confront Bayard, you knew then. It's why you were so careful to tell me the exact time Wilcox had encountered Bayard. Only, he didn't bring the lad straight home, did he?"

"The girl was a whore," said Amanda suddenly, the words a harsh, angry tear ripped from a tightly constricted throat. "A whore, and a traitor."

A strange light shone in her brother's uncanny, alien eyes. "So that makes it all right, does it, what Wilcox did to her? What about the maid, Mary Grant? Or is that all right, too, because she was just a common servant and not a very honest one at that?"

His words fell into a silence Amanda had no intention of breaking. From outside came the fog-muffled clip-clop of hooves, and, nearer at hand, the clatter of a bucket followed by a giggle from one of the housemaids.

In the end it was Sebastian who broke the silence, the anger in his voice having been replaced by a kind of urgency. "Wilcox has developed a taste for it now, Amanda. You do realize that, don't you? He's going to keep doing it. And one day, he will be caught."

"Hopefully not until after they've hanged you."

His face went suddenly, satisfyingly blank. "I've always known you disliked me," he said after a pause. "But I don't think I realized until now just how much you hate me."

"Of course I hate you," she said, practically spitting the words at him. "Why wouldn't I? You, Viscount Devlin, the precious, pampered heir to everything. Everything that should have been mine." She thumped her fist against her chest. "*Mine*. I was my father's firstborn child. While you—" She cut herself off just in time, clenching her teeth together.

"I didn't invent the laws of male primogeniture," he said, his voice a quiet counterpart to hers, his brows drawing together as if in puzzlement as he searched her face, "even if I have benefited from them."

She watched, confused, as a strange smile touched his lips, then faded. "It's funny, but my first thought when it finally all came together was to rush over here and warn you—warn you about how dangerous the man you were married to has become. It wasn't until I started thinking about what you'd said, about how Bayard had passed out before nine when the police have everyone thinking the murder took place between five and eight, that I realized you knew the truth." He drew in a deep breath then let it out in a harsh expulsion of air. "I'm not going to swing for you, Amanda. And I'm not going to let that sick bastard who is your husband keep butchering women."

"You have no proof," she said, as he turned toward the door.

He paused to glance back at her over his shoulder. "I'll find something." His mouth curved into a tight smile, harder and far meaner than the last. "Even if I have to make it up."

~⌒◡

Outside the churchyard of St. Matthew of the Fields, Sir
Henry Lovejoy found the streets of Westminster deserted. Peering hopefully into the murky darkness, he
turned up his collar against the creeping, insidious cold
and wished he'd had the forethought to tell his hackney
driver to wait.

He thought about that girl, Rachel York, coming here
alone on a night such as this. He wondered at the kind
of courage that must have taken—courage, or a passionately held conviction, or maybe a large dose of
both. Yet there was nothing he had discovered yet in
this case that suggested a reason for either.

The Reverend McDermott had been shocked at the
discovery that such a woman had possessed a key to his
church and baffled as to how she might have obtained
it. Yet she had obtained it, and used it to meet the Earl
of Hendon here at ten o'clock, just as Hendon had
claimed. It was why Jem Cummings had seen the bloody
footprints of two men—the first set belonging to Rachel
York's murderer, the second set left, later, by Hendon.

It was always dangerous, Lovejoy knew, to assume a
fact is true simply because it appears obvious. Yet it was
a mistake all too often made—a mistake he had made.
And because of it, they'd spent the last week chasing an
innocent man.

The rattle of carriage wheels over rough cobbles
brought Lovejoy's head around as a dark, rawboned job
horse and hackney emerged from the gloom. There was
a shout, and the jarvey pulled up.

The carriage's near door flew open. "Sir Henry. There
you are." Edward Maitland appeared in the open doorway. "I was hoping to catch you before you left the
church. We've a report that Viscount Devlin has been

staying at an inn near Tothill Fields. A place called the Rose and Crown. I've sent some lads to watch the place, but I thought you'd like to be there when the arrest is made."

Lovejoy scrambled up into the carriage's musty interior. "There've been some new developments in the case," he said as the carriage took off again with a jerk. He gave the constable a quick summary of his meeting with the sexton and the Reverend McDermott. "What it means, of course," he said, wrapping up, "is that in all likelihood Rachel York wasn't killed until sometime after eight—probably more like ten o'clock. And since we know Lord Devlin arrived at his club shortly before nine, his lordship couldn't possibly have had enough time to kill the girl here in Westminster, rush home to Brook Street, change his clothes, and still appear in St. James's Street when he did."

The swinging carriage lamp threw irregular patterns of light and shadow over the set features of the constable's face. "Just because we don't see how he could have done it doesn't mean he didn't do it," said Maitland. "Besides, you're forgetting what he did to Constable Simplot."

Lovejoy bit back what he'd been about to say. It was true, he had been forgetting Simplot. Lovejoy sighed. "How is the lad?"

"Still out of his head with fever. They don't think he'll last the night. It's a miracle he's lived as long as he has."

Lovejoy nodded, his thoughts running back over what had happened that Wednesday afternoon in Brook Street. Here was one aspect of the case he had yet to consider. Why would a privileged young nobleman from a powerful, wealthy family deliberately attack and attempt to kill a constable in order to escape

arrest for a crime of which he knew himself to be innocent? It made no sense.

Yet when it came to the young Viscount's arrest,
Lovejoy realized with a sigh, it mattered as little as the
sexton's discovery of the key. For Lovejoy was also forgetting Charles, Lord Jarvis. As far as Lord Jarvis was
concerned, Devlin's innocence or guilt had never been
an issue. The Viscount had been tried and found guilty
by the press and the streets, and the shocked populous
of London wanted him brought to justice.

For the son of a peer of the realm to be seen getting
away with murder would have been a volatile situation,
at any time. Now, with the King declared mad and the
Prince about to be created Regent, the situation could
become dangerous. And Jarvis had been more than
clear about what was at stake: Devlin was to be brought
in before tomorrow's ceremony, or Lovejoy's position
as Queen Square magistrate would be forfeit.

Chapter 58

Life is full of scary things, Kat Boleyn's father used to tell her. Scary things, like the steadily approaching tramp of marching soldiers and the silhouette of a rope dangling against a misty morning sky. Or the dark muzzle of a gun, gripped in the hand of a smiling man.

"Why?" she said now, her gaze on the man before her. Life might be full of scary things, but she'd learned long ago to hide her fears behind a smooth face and a steady voice. "What do you want with me?"

He was one of those men whose lips seemed perpetually curved into a faint smile. But at her words the smile slipped, as if he'd anticipated meek obedience or fearful hysteria, and found the calm directness of her question disconcerting.

"All I need from you, my dear, is cooperation." The smile was back in place now, serene, confident. He nodded toward Tom. "You know this lad, do you?"

Kat's gaze met that of the boy who stood stiffly at her side. Tom stared back at her, his dark eyes alert. "Yes," she said.

"Good. Then he can be trusted to deliver a message." With his free hand, Wilcox retrieved a folded note from an inner pocket and held it out to Tom. "Take this to Viscount Devlin. The note will give him the particulars he needs, but I am relying on you to convey to his lordship the gravity of the situation. I trust I do make myself clear?"

Kat sucked in a quick gasp just as quickly stifled, for she understood all too clearly what Wilcox intended. He was setting a trap to catch Sebastian and she was to be the bait.

Fear welled within her, hot and trembling, but she forced it down. Fear interfered with one's ability to think, and she needed to think clearly. It occurred to her that whatever Wilcox's carefully arranged plan, she could destroy it in an instant simply by refusing to go with him. Except there was something in Wilcox's eyes that gave her pause. A man like this could kill without second thoughts or remorse. Kat knew what it would do to Sebastian, if he felt himself responsible for her death. A man driven by that kind of rage and guilt could make mistakes. Fatal mistakes.

She drew in a deep, cold breath of the smoke-fouled night air, felt the acrid burn of it tear at her throat. It tasted bitter in her mouth, bitter as fear. As if he could smell her fear, Wilcox's smile widened.

It was the smile that decided her—the smile, and the man's self-assured confidence in the success of whatever strategy he had devised to ensnare Sebastian St. Cyr. He obviously thought his plan infallible. But Kat knew Sebastian, knew the uncanny, animal-like keenness of his senses and the swiftness of his reflexes. Sebastian might be walking into a trap, but at least he would know it.

And so for the second time that evening, she met Tom's gaze and held it, and slowly nodded. She could only hope he understood.

For a moment longer, Tom hesitated. Then he reached for the note and darted out into the street, brushing past Wilcox on the way. But on the cobbles the boy suddenly stopped, swinging back around, one hand coming up to clutch his hat tighter to his head. "And if'n the gov'nor don't come?"

"Remind him what happened to Rachel York and Mary Grant," said Wilcox, taking Kat's arm and drawing her close to him with a firm grip. "He'll come."

~

Sebastian was changing his clothes in his room at the Rose and Crown when Tom came hurtling through the door, bringing with him the cold stench of the foggy night.

"God save us, gov'nor, but 'e's nabbed her," panted the boy, his eyes wide, his thin chest jerking with the effort to draw breath. "E's nabbed Miss Kat."

Sebastian whipped about. "*What*? What are you saying?"

"Yer nevy's papa. Lord Wilcox. Grabbed her right outside her 'ouse, he did, and give me this 'ere message for you. Said I was to tell you—"

Sebastian snatched the sealed missive from the boy's outstretched hand and tore it open, his gaze scanning the cramped lines.

I have in my possession an item which I believe is of considerable interest to you. You may claim this item in person at the Prosperity Trading Company warehouse, below the Hermitage Dock. The rapidity of your response will ensure that the item remains undamaged.

Needless to say, you will come alone and unarmed. The consequences otherwise would be swift and unfortunate.

Sebastian felt a torrent of rage and fear sweep through him, a sick mingling of hot and cold that stole his breath and twisted at something vital deep within him. He knew Tom was still speaking, but the words were lost in the roaring in Sebastian's ears.

He lifted his head to look directly at the boy. "What? Say that again."

Something in Sebastian's face made the boy take a step back, his nostrils flaring as he sucked in a deep breath and swallowed hard. "It's 'im, isn't it? He's the cove what you've been lookin' for, the one what's been killin' them women. 'E said I was to remind you o' what happened to them other two morts. Rachel York and Mary Grant."

"*Oh, Jesus.*" Sebastian flung aside the note and grabbed his boots.

Behind him, Tom darted forward to pick up the fallen paper, his mouth moving soundlessly as he struggled to decipher the words. He looked up, his brows twitching together, his breathing still ragged. "You can't be meaning to go there? To this wharf?"

Sebastian shoved one foot into a boot. He hadn't realized the boy knew how to read. "What would you suggest I do instead?"

"But it's a trap!"

"So I am aware."

"What you thinkin' yer gonna do? Just walk into it?"

"Not if I can help it." He paused to grasp the boy's shoulders. "But in case something should happen to me, I want you to go to my father, the Earl of Hendon. Tell him as much of the tale as you can."

Tom's nostrils flared as he jerked in air. "No earl's gonna believe me! Not some snatcher off the streets."

"Show him the note. It's a pity it isn't signed, but then, Wilcox is no fool."

An unexpected gleam of delight danced in the boy's eyes. "I lifted—" He broke off when Sebastian held up a warning hand. "What is it? What'd you 'ear?"

Coat in hand, Sebastian crossed swiftly to listen at the door. "Did someone follow you here?" The sounds were distant but unmistakable: a quickly hushed whisper, the soft and careful tread of men upon the stairs.

"No." Tom's eyes went wide. "But I seen a beak sittin' in the taproom when I come in. I got the feelin' 'e was waitin' for someone."

The footsteps were in the hall now.

Sebastian shrugged into his coat and started across the room. "I think we'll go out the window," he said, just as glass shattered and the casement frame flew in on a gust of cold, smoke-tinged air.

"Bloody hell," swore Sebastian. Snatching up the straight-backed chair from the table, he smashed it into the chest of the black-bearded man whose bulky torso had appeared at the shattered window. The man gave a grunt and disappeared. Sebastian was swinging what was left of the chair at a second man's gut when he heard a key grating in the door behind him. He swore again. *Damn* that innkeeper.

Chair still in hand, Sebastian spun to the door and found himself facing the big, blond-headed constable he remembered from that fatal night in Brook Street. "Tom, *run*," said Sebastian over his shoulder as he and Edward Maitland circled each other, both men crouched and watchful. "Get to my father. Goddamn it," he cried, when the boy simply stood there slack mouthed and frozen. "I said, run!"

The boy whirled toward the door.

Something hard and solid slammed into the side of

Sebastian's head. He staggered and tried to turn, but the world began to go black. The last thing he saw was the skinny, flailing arms of the boy, Tom, held fast in the hands of Sir Henry Lovejoy.

Chapter 59

Sebastian came awake to a sense of movement, to the clip-clop of horses' hooves and the clatter of carriage wheels jolting over uneven paving.

Through a dizzying spiral of pain, his thoughts flew at once to Kat. The horror of what he knew Wilcox would do to her was so powerful he was nearly shaking with the need to control it, with the need to keep himself from lashing out in mindless, useless frustration. He forced himself to keep his eyes closed and lie still, fighting down a wave of nausea that burned sour in his throat as he concentrated all his senses on the task of understanding the situation in which he now found himself.

He lay on the cracked leather seat of an old carriage. The forward seat. Rough ropes bit into his wrists, binding them together before him. His ankles were bound as well. But he could detect the steady breathing of only one other person in the carriage with him, a man who sat quiet and alert on the opposite seat. One man.

Which man?

Sebastian opened his eyes to find Sir Henry Lovejoy regarding him through narrowed, watchful brown eyes. "Well," said Sebastian in a pleasantly conversational tone, "I wouldn't have expected the Beau Brummell of Queen Square to willingly miss this."

"If you are referring to Senior Constable Maitland, he is currently otherwise occupied. Conveying two of his fellow constables to the surgeon, to be precise."

Fighting down a fresh wave of nauseous dizziness, Sebastian shifted his weight slightly and discovered that in addition to being tied together, his wrists were also tethered to a ring bolted to the carriage floor. He tightened his jaw against a violent upswelling of rage, but some hint of his feelings must have shown on Sebastian's face because he noticed the magistrate sink back farther into his corner, his eyes wide and watchful.

Sebastian showed his teeth in a smile. "You aren't afraid I'll murder you between here and the Public Office? Cut off your head and take a bath in your blood and do all manner of other ungodly things to your person?"

Lovejoy was not amused. "I think not."

Sebastian glanced out the window as the carriage swung around a corner. The foggy void of the night swirled about them. "And the boy?" he asked casually.

"If you mean that appallingly foul-mouthed urchin who was taken up in your company, he slipped out of my grip and darted off as we were leaving the inn."

It was a crumb of comfort, pitifully small. There were too many things that could go wrong. Hendon could refuse to see the boy, or simply refuse to believe him. And even if the Earl did believe the boy's tale, what then? Whether Hendon sent a party of constables to the wharf, or went himself, the result would be disastrous. Martin Wilcox might be a murderer, but he was no fool and he knew what was at stake. The trap he had laid for Sebastian would be cleverly, carefully planned and orchestrated so that, whatever the outcome, Kat would die. Wilcox couldn't afford to let her live to tell the tale.

Sebastian fixed Sir Henry Lovejoy with an intense stare. "You must let me go."

The little magistrate thrust his hands into his pockets and settled deeper into his overcoat, as if bothered by the cold that seeped up from the straw-strewn floorboards and whistled in with the wind through the cracked windows. "It might be some consolation for you to know that I have reason to believe that you are indeed innocent of the deaths of those two women, Rachel York and Mary Grant. However, once the formalities are satisfied—"

"You don't understand," said Sebastian, his voice low and earnest. "You need to let me go *now*. The man who killed those women has taken another one, Kat Boleyn. If I don't get to her in time, he'll kill her, too."

The carriage lurched suddenly, slowing to a crawl as a thickening press of bodies engulfed them. At first Sebastian thought it another bread riot. Then he heard a cry, "Huzzah for Florizel," and saw the laughter and bright expectation in the swell of upturned faces shining in the golden light of the carriage lamps, and he understood. This was not a mob, but a crowd of revelers celebrating the installation of the Prince as Regent, which was to take place in the morning. They genuinely believed their hard-pressed, desperate lives were finally going to take a turn for the better. They didn't understand that nothing would really change, that they were simply replacing an earnest but mad old king with a vain, pleasure-loving, self-indulgent prince who gave far more thought to the cut of his coats than to the spiraling cost of bread; who had never heard the wail of a child starving in the cold, never seen those stacks of pitifully small, white-shrouded bodies waiting for the quicklime of the poor hole.

"There is still the matter of Constable Simplot," said Sir Henry. "While I can understand—"

"*Goddamn it*," Sebastian swore, coming half upright

only to be thrown off balance by his bound ankles. "I didn't attack your bloody constable. Why would I? Did you not hear what I said? A woman is going to *die*. Tonight."

A string of firecrackers went off next to the carriage, startling the horse and bringing a roar of excitement from the crowd. "If that is true," said Lovejoy, his nervous gaze darting to the window, "then tell me where this man is keeping her. I'll send constables after them."

Sebastian let out a harsh laugh. "She's bait in a trap set for me. If your constables go charging in there, she'll die."

"I think you underestimate the capabilities of my constables."

"Do I?"

"This man—the one you say is killing these women. Who is he?"

"My brother-in-law. Lord Wilcox."

The magistrate's lips parted as if on a gasp, but he kept his features otherwise admirably controlled. Still, it was several moments before he said, "And your proof?"

Sebastian had to beat back an uncharacteristic welling of frustration and despair. Proof? He had none. "The only proof I have is that he has taken Kat Boleyn."

"And your proof of that?"

A sudden explosion of fireworks ripped through the night, filling the street with a shower of sparks that glowed eerily in the heavy fog. "I have none."

Lovejoy nodded, the light of a new burst of fireworks winking on the lenses of his eyeglasses. "And if you walk into this trap you say Lord Wilcox has set for you? How will that save her?"

"I have no intention of falling neatly into Wilcox's trap."

"Yet you might. If you will simply tell me—"

"Goddamn you!" Sebastian cried, yanking painfully, uselessly, at the ropes that tethered him. "You stupid, bloody-minded, self-congratulating bastard. Every minute you keep me here, you are *killing* her."

Sebastian went suddenly still, his chest jerking on a quick intake of cold, smoke-fouled air as he carefully trained his gaze away from the window through which he had seen, briefly, the small, thin arm of a boy who clung to the back of the carriage.

"I understand your frustration," said Sir Henry with a plodding calm that made Sebastian want to scream. "But the law—" He broke off as the hackney's near door jerked open and a small, roughly dressed body appeared on the step. "I say—" he began, then broke off again when Tom swung up into the carriage. The flaring glow from an explosion of fireworks gleamed bright and dangerous on the blade he held gripped tightly in one fist.

"Make a sound or move a whisker," said the boy fiercely, "an' I'll slit yer gullet."

"Heaven preserve us," said Sir Henry, one hand groping for the strap as the carriage gave a sudden lurch.

"I know I didn't do what you done told me," Tom said as he leapt to slice through the ropes at Sebastian's wrists.

"Thank God for that." Sebastian flung aside the remnants of the ropes while the boy crouched to cut the bindings at his ankles. Careful to keep one eye on the white-faced magistrate, Sebastian gripped Tom's shoulder, his hand tightening in a spasm of wordless gratitude as the boy rose to his feet. "But do it now, lad. Quickly. And this time, don't look back."

Tom's head jerked, his face settling into stubborn lines. "I'm coming with you."

Sebastian urged him toward the door. "No. You have your instructions. I expect you to follow them."

"But—"

The need for haste welled up within Sebastian, so fierce and white-hot, it burned in his chest as he swallowed down the impulse to scream at the boy. "Something might go wrong," said Sebastian, struggling to keep his voice calm and steady while every fiber of his being hummed with desperate impatience. "If it does, I'm counting on you to see this bastard brought to justice." Conscious of the magistrate's wrathful presence, Sebastian chose his words carefully. "You know what I need you to do. Can you do it? *Can* you?"

The boy hesitated, his throat working as he swallowed, hard. Then he ducked his head and nodded. "Aye, guv'nor. I'll do it." He pressed the handle of his knife into Sebastian's fist. " 'Ere. You might be needin' this," he said, and, without looking back, slipped off the step into the crowd.

Sebastian watched the small figure disappear into the surging, cheering press of humanity. Then he tucked the knife away in his boot, and prepared to follow.

"This woman," said Sir Henry suddenly. "Tell me where she's being kept."

Sebastian paused at the open door, one hand tightening on the frame as he glanced back. "I think not," he said, and dropped off the step to be swallowed up by the night.

Chapter 60

*T*he Prosperity Trading Company's warehouse fronted one of the basins lying just below Parson's Stairs and the Hermitage Dock.

Sebastian took a hackney as far as Burr Street, then worked his way on foot toward the river. Crowded by day with seamen and stevedores, the wharves after dark were a dangerous labyrinth patrolled by the river police and private guards hired by ship owners and trading companies desperate to control the swarms of thieves who could empty a warehouse or a ship's hold in a night, and slit a man's throat for the coat on his back.

But tonight Sebastian seemed to have the riverfront to himself, moving through fog foul with the stench of salt and river sludge mingling with the odors of the nearby tanneries and soap factories. He could hear the slap of the incoming tide and the occasional muffled boom of distant fireworks from Tower Hill and the Bridge, but the thickness of the fog brought its own special hush to the world, magnifying the sound of his breathing until it grated loud and harsh in his ears.

The warehouse he sought lay midway down a row that loomed before him from out of the gloom. Two stories high and built of rough stone, it butted to the south against another warehouse, while to the left an alley just wide enough for a cart separated it from the next row of buildings, ancient relics of soot-darkened brick.

As he neared the row, Sebastian could see a faint glow of light shining through the Prosperity Trading Company warehouse's arched, brick-faced windows, but they were set high in the thick stone walls, too high for anyone to look through. In the center of the wall facing the narrow lane, a set of double doors sturdily built of thick planks gave access to the warehouse's ground floor. The door's heavy padlock hung dark and undisturbed against the peeling painted wood.

The padlock was both an acknowledgement and a mocking warning, Sebastian thought; it was Wilcox's way of saying, *I know you have no intention of walking blindly into my trap. But make no mistake, I'm ready for you. And whereas I know this warehouse very, very well, you, my friend, do not.*

Sebastian knew the price of arrogance. It was his own arrogance, after all—his belief in his ability to catch Rachel's killer—that had led Kat to this deserted warehouse and the terrors she must now be facing as she waited, live bait in a monster's trap. But he kept telling himself that however arrogant Wilcox might be, the man was no fool. He would know he needed Kat alive if he were to have any hope of surviving the confrontation to come.

Looking up, Sebastian scanned the windows on the upper floor and found them barred, like those of the ground floor, with stout iron grills. But there would be another set of doors, he knew, on the water side.

Soft footed, trying to control even the rasp of his breathing, he slipped down the side alley, toward the water. As he passed a pile of empty packing crates and broken barrels, a rat scuttled, squealing before him.

He stopped, his ears straining to catch any hint of

sound, any indication that Wilcox, waiting within the stone fastness of the warehouse, had heard. A faint breath of air heavy with the scents of the sea lifted off the basin, its heaving black waters all but obscured by the freezing fog that hung low and thick. The high dark hulks and swaying masts of the ships that lay anchored there were mere shadows in the night, quiet and ghostlike.

Treading carefully over the rough weathered planks of the open dock, Sebastian crept toward the waterfront doors. They bore no padlock, but then, they were normally barred from within anyway. Reaching out, he applied just enough pressure against the first panel to tell him what he had already guessed: these doors, too, were locked.

He could hear the slap of water beneath him, for the warehouses here, as along so many of the basins and canals lining the river, were built over the water. There would be a trapdoor in the planked floor of the warehouse to give direct access to lighters and barges. A way of entry, perhaps, but one which would give too much of the advantage to the man waiting within. Sebastian needed to find some approach that would give him a visual advantage. He needed to come in from above.

A second set of loading doors opened from the dock to the upper floor, where a stout beam thrusting out from the wall could be used to hoist goods. But the beam was bare now of both winch and pulley, and Sebastian had no rope to climb up to it. A nearby pile of crates virtually blocked the wharf ahead of him, but they were neither near enough to the door, nor high enough to enable him to reach it. He had to find another way in.

Retracing his steps to the front of the warehouse, he scanned the building's flat roofline. The warehouse beside it was older and larger, but of roughly the same height. Its door, like that of the Prosperity Trading Company, was padlocked.

Sebastian retrieved one of the broken barrels from the alley. Even empty, the iron-banded oak weighed some forty or fifty pounds. Heaving it over his head, he brought the iron edge down on the padlock once, then again, smiling grimly as he felt the lock sheer away from the door, hasp and all.

In the stillness of the fog-shrouded night, the resultant clatter sounded unnaturally loud. Sebastian paused, his breath coming in pants as he listened to the slosh of the incoming tide against the wharfs.

Slipping between the heavy doors, he paused again, waiting for his eyes to adjust to the gloom. It was true he could cope better than most men with the darkness of the night. But his eyes still needed some light to see, and the dense fog obliterated all hint of moon and stars, even the reflected lights of the city around them.

He inched his way across a floor crowded with crates and barrels that perfumed the air with the heavy scents of their contents: tea from India, sables from Russia, baled cotton from the Carolinas. A faint glow showed him a central well some eight to ten feet square, faintly lit from above by a grimy skylight and edged along one side by a steep, straight stair.

He climbed the steps in a light-footed rush that brought him to an upper floor crowded, like the one below, with packing cases and bales. Overhead, the skylight showed only as a dark gray square against the black of the ceiling. There would be tools, he knew, kept here on the upper floor by the warehouse crew. Precious minutes ticked by as he searched, first at the top of the steps, then along the unrailed edge.

He found them at last in a wooden crate left near the front wall. Tossing aside hammers, lengths of chain, and a coil of rope, he grasped a small pry bar, which he thrust into the waistband of his breeches. Then, by shifting some of the crates, he was able to climb within an arm's reach of the skylight.

Set into a large raised wooden frame, the skylight was made up of some half-dozen sections hinged so that they could be raised for ventilation. Feeling along the edge, Sebastian located the clasp of the section above his head and carefully eased it open.

Thick with the smell of sulfur and coal smoke and the scents of the sea, the night swirled in around him. Grasping the edge of the frame, Sebastian levered himself up through the small square opening and onto the roof.

He lay still for a moment, his breath showing white as he listened to the distant boom of fireworks lost in the night. Slowly, he rolled to his feet and crossed the slate expanse to drop lightly down onto the roof of the adjoining warehouse.

Here, the skylight glowed with a faint golden light. But as he inched toward it, he saw that the glass was too clouded and grimy to show more than the vague shapes of the objects below. There was always a chance, he knew, that Wilcox awaited him here on the upper floor. But most men feared the dark, and the source of light from within the building obviously came from the ground floor, site of the warehouse's two main entrances and the water door.

Slipping the pry bar between the skylight's frame and base, Sebastian applied a gentle pressure and felt a slight give as the inner catch began to loosen. He tried again, increasing the pressure, and heard the rending timbers whine in protest.

He immediately eased up on the bar, the night air cold against his sweat-dampened face. Sitting back on his heels, he considered his options. Impossible to break the skylight's frame or shatter the glass without announcing his arrival. But besides the trapdoor leading up from the water, there remained only one other entrance to the warehouse: the dockside doors to the upper floor.

His gaze focused on the crumbling chimney of the fireplace used to warm the warehouse's small counting office. He stared at it for a moment, then retraced his steps to the adjacent roof. Dropping lightly through the open skylight, he retrieved one of the coils of rope he had seen there, along with a stout length of iron.

He was conscious, again, of the relentless passage of time. Lashing one end of the rope to the chimney, Sebastian wound the other end around his waist and lowered himself carefully over the warehouse's back wall, the rough planks of the dock some twenty feet below lost in the mists swirling in from the water. Straightening his legs as a brace, he levered away from the wall and walked crabwise down the rough stone until he came to the double doors that gave access to the upper floor. A stout lintel ran just below the door, forming a ledge against which he was able to brace his weight while he applied subtle pressure to the doors. The panels gave for about an inch, then stopped. These doors, too, were secured from the inside by a bar.

Shifting his weight, Sebastian retrieved the pry bar from his waistband and thrust its end between the two doors, wedging them open far enough that he was able to slip the length of iron rod in beneath the pivot bar and lever it up. He felt it catch for a moment, then drop away with a clatter that had him cursing silently into the night.

The near door swung open to a gentle nudge that drew no shriek of protest from the hinges. He eased himself inside, deftly closing the doors behind him against any sliver of light or sudden draft of cold air that might betray his presence ... if the clatter of the falling bar hadn't already done that.

The atmosphere here was redolent with the warm, exotic scent of coffee. Surrounded by towering stacks of bulging burlap bags, Sebastian crept toward the golden pool of light that was the central opening. The well was large, some eight to ten feet across, and configured much like that of the adjoining warehouse, with a straight flight of stairs running up one side. He could see a huge overhead beam to which was mounted a stout pulley wound with a thick rope. One end of the rope ran down, diagonally, out of Sebastian's line of vision, but the other hung straight and tautly weighted. As he watched, it quivered slightly, as if the weight suspended from it had moved.

With a sick sense of dread clawing at his guts, Sebastian crept toward the unrailed edge of the well to where he could look down upon the scene Martin Wilcox had prepared for him.

Three lanterns were clustered together, their light shuttered so that they threw only a narrow, concentrated beam that illuminated the area directly before them while leaving the rest of the warehouse shrouded in darkness. And in that shaft of light, Wilcox had hung Kat.

Her wrists were bound together, and it was from these that she hung suspended from the great overhead pulley, her fingers twisting around to grasp painfully at the rope in an attempt to relieve the strain on her arms and shoulders. As he watched, she pivoted slowly, swinging around so that he could see the fear and the pain in her eyes, her lips drawn back in a harsh rictus around the gag that held her mouth ajar. Her ankles had been tied, too, with more rope wound around her legs, pinning the torn cloth of her velvet riding habit tightly against her.

She hung suspended some three or four feet above where the floor should have been, except that Wilcox had positioned her directly above the trapdoor to the basin and the trapdoor was now open. Through it, Sebastian could see the shimmering blackness of lapping waves as the tide rose with the night.

It was a diabolical trap, delicately baited. Whether Sebastian had entered the warehouse through one of the two ground-floor entrances, or whether he came up through the trapdoor or down the stairs, he could not reach Kat without being caught in the light. Yet because of the way the lanterns set up, Wilcox kept for himself the protective cover of darkness. He also controlled the rope by which Kat Boleyn hung suspended. The only way Sebastian could free her would be to cut her loose. Yet, bound as she was, even if he were to plunge with her into the dark icy waters below, she would in all probability drown before he could get her to shore.

There was only one move Sebastian could make. He acted swiftly, calculating the position of the lamps and the distance to the rope. Quietly hefting one of the large bags of coffee beans, he eased it over to the edge of the well. He was just stepping back when a board creaked, betrayingly, beneath his foot.

He froze, but the damage was already done. Martin Wilcox's amused voice came from out of the darkness below. "You may as well show yourself, Devlin. I know you're there."

There was a pause, during which Sebastian shrugged off his coat and clenched Tom's knife between his teeth. Into the silence, Wilcox said, "Let me rephrase that. If you don't come down, now, your whore here goes in the river. You hear that, Devlin? All I need do is cut the rope, and she's fish bait."

Sebastian gave the coffee sack a hard shove that carried it over the edge of the central well to plummet straight down on the triangle of lamps below.

It landed with a shattering crash that plunged the warehouse into darkness just as Sebastian leapt from the well's edge.

One hand clutched only air, cold and empty. But his right hand caught the rope and closed on it, his arm wrenching in his shoulder as it took all his weight. The impact of the sideways lunge set the rope to swinging, but the movement was slight, too slight. He kicked his legs to make it swing farther, the fibers of the rope burning his hand through the leather of his glove as he slid down to Kat.

He could hear the frightened strain of her breathing. Still gripping the rope with one hand, he closed his free arm around her in a swift, fierce embrace that drew her shivering body back against his chest as he kicked again, swinging them back and forth on the end of the rope like a pendulum. Then, wrapping one leg around her hips to keep them together, he slipped the knife from his teeth and, when the arc of their swing neared its apogee, he reached up and sliced through the rope.

Gritting his teeth, Sebastian hacked at the heavy fibers, the last strands unraveling as he prayed that he hadn't miscalculated the angle of the arc, that the rope wouldn't give way at the precise moment they were over the open trap to plunge them into the freezing black waters below.

With a half-catching jerk, the rope unraveled and snapped, hurtling them downward just as a blunderbuss exploded in a deafening roar of fire and smoke.

Chapter 61

Sebastian felt the pain of the shot rip like fire through the flesh of his thigh, just before they hit the floor-boards. At the last instant he managed to twist so that Kat fell half on top of him and he absorbed most of the impact himself.

He rolled, shifting her weight so that she lay within the protective curve of his body. He could hear the rasp of her breathing, open mouthed behind the gag, but he had no way of knowing if she had taken any of the shot herself. Bringing his lips close to her ear, he whispered softly, "Lie still."

He felt rather than saw her nodded response, for without the lanterns and surrounded as they were by towering piles of crates and wool bales, the blackness of the night seemed nearly complete.

Moving swiftly in the dark, he sliced through the ropes binding her ankles and tore away the coils wrap-ping her legs. Cautiously, he ran his hands up over her body. It was just below her ribs he felt the warm sticky wetness of blood.

His heart thudding painfully in his chest, he ripped the cravat from his neck and pressed the quickly folded cloth against her side, unable in the thick, unfamiliar blackness of the foggy night to gauge the seriousness of the wound. Holding the cloth tight with one hand, he worked awkwardly to slice the ropes from her wrists before moving to ease the gag from her mouth.

Her hand caught at his, squeezed his fingers in a silent, trembling communication, then slid away to flutter down to her bloody side.

One cheek pressed against her hair, Sebastian willed his breathing to still as he strained to penetrate the hushed blackness of night. He knew that at the time of the blunderbuss's firing, Wilcox had been hidden amongst the crates back beneath the stairs. But he couldn't be certain the man hadn't moved since then. And while Sebastian doubted Wilcox's ability to reload a blunderbuss in the dark, there was no way of knowing how many firearms he had with him. Even Kat wouldn't know if the man had hidden a stash of carbines or pistols at various points about the warehouse before he brought her here.

If he'd been alone, Sebastian would have taken the offensive, trusting his training and the unnatural quickness of his senses to even out the disadvantages of being unarmed and unfamiliar with his surroundings. But he couldn't leave Kat, alone and vulnerable and hurt.

Yet as the silence in the warehouse stretched out, a dark and tangible thing, Sebastian realized he couldn't afford to wait for Wilcox to make the next move, either. He had no way of knowing how badly Kat was injured, but he could feel her life's blood seeping hot and wet through the thick folds of his cravat, could smell the coppery tang mingling with the scents of salt and lanolin that lay so heavy on the night air.

He took her hand in his and pressed it to the cloth at her side, then slipped his own hand away. Dipping his head, he brushed her cheek with his lips and found her face cold and unnaturally clammy. *I'm not leaving you,* he was telling her, although he had no way of knowing whether or not she understood.

He could feel the cold dampness rising up from the water through the opening beside them, for their fall had brought them heart-stoppingly close to the edge of the trapdoor. The faint outline of a stack of coffee sacks showed near the opening's edge. Moving by slow degrees, he was able to shift his weight until his shoulder touched one of the sacks.

Gritting his teeth, he heaved, tipping the coffee over the edge. Then he rolled quickly away, taking Kat with him as the heavy bag flopped down to tumble some eight feet or more before sliding into the black water with a long and satisfyingly loud plop.

Her trembling body held tight against his, Sebastian waited for another explosion of gunfire. But there was only a silence filled with the wash of ripples radiating out to slop against the timber supports before fading away into nothing.

Wilcox's voice came to him, low and mocking from out of the shadows to his left. "A pitiful ruse, Devlin. What were you expecting me to do? Carelessly venture forth on the assumption you'd slipped away?"

Unwilling to give away their own position, Sebastian smiled grimly into the night. So the bastard *had* moved to a new position, behind the bales of Australian wool that lay between Sebastian and the doors leading out to the loading dock.

"An interesting standoff," Wilcox continued. "One might be tempted to say I've lost the advantage. Except that I can smell blood, Devlin. Yours, I wonder? Or hers? I can afford to wait out the night. Can you?"

Kat's hand snaked out, suddenly, to touch Sebastian's arm. "*Sebastian*," she whispered.

But he had already seen it himself: a faint glow of or-

ange growing steadily brighter behind the stack of wool
bales near the base of the stairs. A spark from the blunderbuss's explosion must have landed to smolder
amidst the lanolin-rich bales. A breath of air stirred by
the draft rising off the open trapdoor brought with it the
faintest hint of burning raw wool, pungent and unmistakable. Then the entire pile burst into flames.

As Sebastian watched, the flames leapt high, carried
by the updraft from the open water door. With a
whoosh, the old timbers of the staircase caught, coming
alive with a crackling dance of fire that sent black
smoke roiling through the building.

He heard Kat suck in her breath on a stifled gasp and
knew the full implications of the fire were not lost upon
her. Wilcox was between them and the double doors
leading to the water's edge. With the stairs to the second
story aflame and the main entrance to the lane padlocked
on the outside, the only other way out of the building was
through the trapdoor. But it was an eight-foot drop into
the icy cold waters of the basin; half-fainting from loss of
blood and weighed down by the heavy velvet train of her
riding habit, Kat would surely drown.

All around them, the warehouse and its contents
were going up like a pitch-soaked torch. Here on the
floor, near the open trapdoor, the air was still relatively
clear, but it wouldn't be for long. They had to get out,
now.

From the sound of Wilcox's hacking cough, Sebastian
realized the man was moving again. The bar on the
dockside doors gave a metallic shriek as it was yanked
back. For a moment, the swirling black smoke parted.
He saw the doors open, a man's form showing dark and
solid against the foggy night sky. Then it was gone.

Kat's fingers curled around Sebastian's arm, gripping
tight. In the eerie red glow of the fire he could now see

her quite clearly. The entire side of her riding habit was dark with blood.

"Christ." No longer constrained by the fear of drawing Wilcox's gunfire, Sebastian moved quickly, tearing long strips of cloth from her train and tying them tightly around the wound. "We're going to have to follow him out that door. You realize that, don't you?"

Kat shook her head, her eyes wide in a pale face. "No. He still has a pistol. If we go through that door, he'll be waiting for us."

Sebastian gathered her into his arms. "We've no choice." He had to shout to be heard above the roar of the fire. "The doors to the lane are padlocked from the outside."

"Then break the lock."

Sebastian glanced toward the front of the building. Already, the smoke was so thick that each breath burned his throat and tore at his lungs. "I can try."

Coughing badly, he carried her to where she could catch a breath of the fresh air flowing in from the gap beneath the two front doors. Casting about in the thickening smoke, he found a heavy sea chest, bound with brass but small enough that he could grasp it with both hands. Using the end of the chest as a battering ram, he slammed it against the juncture of the heavy wooden doors. His aim was to break the lock, or at least tear off the hasp. He could feel the heat of the flames searing his back, sucking the air from his lungs. Gritting his teeth, he slammed the chest into the doors a second time, and heard a satisfying crack.

With all his strength, he rammed the doors a third time. The chest shattered in his hands.

"It's no use," he cried, heaving the chest aside. "We have to go out the back."

He bent to lift Kat into his arms, but she clutched his

chest and shook her head. "Leave me. Without me, you can slip through the water door."

He met her gaze, his chest jerking for breath beneath her spread fingers. "I'm not leaving you. So you may as well give over trying to be so bloody noble and simply accept that it's my turn."

There was an instant's silence; then he heard her answering laugh, faint but true.

With a tearing roar, the great overhanging beam from the central well collapsed in a violent shower of sparks. "Bloody hell," Sebastian swore.

Clutching Kat to him, dodging fiery bales and falling debris, he sprinted across the warehouse floor. For one wretched moment he thought he'd become disoriented and lost his way in the thickening smoke. Then he saw the open doorway framing a rectangle of gray mist beyond, and he burst through into the cool, lifegiving air of the night.

He'd expected to find Wilcox there on the dock, beside the basin. But the dock stretched out empty before them.

"He must have heard you trying to break through the front doors and gone around," said Kat, coughing badly.

"Maybe." Sebastian's own voice was a pained rasp. Or maybe Wilcox was simply waiting for them at the end of that long dark alleyway that ran along the north side of the warehouse.

"Set me down. I can walk," she said.

"Are you certain?"

"Yes." She pushed away from him so that her feet slid to the ground. Then she said, "Sorry. A miscalculation," and fainted dead away.

Swinging her up into his arms again, Sebastian turned south, away from the alley and the dangers that might lurk there. He'd thought the pile of crates at the juncture of the two buildings only partially obstructed the dock, but he saw now that he was wrong, that the way was blocked completely. He had no choice but to go north.

By now, the flames were shooting from the warehouse's upper story. One by one, the windows began to shatter, the night filling with the sound of breaking glass as the splintered shards rained down around them. Sheltering Kat with his own body, broken glass crunching beneath his boots, Sebastian ran. As he ducked past the mouth of the alleyway, he saw it filled with smoke and leaping flames from the burning building beside it. If Wilcox had been there, waiting, the heat and breaking glass would have driven him back.

The fire roaring behind him, Sebastian kept to the strip of narrow dock running along the edge of the basin. Passing the row of ancient brick warehouses, he worked his way north. The black waters of the basin reflected the leaping flames, while the fog caught the glow of savage orange until it seemed that the very night around him was afire.

He could see another passageway ahead, leading off to the left, that he hoped would take him inland. Then his heel caught on an uneven plank and he stumbled, going down as his wounded leg gave way beneath him in a spasm of pain, white hot and nearly blinding.

He sank to his knees, Kat still held, insensible, in his arms. He was aware of the distant heat of the fire and the ache in his seared lungs as he struggled to suck in air. Gathering his strength, he was about to push up again when he heard the click of a pistol's hammer being drawn back, and Wilcox's voice saying, "Bad choice, Devlin."

Chapter 62

*M*artin Wilcox stepped out of the smoke-swirled darkness, a flintlock pistol gripped in one hand. His driving cloak was gone; soot stained the starched white linen of his cravat, and falling cinders had singed the Bath superfine of his inimitably cut coat. But his voice was still oddly pleasant, almost conversational.

"It all comes down to choices. Doesn't it, Devlin?" he said. "The choice you made to stay in London and stir up trouble, for instance, when any reasonable, prudent man would have fled abroad. The choice you made to come here tonight and walk into my little trap. And then there's the choice you faced just now. By sacrificing the girl, you might have escaped me. But that's not a choice a man like you could live with, is it? It's what makes you so fatally predictable."

Sebastian felt the planks of the dock rough beneath his knees, the cold air blowing in from the basin cool against the film of sweat on his face as he watched Wilcox walk up to him. "And what of your choices, Wilcox? Your choice to kill Rachel York rather than pay for whatever she was offering to sell to you. Was that so wise?"

Wilcox kept coming until he stood just feet away, the pistol held straight-armed before him. "Ah, but you see,

I thought our dear Rachel had made an unwise choice herself. When I heard she'd gone to meet Hendon that night, I assumed she'd found a higher bidder for her wares. So I followed, expecting to recover the evidence of my little insurance scheme. Instead, what do I find but your mother's most interesting affidavit. It was a surprise, believe me."

"Insurance scheme—?" Sebastian began, only to break off as he suddenly understood. "Of course. The story you carried to Hendon last year about an embarrassing sexual peccadillo was an invention, designed to extricate yourself from an awkward situation. How long *have* you been caught in Leo Pierrepont's web?"

Wilcox's habitual smile never slipped. "Three years. I'm the one who tipped Pierrepont off as to our intentions in Spain." He said it as if he were proud of it.

"So that's the reason you tracked down Rachel's maid, Mary Grant? To recover whatever evidence Rachel took from Pierrepont that would have proved your involvement with the French went back much further than anyone supposed."

"That's right. I doubt the stupid fool even realized the value of what she had."

"But that didn't stop you from killing her."

"One could never be sure," he said, smiling through his teeth. "The evidence against myself I destroyed at once, of course. But the other documents I kept. One never knows when such things might prove useful. Where you made your mistake was in taking your mother's affidavit from my library. Until I found it missing, I'd no notion you'd tweaked onto me."

Sebastian looked up into his brother-in-law's face, and laughed. "I don't have the affidavit. Do you mean to tell me you've lost it? How ... careless of you."

Wilcox's hand tightened convulsively around the pistol's handle, then relaxed. "An interesting tactic. You think to unnerve me, I take it?" He shook his head. "It won't work." The man's face suddenly hardened, his normally placid, smiling features twisting in a way that reminded Sebastian of Bayard. "Set the girl down on the dock—but don't get up. Back away from her on your knees."

His gaze still focused on Wilcox's face, Sebastian eased Kat down onto the dock. She let out a soft sigh, then lay still as he shifted away from her, repositioning his weight subtly so that he came up into a crouch.

Wilcox smiled. "There. I need a clean shot. Wouldn't want to confuse the authorities when I present them with your dead body. And the mutilated corpse of your last victim, of course," he added, his gaze flicking significantly toward Kat. "They'll be so pleased."

Sebastian had his good leg under him, his muscles tensed, ready to spring, as he watched Wilcox's eyes.

"No one actually *cares* who killed those women. You understand that, don't you? No fire burns within the collective metropolitan bosom to see justice done. People simply want to feel safe, and with you dead, they will. I'll be a hero. Ironic, isn't it?"

Sebastian saw the flicker in Wilcox's eyes the instant before his finger tightened on the pistol's trigger.

Sebastian dove forward, twisting his body sideways as he flung up his left arm. His open palm slammed into Wilcox's extended wrist, knocking it up just as the pistol exploded fire and smoke into the night.

Sebastian felt a searing heat tear across his upper arm. Then his right shoulder slammed into Wilcox at midthigh. He wrapped his good arm around the back of the bastard's knees and yanked, although the sheer momentum of the lunge would have been enough by itself to knock him over.

Wilcox went down hard, his back hitting the dock with a thump that drove the air from his lungs in a huff as Sebastian landed on top of him. Still gasping for breath, Wilcox swung the empty flintlock like a club, bashing its heavy weight down on Sebastian's back.

Swearing harshly, Sebastian grabbed the man's pistol hand in a brutal grip and yanked it over his head, tightening his grip until Wilcox relaxed his hold on the pistol in a spasm of pain. Then he went suddenly, utterly still.

"So you've overpowered me," he said, panting, the light from the distant fire gleaming in his eyes as he smiled up at Sebastian. "What now, hmm? You do realize that you've no proof of what I did to those women. None. Even the scratches that bitch left on my neck have healed. It'll simply be your word against mine. And who would believe you?"

"You're forgetting Kat Boleyn."

"What? The word of a whore? Against that of a friend of the Crown Prince himself?" Wilcox smiled. "I don't think so." Still smiling, he twisted his lower body and drove his knee up, straight into Sebastian's wounded thigh.

The pain exploded in a fireball that made Sebastian gasp. For an instant his vision blurred and his head swam, and his hold on Wilcox relaxed just enough to enable the man to clamber backward from beneath him.

Rolling over, Wilcox made it as far as his hands and knees before Sebastian lunged after him. They teetered for a moment at the edge of the dock, then went over together.

Sebastian lost his grip on Wilcox as they fell. Wilcox slammed into the water in an awkward, crumpled heap. But Sebastian managed to straighten his body so that he hit feet first. He plunged deep into the cold, black water, then shot back to the surface, treading water heavily, weighed down by the awkwardness of boots and rough breeches, the wounds in his shoulder and thigh on fire.

He could hear his brother-in-law coughing and gasping, see the white of his cravat and waistcoat glowing out of the darkness of the night. Sebastian swam toward him. For a moment the man's fat head disappeared beneath black water sheened with orange by the distant fire. Then he floundered up again, arms and legs thrashing, his eyes opening wide in his pale face when he saw Sebastian.

"Help me! For God's sake, *help me*. I can't swim." One of his flailing hands caught at Sebastian's neck, clutching, strangling.

"Let go of me, you fool. You'll drown us both."

But Wilcox was beyond reason. "You can't let me drown," he sputtered, his grip on Sebastian tightening, frantic.

Sucking in a deep breath, Sebastian dove, twisting under Wilcox's arm to break the man's grip. This time, he was careful to surface behind the floundering man's back. With a straight arm, Sebastian reached out and grasped the back of Wilcox's collar. It was a standard lifesaving maneuver; Sebastian had only to pull the man in close, wrap a bent elbow beneath Wilcox's chin to keep his head above water, and swim toward the dock.

He could hear in the distance the roar of the flames consuming the warehouse and, more distant still, the frantic *clang-clang* of the fire bell. Sebastian tightened his grip on the back of Wilcox's coat. But he kept his arm straight.

It all comes down to choices, the man had said. And the choice Sebastian now faced lay dark and murky before him. Because Wilcox was right: there was no proof of what the man had done, nothing linking him to the twisted slaying of those two women, nothing to stop him from doing it again, and again.

Other considerations whispered to his conscience: if saved from the water, Wilcox might still somehow manage to best Sebastian and attack Kat. But Sebastian knew that wasn't the real issue. He had learned long ago that the line between right and wrong, between good and evil, isn't always sharply drawn. But he still believed that the line existed, nonetheless. He'd set out, barely a week ago, to prove himself unjustly accused of a heinous crime. Only gradually had his purpose shifted. And he knew that while he might never be able to prove his own innocence, he could at least fulfill a promise made to a woman too long dead to hear.

From somewhere near at hand came the sound of a man's shout. But it didn't matter. Sebastian had made his choice. Opening his hand, he let the coat of Bath superfine slip through his fingers.

Chapter 63

*F*rom where he stood at the edge of the dock, Sir Henry Lovejoy watched the Viscount climb the rough ladder from the water below. As he reached the top, Devlin looked up, his uncanny eyes gleaming yellow in the reflected fire's light.

The two men stared at each other, Devlin's breath coming so hard and fast that the coarse cloth of his water-soaked, bloodstained shirt shuddered with each lifting of his chest. It was Devlin who spoke first.

"The boy, Tom? Where is he?"

"Quite safe. I intercepted him just outside your father's house in Grosvenor Square. That's right," he added, when Devlin's eyebrows twitched together. "I overheard your instructions to the lad back at the Rose and Crown."

"And?"

Lovejoy cleared his throat. "I found Wilcox's note in his pocket."

"The note was unsigned."

"Yes. I admit I initially found it difficult to credence the lad's rather long and tangled tale. But he'd had the forethought to liberate his lordship's pocketbook, which lent considerable weight to his story."

Levering himself up onto the dock, his wet clothes

clinging to his lean frame, the Viscount went to crouch beside the crumpled, bloody form of the woman. Love-joy didn't move. "Is she . . ."

"No." Her blood streaming over his hands, Devlin lifted the woman gently into his arms. The wind caught her long dark hair, blowing it loose across his face. She stirred, her voice a hoarse murmur, and he nuzzled his lips against her ear, whispering reassurances.

Then his gaze lifted, again, to meet Lovejoy's. "How much did you overhear? Just now."

And Sir Henry Lovejoy, that hardheaded stickler for the processes of the law and the sanctity of truth, who had arrived at the basin's edge only in time to watch Wilcox's head first disappear beneath the black waters, smiled tightly and said, "Enough."

Chapter 64

Sebastian watched Kat breathe, watched the gentle rise and fall of her breasts beneath lace-trimmed sheets, watched the flicker of golden candlelight over the pale skin of her eyelids, closed now in gentle sleep.

He stood beside the bed, his dressing gown thrown casually over his shoulders. Around them, the Brook Street house settled into the hush of the night. It seemed oddly strange, to be here again in his own house, to be wearing freshly laundered linen and fine silk. He was here, and safe, and yet the coiled sense of alertness, the driving restlessness remained.

"She's going to be fine, Sebastian," said Paul Gibson, coming to stand beside him. "I'll stay with her. But you need to get some rest. You've lost a fair amount of blood yourself."

Sebastian nodded. Beneath the bandages, his shoulder and leg throbbed with a fiery ache that seemed to radiate out and blend with every cut and bruise he'd acquired over the past week. He felt as if he hadn't slept in a lifetime. "Call me if she wakes."

"Of course."

Turning toward his room, Sebastian became aware of the sound of a man's loud, angry voice drifting up from the hall below.

"Damn your impudence," swore the Earl of Hendon. "And to hell with your instructions. *I want to see my son.*"

Sebastian paused at the top of the stairs. "Father."

Hendon looked up, a succession of emotions chasing one another across the features of his white, anguished face as he watched Sebastian limp down the stairs toward him. But all he said was, "I'd heard you were hurt."

"It's nothing," said Sebastian, and led the way into the drawing room.

Hendon closed the door carefully behind him. "I've had a meeting with Lord Jarvis and Sir Henry Lovejoy, concerning these recent revelations about Wilcox. The situation is delicate, particularly with the Prince's installation as Regent to take place tomorrow. For an intimate of the Prince to be implicated in such heinous crimes at this time . . ."

"Devilishly inconvenient. So what is Jarvis proposing? I'm confident he's come up with some solution."

At the levity in Sebastian's tone, the Earl's features settled into a deep frown. "As a matter of fact, the suggestion was mine. The murders of Rachel York and Mary Grant will be attributed to the Frenchman, Leo Pierrepont."

"Of course. Cooperative of him to have fled the country." Sebastian went to stand before the hearth, his gaze on the fire. "And Wilcox's death?"

"The work of the cutthroats and thieves who set fire to the warehouse. The riverfront can be a dangerous place at night."

"Amanda will be pleased. No opprobrium attached to the family name to interfere with Stephanie's come out next year." Sebastian glanced around. "You do realize that Amanda knew?"

"What? That Wilcox had butchered those two women? That I can't believe. Even of Amanda."

Sebastian smiled grimly. "Unlike you, however, she was unaware of her husband's French connections."

Sebastian wasn't expecting an apology from his father and he didn't get one. Sebastian waited, instead, for the inevitable question.

Hendon cleared his throat. "It was Wilcox who took Lady Hendon's affidavit from Rachel York's body, I assume?"

"Yes. Although I gather from something he said it's gone missing again. He thought I'd taken it."

Hendon stood very still, beads of moisture showing on his temples, as if he were hot. "You don't have it?"

"No."

The Earl turned away, one hand scrubbing across his face as he struggled to absorb this. It was a moment before he said gruffly, "And the woman? I understand her injuries are serious."

"She's lost a lot of blood, but the doctor says nothing vital was hit. Barring infection, she should recover."

Hendon worked his lower jaw back and forth in that way he had. "She told you, I presume, what passed between us six years ago."

Sebastian stared at his father.

"I did what I thought was right at the time," Hendon said, his voice brusque. "I still think it was right. Such a marriage would have ruined your life. Thank God she finally saw that herself."

"How much, precisely, did you offer her?" Sebastian asked, his voice low and dangerous.

"Twenty thousand pounds. There aren't many women who'd turn down a chance at that kind of money."

"She turned you down?"

"Why, yes. You mean, she *didn't* tell you?"

"No. No, she didn't."

Kat came awake slowly. The fiery pain she remembered from the night before had gone, leaving a dull ache that throbbed down her side.

The room with its dusky blue silken hangings and gilded furniture was unfamiliar, but she recognized the man in doeskin breeches and top boots who sat, arms crossed at his chest, in a tapestry-covered chair beside the bed. He must have sensed her gaze upon him because he turned, his hand reaching to cover hers on the counterpane.

"I knew you'd come for me," she said, surprised to discover her throat raw, her voice husky from the fire.

Devlin's hand tightened around hers. "*Kat.* Dear God. I am so sorry."

She smiled, because it was so like him to blame himself for what had happened to her, to blame himself for having involved her in his struggle to make sense of Rachel's death. And then her smile faded because he didn't know—she hoped he would never know—how deeply she had been involved in the events surrounding Rachel's death even before he came to her for help.

"I had a long talk with Hendon last night," he said, his brows drawing together, his jaw held unexpectedly tight. "Why didn't you tell me the truth?"

"Which truth is that?" She kept her voice even, although her heart had begun to thud uncomfortably in her chest. "There are many truths, more than a few of which are best not told."

"The truth about what happened six years ago."

"Ah. That one." She laughed softly, hoping to turn away any more questions. But he continued to stare at her in that compelling way of his, and she knew he would demand an answer. She sought to frame it in the lightest terms possible. "Telling you would have been counterproductive. That sort of noble sacrifice only achieves its object when masked."

One corner of his mouth lifted in a ghost of a smile. "You need to curb this unfortunate predilection of yours for martyrdom."

Her hand twisted beneath his, held him tight. "He was right, you know. Your father. He said if I really loved you, I wouldn't marry you."

His eyes had always fascinated her. Wild and fiercely intelligent, they glittered now with anger and hurt. "And so you lied to me. For my own good."

"Yes."

"Damn you." He pushed up from the chair and swung away, only to turn again, nostrils flaring, chest jerking with the passion of his breathing. "I would have made you my *wife*. You had no right to make that kind of decision without me."

She struggled to sit up, her shaky hand sinking into the featherbed beneath her. "Oh, Sebastian. Don't you see? I'm the only one who could."

A silence fell between them, taut and sad. She could hear the cry of a vendor hawking his wares in the street outside, and, nearer, the soft fall of ash on the hearth. She let her gaze rove over the man before her, over the familiar, proud bones of his face, the lean, beautiful length of his body. And because she loved him so much, because she would always love him, she forced herself to say what needed to be said, although the words tore open every old bleeding wound she'd hidden away so deep within her. "And I would do it again," she whispered, "because you are who you are, while I am . . . what I am."

His head jerked back, his lips pulling into a thin, hard line. "I can change what you are."

"By making me the future Lady Hendon?" Kat shook her head. "That would only change my name, not what I *am*—what people would see when they looked at me."

"You think I give a damn about other people?"

"No. But I care. I care what other people think of you. Nothing you can do would ever raise me up to your level, Sebastian; I would only drag you down to mine. And that I refuse to do."

He stared at her, his strange yellow eyes fierce and hard. Then he sucked in a quick breath and for a moment she saw a flash of his soul, a hint of the vulnerability she knew he kept hidden deep within him, and it ripped at her heart. "You could have said that six years ago, instead of driving me away with a lie."

"Oh, Sebastian. Don't you see? I had to drive you away. I knew if I told you the truth, you'd try to change my mind, that you wouldn't accept it. And I knew, too, that I wouldn't have the strength to hold out against you."

He came to stand beside her. It wasn't until he gently touched her cheek and she saw the sheen of wetness on his fingertips that she realized she was crying. "I'm not accepting it now," he said.

She shook her head, although she couldn't quite stop herself from bringing up her hand to cradle his palm against her cheek. "I'll not be changing my mind."

He smiled then, the smile she loved, the one that made him look both boyish and a little bit wicked. "I can be patient."

~~

"The mantle should be of silk-trimmed paramatta, I think," said Amanda, holding the pattern card so that it caught the weak morning light streaming in her drawing room windows. "With crepe." She handed the card back to her dressmaker and reached for the next design. "But on this one we'll have the bodice covered with crepe, with cuffs and collar of deep lawn."

"Yes, my lady."

Amanda sighed. It was always such a bother, this business of assembling the accouterments of deep mourning. Black petticoats and stockings, handkerchiefs with black borders in cambric and silk . . . The list seemed endless. All the servants would need to be outfitted as well, of course, although Amanda intended to look into dyeing some of their existing clothing black. She'd heard Indian logwood worked quite well. Thank heavens Stephanie would be out of mourning before she was due to be presented at Court the following Season. Amanda herself, of course, would be in half mourning for another year or two beyond that.

The commotion in the hall below surprised her. Then she heard her father's voice, and understood.

"Send the woman away," said Hendon, appearing in the entrance to the morning room.

Amanda nodded to the dressmaker, who collected her pattern cards and samples, and scampered out the doorway.

"Where is it?" Hendon demanded the instant the door shut behind the dressmaker.

Amanda settled back against the damask cushions of her chair and stared up at her father with a placid, well-composed face. "Where is what?"

"Don't play me for a fool. Your mother's affidavit. Wilcox thought Sebastian had taken it. And since I disremember hearing of your having any break-ins recently, the conclusion is obvious."

Amanda held herself quite still. "Is it?"

Hendon stared at her from across the room, dark color suffusing his face, his chest rising and falling with his agitated breathing. It was a moment before he spoke. His voice was crisp, but surprisingly calm and even. "So that's the way we're going to play it, is it? Very well. But mark my words." He raised one hand to jab a thick finger into the air between them. "If I can hush up your precious husband's nasty little activities, I can also lay them bare to the world. And I don't think the consequences of that would be pleasant—for either you or for your children."

Amanda surged to her feet, rage thrumming through her so hard and fast she was trembling with it. "You would do that? You would do that to your own grand-children?"

Hendon stared back at her, his jaw set. "I would do anything to protect the succession. Do you understand? Anything."

"Yes. Well." She gave a torn laugh. "We've already seen that, haven't we?"

Chapter 65

$\mathcal{A}$t the hour appointed for the installation of the Prince of Wales as Regent, the sun broke through the clouds that had been shrouding the city and a light wind blew the dirty remnants of the fog away.

Restless and still technically a fugitive from justice for the attack on Constable Simplot, Sebastian pushed through the rabble massing in the streets. He was crossing Piccadilly when Sir Henry Lovejoy hailed him from the open window of a passing hackney. "If I might have a word, my lord?"

Nodding, Sebastian waited while the little magistrate paid off the jarvey. Together, they entered the park and turned toward the lagoon to walk along in silence until the crowds thinned around them.

Lovejoy said, "I thought you should know that Constable Simplot regained consciousness last night. His fever has broken and the doctors say the prognosis for his recovery is quite promising."

"The man must have the constitution of an ox."

An unexpected smile played about the magistrate's thin lips. "That is roughly the opinion of his doctors." The smile faded. "He's told us what happened that afternoon, on Brook Street. Needless to say, Chief Constable Maitland has been dismissed from his duties."

Sebastian nodded. He supposed he should feel relieved that the young constable had survived to give witness to the truth. Perhaps in time, Sebastian thought, he would feel relief. But at the moment he simply felt numb, as if it had all happened long ago in someone else's lifetime.

"I was most impressed," Sir Henry was saying, "by the way you went about the task of discovering the true identity of the killer. Your investigative abilities are quite remarkable, my lord. If you weren't a nobleman, you'd make a fine detective."

Sebastian laughed.

"Some cases, of course, are more difficult for our office to deal with than others," said Lovejoy. "Particularly those cases involving the royal family or members of the nobility." He cleared his throat uncomfortably and squinted off into the distance. "I was wondering ... given your talents and abilities, if you might be interested in occasionally cooperating with our office on such exceptional cases? On a purely unofficial basis, of course."

"No," said Sebastian baldly.

Lovejoy nodded, his chin held tight against his chest. "Yes, of course. I understand. It's a passion not many feel, that driving need to see justice done in this world. To stand on the side of the weak and disadvantaged against the influential and powerful, and fight to right a terrible wrong. It's such a pervasive, grinding thing, injustice. And unfortunately all too common. I suppose the only way most people can tolerate it is by simply shrugging their shoulders and ignoring it, and going on living their own lives. Unless, of course, the injustice falls on them, or those they love."

"I know what you're trying to do," said Sebastian. "But you are wrong about me. What I did was motivated by self-interest. Nothing more."

"Of course." They had reached the lagoon now. Lovejoy paused, his eyes narrowing as he stared out over the wind-ruffled water. "I looked into the records of your service in Portugal," he said after a moment. "I know why you sold out."

Beside them, a drake lifted off the water. Sebastian narrowed his eyes, watching it rise up, its outstretched wings beating against the blue winter sky. "You read too much into that."

"Do I?"

Sebastian swung his head to look at the man beside him. "I killed him. You know that, don't you?" They both understood it was Wilcox of whom they now spoke.

"You let him die. There is a difference. We are taught that to take another life is wrong, yet the state does it, and calls it justice. Soldiers on the battlefield kill, and are named heroes." The little magistrate turned up his collar against the cold wind blowing off the sunlit waters. "What you did was wrong. But it's a sin we both share, and a choice that I, for one, am glad you made."

Choices, the man had said. *It all comes down to choices. . . .*

In the distance, a cannon boomed, and another. Then they heard a roar as tens of thousands of voices raised together in a cheer.

"So," said Sir Henry Lovejoy. "The Regency begins."

~

"No, wait!" George, Prince of Wales and soon to be Prince Regent, sucked in a desperate gasp of air and flung out one fat, beringed hand to grasp the red lacquered back of a nearby chair. "I can't go out there yet. I can't breathe. *Oh, God.* Do you think it's my heart? I feel a series of palpitations coming on. Where is Dr. Herberden?"

Charles, Lord Jarvis, wrenched the stopper from a vial of smelling salts and waved the pungent concoction back and forth beneath his prince's pale nostrils. "Here, here, Your Royal Highness. You'll be fine. An understandable attack of nerves, that's all," he said soothingly, then whispered in an urgent undertone to one of the Prince's gentlemen, "Loosen his corset."

From his position near the door, the Earl of Hendon slipped a watch from his waistcoat pocket and frowned. The Privy Council had already been kept waiting for an hour. But then, everyone at Court was accustomed to waiting for the Prince. There was no reason to expect his installation as Regent to be any different.

The Prince was breathing better now, but Jarvis shook his head at the Earl of Hendon and pressed a glass of wine into the Prince's trembling hands.

It hadn't been an easy thing, shepherding the Prince toward his new position as Regent while simultaneously maneuvering to keep the Whigs out of government. That girl's murder coupled with the apparent involvement of Hendon's son had come perilously close to scuttling the entire scheme. But in the end all had come off as planned. The Whigs had been discredited, Perceval and the Tories would remain in power, and the war would continue until the French were finally, irrevocably crushed. Soon, there would be no one left in all the world to challenge British supremacy. Unconquerable and all-powerful, Britannia would take her divinely ordained position as the New and Final Rome. It was to be the happy fate of Jarvis's own generation of Englishmen to witness the final inauguration of an empire that would last a thousand years and more into the future.

"Jarvis?" The Prince's voice rose in a peevish whine. "Where is Jarvis?"

"Here," said Jarvis, easing the wineglass from his prince's plump fingers. "Shall we go, Your Highness? England and your destiny await you."

Author's Note

Although it would not have been recognized in the early nineteenth century, the unusual abilities displayed by Sebastian St. Cyr are characteristic of Bithil Syndrome, a little-known but very real genetic mutation found in certain families of Welsh descent.

Bithil Syndrome is marked by astonishingly acute eyesight and hearing, and an abnormal sensitivity to light that allows those with this genetic variation to see clearly in the dark. Other characteristics of the syndrome include extraordinarily quick reflexes, a misshapen vertebra in the lower back, and yellow eyes, the eye color being recessive to both blue and brown.

Although rare, Bithil Syndrome is nevertheless quite ancient, having been discovered in at least one individual known to have died in Wales some ten thousand years ago. In the eighteenth and nineteenth centuries, immigrant Welsh families carried this mutation to North America, where it can be found today, particularly in the southeastern United States amongst families of mixed Cherokee and Welsh descent.

Keep reading for an excerpt from
C. S. Harris's Sebastian St. Cyr Mystery. . .

WHY KINGS CONFESS

Available in paperback!

Chapter 1

*P*aul Gibson lurched down the dark, narrow lane, his face raw from the cold, his fingers numb. There were times when he wandered these alleyways lost in brightly hued reveries of opium-induced euphoria. But not tonight. Tonight, Gibson clenched his jaw and tried to focus on the tap-tap of his wooden leg on the icy cobbles, the reedy wail of a babe carried on the night wind—anything that might distract his mind from the restless, hungering need that drenched his thin frame with sweat and tormented him with ghosts of what could be.

When he first noticed the woman, he thought her an apparition, a mirage of gray wool and velvet lying crumpled beside the entrance to a fetid passageway. But as he drew nearer, he saw pale flesh and the gleaming, dark wetness of blood, and knew she was only too real.

He drew up sharply, the dank, briny air of the nearby Thames rasping in his throat. Cat's Hole, they called this narrow lane, a refuge for thieves, prostitutes and all the desperate, dispossessed of England and beyond. He could feel his heart pounding; the stars glittered like shards of broken glass in the thin slice of cold black sky visible between the looming rooftops above. He hesitated perhaps longer than he should have. But he was a surgeon, his life dedicated to the care of others.

He pushed himself forward again.

She lay curled half on her side, one hand flung out palm up, eyes closed. He hunkered down awkwardly beside her, fingertips searching for a pulse in her slim neck. Her face was delicately boned and framed by a riot of long, flame red hair, her lashes dark and thick against the pale flesh of her smooth cheeks, her lips purple-blue with cold. Or death.

But at his touch, her eyelids fluttered open, her chest jerking on a sob and a broken, whispered prayer. *"Sainte Marie, Mère de Dieu, priez pour nous pauvres pécheurs . . ."*

"It's all right; I'm here to help you," he said gently, wondering if she could even understand him. "Where are you hurt?"

The entire side of her head, he now saw, was matted with blood. Wide-eyed and frightened, she fixed her gaze on him. Then her focus shifted to where the black mouth of the passage yawned beside them. "Damion . . ." Her hand jerked up to clutch his sleeve. "Is he all right?"

Gibson followed her gaze. The man's body was more difficult to discern, a dark, motionless mass deep in the shadows. Gibson shook his head. "I don't know."

Her grip on his arm twisted convulsively. "Go to him. Please."

Nodding, Gibson surged upright, staggering slightly as his wooden peg took his weight and the phantom pains of a long-gone limb ripped through him.

The passage reeked of rot and excrement and the familiar coppery stench of spilled blood. The man lay sprawled on his back beside a pile of broken hogsheads and crates. It was with difficulty that Gibson picked out the once snowy-white folds of a cravat, the silken sheen of what had been a fine waistcoat but was now a blood-soaked mess, horribly ripped.

"Tell me," said the woman. "Tell me he lives."

But Gibson could only stare at the body before him. The man's eyes were wide and sightless, his handsome young face pallid, his outflung arms stiffening in the cold. Someone had hacked open the corpse's chest with a ruthless savagery that spoke of rage tinged with madness. And where the heart should have been gaped only an open cavity.

Bloody and empty.

Chapter 2

*T*he dream began as it often did, with the sun shining golden warm and the laughter of children at play floating on an orange blossom–scented breeze.

Sebastian St. Cyr, Viscount Devlin, moved restlessly in his sleep, for he knew only too well what was to come. The thunder of galloping horses. A shouted order. The hiss of sabers drawn with deadly purpose from well-oiled scabbards. He gave a low moan.

"Devlin?"

Laughter turned to screams of terror. His vision filled with slashing hooves and bare steel stained dark with innocent blood.

"Devlin."

He opened his eyes, his chest jerking as he sucked in a deep, ragged breath. He felt his wife's gentle fingertips touch his lips. Her face rose above him in the darkness, her features pale in the glow of the fire that still burned warm on the bedroom hearth. "It's a dream," she whispered, although he saw the worry that drew together her dark brows. "Just a dream."

For a moment he could only stare at her, lost in the past. Then he folded his arms around her and drew her close so that she could no longer see his face. It was a dream, yes. But it was also a memory, one he had never shared with anyone.

"Did I wake you?" he asked, his voice a hoarse rasp. "I'm sorry."

She shook her head, her weight shifting as she sought in vain for a comfortable position, for she was nearly nine months heavy with his child. "Your son keeps kicking me."

Smiling, he placed his hand on the taut mound of her belly and felt a strong heel grind against his palm. "Shockingly ill-mannered of her."

"I think he's beginning to find it a wee bit crowded in there."

"There is a solution."

She laughed, a low, husky sound that caught without warning at his heart, then twisted. As much as he yearned to hold this child in his arms, thoughts of the looming birth inevitably brought a sense of disquiet that came perilously close to fear. He'd read once that more than one in ten women died in childbirth. Hero's own mother had lost babe after babe—before nearly dying herself.

Yet he heard no echo of his own terror in Hero's calm voice when she said, "Not long now."

He felt the babe kick one last time, then settle as Hero snuggled beside him. He brushed his lips against her temple and murmured, "Try to sleep."

"You sleep," she said, still smiling.

He watched her eyelids drift closed, her breathing slow. Yet the tension that thrummed within him remained, and he found himself wondering if it was the coming babe that had sent his unconscious thoughts drifting back to a time he wished so desperately to forget. A cold wind stirred the heavy velvet drapes at the windows and banged an unlatched shutter somewhere in the darkness. There were nights when the high, arid mountains and ancient stone-walled villages of Spain and Portugal seemed a lifetime away from the London town house sleeping around him. Yet he knew they were not.

He was still awake when an urgent message arrived in Brook Street from Paul Gibson, asking for Sebastian's help.

Ready to find
your next great read?

Let us help.

Visit prh.com/nextread

Visit us at

Visit penguin.com/next read

Penguin